JAMES HILTON'S
three famous novels
complete in one volume

LOST HORIZON
GOOD-BYE, MR. CHIPS
RANDOM HARVEST

JAMES HILTON'S

three famous novels
complete in one volume

Lost Horizon

Good-bye, Mr. Chips

Random Harvest

NELSON DOUBLEDAY, INC.   Garden City, New York

Manufactured in the United States of America.

CONTENTS

Lost Horizon

PREFACE

Lost Horizon was first published on both sides of the Atlantic in the autumn of 1933. Its sale was slow at first, and though it had a few fervent and even notable admirers, by Christmas of that year one might have prophesied that even the ripple it had stirred was already stilled. As this happens to ninety-nine percent of novels, I was not enormously surprised, though I was—dare I now say it?—a little disappointed. But in June, 1934, the story received the Hawthornden Prize, which is given yearly in England for an imaginative work written by a British author under the age of forty-one. The result was in the nature of a resurrection; the sale of the original English edition began to gather momentum, while in America the publishers took the almost unique step of issuing the book afresh. Such a second chance was well taken, for during the past two years seventeen editions have been printed. This, the eighteenth, makes a permanent one.

I recount these details without vainglory, though I cannot pretend to be indifferent over them. There is certainly no book of mine whose success I ever desired more keenly, for *Lost Horizon* was, in part, the expression of a mood for which I had always hoped to find sympathizers. I found them in thousands, and now, through the medium of the screen version that Frank Capra has made, the same mood, I hope, will find them in millions.

Which leads me to a final remark about this mood. When *Lost Horizon* first appeared three years ago, its message of the peril of war to all that we mean by the word "civilization" was considered topical.

"It will be such a storm as the world has not seen before. There will be no safety by arms, no help from authority, no answer in science. It will rage till every flower of culture is trampled, and all human things are leveled in a vast chaos. . . . The Dark Ages that are to come will cover the whole world in a single pall; there will be neither escape nor sanctuary, save such as are too secret to be found or too humble to be noticed. . . ."

How much happier one would be to dismiss all this as thoroughly
out-of-date, than to admit, as one must, that in 1936 it has become
more terrifyingly up-to-date than ever!

JAMES HILTON

London
August 4, 1936

PROLOGUE

Cigars had burned low, and we were beginning to sample the disillusionment that usually afflicts old school friends who have met again as men and found themselves with less in common than they had believed they had. Rutherford wrote novels; Wyland was one of the Embassy secretaries; he had just given us dinner at Tempelhof—not very cheerfully, I fancied, but with the equanimity which a diplomat must always keep on tap for such occasions. It seemed likely that nothing but the fact of being three celibate Englishmen in a foreign capital could have brought us together, and I had already reached the conclusion that the slight touch of priggishness which I remembered in Wyland Tertius had not diminished with years and an M.V.O. Rutherford I liked more; he had ripened well out of the skinny, precocious infant whom I had once alternately bullied and patronized. The probability that he was making much more money and having a more interesting life than either of us, gave Wyland and me our one mutual emotion—a touch of envy.

The evening, however, was far from dull. We had a good view of the big Luft-Hansa machines as they arrived at the aerodrome from all parts of Central Europe, and towards dusk, when arc-flares were lighted, the scene took on a rich, theatrical brilliance. One of the planes was English, and its pilot, in full flying-kit, strolled past our table and saluted Wyland, who did not at first recognize him. When he did so there were introductions all around, and the stranger was invited to join us. He was a pleasant, jolly youth named Sanders. Wyland made some apologetic remark about the difficulty of identifying people when they were all dressed up in Sibleys and flying-helmets; at which Sanders laughed and answered: "Oh, rather, I know that well enough. Don't forget I was at Baskul." Wyland laughed also, but less spontaneously, and the conversation then took other directions.

Sanders made an attractive addition to our small company, and we all drank a great deal of beer together. About ten o'clock Wyland left us for a moment to speak to some one at a table near by, and Rutherford, into the sudden hiatus of talk, remarked: "Oh, by the way, you mentioned Baskul just now. I know the place slightly. What was it you were referring to that happened there?"

Sanders smiled rather shyly. "Oh, just a bit of excitement we had once when I was in the Service." But he was a youth who could not long refrain from being confidential. "Fact is, an Afghan or an Afridi or somebody ran off with one of our buses, and there was the very devil to pay afterwards, as you can imagine. Most impudent thing I ever heard of. The blighter waylaid the pilot, knocked him out, pinched his kit, and climbed into the cockpit without a soul spotting him. Gave the mechanics the proper signals, too, and was up and away in fine style. The trouble was, he never came back."

Rutherford looked interested. "When did this happen?"

"Oh—must have been about a year ago. May, 'thirty-one. We were evacuating civilians from Baskul to Peshawur owing to the revolution—perhaps you remember the business. The place was in a bit of an upset, or I don't suppose the thing could have happened. Still, it *did* happen—and it goes some way to show that clothes make the man, doesn't it?"

Rutherford was still interested. "I should have thought you'd have had more than one fellow in charge of a plane on an occasion like that?"

"We did, on all the ordinary troop-carriers, but this machine was a special one, built for some maharajah originally—quite a stunt kind of outfit. The Indian Survey people had been using it for high-altitude flights in Kashmir."

"And you say it never reached Peshawur?"

"Never reached there, and never came down anywhere else, so far as we could discover. That was the queer part about it. Of course, if the fellow was a tribesman he might have made for the hills, thinking to hold the passengers for ransom. I suppose they all got killed, somehow. There are heaps of places on the frontier where you might crash and not be heard of afterwards."

"Yes, I know the sort of country. How many passengers were there?"

"Four, I think. Three men and some woman missionary."

"Was one of the men, by any chance, named Conway?"

Sanders looked surprised. "Why, yes, as a matter of fact. 'Glory' Conway—did you know him?"

"He and I were at the same school," said Rutherford a little self-consciously, for it was true enough, yet a remark which he was aware did not suit him.

"He was a jolly fine chap, by all accounts of what he did at Baskul," went on Sanders.

Rutherford nodded. "Yes, undoubtedly . . . but how extraordinary . . . extraordinary . . ." He appeared to collect himself after a spell of mind-wandering. Then he said: "It was never in the papers, or I think I should have read about it. How was that?"

Sanders looked suddenly rather uncomfortable, and even, I imagined, was on the point of blushing. "To tell you the truth," he replied, "I seem to have let out more than I should have. Or perhaps it doesn't matter now—it must be stale news in every mess, let alone in the bazaars. It was hushed up, you see—I mean, about the way the thing happened. Wouldn't have sounded well. The Government people merely gave out that one of their machines was missing, and mentioned the names. Sort of thing that didn't attract an awful lot of attention among outsiders."

At this point Wyland rejoined us, and Sanders turned to him half apologetically. "I say, Wyland, these chaps have been talking about 'Glory' Conway. I'm afraid I spilled the Baskul yarn—I hope you don't think it matters?"

Wyland was severely silent for a moment. It was plain that he was reconciling the claims of compatriot courtesy and official rectitude. "I can't help feeling," he said at length, "that it's a pity to make a mere anecdote of it. I always thought you air fellows were put on your honor not to tell tales out of school." Having thus snubbed the youth, he turned, rather more graciously, to Rutherford. "Of course, it's all right in your case, but I'm sure you realize that it's sometimes necessary for events up on the Frontier to be shrouded in a little mystery."

"On the other hand," replied Rutherford dryly, "one has a curious itch to know the truth."

"It was never concealed from any one who had any real reason for wanting to know it. I was at Peshawur at the time, and I can assure you of that. Did you know Conway well—since schooldays, I mean?"

"Just a little at Oxford, and a few chance meetings since. Did *you* come across him much?"

"At Angora, when I was stationed there, we met once or twice."

"Did you like him?"

"I thought he was clever, but rather slack."

Rutherford smiled. "He was certainly clever. He had a most exciting university career—until war broke out. Rowing Blue and a leading light at the Union and prizeman for this, that, and the other

—also I reckon him the best amateur pianist I ever heard. Amazingly many-sided fellow, the kind, one feels, that Jowett would have tipped for a future premier. Yet, in point of fact, one never heard much about him after those Oxford days. Of course the War cut into his career. He was very young and I gather he went through most of it."

"He was blown up or something," responded Wyland, "but nothing very serious. Didn't do at all badly, got a D.S.O. in France. Then I believe he went back to Oxford for a spell as a sort of don. I know he went East in 'twenty-one. His Oriental languages got him the job without any of the usual preliminaries. He had several posts."

Rutherford smiled more broadly. "Then, of course, that accounts for everything. History will never disclose the amount of sheer brilliance wasted in the routine of decoding F.O. chits and handing round tea at Legation bun-fights."

"He was in the Consular Service, not the Diplomatic," said Wyland loftily. It was evident that he did not care for chaff, and he made no protest when, after a little more badinage of a similar kind, Rutherford rose to go. In any case it was getting late, and I said I would go, too. Wyland's attitude as we made our farewells was still one of official propriety suffering in silence, but Sanders was very cordial and said he hoped to meet us again sometime.

I was catching a transcontinental train at a very dismal hour of the early morning, and, as we waited for a taxi, Rutherford asked me if I would care to spend the interval at his hotel. He had a sitting-room, he said, and we could talk. I said it would suit me excellently, and he answered: "Good. We can talk about Conway, if you like, unless you're completely bored with his affairs."

I said that I wasn't, at all, though I had scarcely known him. "He left at the end of my first term, and I never met him afterwards. But he was extraordinarily kind to me on one occasion. I was a new boy and there was no earthly reason why he should have done what he did. It was only a trivial thing, but I've always remembered it."

Rutherford assented. "Yes, I liked him a good deal too, though I also saw surprisingly little of him, if you measure it in time."

And then there was a somewhat odd silence, during which it was evident that we were both thinking of some one who had mattered to us far more than might have been judged from such casual contacts. I have often found since then that others who met Conway, even quite formally and for a moment, remembered him afterwards with great vividness. He was certainly remarkable as a youth, and to me, who had known him at the hero-worshiping age, his memory is

still quite romantically distinct. He was tall and extremely good looking, and not only excelled at games but walked off with every conceivable kind of school prize. A rather sentimental headmaster once
referred to his exploits as "glorious," and from that arose his nickname. Perhaps only he could have survived it. He gave a Speech
Day oration in Greek, I recollect, and was outstandingly first-rate
in school theatricals. There was something rather Elizabethan about
him—his casual versatility, his good looks, that effervescent combination of mental with physical activities. Something a bit Philip-
Sidneyish. Our civilization doesn't often breed people like that
nowadays. I made a remark of this kind to Rutherford, and he replied: "Yes, that's true, and we have a special word of disparagement
for them—we call them dilettanti. I suppose some people must have
called Conway that, people like Wyland, for instance. I don't much
care for Wyland. I can't stand his type—all that primness and
mountainous self-importance. And the complete head-prefectorial
mind, did you notice it? Little phrases about 'putting people on their
honor' and 'telling tales out of school'—as though the bally Empire
were the Fifth Form at St. Dominic's! But, then, I always fall foul
of these sahib diplomats."

We drove a few blocks in silence, and then he continued: "Still,
I wouldn't have missed this evening. It was a peculiar experience for
me, hearing Sanders tell that story about the affair at Baskul. You
see, I'd heard it before, and hadn't properly believed it. It was part
of a much more fantastic story, which I saw no reason to believe at
all, or well, only one very slight reason, anyway. *Now* there are *two*
very slight reasons. I dare say you can guess that I'm not a particularly gullible person. I've spent a good deal of my life traveling about,
and I know there are queer things in the world—if you see them
yourself, that is, but not so often if you hear of them second-hand.
And yet . . ."

He seemed suddenly to realize that what he was saying could not
mean very much to me, and broke off with a laugh. "Well, there's
one thing certain—I'm not likely to take Wyland into my confidence.
It would be like trying to sell an epic poem to *Tit-Bits*. I'd rather try
my luck with you."

"Perhaps you flatter me," I suggested.

"Your book doesn't lead me to think so."

I had not mentioned my authorship of that rather technical work
(after all, a neurologist's is not everybody's "shop"), and I was
agreeably surprised that Rutherford had even heard of it. I said as

much, and he answered: "Well, you see, I was interested, because amnesia was Conway's trouble at one time."

We had reached the hotel and he had to get his key at the bureau. As we went up to the fifth floor he said: "All this is mere beating about the bush. The fact is, Conway isn't dead. At least he wasn't a few months ago."

This seemed beyond comment in the narrow space and time of an elevator ascent. In the corridor a few seconds later I responded: "Are you sure of that? How do you know?"

And he answered, unlocking his door: "Because I traveled with him from Shanghai to Honolulu in a Jap liner last November." He did not speak again till we were settled in armchairs and had fixed ourselves with drinks and cigars. "You see, I was in China in the autumn on a holiday. I'm always wandering about. I hadn't seen Conway for years. We never corresponded, and I can't say he was often in my thoughts, though his was one of the few faces that have always come to me quite effortlessly if I tried to picture it. I had been visiting a friend in Hankow and was returning by the Pekin express. On the train I chanced to get into conversation with a very charming Mother Superior of some French sisters of charity. She was traveling to Chung-Kiang, where her convent was, and, because I knew a little French, she seemed to enjoy chattering to me about her work and affairs in general. As a matter of fact, I haven't much sympathy with ordinary missionary enterprise, but I'm prepared to admit, as many people are nowadays, that the Romans stand in a class by themselves, since at least they work hard and don't pose as commissioned officers in a world full of other ranks. Still, that's by the by. The point is that this lady, talking to me about the mission hospital at Chung-Kiang, mentioned a fever case that had been brought in some weeks back, a man who they thought must be a European, though he could give no account of himself and had no papers. His clothes were native, and of the poorest kind, and when taken in by the nuns he had been very ill indeed. He spoke fluent Chinese, as well as pretty good French, and my train companion assured me that before he realized the nationality of the nuns, he had also addressed them in English with a refined accent. I said I couldn't imagine such a phenomenon, and chaffed her gently about being able to detect a refined accent in a language she didn't know. We joked about these and other matters, and it ended by her inviting me to visit the mission if ever I happened to be thereabouts. This, of course, seemed then as unlikely as that I should climb Everest, and when the train reached Chung-Kiang I shook hands with genuine regret that our chance contact had come to an end. As it happened, though, I was back in Chung-Kiang within a few hours. The train broke down a mile or two further on, and with much difficulty pushed us back to the station, where we learned that a relief engine could not possibly arrive for twelve hours. That's the sort of thing that often happens on Chinese railways. So there was half a day to be lived through in Chung-Kiang—which made me decide to take the good lady at her word and call at the mission.

"I did so, and received a cordial, though naturally a somewhat astonished, welcome. I suppose one of the hardest things for a non-Catholic to realize is how easily a Catholic can combine official rigidity with non-official broad-mindedness. Is that too complicated? Anyhow, never mind, those mission people made quite delightful company. Before I'd been there an hour I found that a meal had been prepared, and a young Chinese Christian doctor sat down with me to it and kept up a conversation in a jolly mixture of French and English. Afterwards, he and the Mother Superior took me to see the hospital, of which they were very proud. I had told them I was a writer, and they were simple-minded enough to be a-flutter at the thought that I might put them all into a book. We walked past the beds while the doctor explained the cases. The place was spotlessly clean and looked to be very competently run. I had forgotten all about the mysterious patient with the refined English accent till the Mother Superior reminded me that we were just coming to him. All I could see was the back of the man's head; he was apparently asleep. It was suggested that I should address him in English, so I said 'Good afternoon,' which was the first and not very original thing I could think of. The man looked up suddenly and said 'Good afternoon' in answer. It was true; his accent was educated. But I hadn't time to be surprised at that, for I had already recognized him, despite his beard and altogether changed appearance and the fact that we hadn't met for so long. He was Conway. I was certain he was, and yet, if I'd paused to think about it, I might well have come to the conclusion that he couldn't possibly be. Fortunately I acted on the impulse of the moment. I called out his name and my own, and though he looked at me without any definite sign of recognition, I was positive I hadn't made any mistake. There was an odd little twitching of the facial muscles that I had noticed in him before, and he had the same eyes that at Balliol we used to say were so much more of a Cambridge blue than an Oxford. But besides all that, he was a man one simply didn't make mistakes about—to see him once was to know him always. Of course the doctor and the Mother Supe-

rior were greatly excited. I told them that I knew the man, that he
was English, and a friend of mine, and that if he didn't recognize
me, it could only be because he had completely lost his memory.
They agreed, in a rather amazed way, and we had a long consulta-
tion about the case. They weren't able to make any suggestions as
to how Conway could possibly have arrived at Chung-Kiang in his
condition.

"To make the story brief, I stayed there over a fortnight, hoping
that somehow or other I might induce him to remember things. I
didn't succeed, but he regained his physical health, and we talked
a good deal. When I told him quite frankly who I was and who he
was, he was docile enough not to argue about it. He was quite cheerful, even, in a vague sort of way, and seemed glad enough to have
my company. To my suggestion that I should take him home, he
simply said that he didn't mind. It was a little unnerving, that apparent lack of any personal desire. As soon as I could I arranged for
our departure. I made a confidant of an acquaintance in the consular
office at Hankow, and thus the necessary passport and so on were
made out without the fuss there might otherwise have been. Indeed,
it seemed to me that for Conway's sake the whole business had better
be kept free from publicity and newspaper headlines, and I'm glad
to say I succeeded in that. It would have been jam, of course, for
the press.

"Well, we made our exit from China in quite a normal way. We
sailed down the Yang-tse to Nanking, and then took train for Shanghai. There was a Jap liner leaving for 'Frisco that same night, so we
made a great rush and got on board."

"You did a tremendous lot for him," I said.

Rutherford did not deny it. "I don't think I should have done quite
as much for any one else," he answered. "But there was something
about the fellow, and always had been—it's hard to explain, but it
made one enjoy doing what one could."

"Yes," I agreed. "He had a peculiar charm, a sort of winsomeness
that's pleasant to remember even now when I picture it, though, of
course, I think of him still as a schoolboy in cricket flannels."

"A pity you didn't know him at Oxford. He was just brilliant—
there's no other word. After the War people said he was different.
I, myself, think he was. But I can't help feeling that with all his gifts
he ought to have been doing bigger work. All that Britannic Majesty
stuff isn't my idea of a great man's career. And Conway was—or
should have been—*great*. You and I have both known him, and I
don't think I'm exaggerating when I say it's an experience we shan't

ever forget. And even when he and I met in the middle of China, with his mind a blank and his past a mystery, there was still that queer core of attractiveness in him."

Rutherford paused reminiscently and then continued: "As you can imagine, we renewed our old friendship on the ship. I told him as much as I knew about himself, and he listened with an attention that might almost have seemed a little absurd. He remembered everything quite clearly since his arrival at Chung-Kiang, and another point that may interest you is that he hadn't forgotten languages. He told me, for instance, that he knew he must have had something to do with India, because he could speak Hindostani.

"At Yokohama the ship filled up, and among the new passengers was Sieveking, the pianist, *en route* for a concert tour in the States. He was at our dining table and sometimes talked with Conway in German. That will show you how outwardly normal Conway was. Apart from his loss of memory, which didn't show in ordinary intercourse, there couldn't have seemed much wrong with him.

"A few nights after leaving Japan, Sieveking was prevailed upon to give a piano recital on board, and Conway and I went to hear him. He played well, of course, some Brahms and Scarlatti, and a lot of Chopin. Once or twice I glanced at Conway and judged that he was enjoying it all, which appeared very natural, in view of his own musical past. At the end of the program the show lengthened out into an informal series of encores which Sieveking bestowed, very amiably, I thought, upon a few enthusiasts grouped round the piano. Again he played mostly Chopin; he rather specializes in it, you know. At last he left the piano and moved towards the door, still followed by admirers, but evidently feeling that he had done enough for them. In the meantime a rather odd thing was beginning to happen. Conway had sat down at the keyboard and was playing some rapid, lively piece that I didn't recognize, but which drew Sieveking back in great excitement to ask what it was. Conway, after a long and rather strange silence, could only reply that he didn't know. Sieveking exclaimed that that was incredible, and grew more excited still. Conway then made what appeared to be a tremendous physical and mental effort to remember, and said at last that the thing was a Chopin study. I didn't think myself it could be, and I wasn't surprised when Sieveking denied it absolutely. Conway, however, grew suddenly quite indignant about the matter—which startled me, because up to then he had shown so little emotion about anything. 'My dear fellow,' Sieveking remonstrated, 'I know everything of Chopin's that exists, and I can assure you that he never wrote what you have just played. He might well have done so, because it's utterly in his style, but he just didn't. I challenge you to show me the score in any of the editions.' To which Conway replied at length: 'Oh, yes, I remember now, it was never printed. I only know it myself from meeting a man who used to be one of Chopin's pupils. . . . Here's another unpublished thing I learned from him.'"

Rutherford steadied me with his eyes as he went on: "I don't know if you're a musician, but even if you're not, I dare say you'll be able to imagine something of Sieveking's excitement, and mine, too, as Conway continued to play. To me, of course, it was a sudden and quite mystifying glimpse into his past, the first clew of any kind that had escaped. Sieveking was naturally engrossed in the musical problem, which was perplexing enough, as you'll realize when I remind you that Chopin died in 1849.

"The whole incident was so unfathomable, in a sense, that perhaps I should add that there were at least a dozen witnesses of it, including a Californian university professor of some repute. Of course, it was easy to say that Conway's explanation was chronologically impossible, or almost so; but there was still the music itself to be explained. If it wasn't what Conway said it was, then what *was* it? Sieveking assured me that if those two pieces were published, they would be in every virtuoso's repertoire within six months. Even if this is an exaggeration, it shows Sieveking's opinion of them. After much argument at the time, we weren't able to settle anything, for Conway stuck to his story, and as he was beginning to look fatigued, I was anxious to get him away from the crowd and off to bed. The last episode was about making some phonograph records. Sieveking said he would fix up all arrangements as soon as he reached America, and Conway gave his promise to play before the microphone. I often feel it was a great pity, from every point of view, that he wasn't able to keep his word."

Rutherford glanced at his watch and impressed on me that I should have plenty of time to catch my train, since his story was practically finished. "Because that night—the night after the recital —he got back his memory. We had both gone to bed and I was lying awake, when he came into my cabin and told me. His face had stiffened into what I can only describe as an expression of overwhelming sadness—a sort of universal sadness, if you know what I mean—something remote or impersonal, a *Wehmut* or *Weltschmerz*, or whatever the Germans call it. He said he could call to mind everything, that it had begun to come back to him during Sieveking's playing, though only in patches at first. He sat for a long while on the edge of my bed, and I let him take his own time and make his own method of telling me. I said that I was glad his memory had returned, but sorry if he already wished that it hadn't. He looked up then and paid me what I shall always regard as a marvelously high compliment. 'Thank God, Rutherford,' he said, 'you are capable of imagining things.' After a while I dressed and persuaded him to do the same, and we walked up and down the boat deck. It was a calm night, starry and very warm, and the sea had a pale, sticky look, like condensed milk. Except for the vibration of the engines, we might have been pacing an esplanade. I let Conway go on in his own way, without questions at first. Somewhere about dawn he began to talk consecutively, and it was breakfast-time and hot sunshine when he had finished. When I say 'finished' I don't mean that there was nothing more to tell me after that first confession. He filled in a good many important gaps during the next twenty-four hours. He was very unhappy, and couldn't have slept, so we talked almost constantly. About the middle of the following night the ship was due to reach Honolulu. We had drinks in my cabin the evening before; he left me about ten o'clock, and I never saw him again."

"You don't mean—" I had a picture in mind of a very calm, deliberate suicide I once saw on the mailboat from Holyhead to Kingstown. Rutherford laughed. "Oh, Lord, no—he wasn't that sort. He just gave me the slip. It was easy enough to get ashore, but he must have found it hard to avoid being traced when I set people searching for him, as of course I did. Afterwards I learned that he'd managed to join the crew of a banana-boat going south to Fiji."

"How did you get to know that?"

"Quite straightforwardly. He wrote to me, three months later, from Bangkok, enclosing a draft to pay the expenses I'd been put to on his account. He thanked me and said he was very fit. He also said he was about to set out on a long journey—to the northwest. That was all."

"Where did he mean?"

"Yes, it's pretty vague, isn't it? A good many places must lie to the northwest of Bangkok. Even Berlin does, for that matter."

Rutherford paused and filled up my glass and his own. It had been a queer story—or else he had made it seem so; I hardly knew which. The music part of it, though puzzling, did not interest me so much as the mystery of Conway's arrival at that Chinese mission hospital; and I made this comment. Rutherford answered that in point of fact they were both parts of the same problem. "Well, how *did* he get to Chung-Kiang?" I asked. "I suppose he told you all about it that night on the ship?"

"He told me something about it, and it would be absurd of me, after letting you know so much, to be secretive about the rest. Only, to begin with, it's a longish sort of tale, and there wouldn't be time even to outline it before you'd have to be off for your train. And besides, as it happens, there's a more convenient way. I'm a little diffident about revealing the tricks of my dishonorable calling, but the truth is, Conway's story, as I pondered over it afterwards, appealed to me enormously. I had begun by making simple notes after our various conversations on the ship, so that I shouldn't forget details; later, as certain aspects of the thing began to grip me, I had the urge to do more, to fashion the written and recollected fragments into a single narrative. By that I don't mean that I invented or altered anything. There was quite enough material in what he told me: he was a fluent talker and had a natural gift for communicating an atmosphere. Also, I suppose, I felt I was beginning to understand the man himself." He went to an attaché-case and took out a bundle of typed manuscript. "Well, here it is, anyhow, and you can make what you like of it."

"By which I suppose you mean that I'm not expected to believe it?"

"Oh, hardly so definite a warning as that. But mind, if you *do* believe, it will be for Tertullian's famous reason—you remember?—*quia impossibile est*. Not a bad argument, maybe. Let me know what you think, at all events."

I took the manuscript away with me and read most of it on the Ostend express. I intended returning it with a long letter when I reached England, but there were delays, and before I could post it I got a short note from Rutherford to say that he was off on his wanderings again and would have no settled address for some months. He was going to Kashmir, he wrote, and thence "east." I was not surprised.

CHAPTER ONE

During that third week of May the situation in Baskul had become much worse and, on the 20th, Air Force machines arrived by arrangement from Peshawur to evacuate the white residents. These numbered about eighty, and most were safely transported across the mountains in troop-carriers. A few miscellaneous aircraft were also employed, among them being a cabin machine lent by the Maharajah of Chandapore. In this, about 10 A.M., four passengers embarked: Miss Roberta Brinklow, of the Eastern Mission; Henry D. Barnard, an American; Hugh Conway, H.M. Consul; and Captain Charles Mallinson, H.M. Vice-Consul.

These names are as they appeared later in Indian and British newspapers.

Conway was thirty-seven. He had been at Baskul for two years, in a job which now, in the light of events, could be regarded as a persistent backing of the wrong horse. A stage of his life was finished; in a few weeks' time, or perhaps after a few months' leave in England, he would be sent somewhere else. Tokio or Teheran, Manila or Muscat; people in his profession never knew what was coming. He had been ten years in the Consular Service, long enough to assess his own chances as shrewdly as he was apt to do those of others. He knew that the plums were not for him; but it was genuinely consoling, and not merely sour grapes, to reflect that he had no taste for plums. He preferred the less formal and more picturesque jobs that were on offer, and as these were often not good ones, it had doubtless seemed to others that he was playing his cards rather badly. Actually, he felt he had played them rather well; he had had a varied and moderately enjoyable decade.

He was tall, deeply bronzed, with brown, short cropped hair and slate-blue eyes. He was inclined to look severe and brooding until he laughed, and then (but it happened not so very often) he looked boyish. There was a slight nervous twitch near the left eye which was usually noticeable when he worked too hard or drank too much, and as he had been packing and destroying documents throughout

the whole of the day and night preceding the evacuation, the twitch
was very conspicuous when he climbed into the aeroplane. He was
tired out, and overwhelmingly glad that he had contrived to be sent
in the maharajah's luxurious air liner instead of in one of the crowded
troop-carriers. He spread himself indulgently in the basket seat as
the plane soared aloft. He was the sort of man who, being used to
major hardships, expects minor comforts by way of compensation.
Cheerfully he might endure the rigors of the road to Samarkand, but
from London to Paris he would spend his last tenner on the Golden
Arrow.

It was after the flight had lasted more than an hour that Mallinson
said he thought the pilot wasn't keeping a straight course. Mallinson
sat immediately in front. He was a youngster in his middle twenties,
pink-cheeked, intelligent without being intellectual, beset with public school limitations, but also with their excellences. Failure to pass
an examination was the chief cause of his being sent to Baskul, where
Conway had had six months of his company and had grown to like
him.

But Conway did not want to make the effort that an aeroplane
conversation demands. He opened his eyes drowsily and replied that
whatever the course taken, the pilot presumably knew best.

Half an hour later, when weariness and the drone of the engine
had lulled him nearly to sleep, Mallinson disturbed him again. "I say,
Conway, I thought Fenner was piloting us?"

"Well, isn't he?"

"The chap turned his head just now and I'll swear it wasn't he."

"It's hard to tell, through that glass panel."

"I'd know Fenner's face anywhere."

"Well, then, it must be some one else. I don't see that it matters."

"But Fenner told me definitely that he was taking this machine."

"They must have changed their minds and given him one of the
others."

"Well, who is this man, then?"

"My dear boy, how should I know? You don't suppose I've memo-
rized the face of every flight-lieutenant in the Air Force, do you?"

"I know a good many of them, anyway, but I don't recognize this
fellow."

"Then he must belong to the minority whom you don't know."
Conway smiled and added: "When we arrive in Peshawur very soon
you can make his acquaintance and ask him all about himself."

"At this rate we shan't get to Peshawur at all. The man's right off his course. And I'm not surprised, either—flying so damned high he can't see where he is."

Conway was not bothering. He was used to air travel, and took things for granted. Besides, there was nothing particular he was eager to do when he got to Peshawur, and no one particular he was eager to see; so it was a matter of complete indifference to him whether the journey took four hours or six. He was unmarried; there would be no tender greetings on arrival. He had friends, and a few of them would probably take him to the club and stand him drinks; it was a pleasant prospect, but not one to sigh for in anticipation.

Nor did he sigh retrospectively, when he viewed the equally pleasant, but not wholly satisfying vista of the past decade. Changeable, fair intervals, becoming rather unsettled; it had been his own meteorological summary during that time, as well as the world's. He thought of Baskul, Pekin, Macao, and the other places—he had moved about pretty often. Remotest of all was Oxford, where he had had a couple of years of donhood after the War, lecturing on Oriental History, breathing dust in sunny libraries, cruising down the High on a push-bicycle. The vision attracted, but did not stir him; there was a sense in which he felt that he was still a part of all that he might have been.

A familiar gastric lurch informed him that the plane was beginning to descend. He felt tempted to rag Mallinson about his fidgets, and would perhaps have done so had not the youth risen abruptly, bumping his head against the roof, and waking Barnard, the American, who had been dozing in his seat at the other side of the narrow gangway. "My God!" Mallinson cried, peering through the window. "Look down there!"

Conway looked. The view was certainly not what he had expected, if, indeed, he had expected anything. Instead of the trim, geometrically laid-out cantonments and the larger oblongs of the hangars, nothing was visible but an opaque mist veiling an immense, sun-brown desolation. The plane, though descending rapidly, was still at a height unusual for ordinary flying. Long, corrugated mountain-ridges could be picked out, perhaps a mile or so closer than the cloudier smudge of the valleys. It was typical Frontier scenery, though Conway had never viewed it before from such an altitude. It was also, which struck him as odd, nowhere that he could imagine near Peshawur. "I don't recognize this part of the world," he commented. Then, more privately, for he did not wish to alarm the others, he added into Mallinson's ear: "Looks as if you're right. The man's lost his way."

The plane was swooping down at a tremendous speed, and as it did so, the air grew hotter; the scorched earth below was like an oven with the door suddenly opened. One mountain top after another lifted itself above the horizon in craggy silhouette; now the flight was along a curving valley, the base of which was strewn with rocks and the débris of dried-up watercourses. It looked like a floor littered with nut-shells. The plane bumped and tossed in air-pockets as uncomfortably as a row-boat in a swell. All four passengers had to hold on to their seats.

"Looks like he wants to land!" shouted the American hoarsely.

"He can't!" Mallinson retorted. "He'd be simply mad if he tried to! He'll crash and then—"

But the pilot did land. A small cleared space opened by the side of a gully, and with considerable skill the machine was jolted and heaved to a standstill. What happened after that, however, was more puzzling and less reassuring. A swarm of bearded and turbanned tribesmen came forward from all directions, surrounding the machine and effectively preventing any one from getting out of it except the pilot. The latter clambered to earth and held excited colloquy with them, during which proceeding it became clear that, so far from being Fenner, he was not an Englishman at all, and possibly not even a European. Meanwhile cans of gasoline were fetched from a dump close by, and emptied into the exceptionally capacious tanks. Grins and disregarding silence met the shouts of the four imprisoned passengers, while the slightest attempt to alight provoked a menacing movement from a score of rifles. Conway, who knew a little Pushtu, harangued the tribesmen as well as he could in that language, but without effect; while the pilot's sole retort to remarks addressed to him in any language was a significant flourish of his revolver. Midday sunlight, blazing on the roof of the cabin, grilled the air inside till the occupants were almost fainting with the heat and with the exertion of their protests. They were quite powerless; it had been a condition of the evacuation that they should carry no arms.

When the tanks were at last screwed up, a gasoline can filled with tepid water was handed through one of the cabin windows. No questions were answered, though it did not appear that the men were personally hostile. After a further parley the pilot climbed back into the cockpit, a Pathan clumsily swung the propeller, and the flight was resumed. The take-off, in that confined space and with the extra gasoline load, was even more skillful than the landing. The plane rose high into the hazy vapors; then turned east, as if setting a course. It was midafternoon.

A most extraordinary and bewildering business! As the cooler air refreshed them, the passengers could hardly believe that it had really happened; it was an outrage to which none could recall any parallel, or suggest any precedent, in all the turbulent records of the Frontier. It would have been incredible, indeed, had they not been victims of it themselves. It was quite natural that high indignation should follow incredulity, and anxious speculation only when indignation had worn itself out. Mallinson then developed the theory which, in the absence of any other, they found easiest to accept. They were being kidnaped for ransom. The trick was by no means new in itself, though this particular technique must be regarded as original. It was a little more comforting to feel that they were not making entirely virgin history; after all, there had been kidnapings before, and a good many of them had ended up all right. The tribesmen kept you in some lair in the mountains till the Government paid up and you were released. You were treated quite decently, and as the money that had to be paid wasn't your own, the whole business was only unpleasant while it lasted. Afterwards, of course, the Air people sent a bombing squadron, and you were left with one good story to tell for the rest of your life. Mallinson enunciated the proposition a shade nervously; but Barnard, the American, chose to be heavily facetious. "Well, gentlemen, I dare say this is a cute idea on somebody's part, but I can't exactly see that your Air Force has covered itself with glory. You Britishers make jokes about the holdups in Chicago and all that, but I don't recollect any instance of a gunman running off with one of Uncle Sam's aeroplanes. And I should like to know, by the way, what this fellow did with the real pilot. Sandbagged him, I bet." He yawned. He was a large, fleshy man, with a hard-bitten face in which good-humored wrinkles were not quite offset by pessimistic pouches. Nobody in Baskul had known much about him except that he had arrived from Persia, where it was presumed he had something to do with oil.

Conway meanwhile was busying himself with a very practical task. He had collected every scrap of paper that they all had, and was composing messages in various native languages to be dropped to earth at intervals. It was a slender chance, in such sparsely populated country, but worth taking.

The fourth occupant, Miss Brinklow, sat tight-lipped and straight-backed, with few comments and no complaints. She was a small, rather leathery woman, with an air of having been compelled to attend a party at which there were goings-on that she could not wholly approve.

Conway had talked less than the two other men, for translating
SOS messages into dialects was a mental exercise requiring concentration. He had, however, answered questions when asked, and had
agreed, tentatively, with Mallinson's kidnaping theory. He had also
agreed, to some extent, with Barnard's strictures on the Air Force.
"Though one can see, of course, how it may have happened. With
the place in commotion as it was, one man in flying-kit would look
very much like another. No one would think of doubting the *bona
fides* of any man in the proper clothes who looked as if he knew
his job. And this fellow *must* have known it—the signals, and so forth.
Pretty obvious, too, that he knows how to fly . . . still, I agree with
you that it's the sort of thing that some one ought to get into hot
water about. And somebody will, you may be sure, though I suspect
he won't deserve it."

"Well, sir," responded Barnard, "I certainly do admire the way you
manage to see both sides of the question. It's the right spirit to have,
no doubt, even when you're being taken for a ride."

Americans, Conway reflected, had the knack of being able to say
patronizing things without being offensive. He smiled tolerantly, but
did not continue the conversation. His tiredness was of a kind that
no amount of possible peril could stave off. Towards late afternoon,
when Barnard and Mallinson, who had been arguing, appealed to
him on some point, it appeared that he had fallen asleep.

"Dead beat," Mallinson commented. "And I don't wonder at it,
after these last few weeks."

"You're his friend?" queried Barnard.

"I've worked with him at the Consulate. I happen to know that
he hasn't been in bed for the last four nights. As a matter of fact,
we're damned lucky in having him with us in a tight corner like
this. Apart from knowing the languages, he's got a sort of way with
him in dealing with people. If any one can get us out of the mess,
he'll do it. He's pretty cool about most things."

"Well, let him have his sleep, then," agreed Barnard.

Miss Brinklow made one of her rare remarks. "I think he *looks*
like a very brave man," she said.

Conway was far less certain that he *was* a very brave man. He
had closed his eyes in sheer physical fatigue, but without actually
sleeping. He could hear and feel every movement of the plane, and
he heard also, with mixed feelings, Mallinson's eulogy of himself. It
was then that he had his doubts, recognizing a tight sensation in his
stomach which was his own bodily reaction to a disquieting mental

survey. He was not, as he knew well from experience, one of those persons who love danger for its own sake. There was an aspect of it which he sometimes enjoyed, an excitement, a purgative effect upon sluggish emotions, but he was far from fond of risking his life. Twelve years earlier he had grown to hate the perils of trench warfare in France, and had several times avoided death by declining to attempt valorous impossibilities. Even his D.S.O. had been won, not so much by physical courage, as by a certain hardly developed technique of endurance. And since the War, whenever there had been danger again, he had faced it with increasing lack of relish unless it promised extravagant dividends in thrills.

He still kept his eyes closed. He was touched, and a little dismayed, by what he had heard Mallinson say. It was his fate in life to have his equanimity always mistaken for pluck, whereas it was actually something much more dispassionate and much less virile. They were all in a damnably awkward situation, it seemed to him, and so far from being full of bravery about it, he felt chiefly an enormous distaste for whatever trouble might be in store. There was Miss Brinklow, for instance. He foresaw that in certain circumstances he would have to act on the supposition that because she was a woman she mattered far more than the rest of them put together, and he shrank from a situation in which such disproportionate behavior might be unavoidable.

Nevertheless, when he showed signs of wakefulness, it was to Miss Brinklow that he spoke first. He realized that she was neither young nor pretty—negative virtues, but immensely helpful ones in such difficulties as those in which they might soon find themselves. He was also rather sorry for her, because he suspected that neither Mallinson nor the American liked missionaries, especially female ones. He himself was unprejudiced, but he was afraid she would find his open mind a less familiar and therefore an even more disconcerting phenomenon. "We seem to be in a queer fix," he said, leaning forward to her ear, "but I'm glad you're taking it calmly. I don't really think anything dreadful is going to happen to us."

"I'm certain it won't if you can prevent it," she answered; which did not console him.

"You must let me know if there is anything we can do to make you more comfortable."

Barnard caught the word. "Comfortable?" he echoed raucously. "Why, of course we're comfortable. We're just enjoying the trip. Pity we haven't a pack of cards—we could play a rubber of bridge."

Conway welcomed the spirit of the remark, though he disliked bridge. "I don't suppose Miss Brinklow plays," he said, smiling.

But the missionary turned round briskly to retort: "Indeed I do, and I could never see any harm in cards at all. There's nothing against them in the Bible."

They all laughed, and seemed obliged to her for providing an excuse. At any rate, Conway thought, she wasn't hysterical.

All afternoon the plane had soared through the thin mists of the upper atmosphere, far too high to give clear sight of what lay beneath. Sometimes, at longish intervals, the veil was torn for a moment, to display the jagged outline of a peak, or the glint of some unknown stream. The direction could be determined roughly from the sun; it was still east, with occasional twists to the north; but where it had led depended on the speed of travel, which Conway could not judge with any accuracy. It seemed likely, though, that the flight must already have exhausted a good deal of the gasoline; though that again depended on uncertain factors. Conway had no technical knowledge of aircraft, but he was sure that the pilot, whoever he might be, was altogether an expert. That halt in the rock-strewn valley had demonstrated it, and also other incidents since. And Conway could not repress a feeling that was always his in the presence of any superb and indisputable competence. He was so used to being appealed to for help that mere awareness of some one who would neither ask nor need it was slightly tranquilizing, even amidst the greater perplexities of the future. But he did not expect his companions to share such a tenuous emotion. He recognized that they were likely to have far more personal reasons for anxiety than he had himself. Mallinson, for instance, was engaged to a girl in England; Barnard might be married; Miss Brinklow had her work, vocation, or however she might regard it. Mallinson, incidentally, was by far the least composed; as the hours passed he showed himself increasingly excitable—apt, also, to resent to Conway's face the very coolness which he had praised behind his back. Once, above the roar of the engine, a sharp storm of argument arose. "Look here," Mallinson shouted angrily, "are we bound to sit here twiddling our thumbs while this maniac does everything he damn well wants? What's to prevent us from smashing that panel and having it out with him?"

"Nothing at all," replied Conway, "except that he's armed and we're not, and that in any case, none of us would know how to bring the machine to earth afterwards."

"It can't be very hard, surely. I dare say you could do it."

"My dear Mallinson, why is it always *me* you expect to perform these miracles?"

"Well, anyway, this business is getting hellishly on my nerves. Can't we *make* the fellow come down?"

"How do you suggest it should be done?"

Mallinson was becoming more and more agitated. "Well, he's *there*, isn't he? About six feet away from us, and we're three men to one! Have we got to stare at his damned back all the time? At least we might force him to tell us what the game is."

"Very well, we'll see." Conway took a few paces forward to the partition between the cabin and the pilot's cockpit, which was situated in front and somewhat above. There was a pane of glass, about six inches square and made to slide open, through which the pilot, by turning his head and stooping slightly, could communicate with his passengers. Conway tapped on this with his knuckles. The response was almost comically as he had expected. The glass panel slid sideways and the barrel of a revolver obtruded. Not a word; just that. Conway retreated without arguing the point, and the panel slid back again.

Mallinson, who had watched the incident, was only partly satisfied. "I don't suppose he'd have dared to shoot," he commented. "It's probably bluff."

"Quite," agreed Conway, "but I'd rather leave you to make sure."

"Well, I do feel we ought to put up some sort of a fight before giving in tamely like this."

Conway was sympathetic. He recognized the convention, with all its associations of red-coated soldiers and school history books, that Englishmen fear nothing, never surrender, and are never defeated. He said: "Putting up a fight without a decent chance of winning is a poor game, and I'm not that sort of hero."

"Good for you, sir," interposed Barnard heartily. "When somebody's got you by the short hairs you may as well give in pleasantly and admit it. For my part I'm going to enjoy life while it lasts and have a cigar. I hope you don't think a little bit of extra danger matters to us?"

"Not so far as I'm concerned, but it might bother Miss Brinklow."

Barnard was quick to make amends. "Pardon me, madam, but do you mind if I smoke?"

"Not at all," she answered graciously. "I don't do so myself, but I just love the smell of a cigar."

Conway felt that of all the women who could possibly have made such a remark, she was easily the most typical. Anyhow, Mallinson's

excitement had calmed a little, and to show friendliness he offered
him a cigarette, though he did not light one himself. "I know how
you feel," he said gently. "It's a bad outlook, and it's all the worse,
in some ways, because there isn't much we can do about it."

"And all the better, too, in other ways," he could not help adding
to himself. For he was still immensely fatigued. There was also in
his nature a trait which some people might have called laziness,
though it was not quite that. No one was capable of harder work,
when it had to be done, and few could better shoulder responsibility;
but the facts remained that he was not passionately fond of activity,
and did not enjoy responsibility at all. Both were included in his
job, and he made the best of them, but he was always ready to give
way to any one else who could function as well or better. It was
partly this, no doubt, that had made his success in the Service less
striking than it might have been. He was not ambitious enough to
shove his way past others, or to make an important parade of doing
nothing when there was really nothing doing. His despatches were
sometimes laconic to the point of curtness, and his calm in emergencies, though admired, was often suspected of being too sincere.
Authority likes to feel that a man is imposing some effort on himself, and that his apparent nonchalance is only a cloak to disguise
an outfit of well-bred emotions. With Conway the dark suspicion
had sometimes been current that he really was as unruffled as he
looked, and that whatever happened, he did not give a damn.
But this, too, like the laziness, was an imperfect interpretation. What
most observers failed to perceive in him was something quite baf-
flingly simple—a love of quietness, contemplation, and being alone.

Now, since he was so inclined and there was nothing else to do, he
leaned back in the basket chair and went definitely to sleep. When
he woke he noticed that the others, despite their various anxieties,
had likewise succumbed. Miss Brinklow was sitting bolt upright with
her eyes closed, like some rather dingy and outmoded idol; Mallinson
had lolled forward in his place with his chin in the palm of a hand.
The American was even snoring. Very sensible of them all, Conway
thought; there was no point in wearying themselves with shouting.
But immediately he was aware of certain physical sensations in
himself, slight dizziness and heart-thumping and a tendency to in-
hale sharply and with effort. He remembered similar symptoms once
before—in the Swiss Alps.

Then he turned to the window and gazed out. The surrounding
sky had cleared completely, and in the light of late afternoon there
came to him a vision which, for the instant, snatched the remaining

breath out of his lungs. Far away, at the very limit of distance, lay range upon range of snow-peaks, festooned with glaciers, and floating, in appearance, upon vast levels of cloud. They compassed the whole arc of the circle, merging towards the west in a horizon that was fierce, almost garish in coloring, like an impressionist back-drop done by some half-mad genius. And meanwhile, the plane, on that stupendous stage, was droning over an abyss in face of a sheer white wall that seemed part of the sky itself until the sun caught it. Then, like a dozen piled-up Jungfraus seen from Mürren, it flamed into superb and dazzling incandescence.

Conway was not apt to be easily impressed, and as a rule he did not care for "views," especially the more famous ones for which thoughtful municipalities provide garden seats. Once, on being taken to Tiger Hill, near Darjeeling, to watch the sunrise upon Everest, he had found the highest mountain in the world a definite disappointment. But this fearsome spectacle beyond the window pane was of different caliber; it had no air of posing to be admired. There was something raw and monstrous about those uncompromising ice-cliffs, and a certain sublime impertinence in approaching them thus. He pondered, envisaging maps, calculating distances, estimating times and speeds. Then he became aware that Mallinson had wakened also. He touched the youth on the arm.

CHAPTER TWO

It was typical of Conway that he let the others waken for themselves, and made small response to their exclamations of astonishment; yet later, when Barnard sought his opinion, gave it with something of the detached fluency of a university professor elucidating a problem. He thought it likely, he said, that they were still in India; they had been flying east for several hours, too high to see much, but probably the course had been along some river valley, one stretching roughly east and west. "I wish I hadn't to rely on memory, but my impression is that the valley of the upper Indus fits in well enough. That would have brought us by now to a very spectacular part of the world, and, as you see, so it has."

"You know where we are, then?" Barnard interrupted.

"Well, no—I've never been anywhere near here before, but I wouldn't be surprised if that mountain is Nanga Parbat, the one Mummery lost his life on. In structure and general lay-out it seems in accord with all I've heard about it."

"You are a mountaineer yourself?"

"In my younger days I was keen. Only the usual Swiss climbs, of course."

Mallinson intervened peevishly: "There'd be more point in discussing where we're going to. I wish to God somebody could tell us."

"Well, it looks to me as if we're heading for that range yonder," said Barnard. "Don't you think so, Conway? You'll excuse me calling you that, but if we're all going to have a little adventure together, it's a pity to stand on ceremony."

Conway thought it very natural that any one should call him by his own name, and found Barnard's apologies for so doing a trifle needless. "Oh, certainly," he agreed, and added: "I think that range must be the Karakorams. There are several passes if our man intends to cross them."

"Our man?" exclaimed Mallinson. "You mean our maniac! I reckon it's time we dropped the kidnaping theory. We're far past the Frontier country by now, there aren't any tribes living around here. The only explanation I can think of is that the fellow's a raving lunatic. Would anybody except a lunatic fly into this sort of country?"

"I know that nobody except a damn fine airman *could*," retorted Barnard. "I never was great at geography, but I understand that these are reputed to be the highest mountains in the world, and if that's so, it'll be a pretty first-class performance to cross them."

"And also the will of God," put in Miss Brinklow unexpectedly.

Conway did not offer his opinion. The will of God or the lunacy of man—it seemed to him that you could take your choice, if you wanted a good enough reason for most things. Or, alternatively (and he thought of it as he contemplated the small orderliness of the cabin against the window background of such frantic natural scenery), the will of man and the lunacy of God. It must be satisfying to be quite certain which way to look at it. Then, while he watched and pondered, a strange transformation took place. The light turned to bluish over the whole mountain, with the lower slopes darkening to violet. Something deeper than his usual aloofness rose in him—not quite excitement, still less fear, but a sharp intensity of expectation. He said: "You're quite right, Barnard, this affair grows more and more remarkable."

"Remarkable or not, I don't feel inclined to propose a vote of thanks about it," Mallinson persisted. "We didn't ask to be brought here, and Heaven knows what we shall do when we get *there*, wherever *there* is. And I don't see that it's any less of an outrage because the fellow happens to be a stunt flyer. Even if he is, he can be just as much a lunatic. I once heard of a pilot going mad in mid-air. This fellow must have been mad from the beginning. That's my theory, Conway."

Conway was silent. He found it irksome to be continually shouting above the roar of the machine, and after all, there was little point in arguing possibilities. But when Mallinson pressed for an opinion, he said: "Very well-organized lunacy, you know. Don't forget the landing for gasoline, and also that this was the only machine that could climb to such a height."

"That doesn't prove he isn't mad. He may have been mad enough to plan everything."

"Yes, of course, that's possible."

"Well, then, we've got to decide on a plan of action. What are we going to do when he comes to earth? If he doesn't crash and kill us all, that is. What are we going to *do*? Rush forward and congratulate him on his marvelous flight, I suppose."

"Not on your life," answered Barnard. "I'll leave you to do all the rushing forward."

Again Conway was loth to prolong the argument, especially since the American, with his level-headed banter, seemed quite capable of handling it himself. Already Conway found himself reflecting that the party might have been far less fortunately constituted. Only Mallinson was inclined to be cantankerous, and that might partly be due to the altitude. Rarefied air had different effects on people; Conway, for instance, derived from it a combination of mental clarity and physical apathy that was not unpleasant. Indeed, he breathed the clear cold air in little spasms of content. The whole situation, no doubt, was appalling, but he had no power at the moment to resent anything that proceeded so purposefully and with such captivating interest.

And there came over him, too, as he stared at that superb mountain, a glow of satisfaction that there were such places still left on earth, distant, inaccessible, as yet unhumanized. The icy rampart of the Karakorams was now more striking than ever against the northern sky, which had become mouse-colored and sinister; the peaks had a chill gleam; utterly majestic and remote, their very namelessness had dignity. Those few thousand feet by which they fell short of the known giants might save them eternally from the climbing expedition; they offered a less tempting lure to the record-breaker. Conway was the antithesis of such a type; he was inclined to see vulgarity in the Western ideal of superlatives, and "the utmost for the highest" seemed to him a less reasonable and perhaps more commonplace proposition than "the much for the high." He did not, in fact, care for excessive striving, and he was bored by mere exploits.

While he was still contemplating the scene, twilight fell, steeping the depths in a rich, velvet gloom that spread upwards like a dye. Then the whole range, much nearer now, paled into fresh splendor; a full moon rose, touching each peak in succession like some celestial lamp-lighter, until the long horizon glittered against a blue-black sky. The air grew cold and a wind sprang up, tossing the machine uncomfortably. These new distresses lowered the spirits of the passengers; it had not been reckoned that the flight could go on after dusk, and now the last hope lay in the exhaustion of gasoline. That, however, was bound to come soon. Mallinson began to argue about it, and Conway, with some reluctance, for he really did not know, gave as his estimate that the utmost distance might be anything up to a thousand miles, of which they must already have covered most. "Well, where would that bring us?" queried the youth miserably.

"It's not easy to judge, but probably some part of Tibet. If these are the Karakorams, Tibet lies beyond. One of the crests, by the way, must be K2, which is generally counted the second highest mountain in the world."

"Next on the list after Everest," commented Barnard. "Gee, this is some scenery."

"And from a climber's point of view much stiffer than Everest. The Duke of Abruzzi gave it up as an absolutely impossible peak."

"*Oh, God!*" muttered Mallinson testily, but Barnard laughed. "I guess you must be the official guide on this trip, Conway, and I'll admit that if I only had a flask of café cognac I wouldn't care if it's Tibet or Tennessee."

"But what are we going to do about it?" urged Mallinson again. "Why are we here? What can be the point of it all? I don't see how you can make jokes about it."

"Well, it's as good as making a scene about it, young fellow. Besides, if the man *is* off his nut, as you've suggested, there probably *isn't* any point."

"He *must* be mad. I can't think of any other explanation. Can you, Conway?"

Conway shook his head.

Miss Brinklow turned round as she might have done during the interval of a play. "As you haven't asked my opinion, perhaps I oughtn't to give it," she began, with shrill modesty, "but I should like to say that I agree with Mr. Mallinson. I'm sure the poor man can't be quite right in his head. The pilot, I mean, of course. There would be no excuse for him, anyhow, if he were *not* mad." She added, shouting confidentially above the din: "And do you know, this is my first trip in the air! My very first! Nothing would ever induce me to do it before, though a friend of mine tried her very best to persuade me to fly from London to Paris."

"And now you're flying from India to Tibet instead," said Barnard. "That's the way things happen."

She went on: "I once knew a missionary who had been to Tibet. He said the Tibetans were very odd people. They believe we are descended from monkeys."

"Real smart of 'em."

"Oh, dear, no, I don't mean in the modern way. They've had the belief for hundreds of years, it's only one of their superstitions. Of course I'm against all of it myself, and I think Darwin was far worse than any Tibetan. I take my stand on the Bible."

"Fundamentalist, I suppose?"

But Miss Brinklow did not appear to understand the term. "I used to belong to the L.M.S.," she shrieked, "but I disagreed with them about infant baptism."

Conway continued to feel that this was a rather comic remark long after it had occurred to him that the initials were those of the London Missionary Society. Still picturing the inconveniences of holding a theological argument at Euston Station, he began to think that there was something slightly fascinating about Miss Brinklow. He even wondered if he could offer her any article of his clothing for the night, but decided at length that her constitution was probably wirier than his. So he huddled up, closed his eyes, and went quite easily and peacefully to sleep.

And the flight proceeded.

Suddenly they were all wakened by a lurch of the machine. Conway's head struck the window, dazing him for the moment; a returning lurch sent him floundering between the two tiers of seats. It was much colder. The first thing he did, automatically, was to glance at his watch; it showed half-past one, he must have been asleep for some time. His ears were full of a loud, flapping sound, which he took to be imaginary until he realized that the engine had been shut off and that the plane was rushing against a gale. Then he stared through the window and could see the earth quite close, vague and snail-gray, scampering underneath. "He's going to land!" Mallinson shouted; and Barnard, who had also been flung out of his seat, responded with a saturnine: "If he's lucky." Miss Brinklow, whom the entire commotion seemed to have disturbed least of all, was adjusting her hat as calmly as if Dover Harbor were just in sight.

Presently the plane touched ground. But it was a bad landing this time—"Oh, my God, damned bad, *damned* bad!" Mallinson groaned as he clutched at his seat during ten seconds of crashing and swaying. Something was heard to strain and snap, and one of the tires exploded. "That's done it," he added in tones of anguished pessimism. "A broken tail-skid, we'll have to stay where we are now, that's certain."

Conway, never talkative at times of crisis, stretched his stiffened legs and felt his head where it had banged against the window. A bruise, nothing much. He must do something to help these people. But he was the last of the four to stand up when the plane came to rest. "Steady," he called out as Mallinson wrenched open the door of the cabin and prepared to make the jump to earth; and eerily, in the comparative silence, the youth's answer came: "No need to be steady—this looks like the end of the world—there's not a soul about, anyhow."

A moment later, chilled and shivering, they were all aware that this was so. With no sound in their ears save the fierce gusts of wind and their own crunching footsteps, they felt themselves at the mercy of something dour and savagely melancholy—a mood in which both earth and air were saturated. The moon looked to have disappeared behind clouds, and starlight illumined a tremendous emptiness heaving with wind. Without thought or knowledge, one could have guessed that this bleak world was mountain-high, and that the mountains rising from it were mountains on top of mountains. A range of them gleamed on a far horizon like a row of dog-teeth.

Mallinson, feverishly active, was already making for the cockpit. "I'm not scared of the fellow on land, whoever he is," he cried. "I'm going to tackle him right away. . . ."

The others watched apprehensively, hypnotized by the spectacle of such energy. Conway sprang after him, but too late to prevent the investigation. After a few seconds, however, the youth dropped down again, gripping his arm and muttering in a hoarse, sobered staccato: "I say, Conway, it's queer. . . . I think the fellow's ill or dead or something. . . . I can't get a word out of him. Come up and look. . . . I took his revolver, at any rate."

"Better give it to me," said Conway, and though still rather dazed by the recent blow on his head, he nerved himself for action. Of all times and places and situations on earth, this seemed to him to combine the most hideous discomforts. He hoisted himself stiffly into a position from which he could see, not very well, into the enclosed cockpit. There was a strong smell of gasoline, so he did not risk striking a match. He could just discern the pilot, huddled forward, his head sprawling over the controls. He shook him, unfastened his helmet, and loosened the clothes round his neck. A moment later he turned round to report: "Yes, there's something happened to him. We must get him out." But an observer might have added that something had happened to Conway as well. His voice was sharper, more incisive; no longer did he sound to be hovering on the brink of some profound doubtfulness. The time, the place, the cold, his fatigue, were now of less account; there was a job that simply had to be done, and the more conventional part of him was uppermost and preparing to do it.

With Barnard and Mallinson assisting, the pilot was extracted from his seat and lifted to the ground. He was unconscious, not dead. Conway had no particular medical knowledge, but, as to most men who have lived in outlandish places, the phenomena of illness were mostly familiar. "Possibly a heart attack brought on by the high altitude," he diagnosed, stooping over the unknown man. "We can do very little for him out here—there's no shelter from this infernal wind. Better get him inside the cabin, and ourselves too. We haven't an idea where we are, and it's hopeless to make a move until daylight."

The verdict and the suggestion were both accepted without dispute. Even Mallinson concurred. They carried the man into the cabin and laid him full-length along the gangway between the seats. The interior was no warmer than outside, but offered a screen to the flurries of wind. It was the wind, before much time had passed, that became the central preoccupation of them all—the *leit-motif*, as it were, of the whole mournful night. It was not an ordinary wind. It was not merely a strong wind or a cold wind. It was somehow a frenzy that lived all around them, a master stamping and ranting over his own domain. It tilted the loaded machine and shook it viciously, and when Conway glanced through the windows it seemed as if the same wind were whirling splinters of light out of the stars.

The stranger lay inert, while Conway, with difficulty in the dimness and confined space, made what examination he could by the light of matches. But it did not reveal much. "His heart's faint," he said at last, and then Miss Brinklow, after groping in her handbag, created a small sensation. "I wonder if this would be any use to the poor man," she proffered condescendingly. "I never touch a drop myself, but I always carry it with me in case of accidents. And this *is* a sort of accident, isn't it?"

"I should say it was," replied Conway with grimness. He unscrewed the bottle, smelt it, and poured some of the brandy into the man's mouth. "Just the stuff for him. Thanks." After an interval the slightest movement of eyelids was visible. Mallinson suddenly became hysterical. "I can't help it," he cried, laughing wildly. "We all look such a lot of damn fools striking matches over a corpse. . . . And he isn't much of a beauty, is he? Chink, I should say, if he's anything at all."

"Possibly." Conway's voice was level and rather severe. "But he's not a corpse yet. With a bit of luck we may bring him round."

"Luck? It'll be his luck, not ours."

"Don't be too sure. And shut up for the time being, anyhow."

There was enough of the schoolboy still in Mallinson to make him respond to the curt command of a senior, though he was obviously in poor control of himself. Conway, though sorry for him, was more concerned with the immediate problem of the pilot, since he, alone of them all, might be able to give some explanation of their plight. Conway had no desire to discuss the matter further in a merely speculative way; there had been enough of that during the journey. He was uneasy now beyond his continuing mental curiosity, for he was aware that the whole situation had ceased to be excitingly perilous and was threatening to become a trial of endurance ending in catastrophe. Keeping vigil throughout that gale-tormented night, he faced facts none the less frankly because he did not trouble to enunciate them to the others. He guessed that the flight had progressed far beyond the western range of the Himalaya towards the less known heights of the Kuen-Lun. In that event they would by now have reached the loftiest and least hospitable part of the earth's surface, the Tibetan plateau, two miles high even in its lowest valleys, a vast, uninhabited, and largely unexplored region of wind-swept upland. Somewhere they were, in that forlorn country, marooned in far less comfort than on most desert islands. Then abruptly, as if to answer his curiosity by increasing it, a rather awe-inspiring change took place. The moon, which he had thought to be hidden by clouds, swung over the lip of some shadowy eminence and, whilst still not showing itself directly, unveiled the darkness ahead. Conway could see the outline of a long valley, with rounded, sad-looking low hills on either side, jet-black against the deep electric blue of the night-sky. But it was to the head of the valley that his eyes were led irresistibly, for there, soaring into the gap, and magnificent in the full shimmer of moonlight, appeared what he took to be the loveliest mountain on earth. It was an almost perfect cone of snow, simple in outline as if a child had drawn it, and impossible to classify as to size, height, or nearness. It was so radiant, so serenely poised, that he wondered for a moment if it were real at all. Then, while he gazed, a tiny puff clouded the edge of the pyramid, giving life to the vision before the faint rumble of the avalanche confirmed it.

He had an impulse to rouse the others to share the spectacle, but decided after consideration that its effect might not be tranquilizing. Nor was it so, from a common sense view-point; such virgin splendors merely emphasized the facts of isolation and danger. There was quite a probability that the nearest human settlement was hundreds of miles away. And they had no food; they were unarmed except for one revolver; the aeroplane was damaged and almost fuel-less, even if any one had known how to fly. They had no clothes suited to the terrific chills and winds; Mallinson's motoring-coat and his own ulster were quite inadequate, and even Miss Brinklow, woolied and mufflered as for a polar expedition (ridiculous, he had thought, on first beholding her), could not be feeling happy. They were all, too, except himself, affected by the altitude. Even Barnard had sunk into melancholy under the strain. Mallinson was muttering to himself; it was clear what would happen to him if these hardships went on for long. In face of such distressful prospects Conway found himself quite unable to restrain an admiring glance at Miss Brinklow. She was not, he reflected, a normal person; no woman who taught Afghans to sing hymns could be considered so. But she was, after every calamity, still normally abnormal, and he was deeply obliged to her for it. "I hope you're not feeling too bad?" he said sympathetically, when he caught her eye.

"The soldiers during the War had to suffer worse things than this," she replied.

The comparison did not seem to Conway a very valuable one. In point of fact, he had never spent a night in the trenches quite so thoroughly unpleasant, though doubtless many others had. He concentrated his attention on the pilot, now breathing fitfully and sometimes slightly stirring. Probably Mallinson was right in guessing the man Chinese. He had the typical Mongol nose and cheekbones, despite his successful impersonation of a British flight-lieutenant. Mallinson had called him ugly, but Conway, who had lived in China, thought him a fairly passable specimen, though now, in the burnished circle of match-flame, his pallid skin and gaping mouth were not pretty.

The night dragged on, as if each minute were something heavy and tangible that had to be pushed to make way for the next. Moonlight faded after a time, and with it that distant specter of the mountain; then the triple mischiefs of darkness, cold, and wind increased until dawn. As though at its signal, the wind dropped, leaving the world in compassionate quietude. Framed in the pale triangle ahead, the mountain showed again, gray at first, then silver, then pink as the earliest sun rays caught the summit. In the lessening gloom the valley itself took shape, revealing a floor of rock and shingle sloping upwards. It was not a friendly picture, but to Conway, as he surveyed, there came a queer perception of fineness in it, of something that had no romantic appeal at all, but a steely, almost an intellectual quality. The white pyramid in the distance compelled the mind's assent as passionlessly as a Euclidean theorem, and when at last the sun rose into a sky of deep delphinium blue, he felt only a little less than comfortable again.

As the air grew warmer the others wakened, and he suggested carrying the pilot into the open, where the sharp dry air and the

sunlight might help to revive him. This was done, and they began a
second and pleasanter vigil. Eventually the man opened his eyes and
began to speak convulsively. His four passengers stooped over him,
listening intently to sounds that were meaningless except to Conway,
who occasionally made answers. After some time the man became
weaker, talked with increasing difficulty, and finally died. That was
about midmorning.

Conway then turned to his companions. "I'm sorry to say he told
me very little—little, I mean, compared with what we should like to
know. Merely that we are in Tibet, which is obvious. He didn't give
any coherent account of why he had brought us here, but he seemed
to know the locality. He spoke a kind of Chinese that I don't understand very well, but I think he said something about a lamasery near
here, along the valley, I gathered, where we could get food and
shelter. Shangri-La, he called it. *La* is Tibetan for mountain pass. He
was most emphatic that we should go there."

"Which doesn't seem to me any reason at all why we should," said
Mallinson. "After all, he was probably off his head. Wasn't he?"

"You know as much about that as I do. But if we don't go to this
place, where else are we to go?"

"Anywhere you like, I don't care. All I'm certain of is that this
Shangri-La, if it's in that direction, must be a few extra miles from
civilization. I should feel happier if we were lessening the distance,
not increasing it. Damnation, man, aren't you going to get us back?"

Conway replied patiently: "I don't think you properly understand
the position, Mallinson. We're in a part of the world that no one
knows very much about, except that it's difficult and dangerous, even
for a fully equipped expedition. Considering that hundreds of miles
of this sort of country probably surround us on all sides, the notion
of walking back to Peshawur doesn't strike me as very hopeful."

"I don't think I could possibly manage it," said Miss Brinklow
seriously.

Barnard nodded. "It looks as if we're darned lucky, then, if this
lamasery *is* round the corner."

"Comparatively lucky, maybe," agreed Conway. "After all, we've
no food, and as you can see for yourselves, the country isn't the kind
it would be easy to live on. In a few hours we shall all be famished.
And then to-night, if we were to stay here, we should have to face
the wind and the cold again. It's not a pleasant prospect. Our only
chance, it seems to me, is to find some other human beings, and

where else should we begin looking for them except where we've been told they exist?"

"And what if it's a trap?" asked Mallinson, but Barnard supplied an answer. "A nice warm trap," he said, "with a piece of cheese in it, would suit me down to the ground."

They laughed, except Mallinson, who looked distraught and nerve-racked. Finally Conway went on: "I take it, then, that we're all more or less agreed? There's an obvious way along the valley; it doesn't look too steep, though we shall have to take it slowly. In any case, we could do nothing here. We couldn't even bury this man without dynamite. Besides, the lamasery people may be able to supply us with porters for the journey back. We shall need them. I suggest we start at once, so that if we don't locate the place by late afternoon we shall have time to return for another night in the cabin."

"And supposing we *do* locate it?" queried Mallinson, still intransigeant. "Have we any guarantee that we shan't be murdered?"

"None at all. But I think it is a less, and perhaps also a preferable risk to being starved or frozen to death." He added, feeling that such chilly logic might not be entirely suited for the occasion: "As a matter of fact, murder is the very last thing one would expect in a Buddhist monastery. It would be rather less likely than being killed in an English cathedral."

"Like Saint Thomas of Canterbury," said Miss Brinklow, nodding an emphatic agreement, but completely spoiling his point. Mallinson shrugged his shoulders and responded with melancholy irritation: "Very well, then, we'll be off to Shangri-La. Wherever and whatever it is, we'll try it. But let's hope it's not half-way up that mountain."

The remark served to fix their glances on the glittering cone towards which the valley pointed. Sheerly magnificent it looked in the full light of day; and then their gaze turned to a stare, for they could see, far away and approaching them down the slope, the figures of men. "Providence!" whispered Miss Brinklow.

CHAPTER THREE

Part of Conway was always an onlooker, however active might be the rest. Just now, while waiting for the strangers to come nearer, he refused to be fussed into deciding what he might or mightn't do in any number of possible contingencies. And this was not bravery, or coolness, or any especially sublime confidence in his own power to make decisions on the spur of the moment. It was, if the worst view be taken, a form of indolence, an unwillingness to interrupt his mere spectator's interest in what was happening.

As the figures moved down the valley they revealed themselves to be a party of a dozen or more, carrying with them a hooded chair. In this, a little later, could be discerned a person robed in blue. Conway could not imagine where they were all going, but it certainly seemed providential, as Miss Brinklow had said, that such a detachment should chance to be passing just there and then. As soon as he was within hailing distance he left his own party and walked ahead, though not hurriedly, for he knew that Orientals enjoy the ritual of meeting and like to take their time over it. Halting when a few yards off, he bowed with due courtesy. Much to his surprise the robed figure stepped from the chair, came forward with dignified delibera- tion, and held out his hand. Conway responded, and observed an old or elderly Chinese, gray-haired, clean-shaven, and rather pallidly decorative in a silk embroidered gown. He in his turn appeared to be submitting Conway to the same kind of ready reckoning. Then, in precise and perhaps too accurate English, he said: "I am from the lamasery of Shangri-La."

Conway bowed again, and after a suitable pause began to explain briefly the circumstances that had brought him and his three com- panions to such an unfrequented part of the world. At the end of the recital the Chinese made a gesture of understanding. "It is indeed remarkable," he said, and gazed reflectively at the damaged aero- plane. Then he added: "My name is Chang, if you would be so good as to present me to your friends."

Conway managed to smile urbanely. He was rather taken with this latest phenomenon, a Chinese who spoke perfect English and

observed the social formalities of Bond Street amidst the wilds of
Tibet. He turned to the others, who had by this time caught up and
were regarding the encounter with varying degrees of astonishment.
"Miss Brinklow . . . Mr. Barnard, who is an American . . . Mr.
Mallinson . . . and my own name is Conway. We are all glad to see
you, though the meeting is almost as puzzling as the fact of our being
here at all. Indeed, we were just about to make our way to your
lamasery, so it is doubly fortunate. If you could give us directions for
the journey—"

"There is no need for that. I shall be delighted to act as your
guide."

"But I could not think of putting you to such trouble. It is exceedingly kind of you, but if the distance is not far—"

"It is not far, but it is not easy, either. I shall esteem it an honor
to accompany you and your friends."

"But really—"

"I must insist."

Conway thought that the argument, in its context of place and
circumstance, was in some danger of becoming ludicrous. "Very
well," he responded. "I'm sure we are all most obliged."

Mallinson, who had been somberly enduring these pleasantries,
now interposed with something of the shrill acerbity of the barrack-
square. "Our stay won't be long," he announced curtly. "We shall pay
for anything we have, and we should like to hire some of your men
to help us on our journey back. We want to return to civilization as
soon as possible."

"And are you so very certain that you are away from it?"

The query, delivered with much suavity, only stung the youth to
further sharpness. "I'm quite sure I'm far away from where I want
to be, and so are we all. We shall be grateful for temporary shelter,
but we shall be more grateful still if you'll provide means for us to
return. How long do you suppose the journey to India will take?"

"I really could not say at all."

"Well, I hope we're not going to have any trouble about it. I've
had some experience of hiring native porters, and we shall expect
you to use your influence to get us a square deal."

Conway felt that most of all this was rather needlessly truculent,
and he was just about to intervene when the reply came, still with
immense dignity: "I can only assure you, Mr. Mallinson, that you
will be honorably treated and that ultimately you will have no
regrets."

"*Ultimately?*" Mallinson exclaimed, pouncing on the word, but there was greater ease in avoiding a scene since wine and fruit were now on offer, having been unpacked by the marching party, stocky Tibetans in sheepskins, fur hats, and yak-skin boots. The wine had a pleasant flavor, not unlike a good hock, while the fruit included mangoes, perfectly ripened and almost painfully delicious after so many hours of fasting. Mallinson ate and drank with incurious relish; but Conway, relieved of immediate worries and reluctant to cherish distant ones, was wondering how mangoes could be cultivated at such an altitude. He was also interested in the mountain beyond the valley; it was a sensational peak, by any standards, and he was surprised that some traveler had not made much of it in the kind of book that a journey in Tibet invariably elicits. He climbed it in mind as he gazed, choosing a route by *col* and *couloir* until an exclamation from Mallinson drew his attention back to earth; he looked round then and saw that the Chinese had been earnestly regarding him. "You were contemplating the mountain, Mr. Conway?" came the enquiry.

"Yes. It's a fine sight. It has a name, I suppose?"

"It is called Karakal."

"I don't think I ever heard of it. Is it very high?"

"Over twenty-eight thousand feet."

"Indeed? I didn't realize there would be anything on that scale outside the Himalaya. Has it been properly surveyed? Whose are the measurements?"

"Whose would you expect, my dear sir? Is there anything incompatible between monasticism and trigonometry?"

Conway savored the phrase and replied: "Oh, not at all—not at all." Then he laughed politely. He thought it a poorish joke, but one perhaps worth making the most of. Soon after that the journey to Shangri-La was begun.

All morning the climb proceeded, slowly and by easy gradients; but at such height the physical effort was considerable, and none had energy to spare for talk. The Chinese traveled luxuriously in his chair, which might have seemed unchivalrous had it not been absurd to picture Miss Brinklow in such a regal setting. Conway, whom the rarefied air troubled less than the rest, was at pains to catch the occasional chatter of the chair-bearers. He knew a very little Tibetan, just enough to gather that the men were glad to be returning to the lamasery. He could not, even had he wished, have continued converse with their leader, since the latter, with eyes closed and face half hidden behind curtains, appeared to have the knack of instant and well-timed sleep.

Meanwhile the sun was warm; hunger and thirst had been appeased, if not satisfied; and the air, clean as from another planet, was more precious with every intake. One had to breathe consciously and deliberately, which, though disconcerting at first, induced after a time an almost ecstatic tranquillity of mind. The whole body moved in a single rhythm of breathing, walking, and thinking; the lungs, no longer discreet and automatic, were disciplined to harmony with mind and limb. Conway, in whom a mystical strain ran in curious consort with skepticism, found himself not unhappily puzzled over the sensation. Once or twice he spoke a cheerful word to Mallinson, but the youth was laboring under the strain of the ascent. Barnard also gasped asthmatically, while Miss Brinklow was engaged in some grim pulmonary warfare which for some reason she made efforts to conceal. "We're nearly at the top," Conway said encouragingly.

"I once ran for a train and felt just like this," she answered.

So also, Conway reflected, there were people who considered cider was just like champagne. It was a matter of palate.

He was surprised to find that beyond his puzzlement he had few misgivings, and none at all on his own behalf. There were moments in life when one opened wide one's soul just as one might open wide one's purse if an evening's entertainment were proving unexpectedly costly but also unexpectedly novel. Conway, on that breathless morning in sight of Karakal, made just such a willing, relieved, yet not excited response to the offer of new experience. After ten years in various parts of Asia he had attained to a somewhat fastidious valuation of places and happenings; and this, he was bound to admit, promised unusually.

About a couple of miles along the valley the ascent grew steeper, but by this time the sun was overclouded and a silvery mist obscured the view. Thunder and avalanches resounded from the snow-fields above; the air took chill, and then, with the sudden changefulness of mountain regions, became bitterly cold. A flurry of wind and sleet drove up, drenching the party and adding immeasurably to their discomfort; even Conway felt at one moment that it would be impossible to go much further. But shortly afterwards it seemed that the summit of the ridge had been reached, for the chair-bearers halted to readjust their burden. The condition of Barnard and Mallinson, who were both suffering severely, led to continued delay; but the Tibetans were clearly anxious to press on, and made signs that the rest of the journey would be less fatiguing.

After these assurances it was disappointing to see them uncoiling ropes. "Do they mean to hang us already?" Barnard managed to exclaim, with desperate facetiousness; but the guides soon showed that their less sinister intention was merely to link the party together in ordinary mountaineering fashion. When they observed that Conway was familiar with rope-craft, they became much more respectful and allowed him to dispose the party in his own way. He put himself next to Mallinson, with Tibetans ahead and to the rear, and with Barnard and Miss Brinklow and more Tibetans further back still. He was prompt to notice that the men, during their leader's continuing sleep, were inclined to let him deputize. He felt a familiar quickening of authority; if there were to be any difficult business he would give what he knew was his to give—confidence and command. He had been a first-class mountaineer in his time, and was still, no doubt, pretty good. "You've got to look after Barnard," he told Miss Brinklow, half jocularly, half meaning it; and she answered, with the coyness of an eagle: "I'll do my best, but you know, I've never been roped before."

But the next stage, though occasionally exciting, was less arduous than he had been prepared for, and a relief from the lung-bursting strain of the ascent. The track consisted of a traverse cut along the flank of a rock wall whose height above them the mist obscured. Perhaps mercifully it also obscured the abyss on the other side, though Conway, who had a good eye for heights, would have liked to see where he was. The path was scarcely more than two feet wide in places, and the manner in which the bearers maneuvered the chair at such points drew his admiration almost as strongly as did the nerves of the occupant who could manage to sleep through it all. The Tibetans were reliable enough, but they seemed happier when the path widened and became slightly downhill. Then they began to sing amongst themselves, lilting barbaric tunes that Conway could imagine orchestrated by Massenet for some Tibetan ballet. The rain ceased and the air grew warmer. "Well, it's quite certain we could never have found our way here by ourselves," said Conway, intending to be cheerful, but Mallinson did not find the remark very comforting. He was, in fact, acutely terrified, and in more danger of showing it now that the worst was over. "Should we be missing much?" he retorted bitterly. The track went on, more sharply downhill, and at one spot Conway found some edelweiss, the first welcome sign of more hospitable levels. But this, when he announced it, consoled Mallinson even less. "Good God, Conway, d'you fancy you're pottering about the Alps? What sort of hell's kitchen are we making for, that's what I'd like to know? And what's our plan of action when we get to it? *What are we going to do?*"

Conway said quietly: "If you'd had all the experiences I've had, you'd know that there are times in life when the most comfortable thing is to do nothing at all. Things happen to you and you just let them happen. The War was rather like that. One is fortunate if, as on this occasion, a touch of novelty seasons the unpleasantness."

"You're too confoundedly philosophic for me. That wasn't your mood during the trouble at Baskul."

"Of course not, because then there was a chance that I could alter events by my own actions. But now, for the moment at least, there's no such chance. We're here because we're here, if you want a reason. I've usually found it a soothing one."

"I suppose you realize the appalling job we shall have to get back by the way we've come. We've been slithering along the face of a perpendicular mountain for the last hour—I've been taking notice."

"So have I."

"Have you?" Mallinson coughed excitedly. "I dare say I'm being a nuisance, but I can't help it. I'm suspicious about all this. I feel we're doing far too much what these fellows want us to. They're getting us into a corner."

"Even if they are, the only alternative was to stay out of it and perish."

"I know that's logical, but it doesn't seem to help. I'm afraid I don't find it as easy as you do to accept the situation. I can't forget that two days ago we were in the consulate at Baskul. To think of all that has happened since is a bit overwhelming to me. I'm sorry. I'm overwrought. It makes me realize how lucky I was to miss the War; I suppose I should have got hysterical about things. The whole world seems to have gone completely mad all round me. I must be pretty wild myself to be talking to you like this."

Conway shook his head. "My dear boy, not at all. You're twenty-four years old, and you're somewhere about two and a half miles up in the air: those are reasons enough for anything you may happen to feel at the moment. I think you've come through a trying ordeal extraordinarily well, better than I should at your age."

"But don't *you* feel the madness of it all? The way we flew over those mountains and that awful waiting in the wind and the pilot dying and then meeting these fellows, doesn't it all seem nightmarish and incredible when you look back on it?"

"It does, of course."

"Then I wish I knew how you manage to keep so cool about everything."

"Do you really wish that? I'll tell you if you like, though you'll perhaps think me cynical. It's because so much else that I can look back on seems nightmarish too. This isn't the only mad part of the world, Mallinson. After all, if you *must* think of Baskul, do you remember just before we left how the revolutionaries were torturing their captives to get information? An ordinary washing-mangle, quite effective, of course, but I don't think I ever saw anything more comically dreadful. And do you recollect the last message that came through before we were cut off? It was a circular from a Manchester textile firm asking if we knew of any trade openings in Baskul for the sale of corsets! Isn't that mad enough for you? Believe me, in arriving here the worst that can have happened is that we've exchanged one form of lunacy for another. And as for the War, if you'd been in it you'd have done the same as I did, learned how to funk with a stiff lip."

They were still conversing when a sharp but brief ascent robbed them of breath, inducing in a few paces all their earlier strain. Presently the ground leveled, and they stepped out of the mist into clear, sunny air. Ahead, and only a short distance away, lay the lamasery of Shangri-La.

To Conway, seeing it first, it might have been a vision fluttering out of that solitary rhythm in which lack of oxygen had encompassed all his faculties. It was, indeed, a strange and half-incredible sight. A group of colored pavilions clung to the mountainside with none of the grim deliberation of a Rhineland castle, but rather with the chance delicacy of flower-petals impaled upon a crag. It was superb and exquisite. An austere emotion carried the eye upward from milk-blue roofs to the gray rock bastion above, tremendous as the Wetterhorn above Grindelwald. Beyond that, in a dazzling pyramid, soared the snow slopes of Karakal. It might well be, Conway thought, the most terrifying mountainscape in the world, and he imagined the immense stress of snow and glacier against which the rock functioned as a gigantic retaining wall. Someday, perhaps, the whole mountain would split, and a half of Karakal's icy splendor come toppling into the valley. He wondered if the slightness of the risk combined with its fearfulness might even be found agreeably stimulating.

Hardly less an enticement was the downward prospect, for the mountain wall continued to drop, nearly perpendicularly, into a cleft that could only have been the result of some cataclysm in the far past. The floor of the valley, hazily distant, welcomed the eye with greenness; sheltered from winds, and surveyed rather than dominated by the lamasery, it looked to Conway a delightfully favored place, though if it were inhabited its community must be completely isolated by the lofty and sheerly unscalable ranges on the further side. Only to the lamasery did there appear to be any climbable egress at all. Conway experienced, as he gazed, a slight tightening of apprehension; Mallinson's misgivings were not, perhaps, to be wholly disregarded. But the feeling was only momentary, and soon merged in the deeper sensation, half mystical, half visual, of having reached at last some place that was an end, a finality.

He never exactly remembered how he and the others arrived at the lamasery, or with what formalities they were received, unroped, and ushered into the precincts. That thin air had a dream-like texture, matching the porcelain-blue of the sky; with every breath and every glance he took in a deep anesthetizing tranquillity that made him impervious alike to Mallinson's uneasiness, Barnard's witticisms, and Miss Brinklow's coy portrayal of a lady well prepared for the worst. He vaguely recollected surprise at finding the interior spacious, well warmed, and quite clean; but there was no time to do more than notice these qualities, for the Chinese had left his hooded chair and was already leading the way through various antechambers. He was quite affable now. "I must apologize," he said, "for leaving you to yourselves on the way, but the truth is, journeys of that kind don't suit me, and I have to take care of myself. I trust you were not too fatigued?"

"We managed," replied Conway with a wry smile.

"Excellent. And now, if you will come with me, I will show you to your apartments. No doubt you would like baths. Our accommodation is simple, but I hope adequate."

At this point Barnard, who was still affected by shortness of breath, gave vent to an asthmatic chuckle. "Well," he gasped, "I can't say I like your climate yet—the air seems to stick on my chest a bit—but you've certainly got a darned fine view out of your front windows. Do we all have to line up for the bathroom, or is this an American hotel?"

"I think you will find everything quite satisfactory, Mr. Barnard."

Miss Brinklow nodded primly. "I should hope so, indeed."

"And afterwards," continued the Chinese, "I should be greatly honored if you will all join me at dinner."

Conway replied courteously. Only Mallinson had given no sign of his attitude in the face of these unlooked-for amenities. Like Barnard, he had been suffering from the altitude, but now, with an effort, he found breath to exclaim: "And afterwards also, if you don't mind, we'll make our plans for getting away. The sooner the better, so far as I'm concerned."

CHAPTER FOUR

"So you see," Chang was saying, "we are less barbarian than you expected. . . ."

Conway, later that evening, was not disposed to deny it. He was enjoying that pleasant mingling of physical ease and mental alertness which seemed to him, of all sensations, the most truly civilized. So far, the appointments of Shangri-La had been all that he could have wished, certainly more than he could ever have expected. That a Tibetan monastery should possess a system of central heating was not, perhaps, so very remarkable in an age that supplied even Lhasa with telephones; but that it should combine the mechanics of Western hygiene with so much else that was Eastern and traditional, struck him as exceedingly singular. The bath, for instance, in which he had recently luxuriated, had been of a delicate green porcelain, a product, according to inscription, of Akron, Ohio. Yet the native attendant had valeted him in Chinese fashion, cleansing his ears and nostrils, and passing a thin, silk swab under his lower eyelids. He had wondered at the time if and how his three companions were receiving similar attentions.

Conway had lived for nearly a decade in China, not wholly in the bigger cities; and he counted it, all things considered, the happiest part of his life. He liked the Chinese, and felt at home with Chinese ways. In particular he liked Chinese cooking, with its subtle undertones of taste; and his first meal at Shangri-La had therefore conveyed a welcome familiarity. He suspected, too, that it might have contained some herb or drug to relieve respiration, for he not only felt a difference himself, but could observe a greater ease among his fellow guests. Chang, he noticed, ate nothing but a small portion of green salad, and took no wine. "You will excuse me," he had explained at the outset, "but my diet is very restricted; I am obliged to take care of myself."

It was the reason he had given before, and Conway wondered by what form of invalidism he was afflicted. Regarding him now more closely, he found it difficult to guess his age; his smallish and somehow undetailed features, together with the moist clay texture of his

skin, gave him a look that might either have been that of a young
man prematurely old or of an old man remarkably well preserved.
He was by no means without attractiveness of a kind; a certain stylized courtesy hung about him in a fragrance too delicate to be detected till one had ceased to think about it. In his embroidered gown
of blue silk, with the usual side-slashed skirt and tight-ankled trousers, all the hue of water color skies, he had a cold metallic charm
which Conway found pleasing, though he knew it was not everybody's taste.

The atmosphere, in fact, was Chinese rather than specifically Tibetan; and this in itself gave Conway an agreeable sensation of being
at home, though again it was one that he could not expect the others
to share. The room, too, pleased him; it was admirably proportioned,
and sparingly adorned with tapestries and one or two fine pieces of
lacquer. Light was from paper lanterns, motionless in the still air.
He felt a soothing comfort of mind and body, and his renewed speculations as to some possible drug were hardly apprehensive. Whatever
it was, if it existed at all, it had relieved Barnard's breathlessness
and Mallinson's truculence; both had dined well, finding satisfaction
in eating rather than talk. Conway also had been hungry enough,
and was not sorry that etiquette demanded gradualness in approaching matters of importance. He had never cared for hurrying a situation that was itself enjoyable, so that the technique well suited him.
Not, indeed, until he had begun a cigarette did he give a gentle
lead to his curiosity; he remarked then, addressing Chang: "You
seem a very fortunate community, and most hospitable to strangers.
I don't imagine, though, that you receive them often."

"Seldom indeed," replied the Chinese, with measured stateliness.
"It is not a traveled part of the world."

Conway smiled at that. "You put the matter mildly. It looked to
me, as I came, the most isolated spot I ever set eyes on. A separate
culture might flourish here without contamination from the outside
world."

"Contamination, would you say?"

"I use the word in reference to dance bands, cinemas, electric
signs, and so on. Your plumbing is quite rightly as modern as you can
get it, the only certain boon, to my mind, that the East can take from
the West. I often think that the Romans were fortunate; their civilization reached as far as hot baths without touching the fatal knowledge of machinery."

Conway paused. He had been talking with an impromptu fluency
which, though not insincere, was chiefly designed to create and con-

trol an atmosphere. He was rather good at that sort of thing. Only
a willingness to respond to the superfine courtesy of the occasion
prevented him from being more openly curious.

Miss Brinklow, however, had no such scruples. "Please," she said,
though the word was by no means submissive, "will you tell us about
the monastery?"

Chang raised his eyebrows in very gentle deprecation of such im-
mediacy. "It will give me the greatest of pleasure, madam, so far
as I am able. What exactly do you wish to know?"

"First of all, how many are there of you here, and what nationality do you belong to?" It was clear that her orderly mind was func-
tioning no less professionally than at the Baskul mission-house.

Chang replied: "Those of us in full lamahood number about fifty,
and there are a few others, like myself, who have not yet attained
to complete initiation. We shall do so in due course, it is to be hoped.
Till then we are half-lamas, postulants, you might say. As for our
racial origins, there are representatives of a great many nations
among us, though it is perhaps natural that Tibetans and Chinese
make up the majority."

Miss Brinklow would never shirk a conclusion, even a wrong one.
"I see. It's really a native monastery, then. Is your head lama a Tibetan or a Chinese?"

"No."

"Are there any English?"

"Several."

"Dear me, that seems very remarkable." Miss Brinklow paused
only for breath before continuing: "And now, tell me what you all
believe in."

Conway leaned back with somewhat amused expectancy. He had
always found pleasure in observing the impact of opposite mental-
ities; and Miss Brinklow's girl-guide forthrightness applied to la-
maistic philosophy promised to be entertaining. On the other hand,
he did not wish his host to take fright. "That's rather a big question,"
he said, temporizingly.

But Miss Brinklow was in no mood to temporize. The wine, which
had made the others more reposeful, seemed to have given her an
extra liveliness. "Of course," she said with a gesture of magnanimity,
"I believe in the true religion, but I'm broadminded enough to admit
that other people, foreigners, I mean, are quite often sincere in their
views. And naturally in a monastery I wouldn't expect to be agreed
with."

Her concession evoked a formal bow from Chang. "But why not, madam?" he replied in his precise and flavored English. "Must we hold that because one religion is true, all others are bound to be false?"

"Well, of course, that's rather obvious, isn't it?"

Conway again interposed. "Really, I think we had better not argue. But Miss Brinklow shares my own curiosity about the motive of this unique establishment."

Chang answered rather slowly and in scarcely more than a whisper: "If I were to put it into a very few words, my dear sir, I should say that our prevalent belief is in moderation. We inculcate the virtue of avoiding excess of all kinds—even including, if you will pardon the paradox, excess of virtue itself. In the valley which you have seen, and in which there are several thousand inhabitants living under the control of our order, we have found that the principle makes for a considerable degree of happiness. We rule with moderate strictness, and in return we are satisfied with moderate obedience. And I think I can claim that our people are moderately sober, moderately chaste, and moderately honest."

Conway smiled. He thought it well expressed, besides which it made some appeal to his own temperament. "I think I understand. And I suppose the fellows who met us this morning belonged to your valley people?"

"Yes. I hope you had no fault to find with them during the journey?"

"Oh, no, none at all. I'm glad they were more than moderately sure-footed, anyhow. You were careful, by the way, to say that the rule of moderation applied to *them*—am I to take it that it does not apply to your priesthood also?"

But at that Chang could only shake his head. "I regret, sir, that you have touched upon a matter which I may not discuss. I can only add that our community has various faiths and usages, but we are most of us moderately heretical about them. I am deeply grieved that at the moment I cannot say more."

"Please don't apologize. I am left with the pleasantest of speculations." Something in his own voice, as well as in his bodily sensations, gave Conway a renewed impression that he had been very slightly doped. Mallinson appeared to have been similarly affected, though he seized the present chance to remark: "All this has been very interesting, but I really think it's time we began to discuss our plans for getting away. We want to return to India as soon as possible. How many porters can we be supplied with?"

The question, so practical and uncompromising, broke through the crust of suavity to find no sure foothold beneath. Only after a longish interval came Chang's reply: "Unfortunately, Mr. Mallinson, I am not the proper person to approach. But in any case, I hardly think the matter could be arranged immediately."

"But something has *got* to be arranged! We've all got our work to return to, and our friends and relatives will be worrying about us. We simply *must* return. We're obliged to you for receiving us like this, but we really can't slack about here doing nothing. If it's at all feasible, we should like to set out not later than to-morrow. I expect there are a good many of your people who would volunteer to escort us—we should make it well worth their while, of course."

Mallinson ended nervously, as if he had hoped to be answered before saying so much; but he could extract from Chang no more than a quiet and almost reproachful: "But all this, you know, is scarcely in my province."

"Isn't it? Well, perhaps you can do *something*, at any rate. If you could get us a large scale map of the country, it would help. It looks as if we shall have a long journey, and that's all the more reason for making an early start. You have maps, I suppose?"

"Yes, we have a great many."

"We'll borrow some of them, then, if you don't mind. We can return them to you afterwards, I suppose you must have communications with the outer world from time to time. And it would be a good idea to send messages ahead, also, to reassure our friends. How far away is the nearest telegraph line?"

Chang's wrinkled face seemed to have acquired a look of infinite patience, but he did not reply.

Mallinson waited a moment and then continued: "Well, where do you send to when you want anything? Anything civilized, I mean." A touch of scaredness began to appear in his eyes and voice. Suddenly he thrust back his chair and stood up. He was pale, and passed his hand wearily across his forehead. "I'm so tired," he stammered, glancing round the room. "I don't feel that any of you are really trying to help me. I'm only asking a simple question. It's obvious you must know the answer to it. When you had all these modern baths installed, how did they get here?"

There followed another silence.

"You won't tell me, then? It's part of the mystery of everything else, I suppose. Conway, I must say I think you're damned slack. Why don't *you* get at the truth? I'm all in, for the time being—but— to-morrow, mind—we *must* get away to-morrow—it's essential——"

He would have slid to the floor had not Conway caught him and helped him to a chair. Then he recovered a little, but did not speak.

"To-morrow he will be much better," said Chang gently. "The air here is difficult for the stranger at first, but one soon becomes acclimatized."

Conway felt himself waking from a trance. "Things have been a little trying for him," he commented with rather rueful mildness. He added, more briskly: "I expect we're all feeling it somewhat. I think we'd better adjourn this discussion and go to bed. Barnard, will you look after Mallinson? And I'm sure *you're* in need of sleep too, Miss Brinklow." There had been some signal given, for at that moment a servant appeared. "Yes, we'll get along—good night—good night—I shall soon follow." He almost pushed them out of the room, and then, with a scantness of ceremony that was in marked contrast with his earlier manner, turned to his host. Mallinson's reproach had spurred him.

"Now, sir, I don't want to detain you long, so I'd better come to the point. My friend is impetuous, but I don't blame him, he's quite right to make things clear. Our return journey has to be arranged, and we can't do it without help from you or from others in this place. Of course, I realize that leaving to-morrow is impossible, and for my own part I hope to find a minimum stay quite interesting. But that, perhaps, is not the attitude of my companions. So if it's true, as you say, that you can do nothing for us yourself, please put us in touch with some one else who can."

The Chinese answered: "You are wiser than your friends, my dear sir, and therefore you are less impatient. I am glad."

"That's not an answer."

Chang began to laugh, a jerky, high pitched chuckle so obviously forced that Conway recognized in it the polite pretense of seeing an imaginary joke with which the Chinese "saves face" at awkward moments. "I feel sure you have no cause to worry about the matter," came the reply, after an interval. "No doubt in due course we shall be able to give you all the help you need. There are difficulties, as you can imagine, but if we all approach the problem sensibly, and without undue haste—"

"I'm not suggesting haste. I'm merely seeking information about porters."

"Well, my dear sir, that raises another point. I very much doubt whether you will easily find men willing to undertake such a journey. They have their homes in the valley, and they don't care for leaving them to make long and arduous trips outside."

"They can be prevailed upon to do so, though, or else why and where were they escorting you this morning?"

"This morning? Oh, that was quite a different matter."

"In what way? Weren't you setting out on a journey when I and my friends chanced to come across you?"

There was no response to this, and presently Conway continued in a quieter voice: "I understand. Then it was *not* a chance meeting. I had wondered all along, in fact. So you came there deliberately to intercept us. That suggests you must have known of our arrival beforehand. And the interesting question is, *How?*"

His words laid a note of stress amidst the exquisite quietude of the scene. The lantern light showed up the face of the Chinese; it was calm and statuesque. Suddenly, with a small gesture of the hand, Chang broke the strain; pulling aside a silken tapestry he undraped a window leading to a balcony. Then, with a touch upon Conway's arm, he led him into the cold crystal air. "You are clever," he said dreamily, "but not entirely correct. For that reason I should counsel you not to worry your friends by these abstract discussions. Believe me, neither you nor they are in any danger at Shangri-La."

"But it isn't danger we're bothering about. It's delay."

"I realize that. And of course there *may* be a certain delay, quite unavoidably."

"If it's only for a short time, and genuinely unavoidable, then naturally we shall have to put up with it as best we can."

"How very sensible, for we desire nothing more than that you and your companions should enjoy every moment of your stay here."

"That's all very well, and as I told you, in a personal sense I can't say I shall mind a great deal. It's a new and interesting experience, and in any case, we need some rest."

He was gazing upward to the gleaming pyramid of Karakal. At that moment, in bright moonlight, it seemed as if a hand reached high might just touch it; it was so brittle-clear against the blue immensity beyond.

"To-morrow," said Chang, "you may find it even more interesting. And as for rest, if you are fatigued, there are not many better places in the world."

Indeed, as Conway continued to gaze, a deeper repose overspread him, as if the spectacle were as much for the mind as for the eye. There was hardly any stir of wind, in contrast to the upland gales that had raged the night before; the whole valley, he perceived, was a land-locked harbor, with Karakal brooding over it, lighthouse-fashion. The simile grew as he considered it, for there was actually light

on the summit, an ice-blue gleam that matched the splendor it reflected. Something prompted him then to enquire the literal interpretation of the name, and Chang's answer came as a whispered
echo of his own musing. "Karakal, in the valley patois, means Blue
Moon," said the Chinese.

Conway did not pass on his conclusion that the arrival of himself
and party at Shangri-La had been in some way expected by its inhabitants. He had had it in mind that he must do so, and he was
aware that the matter was important; but when morning came his
awareness troubled him so little, in any but a theoretical sense, that
he shrank from being the cause of greater concern in others. One
part of him insisted that there was something distinctly queer about
the place, that the attitude of Chang on the previous evening had
been far from reassuring, and that the party were virtually prisoners
unless and until the authorities chose to do more for them. And it
was clearly his duty to compel them to do this. After all, he was a
representative of the British Government, if nothing else; it was
iniquitous that the inmates of a Tibetan monastery should refuse
him any proper request. . . . That, no doubt, was the normal official
view that would be taken; and part of Conway was both normal
and official. No one could better play the strong man on occasions;
during those final difficult days before the evacuation he had behaved in a manner which (he reflected wryly) should earn him
nothing less than a knighthood and a Henty school prize novel entitled *With Conway at Baskul.* To have taken on himself the leader-
ship of some scores of mixed civilians, including women and
children, to have sheltered them all in a small consulate during a hot-
blooded revolution led by antiforeign agitators, and to have bullied
and cajoled the revolutionaries into permitting a wholesale evacuation by air, it was not, he felt, a bad achievement. Perhaps by
pulling wires and writing interminable reports, he could wangle
something out of it in the next New Year Honors. At any rate it
had won him Mallinson's fervent admiration. Unfortunately, the
youth must now be finding him so much more of a disappointment.
It was a pity, of course, but Conway had grown used to people
liking him only because they misunderstood him. He was not genuinely one of those resolute, strong-jawed, hammer-and-tongs empire
builders; the semblance he had given was merely a little one act
play, repeated from time to time by arrangement with fate and the
Foreign Office, and for a salary which any one could turn up in the
pages of Whitaker.

The truth was, the puzzle of Shangri-La, and of his own arrival there, was beginning to exercise over him a rather charming fascination. In any case he found it hard to feel any personal misgivings. His official job was always liable to take him into odd parts of the world, and the odder they were, the less, as a rule, he suffered from boredom; why, then, grumble because accident, instead of a chit from Whitehall, had sent him to this oddest place of all?

He was, in fact, very far from grumbling. When he rose in the morning and saw the soft lapis blue of the sky through his window, he would not have chosen to be elsewhere on earth either in Peshawur or Piccadilly. He was glad to find that on the others, also, a night's repose had had a heartening effect. Barnard was able to joke quite cheerfully about beds, baths, breakfasts, and other hospitable amenities. Miss Brinklow admitted that the most strenuous search of her apartment had failed to reveal any of the drawbacks she had been well prepared for. Even Mallinson had acquired a touch of half sulky complacency. "I suppose we shan't get away to-day after all," he muttered, "unless somebody looks pretty sharp about it. These fellows are typically Oriental, you can't get them to do anything quickly and efficiently."

Conway accepted the remark. Mallinson had been out of England just under a year; long enough, no doubt, to justify a generalization which he would probably still repeat when he had been out for twenty. And it was true, of course, in some degree. Yet to Conway it did not appear that the Eastern races were abnormally dilatory, but rather that Englishmen and Americans charged about the world in a state of continual and rather preposterous fever-heat. It was a point of view that he hardly expected any fellow Westerner to share, but he was more faithful to it as he grew older in years and experience. On the other hand, it was true enough that Chang was a subtle quibbler and that there was much justification for Mallinson's impatience. Conway had a slight wish that he could feel impatient too; it would have been so much easier for the boy.

He said: "I think we'd better wait and see what to-day brings. It was perhaps too optimistic to expect them to do anything last night."

Mallinson looked up sharply. "I suppose you think I made a fool of myself, being so urgent? I couldn't help it; I thought that Chinese fellow was damned fishy, and I do still. Did you succeed in getting any sense out of him after I'd gone to bed?"

"We didn't stay talking long. He was rather vague and noncommittal about most things."

"We shall jolly well have to keep him up scratch to-day."

"No doubt," agreed Conway, without marked enthusiasm for the prospect. "Meanwhile this is an excellent breakfast." It consisted of pomelo, tea, and chupatties, perfectly prepared and served. Towards the finish of the meal Chang entered and with a little bow began the exchange of politely conventional greetings which, in the English language, sounded just a trifle unwieldy. Conway would have preferred to talk in Chinese, but so far he had not let it be known that he spoke any Eastern tongue; he felt it might be a useful card up his sleeve. He listened gravely to Chang's courtesies, and gave assurances that he had slept well and felt much better. Chang expressed his pleasure at that, and added: "Truly, as your national poet says, 'Sleep knits up the raveled sleeve of care.'"

This display of erudition was not too well received. Mallinson answered with that touch of scorn which any healthy-minded young Englishman must feel at the mention of poetry. "I suppose you mean Shakespeare, though I don't recognize the quotation. But I know another one that says 'Stand not upon the order of your going, but go at once.' Without being impolite, that's rather what we should all like to do. And I want to hunt round for those porters right away, this morning, if you've no objection."

The Chinese received the ultimatum impassively, replying at length: "I am sorry to tell you that it would be of little use. I fear we have no men available who would be willing to accompany you so far from their homes."

"But good God, man, you don't suppose we're going to take that for an answer, do you?"

"I am sincerely regretful, but I can suggest no other."

"You seem to have figgered it all out since last night," put in Barnard. "You weren't nearly so dead sure of things then."

"I did not wish to disappoint you when you were so tired from your journey. Now, after a refreshing night, I am in hope that you will see matters in a more reasonable light."

"Look here," intervened Conway briskly, "this sort of vagueness and prevarication won't do. You know we can't stay here indefinitely. It's equally obvious that we can't get away by ourselves. What, then, do you propose?"

Chang smiled with a radiance that was clearly for Conway alone. "My dear sir, it is a pleasure to make the suggestion that is in my mind. To your friend's attitude there was no answer, but to the demand of a wise man there is always a response. You may recollect that it was remarked yesterday, again by your friend, I believe, that we are bound to have occasional communication with the outside world. That is quite true. From time to time we require certain things from distant *entrepôts,* and it is our habit to obtain them in due course, by what methods and with what formalities I need not trouble you. The point of importance is that such a consignment is expected to arrive shortly, and as the men who make delivery will afterwards return, it seems to me that you might manage to come to some arrangement with them. Indeed I cannot think of a better plan, and I hope, when they arrive—"

"When *do* they arrive?" interrupted Mallinson bluntly.

"The exact date is, of course, impossible to forecast. You have yourself had experience of the difficulty of movement in this part of the world. A hundred things may happen to cause uncertainty, hazards of weather—"

Conway again intervened. "Let's get this clear. You're suggesting that we should employ as porters the men who are shortly due here with some goods. That's not a bad idea as far as it goes, but we must know a little more about it. First, as you've already been asked, when are these people expected? And second, where will they take us?"

"That is a question you would have to put to them."

"Would they take us to India?"

"It is hardly possible for me to say."

"Well, let's have an answer to the other question. When will they be here? I don't ask for a date, I just want some idea whether it's likely to be next week or next year."

"It might be about a month from now. Probably not more than two months."

"Or three, four, or five months," broke in Mallinson hotly. "And you think we're going to wait here for this convoy or caravan or whatever it is to take us God knows where at some completely vague time in the distant future?"

"I think, sir, the phrase 'distant future' is hardly appropriate. Unless something unforeseen occurs, the period of waiting should not be longer than I have said."

"But *two months!* Two months in this place! It's preposterous! Conway, you surely can't contemplate it! Why, two weeks would be the limit!"

Chang gathered his gown about him in a little gesture of finality. "I am sorry. I did not wish to offend. The lamasery continues to offer all of you its utmost hospitality for as long as you have the misfortune to remain. I can say no more."

"You don't need to," retorted Mallinson furiously. "And if you think you've got the whip hand over us, you'll soon find you're damn well mistaken! We'll get all the porters we want, don't worry. You can bow and scrape and say what you like—"

Conway laid a restraining hand on his arm. Mallinson in a temper presented a child-like spectacle; he was apt to say anything that came into his head, regardless alike of point and decorum. Conway thought it readily forgivable in one so constituted and circumstanced, but he feared it might affront the more delicate susceptibilities of a Chinese. Fortunately Chang had ushered himself out, with admirable tact, in good time to escape the worst.

CHAPTER FIVE

They spent the rest of the morning discussing the matter. It was certainly a shock for four persons who in the ordinary course should have been luxuriating in the clubs and mission houses of Peshawur, to find themselves faced instead with the prospect of two months in a Tibetan monastery. But it was in the nature of things that the initial shock of their arrival should have left them with slender reserves either of indignation or astonishment; even Mallinson, after his first outburst, subsided into a mood of half-bewildered fatalism. "I'm past arguing about it, Conway," he said, puffing at a cigarette with nervous irritability. "You know how I feel. I've said all along that there's something queer about this business. It's crooked. I'd like to be out of it this minute."

"I don't blame you for that," replied Conway. "Unfortunately, it's not a question of what any of us would like, but of what we've all got to put up with. Frankly, if these people say they won't or can't supply us with the necessary porters, there's nothing for it but to wait till the other fellows come. I'm sorry to admit that we're so helpless in the matter, but I'm afraid it's the truth."

"You mean we've got to stay here for two months?"

"I don't see what else we can do."

Mallinson flicked his cigarette ash with a gesture of forced nonchalance. "All right, then. Two months it is. And now let's all shout hooray about it."

Conway went on: "I don't see why it should be much worse than two months in any other isolated part of the world. People in our jobs are used to being sent to odd places, I think I can say that of us all. Of course, it's bad for those of us who have friends and relatives. Personally, I'm fortunate in that respect, I can't think of any one who'll worry over me acutely, and my work, whatever it might have been, can easily be done by somebody else."

He turned to the others as if inviting them to state their own cases. Mallinson proffered no information, but Conway knew roughly how he was situated. He had parents and a girl in England; it made things hard.

Barnard, on the other hand, accepted the position with what Conway had learned to regard as an habitual good humor. "Well, I guess I'm pretty lucky, for that matter, two months in the penitentiary won't kill me. As for the folks in my home town, they won't bat an eye. I've always been a bad letter writer."

"You forget that our names will be in the papers," Conway reminded him. "We shall all be posted missing, and people will naturally assume the worst."

Barnard looked startled for the moment; then he replied, with a slight grin: "Oh, yes, that's true, but it don't affect me, I assure you."

Conway was glad it didn't, though the matter remained a little puzzling. He turned to Miss Brinklow, who till then had been remarkably silent; she had not offered any opinion during the interview with Chang. He imagined that she too might have comparatively few personal worries. She said brightly: "As Mr. Barnard says, two months here is nothing to make a fuss about. It's all the same, wherever one is, when one's in the Lord's service. Providence has sent me here. I regard it as a call."

Conway thought the attitude a very convenient one, in the circumstances. "I'm sure," he said encouragingly, "you'll find your mission society pleased with you when you *do* return. You'll be able to give much useful information. We'll all of us have had an experience, for that matter. That should be a small consolation."

The talk then became general. Conway was rather surprised at the ease with which Barnard and Miss Brinklow had accommodated themselves to the new prospect. He was relieved, however, as well; it left him with only one disgruntled person to deal with. Yet even Mallinson, after the strain of all the arguing, was experiencing a reaction; he was still perturbed, but more willing to look at the brighter side of things. "Heaven knows what we shall find to do with ourselves," he exclaimed, but the mere fact of making such a remark showed that he was trying to reconcile himself.

"The first rule must be to avoid getting on each other's nerves," replied Conway. "Happily, the place seems big enough, and by no means overpopulated. Except for servants, we've only seen one of its inhabitants so far."

Barnard could find another reason for optimism. "We won't starve, at any rate, if our meals up to now are a fair sample. You know, Conway, this place isn't run without plenty of hard cash. Those baths, for instance, they cost real money. And I can't see that anybody earns anything here, unless those chaps in the valley have jobs, and even then, they wouldn't produce enough for export. I'd like to know if they work any minerals."

"The whole place is a confounded mystery," responded Mallinson. "I dare say they've got pots of money hidden away, like the Jesuits. As for the baths, probably some millionaire supporter presented them. Anyhow, it won't worry me, once I get away. I must say, though, the view *is* rather good, in its way. Fine winter sport center if it were in the right spot. I wonder if one could get any ski-ing on some of those slopes up yonder?"

Conway gave him a searching and slightly amused glance. "Yesterday, when I found some edelweiss, you reminded me that I wasn't in the Alps. I think it's my turn to say the same thing now. I wouldn't advise you to try any of your Wengen-Scheidegg tricks in this part of the world."

"I don't suppose anybody here has ever seen a ski-jump."

"Or even an ice-hockey match," responded Conway banteringly. "You might try to raise some teams. What about 'Gentlemen *v.* Lamas'?"

"It would certainly teach them to play the game," Miss Brinklow put in with sparkling seriousness.

Adequate comment upon this might have been difficult, but there was no necessity, since lunch was about to be served, and its character and promptness combined to make an agreeable impression. Afterwards, when Chang entered, there was small disposition to continue the squabble. With great tactfulness the Chinese assumed that he was still on good terms with everybody, and the four exiles allowed the assumption to stand. Indeed, when he suggested that they might care to be shown a little more of the lamasery buildings, and that if so, he would be pleased to act as guide, the offer was readily accepted. "Why, surely," said Barnard. "We may as well give the place the once-over while we're here. I reckon it'll be a long time before any of us pay a second visit."

Miss Brinklow struck a more thought-giving note. "When we left Baskul in that aeroplane I'm sure I never dreamed we should ever get to a place like this," she murmured as they all moved off under Chang's escort.

"And we don't know yet why we have," answered Mallinson unforgetfully.

Conway had no race or color prejudice, and it was an affectation for him to pretend, as he sometimes did in clubs and first-class railway carriages, that he set any particular store on the "whiteness" of a lobster-red face under a topee. It saved trouble to let it be so assumed, especially in India, and Conway was a conscientious trouble-saver. But in China it had been less necessary; he had had many Chinese friends, and it had never occurred to him to treat them as inferiors. Hence, in his intercourse with Chang, he was sufficiently unpreoccupied to see in him a mannered old gentleman who might not be entirely trustworthy, but who was certainly of high intelligence. Mallinson, on the other hand, tended to regard him through the bars of an imaginary cage; Miss Brinklow was sharp and sprightly, as with the heathen in his blindness; while Barnard's wise-cracking *bonhomie* was of the kind he would have cultivated with a butler.

Meanwhile the grand tour of Shangri-La was interesting enough to transcend these attitudes. It was not the first monastic institution Conway had inspected, but it was easily the largest and, apart from its situation, the most remarkable. The mere procession through rooms and courtyards was an afternoon's exercise, though he was aware of many apartments passed by, indeed, of whole buildings into which Chang did not offer admission. The party were shown enough, however, to confirm the impressions each one of them had formed already. Barnard was more certain than ever that the lamas were rich; Miss Brinklow discovered abundant evidence that they were immoral. Mallinson, after the first novelty had worn off, found himself no less fatigued than on many sight-seeing excursions at lower altitudes; the lamas, he feared, were not likely to be his heroes.

Conway alone submitted to a rich and growing enchantment. It was not so much any individual thing that attracted him as the gradual revelation of elegance, of modest and impeccable taste, of harmony so fragrant that it seemed to gratify the eye without arresting it. Only indeed by a conscious effort did he recall himself from the artist's mood to the connoisseur's, and then he recognized treasures that museums and millionaires alike would have bargained for, exquisite pearl blue Sung ceramics, paintings in tinted inks preserved for more than a thousand years, lacquers in which the cold and lovely detail of fairyland was not so much depicted as orchestrated. A world of incomparable refinements still lingered tremulously in porcelain and varnish, yielding an instant of emotion before its dissolution into purest thought. There was no boastfulness, no striving after effect, no concentrated attack upon the feelings of the beholder. These delicate perfections had an air of having fluttered into existence like petals from a flower. They would have maddened a collector, but Conway did not collect; he lacked both money and the acquisitive instinct. His liking for Chinese art was an affair of the mind; in a world of increasing noise and hugeness, he turned in private to gentle, precise, and miniature things. And as he passed through room after room, a certain pathos touched him remotely at the thought of Karakal's piled immensity over against such fragile charms.

The lamasery, however, had more to offer than a display of Chinoiserie. One of its features, for instance, was a very delightful library, lofty and spacious, and containing a multitude of books so retiringly housed in bays and alcoves that the whole atmosphere was more of wisdom than of learning, of good manners rather than seriousness. Conway, during a rapid glance at some of the shelves, found much to astonish him; the world's best literature was there, it seemed, as well as a great deal of abstruse and curious stuff that he could not appraise. Volumes in English, French, German, and Russian abounded, and there were vast quantities of Chinese and other Eastern scripts. A section which interested him particularly was devoted to Tibetiana, if it might be so called; he noticed several rarities, among them the *Novo Descubrimento de grao catayo ou dos Regos de Tibet,* by Antonio de Andrada (Lisbon, 1626); Athanasius Kircher's *China* (Antwerp, 1667); Thevenot's *Voyage à la Chine des Pères Grueber et d'Orville;* and Beligatti's *Relazione Inedita di un Viaggio al Tibet.* He was examining the last named when he noticed Chang's eyes fixed on him in suave curiosity. "You are a scholar, perhaps?" came the enquiry.

Conway found it hard to reply. His period of donhood at Oxford gave him some right to assent, but he knew that the word, though the highest of compliments from a Chinese, had yet a faintly priggish sound for English ears, and chiefly out of consideration for his companions he demurred to it. He said: "I enjoy reading, of course, but my work during recent years hasn't supplied many opportunities for the studious life."

"Yet you wish for it?"

"Oh, I wouldn't say all that, but I'm certainly aware of its attractions."

Mallinson, who had picked up a book, interrupted: "Here's something for your studious life, Conway. It's a map of the country."

"We have a collection of several hundreds," said Chang. "They are all open to your inspection, but perhaps I can save you trouble in one respect. You will not find Shangri-La marked on any."

"Curious," Conway made comment. "I wonder why?"

"There is a very good reason, but I am afraid that is all I can say."

Conway smiled, but Mallinson looked peevish again. "Still piling up the mystery," he said. "So far we haven't seen much that any one need bother to conceal."

Suddenly Miss Brinklow came to life out of a mute preoccupation. "Aren't you going to show us the lamas at work?" she fluted, in the tone which one felt had intimidated many a Cook's man. One felt, too, that her mind was probably full of hazy visions of native handicrafts, prayer-mat weaving, or something picturesquely primitive that she could talk about when she got home. She had an extraordinary knack of never seeming very much surprised, yet of always seeming very slightly indignant, a combination of fixities which was not in the least disturbed by Chang's response: "I am sorry to say it is impossible. The lamas are never, or perhaps I should say only very rarely, seen by those outside the lamahood."

"I guess we'll have to miss 'em then," agreed Barnard. "But I do think it's a real pity. You've no notion how much I'd like to have shaken the hand of your head-man."

Chang acknowledged the remark with benign seriousness. Miss Brinklow, however, was not yet to be side-tracked. "What do the lamas do?" she continued.

"They devote themselves, madam, to contemplation and to the pursuit of wisdom."

"But that isn't *doing* anything."

"Then, madam, they do nothing."

"I thought as much." She found occasion to sum up. "Well, Mr. Chang, it's a pleasure being shown all these things, I'm sure, but you won't convince me that a place like this does any real good. I prefer something more practical."

"Perhaps you would like to take tea?"

Conway wondered at first if this were intended ironically, but it soon appeared not; the afternoon had passed swiftly, and Chang, though frugal in eating, had the typical Chinese fondness for tea-drinking at frequent intervals. Miss Brinklow, too, confessed that visiting art galleries and museums always gave her a touch of headache. The party, therefore, fell in with the suggestion, and followed Chang through several courtyards to a scene of quite sudden and unmatched loveliness. From a colonnade steps descended to a garden, in which a lotus pool lay entrapped, the leaves so closely set that they gave an impression of a floor of moist green tiles. Fringing the pool were posed a brazen menagerie of lions, dragons, and unicorns, each offering a stylized ferocity that emphasized rather than offended the surrounding peace. The whole picture was so perfectly proportioned that the eye was entirely unhastened from one part to another; there was no vying or vanity, and even the summit of Karakal, peerless above the blue tiled roofs, seemed to have surrendered within the framework of an exquisite artistry. "Pretty little place," commented Barnard, as Chang led the way into an open pavilion which, to Conway's further delight, contained a harpsichord and a modern grand piano. He found this in some ways the crowning astonishment of a rather astonishing afternoon. Chang answered all his questions with complete candour up to a point; the lamas, he explained, held Western music in high esteem, particularly that of Mozart; they had a collection of all the great European compositions, and some were skilled performers on various instruments.

Barnard was chiefly impressed by the transport problem. "D'you mean to tell me that this pi-anno was brought here by the route we came along yesterday?"

"There is no other."

"Well, that certainly beats everything! Why, with a phonograph and a radio you'd be all fixed complete! Perhaps, though, you aren't yet acquainted with up-to-date music?"

"Oh, yes, we have had reports, but we are advised that the mountains would make wireless reception impossible, and as for a phonograph, the suggestion has already come before the authorities, but they have felt no need to hurry in the matter."

"I'd believe that even if you hadn't told me," Barnard retorted. "I guess that must be the slogan of your society, 'No hurry.'" He laughed loudly and then went on: "Well, to come down to details, suppose in due course your bosses decide that they *do* want a phonograph, what's the procedure? The makers wouldn't deliver here, that's a sure thing. You must have an agent in Pekin or Shanghai or somewhere, and I'll bet everything costs plenty by the time you handle it."

But Chang was no more to be drawn than on a previous occasion. "Your surmises are intelligent, Mr. Barnard, but I fear I cannot discuss them."

So there they were again, Conway reflected, edging the invisible border-line between what might and might not be revealed. He thought he could soon begin to map out that line in imagination, though the impact of a new surprise deferred the matter. For servants were already bringing in the shallow bowls of scented tea, and along with the agile, lithe-limbed Tibetans there had also entered, quite inconspicuously, a girl in Chinese dress. She went directly to the harpsichord and began to play a gavotte by Rameau. The first bewitching twang stirred in Conway a pleasure that was beyond amazement; those silvery airs of eighteenth century France seemed to match in elegance the Sung vases and exquisite lacquers and the lotus-pool beyond; the same death-defying fragrance hung about them, lending immortality through an age to which their spirit was alien. Then he noticed the player. She had the long, slender nose, high cheekbones, and egg-shell pallor of the Manchu; her black hair was drawn tightly back and braided; she looked very finished and miniature. Her mouth was like a little pink convolvulus, and she was quite still, except for her long-fingered hands. As soon as the gavotte was ended, she made a little obeisance and went out.

Chang smiled after her and then, with a touch of personal triumph, upon Conway. "You are pleased?" he queried.

"Who is she?" asked Mallinson, before Conway could reply.

"Her name is Lo-Tsen. She has much skill with Western keyboard music. Like myself, she has not yet attained the full initiation."

"I should think not, indeed!" exclaimed Miss Brinklow. "She looks hardly more than a child. So you have women lamas, then?"

"There are no sex distinctions among us."

"Extraordinary business, this lamahood of yours," Mallinson commented loftily, after a pause. The rest of the tea-drinking proceeded without conversation; echoes of the harpsichord seemed still in the air, imposing a strange spell. Presently, leading the departure from the pavilion, Chang ventured to hope that the tour had been enjoyable. Conway, replying for the others, see-sawed with the customary courtesies. Chang then assured them of his own equal enjoyment, and hoped they would consider the resources of the music room and library wholly at their disposal throughout their stay. Conway, with some sincerity, thanked him again. "But what about the lamas?" he added. "Don't they ever want to use them?"

"They yield place with much gladness to their honored guests."

"Well, that's what I call real handsome," said Barnard. "And what's more, it shows that the lamas do really know we exist. That's a step forward, anyhow, makes me feel much more at home. You've certainly got a swell outfit here, Chang, and that little girl of yours plays the pi-anno very nicely. How old would she be, I wonder?"

"I am afraid I cannot tell you."

Barnard laughed. "You don't give away secrets about a lady's age, is that it?"

"Precisely," answered Chang with a faintly shadowing smile.

That evening, after dinner, Conway made occasion to leave the others and stroll out into the calm, moon-washed courtyards. Shangri-La was lovely then, touched with the mystery that lies at the core of all loveliness. The air was cold and still; the mighty spire of

Karakal looked nearer, much nearer than by daylight. Conway was physically happy, emotionally satisfied, and mentally at ease; but in his intellect, which was not quite the same thing as mind, there was a little stir. He was puzzled. The line of secrecy that he had begun to map out grew sharper, but only to reveal an inscrutable background. The whole amazing series of events that had happened to him and his three chance companions swung now into a sort of focus; he could not yet understand them, but he believed they were somehow to be understood.

Passing along a cloister, he reached the terrace leaning over the valley. The scent of tuberose assailed him, full of delicate associations; in China it was called "the smell of moonlight." He thought whimsically that if moonlight had a sound also, it might well be the Rameau gavotte he had heard so recently; and that set him thinking of the little Manchu. It had not occurred to him to picture women at Shangri-La; one did not associate their presence with the general practice of monasticism. Still, he reflected, it might not be a disagreeable innovation; indeed, a female harpsichordist might be an asset to any community that permitted itself to be (in Chang's words) "moderately heretical."

He gazed over the edge into the blue-black emptiness. The drop was phantasmal; perhaps as much as a mile. He wondered if he would be allowed to descend it and inspect the valley civilization that had been talked of. The notion of this strange culture-pocket, hidden amongst unknown ranges, and ruled over by some vague kind of theocracy, interested him as a student of history, apart from the curious though perhaps related secrets of the lamasery.

Suddenly, on a flutter of air, came sounds from far below. Listening intently, he could hear gongs and trumpets and also (though perhaps only in imagination) the massed wail of voices. The sounds faded on a veer of the wind, then returned to fade again. But the hint of life and liveliness in those veiled depths served only to emphasize the austere serenity of Shangri-La. Its forsaken courts and pale pavilions simmered in repose from which all the fret of existence had ebbed away, leaving a hush as if moments hardly dared to pass. Then, from a window high above the terrace, he caught the rose-gold of lantern light; was it there that the lamas devoted themselves to contemplation and the pursuit of wisdom, and were those devotions now in progress? The problem seemed one that he could solve merely by entering at the nearest door and exploring through gallery and corridor until the truth were his; but he knew that such freedom was illusory, and that in fact his movements were watched.

Two Tibetans had padded across the terrace and were idling near the parapet. Good-humored fellows they looked, shrugging their colored cloaks negligently over naked shoulders. The whisper of gongs and trumpets uprose again, and Conway heard one of the men question his companion. The answer came: "They have buried Talu." Conway, whose knowledge of Tibetan was very slight, hoped they would continue talking; he could not gather much from a single remark. After a pause the questioner, who was inaudible, resumed the conversation, and obtained answers which Conway overheard and loosely understood as follows:

"He died outside."

"He obeyed the high ones of Shangri-La."

"He came through the air over the great mountains with a bird to hold him."

"Strangers he brought, also."

"Talu was not afraid of the outside wind, nor of the outside cold."

"Though he went outside long ago, the valley of Blue Moon remembers him still."

Nothing more was said that Conway could interpret, and after waiting for some time he went back to his own quarters. He had heard enough to turn another key in the locked mystery, and it fitted so well that he wondered he had failed to supply it by his own deductions. It had, of course, crossed his mind, but a certain initial and fantastic unreasonableness about it had been too much for him. Now he perceived that the unreasonableness, however fantastic, was to be swallowed. That flight from Baskul had *not* been the meaningless exploit of a madman. It had been something planned, prepared, and carried out at the instigation of Shangri-La. The dead pilot was known by name to those who lived there; he had been one of them, in some sense; his death was mourned. Everything pointed to a high directing intelligence bent upon its own purposes; there had been, as it were, a single arch of intention spanning the inexplicable hours and miles. But what *was* that intention? For what possible reason could four chance passengers in a British Government aeroplane be whisked away to these trans-Himalayan solitudes?

Conway was somewhat aghast at the problem, but by no means wholly displeased with it. It challenged him in the only way in which he was readily amenable to challenge—by touching a certain clarity of brain that only demanded a sufficient task. One thing he decided instantly; the cold thrill of discovery must not yet be communicated, neither to his companions, who could not help him, nor to his hosts, who doubtless would not.

CHAPTER SIX

"I reckon some folks have to get used to worse places," Barnard remarked towards the close of his first week at Shangri-La, and it was doubtless one of the many lessons to be drawn. By that time the party had settled themselves into something like a daily routine, and with Chang's assistance the boredom was no more acute than on many a planned holiday. They had all become acclimatized to the atmosphere, finding it quite invigorating so long as heavy exertion was avoided. They had learned that the days were warm and the nights cold, that the lamasery was almost completely sheltered from winds, that avalanches on Karakal were most frequent about midday, that the valley grew a good brand of tobacco, that some foods and drinks were more pleasant than others, and that each one of themselves had personal tastes and peculiarities. They had, in fact, discovered as much about each other as four new pupils of a school from which every one else was mysteriously absent. Chang was tireless in his efforts to make smooth the rough places. He conducted excursions, suggested occupations, recommended books, talked with his slow, careful fluency whenever there was an awkward pause at meals, and was on every occasion benign, courteous, and resourceful. The line of demarcation was so marked between information willingly supplied and politely declined that the latter ceased to stir resentment, except fitfully from Mallinson. Conway was content to take note of it, adding another fragment to his constantly accumulating data. Barnard even "jollied" the Chinese after the manner and traditions of a Middle West Rotary convention. "You know, Chang, this is a damned bad hotel. Don't you have any newspapers sent here ever? I'd give all the books in your library for this morning's *Herald-Tribune*." Chang's replies were always serious, though it did not necessarily follow that he took every question seriously. "We have the files of the *Times*, Mr. Barnard, up to a few years ago. But only, I regret to say, the London *Times*."

Conway was glad to find that the valley was not to be "out of bounds," though the difficulties of the descent made unescorted visits impossible. In company with Chang they all spent a whole day inspecting the green floor that was so pleasantly visible from the cliff-edge, and to Conway, at any rate, the trip was of absorbing interest. They traveled in bamboo sedan chairs, swinging perilously over precipices while their bearers in front and to the rear picked a way nonchalantly down the steep track. It was not a route for the squeamish, but when at last they reached the lower levels of forest and foothill the supreme good fortune of the lamasery was everywhere to be realized. For the valley was nothing less than an enclosed paradise of amazing fertility, in which the vertical difference of a few thousand feet spanned the whole gulf between temperate and tropical. Crops of unusual diversity grew in profusion and contiguity, with not an inch of ground untended. The whole cultivated area stretched for perhaps a dozen miles, varying in width from one to five, and though narrow, it had the luck to take sunlight at the hottest part of the day. The atmosphere, indeed, was pleasantly warm even out of the sun, though the little rivulets that watered the soil were ice-cold from the snows. Conway felt again, as he gazed up at the stupendous mountain wall, that there was a superb and exquisite peril in the scene; but for some chance-placed barrier, the whole valley would clearly have been a lake, nourished continually from the glacial heights around it. Instead of which, a few streams dribbled through to fill reservoirs and irrigate fields and plantations with a disciplined conscientiousness worthy of a sanitary engineer. The whole design was almost uncannily fortunate, so long as the structure of the frame remained unmoved by earthquake or landslide.

But even such vaguely future fears could only enhance the total loveliness of the present. Once again Conway was captivated, and by the same qualities of charm and ingenuity that had made his years in China happier than others. The vast encircling *massif* made perfect contrast with the tiny lawns and weedless gardens, the painted tea-houses by the stream, and the frivolously toy-like houses. The inhabitants seemed to him a very successful blend of Chinese and Tibetan; they were cleaner and handsomer than the average of either race, and seemed to have suffered little from the inevitable inbreeding of such a small society. They smiled and laughed as they passed the chaired strangers, and had a friendly word for Chang; they were good-humored and mildly inquisitive, courteous and carefree, busy at innumerable jobs but not in any apparent hurry over them. Altogether Conway thought it one of the pleasantest communities he had ever seen, and even Miss Brinklow, who had been watching for symptoms of pagan degradation, had to admit that everything looked very well "on the surface." She was relieved to find the natives "completely" clothed, even though the women did wear ankle-tight Chinese trousers; and her most imaginative scrutiny of a Buddhist temple revealed only a few items that could be regarded as somewhat doubtfully phallic. Chang explained that the temple had its own lamas, who were under loose control from Shangri-La, though not of the same order. There were also, it appeared, a Taoist and a Confucian temple further along the valley. "The jewel has facets," said the Chinese, "and it is possible that many religions are moderately true."

"I agree with that," said Barnard heartily. "I never did believe in sectarian jealousies. Chang, you're a philosopher, I must remember that remark of yours. 'Many religions are moderately true.' You fellows up on the mountain must be a lot of wise guys to have thought that out. You're right, too, I'm dead certain of it."

"But we," responded Chang dreamily, "are only *moderately* certain."

Miss Brinklow could not be bothered with all that, which seemed to her a sign of mere laziness. In any case she was preoccupied with an idea of her own. "When I get back," she said with tightening lips, "I shall ask my society to send a missionary here. And if they grumble at the expense, I shall just bully them until they agree."

That, clearly, was a much healthier spirit, and even Mallinson, little as he sympathized with foreign missions, could not forbear his admiration. "They ought to send *you*," he said. "That is, of course, if you'd like a place like this."

"It's hardly a question of *liking* it," Miss Brinklow retorted. "One wouldn't like it, naturally—how could one? It's a matter of what one feels one ought to do."

"I think," said Conway, "if I were a missionary I'd choose this rather than quite a lot of other places."

"In that case," snapped Miss Brinklow, "there would be no merit in it, obviously."

"But I wasn't thinking of merit."

"More's the pity, then. There's no good in doing a thing because you like doing it. Look at these people here!"

"They all seem very happy."

"*Exactly*," she answered with a touch of fierceness. She added: "Anyhow, I don't see why I shouldn't make a beginning by studying the language. Can you lend me a book about it, Mr. Chang?"

Chang was at his most mellifluous. "Most certainly, madam, with the greatest of pleasure. And, if I may say so, I think the idea an excellent one."

When they ascended to Shangri-La that evening he treated the matter as one of immediate importance. Miss Brinklow was at first a little daunted by the massive volume compiled by an industrious nineteenth century German (she had more probably imagined some slighter work of a "Brush up your Tibetan" type), but with help from the Chinese and encouragement from Conway she made a good beginning and was soon observed to be extracting grim satisfaction from her task.

Conway, too, found much to interest him, apart from the engrossing problem he had set himself. During the warm, sunlit days he made full use of the library and music room, and was confirmed in his impression that the lamas were of quite exceptional culture. Their taste in books was catholic, at any rate; Plato in Greek touched Omar in English; Nietzsche partnered Newton; Thomas More was there, and also Hannah More, Thomas Moore, George Moore, and even Old Moore. Altogether Conway estimated the number of volumes at between twenty and thirty thousand; and it was tempting to speculate upon the method of selection and acquisition. He sought also to discover how recently there had been additions, but he did not come across anything later than a cheap reprint of *Im Westen Nichts Neues*. During a subsequent visit, however, Chang told him that there were other books published up to about the middle of 1930 which would doubtless be added to the shelves eventually; they had already arrived at the lamasery. "We keep ourselves fairly up-to-date, you see," he commented.

"There are people who would hardly agree with you," replied Conway with a smile. "Quite a lot of things have happened in the world since last year, you know."

"Nothing of importance, my dear sir, that could not have been foreseen in 1920, or that will not be better understood in 1940."

"You're not interested, then, in the latest developments of the world crisis?"

"I shall be very deeply interested—in due course."

"You know, Chang, I believe I'm beginning to understand you. You're geared differently, that's what it is. Time means less to you than it does to most people. If I were in London I wouldn't always be eager to see the latest hour-old newspaper, and you at Shangri-La are no more eager to see a year-old one. Both attitudes seem to me quite sensible. By the way, how long is it since you last had visitors here?"

"That, Mr. Conway, I am unfortunately unable to say."

It was the usual ending to a conversation, and one that Conway found less irritating than the opposite phenomenon from which he had suffered much in his time—the conversation which, try as he would, seemed never to end. He began to like Chang rather more as their meetings multiplied, though it still puzzled him that he met so few of the lamasery personnel; even assuming that the lamas themselves were unapproachable, were there not other postulants besides Chang?

There was, of course, the little Manchu. He saw her sometimes when he visited the music room; but she knew no English, and he was still unwilling to disclose his own Chinese. He could not quite determine whether she played merely for pleasure, or was in some way a student. Her playing, as indeed her whole behavior, was exquisitely formal, and her choice lay always among the more patterned compositions—those of Bach, Corelli, Scarlatti, and occasionally Mozart. She preferred the harpsichord to the piano, but when Conway went to the latter she would listen with grave and almost dutiful appreciation. It was impossible to know what was in her mind; it was difficult even to guess her age. He would have doubted her being over thirty or under thirteen; and yet, in a curious way, such manifest unlikelihoods could neither of them be ruled out as wholly impossible.

Mallinson, who sometimes came to listen to the music for want of anything better to do, found her a very baffling proposition. "I can't think what she's doing here," he said to Conway more than once. "This lama business may be all right for an old fellow like Chang, but what's the attraction in it for a girl? How long has she been here, I wonder?"

"I wonder too, but it's one of those things we're not likely to be told."

"Do you suppose she *likes* being here?"

"I'm bound to say she doesn't appear to *dis*like it."

"She doesn't appear to have feelings at all, for that matter. She's like a little ivory doll more than a human being."

"A charming thing to be like, anyhow."

"As far as it goes."

Conway smiled. "And it goes pretty far, Mallinson, when you come to think about it. After all, the ivory doll has manners, good taste in dress, attractive looks, a pretty touch on the harpsichord, and she doesn't move about a room as if she were playing hockey. Western Europe, so far as I recollect it, contains an exceptionally large number of females who lack those virtues."

"You're an awful cynic about women, Conway."

Conway was used to the charge. He had not actually had a great

deal to do with the other sex, and during occasional leaves in Indian
hill-stations the reputation of cynic had been as easy to sustain as
any other. In truth he had had several delightful friendships with
women who would have been pleased to marry him if he had asked
them—but he had not asked them. He had once got nearly as far
as an announcement in the *Morning Post,* but the girl did not want
to live in Pekin and he did not want to live at Tunbridge Wells,
mutual reluctances which proved impossible to dislodge. So far as
he had had experience of women at all, it had been tentative, intermittent, and somewhat inconclusive. But he was not, for all that, a
cynic about them.

He said with a laugh: "I'm thirty-seven—you're twenty-four. That's
all it amounts to."

After a pause Mallinson asked suddenly: "Oh, by the way, how
old should you say Chang is?"

"Anything," replied Conway lightly, "between forty-nine and a
hundred and forty-nine."

Such information, however, was less trustworthy than much else
that was available to the new arrivals. The fact that their curiosities
were sometimes unsatisfied tended to obscure the really vast quan-
tity of data which Chang was always willing to outpour. There were
no secrecies, for instance, about the customs and habits of the valley
population, and Conway, who was interested, had talks which might
have been worked up into a quite serviceable degree thesis. He was
particularly interested, as a student of affairs, in the way the valley
population was governed; it appeared, on examination, to be a rather
loose and elastic autocracy, operated from the lamasery with a benevolence that was almost casual. It was certainly an established success,
as every descent into that fertile paradise made more evident. Conway was puzzled as to the ultimate basis of law and order; there
appeared to be neither soldiers nor police, yet surely some provision
must be made for the incorrigible? Chang replied that crime was
very rare, partly because only serious things were considered crimes,
and partly because every one enjoyed a sufficiency of everything he
could reasonably desire. In the last resort the personal servants of
the lamasery had power to expel an offender from the valley—though
this, which was considered an extreme and dreadful punishment,
had only very occasionally to be imposed. But the chief factor in
the government of Blue Moon, Chang went on to say, was the incul-
cation of good manners, which made men feel that certain things
were "not done," and that they lost caste by doing them. "You English

inculcate the same feeling," said Chang, "in your public schools, but not, I fear, in regard to the same things. The inhabitants of our valley, for instance, feel that it is 'not done' to be inhospitable to strangers, to dispute acrimoniously, or to strive for priority amongst one another. The idea of enjoying what your English headmasters call the mimic warfare of the playing-field would seem to them entirely barbarous—indeed, a sheerly wanton stimulation of all the lower instincts."

Conway asked if there were never disputes about women.

"Only very rarely, because it would not be considered good manners to take a woman that another man wanted."

"Supposing somebody wanted her so badly that he didn't care a damn whether it was good manners or not?"

"Then, my dear sir, it would be good manners on the part of the other man to let him have her, and also on the part of the woman to be equally agreeable. You would be surprised, Conway, how the application of a little courtesy all round helps to smooth out these problems."

Certainly during visits to the valley Conway found a spirit of good will and contentment that pleased him all the more because he knew that of all the arts that of government has been brought least to perfection. When he made some complimentary remark, however, Chang responded: "Ah, but you see, we believe that to govern perfectly it is necessary to avoid governing too much."

"Yet you don't have any democratic machinery—voting, and so on?"

"Oh, no. Our people would be quite shocked by having to declare that one policy was completely right and another competely wrong."

Conway smiled. He found the attitude a curiously sympathetic one.

Meanwhile, Miss Brinklow derived her own kind of satisfaction from a study of Tibetan; meanwhile, also, Mallinson fretted and groused, and Barnard persisted in an equanimity which seemed almost equally remarkable, whether it were real or simulated.

"To tell you the truth," said Mallinson, "the fellow's cheerfulness is just about getting on my nerves. I can understand him trying to keep a stiff lip, but that continual joking of his begins to upset me. He'll be the life and soul of the party if we don't watch him."

Conway too had once or twice wondered at the ease with which the American had managed to settle down. He replied: "Isn't it rather lucky for us he *does* take things so well?"

"Personally, I think it's damned peculiar. What do you *know* about him, Conway? I mean who he is, and so on."

"Not much more than you do. I understood he came from Persia and was supposed to have been oil-prospecting. It's his way to take things easily—when the air evacuation was arranged I had quite a job to persuade him to join us at all. He only agreed when I told him that an American passport wouldn't stop a bullet."

"By the way, did you ever see his passport?"

"Probably I did, but I don't remember. Why?"

Mallinson laughed. "I'm afraid you'll think I haven't exactly been minding my own business. Why should I, anyhow? Two months in this place ought to reveal all our secrets, if we have any. Mind you, it was a sheer accident, in the way it happened, and I haven't let slip a word to any one else, of course. I didn't think I'd tell even you, but now we've got on to the subject I may as well."

"Yes, of course, but I wish you'd let me know what you're talking about."

"Just this. Barnard was traveling on a forged passport and he isn't Barnard at all."

Conway raised his eyebrows with an interest that was very much less than concern. He liked Barnard, so far as the man stirred him to any emotion at all; but it was quite impossible for him to care intensely who he really was or wasn't. He said: "Well, who do you think he is, then?"

"He's Chalmers Bryant."

"The deuce he is! What makes you think so?"

"He dropped a pocketbook this morning and Chang picked it up and gave it to me, thinking it was mine. I couldn't help seeing it was stuffed with newspaper clippings—some of them fell out as I was handling the thing, and I don't mind admitting that I looked at them. After all, newspaper clippings aren't private, or shouldn't be. They were all about Bryant and the search for him, and one of them had a photograph which was absolutely like Barnard except for a mustache."

"Did you mention your discovery to Barnard himself?"

"No, I just handed him his property without any comment."

"So the whole thing rests on your identification of a newspaper photograph?"

"Well, so far, yes."

"I don't think I'd care to convict any one on that. Of course you might be right—I don't say he couldn't *possibly* be Bryant. If he were, it would account for a good deal of his contentment at being here—he could hardly have found a better place to hide."

Mallinson seemed a trifle disappointed by this casual reception of news which he evidently thought highly sensational. "Well, what are you going to do about it?" he asked.

Conway pondered a moment and then answered: "I haven't much of an idea. Probably nothing at all. What *can* one do, in any case?"

"But dash it all, if the man *is* Bryant—"

"My dear Mallinson, if the man were Nero it wouldn't have to matter to us for the time being! Saint or crook, we've got to make what we can of each other's company as long as we're here, and I can't see that we shall help matters by striking any attitudes. If I'd suspected who he was at Baskul, of course, I'd have tried to get in touch with Delhi about him—it would have been merely a public duty. But now I think I can claim to be *off* duty."

"Don't you think that's rather a slack way of looking at it?"

"I don't care if it's slack so long as it's sensible."

"I suppose that means your advice to me is to forget what I've found out?"

"You probably can't do that, but I certainly think we might both of us keep our own counsel about it. Not in consideration for Barnard or Bryant or whoever he is, but to save ourselves the deuce of an awkward situation when we get away."

"You mean we ought to let him go?"

"Well, I'll put it a bit differently and say we ought to give somebody else the pleasure of catching him. When you've lived quite sociably with a man for a few months, it seems a little out of place to call for the handcuffs."

"I don't think I agree. The man's nothing but a large-scale thief— I know plenty of people who've lost their money through him."

Conway shrugged his shoulders. He admired the simple black-and-white of Mallinson's code; the public school ethic might be crude, but at least it was downright. If a man broke the law, it was every one's duty to hand him over to justice—always provided that it was the kind of law one was not allowed to break. And the law pertaining to checks and shares and balance-sheets was decidedly that kind. Bryant had transgressed it, and though Conway had not taken much interest in the case, he had an impression that it was a fairly bad one of its kind. All he knew was that the failure of the giant Bryant group in New York had resulted in losses of about a hundred million dollars—a record crash, even in a world that exuded records. In some way or other (Conway was not a financial expert)

Bryant had been monkeying on Wall Street, and the result had been a warrant for his arrest, his escape to Europe, and extradition orders against him in half a dozen countries.

Conway said finally: "Well, if you take my tip you'll say nothing about it—not for his sake but for ours. Please yourself, of course, so long as you don't forget the possibility that he mayn't be the fellow at all."

But he was, and the revelation came that evening after dinner. Chang had left them; Miss Brinklow had turned to her Tibetan grammar; the three male exiles faced each other over coffee and cigars. Conversation during the meal would have languished more than once but for the tact and affability of the Chinese; now, in his absence, a rather unhappy silence supervened. Barnard was for once without jokes. It was clear to Conway that it lay beyond Mallinson's power to treat the American as if nothing had happened, and it was equally clear that Barnard was shrewdly aware that something *had* happened.

Suddenly the American threw away his cigar. "I guess you all know who I am," he said.

Mallinson colored like a girl, but Conway replied in the same quiet key: "Yes, Mallinson and I think we do."

"Darned careless of me to leave those clippings lying about."

"We're all apt to be careless at times."

"Well, you're mighty calm about it, that's something."

There was another silence, broken at length by Miss Brinklow's shrill voice: "I'm sure *I* don't know who you are, Mr. Barnard, though I must say I guessed all along you were traveling *incognito*." They all looked at her enquiringly and she went on: "I remember when Mr. Conway said we should all have our names in the papers, you said it didn't affect you. I thought then that Barnard probably wasn't your real name."

The culprit gave a slow smile as he lit himself another cigar. "Madam," he said eventually, "you're not only a smart detective, but you've hit on a really polite name for my present position. I'm traveling *incognito*. You've said it, and you're dead right. As for you boys, I'm not sorry in a way that you've found me out. So long as none of you had an inkling, we could all have managed, but considering how we're fixed it wouldn't seem very neighborly to play the high hat with you now. You folks have been so darned nice to me that I don't want to make a lot of trouble. It looks as if we were all going to be joined together for better or worse for some little time ahead, and it's up to us to help one another out as far as we can. As for what happens afterwards, I reckon we can leave that to settle itself."

All this appeared to Conway so eminently reasonable that he gazed at Barnard with considerably greater interest, and even—though it was perhaps odd at such a moment—a touch of genuine appreciation. It was curious to think of that heavy, fleshy, good-humored, rather paternal looking man as the world's hugest swindler. He looked far more the type that, with a little extra education, would have made a popular headmaster of a prep school. Behind his joviality there were signs of recent strains and worries, but that did not mean that the joviality was forced. He obviously was what he looked—a "good fellow" in the world's sense, by nature a lamb and only by profession a shark.

Conway said: "Yes, that's very much the best thing, I'm certain."

Then Barnard laughed. It was as if he possessed even deeper reserves of good humor which he could only now draw upon. "Gosh, but it's mighty queer," he exclaimed, spreading himself in his chair. "The whole darned business, I mean. Right across Europe, and on through Turkey and Persia to that little one-horse burg! Police after me all the time, mind you—they nearly got me in Vienna! It's pretty exciting at first, being chased, but it gets on your nerves after a bit. I got a good rest at Baskul, though—I thought I'd be safe in the midst of a revolution."

"And so you were," said Conway with a slight smile, "except from bullets."

"Yeah, and that's what bothered me at the finish. I can tell you it was a mighty hard choice—whether to stay in Baskul and get plugged, or accept a trip in your Government's aeroplane and find the bracelets waiting at the other end. I wasn't exactly keen to do either."

"I remember you weren't."

Barnard laughed again. "Well, that's how it was, and you can figger it out for yourself that the change of plan which brought me here, don't worry me an awful lot. It's a first-class mystery, but, speaking personally, there couldn't have been a better one. It isn't my way to grumble as long as I'm satisfied."

Conway's smile became more definitely cordial. "A very sensible attitude, though I think you rather overdid it. We were all beginning to wonder how you managed to be so contented."

"Well, I *was* contented. This ain't a bad place, when you get used to it. The air's a bit snappy at first, but you can't have everything. And it's nice and quiet for a change. Every fall I go down to Palm

Beach for a rest cure, but they don't give it you, those places—you're in the racket just the same. But here I guess I'm having just what the doctor ordered, and it certainly feels grand to me. I'm on a different diet, I can't look at the tape, and my broker can't get me on the telephone."

"I dare say he wishes he could."

"Sure. There'll be a tidy-sized mess to clear up, and I know it."

He said this with such simplicity that Conway could not help responding: "I'm not much of an authority on what people call high finance."

It was a lead, and the American accepted it without the slightest reluctance. "High finance," he said, "is mostly a lot of bunk."

"So I've often suspected."

"Look here, Conway, I'll put it like this. A feller does what he's been doing for years, and what lots of other fellers have been doing, and suddenly the market goes against him. He can't help it, but he braces up and waits for the turn. But somehow the turn don't come as it always used to, and when he's lost ten million dollars or so he reads in some paper that a Swede professor thinks it's the end of the world. Now I ask you, does that sort of thing help markets? Of course, it gives him a bit of a shock, but he still can't help it. And there he is till the cops come—if he waits for 'em. I didn't."

"You claim it was all just a run of bad luck, then?"

"Well, I certainly had a large packet."

"You also had other people's money," put in Mallinson sharply.

"Yeah, I did. And why? Because they all wanted something for nothing and hadn't the brains to get it for themselves."

"I don't agree. It was because they trusted you and thought their money was safe."

"Well, it wasn't safe. It couldn't be. There isn't safety anywhere, and those who thought there was were like a lot of saps trying to hide under an umbrella in a typhoon."

Conway said pacifyingly: "Well, we'll all admit you couldn't help the typhoon."

"I couldn't even pretend to help it—any more than you could help what happened after we left Baskul. The same thing struck me then as I watched you in the aeroplane keeping dead calm while Mallinson here had the fidgets. You knew you couldn't do anything about it, and you weren't caring two hoots. Just like I felt myself when the crash came."

"That's nonsense!" cried Mallinson. "Any one can help swindling. It's a matter of playing the game according to the rules."

"Which is a darned difficult thing to do when the whole game's going to pieces. Besides, there isn't a soul in the world who knows what the rules are. All the professors of Harvard and Yale couldn't tell you 'em."

Mallinson replied rather scornfully: "I'm referring to a few quite simple rules of everyday conduct."

"Then I guess your everyday conduct doesn't include managing trust companies."

Conway made haste to intervene. "We'd better not argue. I don't object in the least to the comparison between your affairs and mine. No doubt we've all been flying blind lately, both literally and in other ways. But we're here now, that's the important thing, and I agree with you that we could easily have had more to grumble about. It's curious, when you come to think about it, that out of four people picked up by chance and kidnaped a thousand miles, three should be able to find some consolation in the business. *You* want a rest-cure and a hiding place; Miss Brinklow feels a call to evangelize the heathen Tibetan."

"Who's the third person you're counting?" Mallinson interrupted. "Not me, I hope?"

"I was including myself," answered Conway. "And my own reason is perhaps the simplest of all—I just rather like being here."

Indeed, a short time later, when he took what had come to be his usual solitary evening stroll along the terrace or beside the lotus-pool, he felt an extraordinary sense of physical and mental settlement. It was perfectly true; he just rather liked being at Shangri-La. Its atmosphere soothed while its mystery stimulated, and the total sensation was agreeable. For some days now he had been reaching, gradually and tentatively, a curious conclusion about the lamasery and its inhabitants; his brain was still busy with it, though in a deeper sense he was unperturbed. He was like a mathematician with an abstruse problem—worrying over it, but worrying very calmly and impersonally.

As for Bryant, whom he decided he would still think of and address as Barnard, the question of his exploits and identity faded instantly into the background, save for a single phrase of his—"the whole game's going to pieces." Conway found himself remembering and echoing it with a wider significance than the American had probably intended; he felt it to be true of more than American banking and trust company management. It fitted Baskul and Delhi and London, war making and empire building, consulates and trade concessions and dinner parties at Government House; there was a reek

of dissolution over all that recollected world, and Barnard's cropper
had only, perhaps, been better dramatized than his own. The whole
game *was* doubtless going to pieces, but fortunately the players were
not as a rule put on trial for the pieces they failed to save. In that
respect financiers were unlucky.

But here, at Shangri-La, all was in deep calm. In a moonless sky
the stars were lit to the full, and a pale blue sheen lay upon the dome
of Karakal. Conway realized then that if by some change of plan the
porters from the outside world were to arrive immediately, he would
not be completely overjoyed at being spared the interval of waiting.
And neither would Barnard, he reflected with an inward smile. It
was amusing, really; and then suddenly he knew that he still liked
Barnard, or he wouldn't have found it amusing. Somehow the loss
of a hundred million dollars was too much to bar a man for; it would
have been easier if he had only stolen one's watch. And after all, how
could any one lose a hundred millions? Perhaps only in the sense in
which a cabinet minister might airily announce that he had been
"given India."

And then again he thought of the time when he would leave
Shangri-La with the returning porters. He pictured the long, arduous
journey, and that eventual moment of arrival at some planter's
bungalow in Sikkim or Baltistan—a moment which ought, he felt,
to be deliriously cheerful, but which would probably be slightly disappointing. Then the first hand-shakings and self-introductions; the
first drinks on clubhouse verandas; sun-bronzed faces staring at him
in barely concealed incredulity. At Delhi, no doubt, interviews with
the Viceroy and the C.I.C.; salaams of turbanned menials; endless
reports to be prepared and sent off. Perhaps even a return to England and Whitehall; deck games on the P. & O.; the flaccid palm
of an under-secretary; newspaper interviews; hard, mocking, sex-
thirsty voices of women—"And is it really true, Mr. Conway, that
when you were in Tibet . . . ?" There was no doubt of one thing; he
would be able to dine out on his yarn for at least a season. But would
he enjoy it? He recalled a sentence penned by Gordon during the
last days at Khartoum—"I would sooner live like a Dervish with the
Mahdi than go out to dinner every night in London." Conway's
aversion was less definite—a mere anticipation that to tell his story in
the past tense would bore him a great deal as well as sadden him a
little.

Abruptly, in the midst of his reflections, he was aware of Chang's
approach. "Sir," began the Chinese, his slow whisper slightly quicken-

ing as he spoke, "I am proud to be the bearer of important news. . . ."

So the porters *had* come before their time, was Conway's first thought; it was odd that he should have been thinking of it so recently. And he felt the pang that he was half prepared for. "Well?" he queried.

Chang's condition was as nearly that of excitement as seemed physically possible for him. "My dear sir, I congratulate you," he continued. "And I am happy to think that I am in some measure responsible—it was after my own strong and repeated recommendations that the High Lama made his decision. He wishes to see you immediately."

Conway's glance was quizzical. "You're being less coherent than usual, Chang. What has happened?"

"The High Lama has sent for you."

"So I gather. But why all the fuss?"

"Because it is extraordinary and unprecedented—even I who urged it did not expect it to happen yet. A fortnight ago you had not arrived, and now you are about to be received by *him!* Never before has it occurred so soon!"

"I'm still rather fogged, you know. I'm to see your High Lama—I realize that all right. But is there anything else?"

"Is it not enough?"

Conway laughed. "Absolutely, I assure you—don't imagine I'm being discourteous. As a matter of fact, something quite different was in my head at first. However, never mind about that now. Of course, I shall be both honored and delighted to meet the gentleman. When is the appointment?"

"Now. I have been sent to bring you to him."

"Isn't it rather late?"

"That is of no consequence. My dear sir, you will understand many things very soon. And may I add my own personal pleasure that this interval—always an awkward one—is now at an end. Believe me, it has been irksome to me to have to refuse you information on so many occasions—extremely irksome. I am joyful in the knowledge that such unpleasantness will never again be necessary."

"You're a queer fellow, Chang," Conway responded. "But let's be going, don't bother to explain any more. I'm perfectly ready and I appreciate your nice remarks. Lead the way."

CHAPTER SEVEN

Conway was quite unruffled, but his demeanor covered an eagerness that grew in intensity as he accompanied Chang across the empty courtyards. If the words of the Chinese meant anything, he was on the threshold of discovery; soon he would know whether his theory, still half formed, were less impossible than it appeared.

Apart from this, it would doubtless be an interesting interview. He had met many peculiar potentates in his time; he took a detached interest in them, and was shrewd as a rule in his assessments. Without self-consciousness he had also the valuable knack of being able to say polite things in languages of which he knew very little indeed. Perhaps, however, he would be chiefly a listener on this occasion. He noticed that Chang was taking him through rooms he had not seen before, all of them rather dim and lovely in lantern light. Then a spiral staircase climbed to a door at which the Chinese knocked, and which was opened by a Tibetan servant with such promptness that Conway suspected he had been stationed behind it. This part of the lamasery, on a higher storey, was no less tastefully embellished than the rest, but its most immediately striking feature was a dry, tingling warmth, as if all the windows were tightly closed and some kind of steam heating plant were working at full pressure. The airlessness increased as he passed on, until at last Chang paused before a door which, if bodily sensation could have been trusted, might well have admitted to a Turkish bath.

"The High Lama," whispered Chang, "will receive you alone." Having opened the door for Conway's entrance, he closed it afterwards so silently that his own departure was almost imperceptible. Conway stood hesitant, breathing an atmosphere that was not only sultry, but full of dusk, so that it was several seconds before he could accustom his eyes to the gloom. Then he slowly built up an impression of a dark-curtained, low-roofed apartment, simply furnished with table and chairs. On one of these sat a small, pale, and wrinkled person, motionlessly shadowed, and yielding an effect as of some fading, antique portrait in chiaroscuro. If there were such a thing as presence divorced from actuality, here it was, adorned with a classic dignity that was more an emanation than an attribute. Conway was curious about his own intense perception of all this, and wondered if it were dependable or merely his reaction to the rich, crepuscular warmth; he felt dizzy under the gaze of those ancient eyes, took a few forward paces, and then halted. The occupant of the chair grew now less vague in outline, but scarcely more corporeal; he was a little old man in Chinese dress, its folds and flounces loose against a flat, emaciated frame. "You are Mr. Conway?" he whispered in excellent English.

The voice was pleasantly soothing, and touched with a very gentle melancholy that fell upon Conway with strange beatitude; though once again the skeptic in him was inclined to hold the temperature responsible.

"I am," he answered.

The voice went on. "It is a pleasure to see you, Mr. Conway. I sent for you because I thought we should do well to have a talk together. Please sit down beside me and have no fear. I am an old man and can do no one any harm."

Conway answered: "I feel it a signal honor to be received by you."

"I thank you, my dear Conway—I shall call you that, according to your English fashion. It is, as I said, a moment of great pleasure for me. My sight is poor, but believe me, I am able to see you in my mind, as well as with my eyes. I trust you have been comfortable at Shangri-La since your arrival?"

"Extremely so."

"I am glad. Chang has done his best for you, no doubt. It has been a great pleasure to him also. He tells me you have been asking many questions about our community and its affairs?"

"I am certainly interested in them."

"Then if you can spare me a little time, I shall be pleased to give you a brief account of our foundation."

"There is nothing I should appreciate more."

"That is what I had thought—and hoped. . . . But first of all, before our discourse . . ."

He made the slightest stir of a hand, and immediately, by what technique of summons Conway could not detect, a servant entered to prepare the elegant ritual of tea-drinking. The little egg-shell bowls of almost colorless fluid were placed on a lacquered tray; Conway, who knew the ceremony, was by no means contemptuous of it. The voice resumed: "Our ways are familiar to you, then?"

Obeying an impulse which he could neither analyze nor find desire to control, Conway answered: "I lived in China for some years."

"You did not tell Chang."

"No."

"Then why am I so honored?"

Conway was rarely at a loss to explain his own motives, but on this occasion he could not think of any reason at all. At length he replied: "To be quite candid, I haven't the slightest idea, except that I must have wanted to tell you."

"The best of all reasons, I am sure, between those who are to become friends. . . . Now tell me, is this not a delicate aroma? The teas of China are many and fragrant, but this, which is a special product of our own valley, is in my opinion their equal."

Conway lifted the bowl to his lips and tasted. The savor was slender, elusive, and recondite, a ghostly bouquet that haunted rather than lived on the tongue. He said: "It is very delightful, and also quite new to me."

"Yes, like a great many of our valley herbs, it is both unique and precious. It should be tasted, of course, very slowly—not only in reverence and affection, but to extract the fullest degree of pleasure. This is a famous lesson that we may learn from Kou Kai Tchou, who lived some fifteen centuries ago. He would always hesitate to reach the succulent marrow when he was eating a piece of sugar-cane, for, as he explained—'I introduce myself gradually into the region of delights.' Have you studied any of the great Chinese classics?"

Conway replied that he was slightly acquainted with a few of them. He knew that the allusive conversation would, according to etiquette, continue until the tea-bowls were taken away; but he found it far from irritating, despite his keenness to hear the history of Shangri-La. Doubtless there was a certain amount of Kou Kai Tchou's reluctant sensibility in himself.

At length the signal was given, again mysteriously, the servant padded in and out, and with no more preamble the High Lama of Shangri-La began:

"Probably you are familiar, my dear Conway, with the general outline of Tibetan history. I am informed by Chang that you have made ample use of our library here, and I doubt not that you have studied the scanty but exceedingly interesting annals of these regions. You will be aware, anyhow, that Nestorian Christianity was widespread throughout Asia during the Middle Ages, and that its memory lingered long after its actual decay. In the seventeenth century a Christian revival was impelled directly from Rome through the agency of those heroic Jesuit missionaries whose journeys, if I may permit myself the remark, are so much more interesting to read of

than those of St. Paul. Gradually the Church established itself over
an immense area, and it is a remarkable fact, not realized by many
Europeans to-day, that for thirty-eight years there existed a Christian mission in Lhasa itself. It was not, however, from Lhasa but
from Pekin, in the year 1719, that four Capuchin friars set out in
search of any remnants of the Nestorian faith that might still be sur-
viving in the hinterland.

"They traveled southwest for many months, by Lanchow and the
Koko-Nor, facing hardships which you will well imagine. Three died
on the way, and the fourth was not far from death when by accident
he stumbled into the rocky defile that remains to-day the only practical approach to the valley of Blue Moon. There, to his joy and surprise, he found a friendly and prosperous population who made haste
to display what I have always regarded as our oldest tradition—that
of hospitality to strangers. Quickly he recovered health and began
to preach his mission. The people were Buddhists, but willing to
hear him, and he had considerable success. There was an ancient
lamasery existing then on this same mountain-shelf, but it was in a
state of decay both physical and spiritual, and as the Capuchin's
harvest increased, he conceived the idea of setting up on the same
magnificent site a Christian monastery. Under his surveillance the
old buildings were repaired and largely reconstructed, and he himself began to live here in the year 1734, when he was fifty-three years
of age.

"Now let me tell you more about this man. His name was Perrault,
and he was by birth a Luxembourger. Before devoting himself to
Far Eastern missions he had studied at Paris, Bologna, and other
universities; he was something of a scholar. There are few existing
records of his early life, but it was not in any way unusual for one
of his age and profession. He was fond of music and the arts, had a
special aptitude for languages, and before he was sure of his vocation
he had tasted all the familiar pleasures of the world. Malplaquet was
fought when he was a youth, and he knew from personal contact the
horrors of war and invasion. He was physically sturdy; during his
first years here he labored with his hands like any other man, tilling
his own garden, and learning from the inhabitants as well as teaching
them. He found gold deposits along the valley, but they did not
tempt him; he was more deeply interested in local plants and herbs.
He was humble and by no means bigoted. He deprecated polygamy,
but he saw no reason to inveigh against the prevalent fondness for
the *tangatse* berry, to which were ascribed medicinal properties, but
which was chiefly popular because its effects were those of a mild

narcotic. Perrault, in fact, became somewhat of an addict himself; it was his way to accept from native life all that it offered which he found harmless and pleasant, and to give in return the spiritual treasure of the West. He was not an ascetic; he enjoyed the good things of the world, and was careful to teach his converts cooking as well as catechism. I want you to have an impression of a very earnest, busy, learned, simple, and enthusiastic person who, along with his priestly functions, did not disdain to put on a mason's overall and help in the actual building of these very rooms. That was, of course, a work of immense difficulty, and one which nothing but his pride and steadfastness could have overcome. Pride, I say, because it was undoubtedly a dominant motive at the beginning—the pride in his own Faith that made him decide that if Gautama could inspire men to build a temple on the ledge of Shangri-La, Rome was capable of no less.

"But time passed, and it was not unnatural that this motive should yield place gradually to more tranquil ones. Emulation is, after all, a young man's spirit, and Perrault, by the time his monastery was well established, was already full of years. You must bear in mind that he had not, from a strict point of view, been acting very regularly; though some latitude must surely be extended to one whose ecclesiastical superiors are located at a distance measurable in years rather than miles. But the folk of the valley and the monks themselves had no misgivings; they loved and obeyed him, and as years went on, came to venerate him also. At intervals it was his custom to send reports to the Bishop of Pekin, but often they never reached him, and as it was to be presumed that the bearers had succumbed to the perils of the journey, Perrault grew more and more unwilling to hazard their lives, and after about the middle of the century he gave up the practice. Some of his earlier messages, however, must have got through, and a doubt of his activities have been aroused, for in the year 1769 a stranger brought a letter written twelve years before, summoning Perrault to Rome.

"He would have been over seventy had the command been received without delay; as it was, he had turned eighty-nine. The long trek over mountain and plateau was unthinkable; he could never have endured the scouring gales and fierce chills of the wilderness outside. He sent, therefore, a courteous reply explaining the situation, but there is no record that his message ever passed the barrier of the great ranges.

"So Perrault remained at Shangri-La, not exactly in defiance of superior orders, but because it was physically impossible for him to fulfill them. In any case he was an old man, and death would proba-

bly soon put an end both to him and his irregularity. By this time
the institution he had founded had begun to undergo a subtle
change. It might be deplorable, but it was not really very astonishing;
for it could hardly be expected that one man unaided should uproot
permanently the habits and traditions of an epoch. He had no Western colleagues to hold firm when his own grip relaxed; and it had
perhaps been a mistake to build on a site that held such older and
differing memories. It was asking too much; but was it not asking
even more to expect a white-haired veteran, just entering the nineties, to realize the mistake that he had made? Perrault, at any rate,
did not then realize it. He was far too old and happy. His followers
were devoted even when they forgot his teaching, while the people
of the valley held him in such reverent affection that he forgave with
ever-increasing ease their lapse into former customs. He was still
active, and his faculties had remained exceptionally keen. At the
age of ninety-eight he began to study the Buddhist writings that
had been left at Shangri-La by its previous occupants, and his intention was then to devote the rest of his life to the composition of
a book attacking Buddhism from the standpoint of orthodoxy. He
actually finished this task (we have his manuscript complete), but
the attack was very gentle, for he had by that time reached the
round figure of a century—an age at which even the keenest acri-
monies are apt to fade.

"Meanwhile, as you may suppose, many of his early disciples had
died, and as there were few replacements, the number resident under the rule of the old Capuchin steadily diminished. From over
eighty at one time, it dwindled to a score, and then to a mere dozen,
most of them very aged themselves. Perrault's life at this time grew
to be a very calm and placid waiting for the end. He was far too old
for disease and discontent; only the everlasting sleep could claim
him now, and he was not afraid. The valley people, out of kindness,
supplied food and clothing; his library gave him work. He had become rather frail, but still kept energy to fulfill the major ceremonial
of his office; the rest of the tranquil days he spent with his books,
his memories, and the mild ecstasies of the narcotic. His mind remained so extraordinarily clear that he even embarked upon a study
of certain mystic practices that the Indians call *yoga*, and which are
based upon various special methods of breathing. For a man of such
an age the enterprise might well have seemed hazardous, and it was
certainly true that soon afterwards, in that memorable year 1789,
news descended to the valley that Perrault was dying at last.

"He lay in this room, my dear Conway, where he could see from

the window the white blurr that was all his failing eyesight gave
him of Karakal; but he could see with his mind also; he could picture the clear and matchless outline that he had first glimpsed half a
century before. And there came to him, too, the strange parade of
all his many experiences, the years of travel across desert and upland,
the great crowds in Western cities, the clang and glitter of Marl-
borough's troops. His mind had straitened to a snow-white calm; he
was ready, willing, and glad to die. He gathered his friends and
servants round him and bade them all farewell; then he asked to
be left alone awhile. It was during such a solitude, with his body
sinking and his mind lifted to beatitude, that he had hoped to give
up his soul . . . but it did not happen so. He lay for many weeks
without speech or movement, and then he began to recover. He was
a hundred and eight."

The whispering ceased for a moment, and to Conway, stirring
slightly, it appeared that the High Lama had been translating, with
fluency, out of a remote and private dream. At length he went on:

"Like others who have waited long on the threshold of death, Perrault had been granted a vision of some significance to take back
with him into the world; and of this vision more must be said later.
Here I will confine myself to his actions and behavior, which were
indeed remarkable. For instead of convalescing idly, as might have
been expected, he plunged forthwith into rigorous self-discipline
somewhat curiously combined with narcotic indulgence. Drug-tak-
ing and deep-breathing exercises—it could not have seemed a very
death-defying regimen; yet the fact remains that when the last of the
old monks died, in 1794, Perrault himself was still living.

"It would almost have brought a smile had there been any one
at Shangri-La with a sufficiently distorted sense of humor. The
wrinkled Capuchin, no more decrepit than he had been for a dozen
years, persevered in a secret ritual he had evolved, while to the folk
of the valley he soon became veiled in mystery, a hermit of uncanny
powers who lived alone on that formidable cliff. But there was still a
tradition of affection for him, and it came to be regarded as meri-
torious and luck-bringing to climb to Shangri-La and leave a simple
gift, or perform some manual task that was needed there. On all
such pilgrims Perrault bestowed his blessing—forgetful, it might be,
that they were lost and straying sheep. For 'Te Deum Laudamus'
and 'Om Mane Padme Hum' were now heard equally in the temples
of the valley.

"As the new century approached, the legend grew into a rich and
fantastic folk-lore—it was said that Perrault had become a god, that

he worked miracles, and that on certain nights he flew to the summit of Karakal to hold a candle to the sky. There is a paleness always on the mountain at full moon; but I need not assure you that neither Perrault nor any other man has ever climbed there. I mention it, even though it may seem unnecessary, because there is a mass of unreliable testimony that Perrault did and could do all kinds of impossible things. It was supposed, for instance, that he practiced the art of self-levitation, of which so much appears in accounts of Buddhist mysticism; but the more sober truth is that he made many experiments to that end, but entirely without success. He did, however, discover that the impairment of ordinary senses could be somewhat offset by a development of others; he acquired skill in telepathy which was perhaps remarkable, and though he made no claim to any specific powers of healing, there was a quality in his mere presence that was helpful in certain cases.

"You will wish to know how he spent his time during these unprecedented years. His attitude may be summed up by saying that, as he had not died at a normal age, he began to feel that there was no discoverable reason why he either should or should not do so at any definite time in the future. Having already proved himself abnormal, it was as easy to believe that the abnormality might continue as to expect it to end at any moment. And that being so, he began to behave without care for the imminence with which he had been so long preoccupied; he began to live the kind of life that he had always desired, but had so rarely found possible; for he had kept at heart and throughout all vicissitudes the tranquil tastes of a scholar. His memory was astonishing; it appeared to have escaped the trammels of the physical into some upper region of immense clarity; it almost seemed that he could now learn *everything* with far greater ease than during his student days he had been able to learn *anything*. He was soon, of course, brought up against a need for books, but there were a few he had had with him from the first, and they included, you may be interested to hear, an English grammar and dictionary and Florio's translation of Montaigne. With these to work on he contrived to master the intricacies of your language, and we still possess in our library the manuscript of one of his first linguistic exercises—a translation of Montaigne's essay on Vanity into Tibetan —surely a unique production."

Conway smiled. "I should be interested to see it sometime, if I might."

"With the greatest of pleasure. It was, you may think, a singularly unpractical accomplishment, but recollect that Perrault had reached a singularly unpractical age. He would have been lonely without some such occupation—at any rate until the fourth year of the nineteenth century, which marks an important event in the history of our foundation. For it was then that a second stranger from Europe arrived in the valley of Blue Moon. He was a young Austrian named Henschell who had soldiered against Napoleon in Italy—a youth of noble birth, high culture, and much charm of manner. The wars had ruined his fortunes, and he had wandered across Russia into Asia with some vague intention of retrieving them. It would be interesting to know how exactly he reached the plateau, but he had no very clear idea himself; indeed, he was as near death when he arrived here as Perrault himself had once been. Again the hospitality of Shangri-La was extended, and the stranger recovered—but there the parallel breaks down. For Perrault had come to preach and proselytize, whereas Henschell took a more immediate interest in the gold deposits. His first ambition was to enrich himself and return to Europe as soon as possible.

"But he did not return. An odd thing happened—though one that has happened so often since that perhaps we must now agree that it cannot be very odd after all. The valley, with its peacefulness and its utter freedom from worldly cares, tempted him again and again to delay his departure, and one day, having heard the local legend, he climbed to Shangri-La and had his first meeting with Perrault.

"That meeting was, in the truest sense, historic. Perrault, if a little beyond such human passions as friendship or affection, was yet endowed with a rich benignity of mind which touched the youth as water upon a parched soil. I will not try to describe the association that sprang up between the two; the one gave utmost adoration, while the other shared his knowledge, his ecstasies, and the wild dream that had now become the only reality left for him in the world."

There was a pause, and Conway said very quietly: "Pardon the interruption, but that is not quite clear to me."

"I know." The whispered reply was completely sympathetic. "It would be remarkable indeed if it were. It is a matter which I shall be pleased to explain before our talk is over, but for the present, if you will forgive me, I will confine myself to simpler things. A fact that will interest you is that Henschell began our collections of Chinese art, as well as our library and musical acquisitions. He made a remarkable journey to Pekin and brought back the first consignment in the year 1809. He did not leave the valley again, but it was his ingenuity which devised the complicated system by which the lamasery has ever since been able to obtain anything needful from the outer world."

"I suppose you found it easy to make payment in gold?"

"Yes, we have been fortunate in possessing supplies of a metal which is held in such high esteem in other parts of the world."

"Such high esteem that you must have been very lucky to escape a gold rush."

The High Lama inclined his head in the merest indication of agreement. "That, my dear Conway, was always Henschell's fear. He was careful that none of the porters bringing books and art treasures should ever approach too closely; he made them leave their burdens a day's journey outside, to be fetched afterwards by our valley folk themselves. He even arranged for sentries to keep constant watch on the entrance to the defile. But it soon occurred to him that there was an easier and more final safeguard."

"Yes?" Conway's voice was guardedly tense.

"You see there was no need to fear invasion by an army. That will never be possible, owing to the nature and distances of the country. The most ever to be expected was the arrival of a few half-lost wanderers who, even if they were armed, would probably be so weakened as to constitute no danger. It was decided, therefore, that henceforward strangers might come as freely as they chose—with but one important proviso.

"And, over a period of years, such strangers did come. Chinese merchants, tempted into the crossing of the plateau, chanced occasionally on this one traverse out of so many others possible to them. Nomad Tibetans, wandering from their tribes, strayed here sometimes like weary animals. All were made welcome, though some reached the shelter of the valley only to die. In the year of Waterloo two English missionaries, traveling overland to Pekin, crossed the ranges by an unnamed pass and had the extraordinary luck to arrive as calmly as if they were paying a call. In 1820 a Greek trader, accompanied by sick and famished servants, was found dying at the topmost ridge of the pass. In 1822 three Spaniards, having heard some vague story of gold, reached here after many wanderings and disappointments. Again, in 1830, there was a larger influx. Two Germans, a Russian, an Englishman, and a Swede made the dreaded crossing of the Tian-Shans, impelled by a motive that was to become increasingly common—scientific exploration. By the time of their approach a slight modification had taken place in the attitude of Shangri-La towards its visitors—not only were they now welcomed if they chanced to find their way into the valley, but it had become customary to meet them if they ever ventured within a certain radius. All this was for a reason I shall later discuss, but the point is of importance as showing that the lamasery was no longer hospitably indifferent; it had already both a need and a desire for new arrivals. And indeed in the years to follow it happened that more than one party of explorers, glorying in their first distant glimpse of Karakal, encountered messengers bearing a cordial invitation—and one that was rarely declined.

"Meanwhile the lamasery had begun to acquire many of its present characteristics. I must stress the fact that Henschell was exceedingly able and talented, and that the Shangri-La of to-day owes as much to him as to its founder. Yes, quite as much, I often think. For his was the firm yet kindly hand that every institution needs at a certain stage of its development, and his loss would have been altogether irreparable had he not completed more than a life-work before he died."

Conway looked up to echo rather than question those final words. *"He died!"*

"Yes. It was very sudden. He was killed. It was in the year of your Indian Mutiny. Just before his death a Chinese artist had sketched him, and I can show you that sketch now—it is in this room."

The slight gesture of the hand was repeated, and once again a servant entered. Conway, as a spectator in a trance, watched the man withdraw a small curtain at the far end of the room and leave a lantern swinging amongst the shadows. Then he heard the whisper inviting him to move, and it was extraordinary how hard it was to do so.

He stumbled to his feet and strode across to the trembling circle of light. The sketch was small, hardly more than a miniature in colored inks, but the artist had contrived to give the flesh-tones a waxwork delicacy of texture. The features were of great beauty, almost girlish in modeling, and Conway found in their winsomeness a curiously personal appeal, even across the barriers of time, death, and artifice. But the strangest thing of all was one that he realized only after his first gasp of admiration: the face was that of a young man.

He stammered as he moved away: "But—you said—this was done just before his death?"

"Yes. It is a very good likeness."

"Then if he died in the year you said—"

"He did."

"And he came here, you told me, in 1803, when he was a youth?"

"Yes."

Conway did not answer for a moment; presently, with an effort, he collected himself to say: "And he was killed, you were telling me?"

"Yes. An Englishman shot him. It was a few weeks after the Englishman had arrived at Shangri-La. He was another of those explorers."

"What was the cause of it?"

"There had been a quarrel—about some porters. Henschell had just told him of the important proviso that governs our reception of guests. It was a task of some difficulty, and ever since, despite my own enfeeblement, I have felt constrained to perform it myself."

The High Lama made another and longer pause, with just a hint of enquiry in his silence; when he continued, it was to add: "Perhaps you are wondering, my dear Conway, what that proviso may be?"

Conway answered slowly and in a low voice: "I think I can already guess."

"Can you, indeed? And can you guess anything else after this long and curious story of mine?"

Conway dizzied in brain as he sought to answer the question; the room was now a whorl of shadows with that ancient benignity at its center. Throughout the narrative he had listened with an intentness that had perhaps shielded him from realizing the fullest implications of it all; now, with the mere attempt at conscious expression, he was flooded over with amazement, and the gathering certainty in his mind was almost stifled as it sprang to words. "It seems impossible," he stammered. "And yet I can't help thinking of it—it's astonishing—and extraordinary—and quite incredible—and yet not *absolutely* beyond my powers of belief—"

"What is, my *son*?"

And Conway answered, shaken with an emotion for which he knew no reason and which he did not seek to conceal: "*That you are still alive, Father Perrault.*"

CHAPTER EIGHT

There had been a pause, imposed by the High Lama's call for further refreshment; Conway did not wonder at it, for the strain of such a long recital must have been considerable. Nor was he himself ungrateful for the respite. He felt that the interval was as desirable from an artistic as from any other point of view, and that the bowls of tea, with their accompaniment of conventionally improvised courtesies, fulfilled the same function as a *cadenza* in music. This reflection brought out (unless it were mere coincidence) an odd example of the High Lama's telepathic powers, for he immediately began to talk about music and to express pleasure that Conway's taste in that direction had not been entirely unsatisfied at Shangri-La. Conway answered with suitable politeness and added that he had been surprised to find the lamasery in possession of such a complete library of European composers. The compliment was acknowledged between slow sips of tea. "Ah, my dear Conway, we are fortunate in that one of our number is a gifted musician—he was, indeed, a pupil of Chopin's—and we have been happy to place in his hands the entire management of our salon. You must certainly meet him."

"I should like to. Chang, by the way, was telling me that your favorite Western composer is Mozart."

"That is so," came the reply. "Mozart has an austere elegance which we find very satisfying. He builds a house which is neither too big nor too little, and he furnishes it in perfect taste."

The exchange of comments continued until the tea-bowls were taken away; by that time Conway was able to remark quite calmly: "So, to resume our earlier discussion, you intend to keep us? That, I take it, is the important and invariable proviso?"

"You have guessed correctly, my son."

"In other words, we are to stay here for ever?"

"I should greatly prefer to employ your excellent English idiom and say that we are all of us here 'for good.'"

"What puzzles me is why we four, out of all the rest of the world's inhabitants, should have been chosen."

Relapsing into his earlier and more consequential manner, the

High Lama responded: "It is an intricate story, if you would care to hear it. You must know that we have always aimed, as far as possible, to keep our numbers in fairly constant recruitment—since, apart from any other reasons, it is pleasant to have with us people of various ages and representative of different periods. Unfortunately, since the recent European War and the Russian Revolution, travel and exploration in Tibet have been almost completely held up; in fact, our last visitor, a Japanese, arrived in 1912, and was not, to be candid, a very valuable acquisition. You see, my dear Conway, we are not quacks or charlatans; we do not and cannot guarantee success; some of our visitors derive no benefit at all from their stay here; others merely live to what might be called a normally advanced age and then die from some trifling ailment. In general we have found that Tibetans, owing to their being inured to both the altitude and other conditions, are much less sensitive than outside races; they are charming people, and we have admitted many of them, but I doubt if more than a few will pass their hundredth year. The Chinese are a little better, but even among them we have a high percentage of failures. Our best subjects, undoubtedly, are the Nordic and Latin races of Europe; perhaps the Americans would be equally adaptable, and I count it our great good fortune that we have at last, in the person of one of your companions, secured a citizen of that nation. But I must continue with the answer to your question. The position was, as I have been explaining, that for nearly two decades we had welcomed no new-comers, and as there had been several deaths during that period, a problem was beginning to arise. A few years ago, however, one of our number came to the rescue with a novel idea; he was a young fellow, a native of our valley, absolutely trustworthy and in fullest sympathy with our aims; but, like all the valley people, he was denied by nature the chance that comes more fortunately to those from a distance. It was he who suggested that he should leave us, make his way to some surrounding country, and bring us additional colleagues by a method which would have been impossible in an earlier age. It was in many respects a revolutionary proposal, but we gave our consent after due consideration. For we must move with the times, you know, even at Shangri-La."

"You mean that he was sent out deliberately to bring some one back by air?"

"Well, you see, he was an exceedingly gifted and resourceful youth, and we had great confidence in him. It was his own idea, and we allowed him a free hand in carrying it out. All we knew definitely was that the first stage of his plan included a period of tuition at an American flying-school."

"But how could he manage the rest of it? It was only by chance that there happened to be that aeroplane at Baskul—"

"True, my dear Conway—many things are by chance. But it happened, after all, to be just the chance that Talu was looking for. Had he not found it, there might have been another chance in a year or two—or perhaps, of course, none at all. I confess I was surprised when our sentinels gave news of his descent on the plateau. The progress of aviation is rapid, but it had seemed likely to me that much more time would elapse before an average machine could make such a crossing of the mountains."

"It wasn't an average machine. It was a rather special one, made for mountain-flying."

"Again by chance? Our young friend was indeed fortunate. It is a pity that we cannot discuss the matter with him—we were all grieved at his death. You would have liked him, Conway."

Conway nodded slightly; he felt it very possible. He said, after a silence: "But what's the idea behind it all?"

"My son, your way of asking that question gives me infinite pleasure. In the course of a somewhat long experience it has never before been put to me in tones of such calmness. My revelation has been greeted in almost every conceivable manner—with indignation, distress, fury, disbelief, and hysteria—but never until this night with mere interest. It is, however, an attitude that I most cordially welcome. To-day you are interested; to-morrow you will feel concern; eventually, it may be, I shall claim your devotion."

"That is more than I should care to promise."

"Your very doubt pleases me—it is the basis of profound and significant faith. . . . But let us not argue. You are interested, and that, from you, is much. All I ask in addition is that what I tell you now shall remain, for the present, unknown to your three companions."

Conway was silent.

"The time will come when they will learn, like you, but that moment, for their own sakes, had better not be hastened. I am so certain of your wisdom in this matter that I do not ask for a promise; you will act, I know, as we both think best. . . . Now let me begin by sketching for you a very agreeable picture. You are still, I should say, a youngish man by the world's standards; your life, as people say, lies ahead of you; in the normal course you might expect twenty or thirty years of only slightly and gradually diminishing activity. By no means a cheerless prospect, and I can hardly expect you to see it as I do—as a slender, breathless, and far too frantic interlude. The first quarter-century of your life was doubtless lived under the cloud of being too young for things, while the last quarter-century would normally be shadowed by the still darker cloud of being too old for them; and between those two clouds, what small and narrow sunlight illumines a human lifetime! But you, it may be, are destined to be more fortunate, since by the standards of Shangri-La your sunlit years have scarcely yet begun. It will happen, perhaps, that decades hence you will feel no older than you are to-day—you may preserve, as Henschell did, a long and wondrous youth. But that, believe me, is only an early and superficial phase. There will come a time when you will age like others, though far more slowly, and into a condition infinitely nobler; at eighty you may still climb to the pass with a young man's gait, but at twice that age you must not expect the whole marvel to have persisted. We are not workers of miracles; we have made no conquest of death or even of decay. All we have done and can sometimes do is to slacken the *tempo* of this brief interval that is called life. We do this by methods which are as simple here as they are impossible elsewhere; but make no mistake; the end awaits us all.

"Yet it is, nevertheless, a prospect of much charm that I unfold for you—long tranquillities during which you will observe a sunset as men in the outer world hear the striking of a clock, and with far less care. The years will come and go, and you will pass from fleshly enjoyments into austerer but no less satisfying realms; you may lose the keenness of muscle and appetite, but there will be gain to match your loss; you will achieve calmness and profundity, ripeness and wisdom, and the clear enchantment of memory. And, most precious of all, you will have Time—that rare and lovely gift that your Western countries have lost the more they have pursued it. Think for a moment. You will have time to read—never again will you skim pages to save minutes, or avoid some study lest it prove too engrossing. You have also a taste for music—here, then, are your scores and instruments, with Time, unruffled and unmeasured, to give you their richest savor. And you are also, we will say, a man of good fellowship—does it not charm you to think of wise and serene friendships, a long and kindly traffic of the mind from which death may not call you away with his customary hurry? Or, if it is solitude that you prefer, could you not employ our pavilions to enrich the gentleness of lonely thoughts?"

The voice made a pause which Conway did not seek to fill.

"You make no comment, my dear Conway. Forgive my eloquence—

I belong to an age and a nation that never considered it bad form
to be articulate. . . . But perhaps you are thinking of wife, parents,
children, left behind in the world? Or maybe ambitions to do this or
that? Believe me, though the pang may be keen at first, in a decade
from now even its ghost will not haunt you. Though in point of fact,
if I read your mind correctly, you have no such griefs."

Conway was startled by the accuracy of the judgment. "That's so,"
he replied. "I'm unmarried; I have few close friends and no ambitions."

"No ambitions? And how have you contrived to escape those widespread maladies?"

For the first time Conway felt that he was actually taking part
in a conversation. He said: "It always seemed to me in my profession
that a good deal of what passed for success would be rather disagreeable, apart from needing more effort than I felt called upon to make.
I was in the Consular Service—quite a subordinate post, but it suited
me well enough."

"Yet your soul was not in it?"

"Neither my soul nor my heart nor more than half my energies.
I'm naturally rather lazy."

The wrinkles deepened and twisted till Conway realized that the
High Lama was very probably smiling. "Laziness in doing stupid
things can be a great virtue," resumed the whisper. "In any case,
you will scarcely find us exacting in such a matter. Chang, I believe,
explained to you our principle of moderation, and one of the things
in which we are always moderate is activity. I myself, for instance,
have been able to learn ten languages; the ten might have been
twenty had I worked immoderately. But I did not. And it is the same
in other directions; you will find us neither profligate nor ascetic.
Until we reach an age when care is advisable, we gladly accept the
pleasures of the table, while—for the benefit of our younger colleagues—the women of the valley have happily applied the principle
of moderation to their own chastity. All things considered, I feel sure
you will get used to our ways without much effort. Chang, indeed,
was very optimistic—and so, after this meeting, am I. But there is,
I admit, an odd quality in you that I have never met in any of our
visitors hitherto. It is not quite cynicism, still less bitterness; perhaps
it is partly disillusionment, but it is also a clarity of mind that I
should not have expected in any one younger than—say, a century
or so. It is, if I had to put a single word to it, passionlessness."

Conway answered: "As good a word as most, no doubt. I don't
know whether you classify the people who come here, but if so, you

can label me '1914-1918.' That makes me, I should think, a unique specimen in your museum of antiquities—the other three who arrived along with me don't enter the category. I used up most of my passions and energies during the years I've mentioned, and though I don't talk much about it, the chief thing I've asked from the world since then is to leave me alone. I find in this place a certain charm and quietness that appeals to me, and no doubt, as you remark, I shall get used to things."

"Is that all, my son?"

"I hope I am keeping well to your own rule of moderation."

"You are clever—as Chang told me, you are very clever. But is there nothing in the prospect I have outlined that tempts you to any stronger feeling?"

Conway was silent for an interval and then replied: "I was deeply impressed by your story of the past, but to be candid, your sketch of the future interests me only in an abstract sense. I can't look so far ahead. I should certainly be sorry if I had to leave Shangri-La tomorrow, or next week, or perhaps even next year; but how I shall feel about it if I live to be a hundred isn't a matter to prophesy. I can face it, like any other future, but in order to make me keen it must have a point. I've sometimes doubted whether life itself has any; and if not, long life must be even more pointless."

"My friend, the traditions of this building, both Buddhist and Christian, are very reassuring."

"Maybe. But I'm afraid I still hanker after some more definite reason for envying the centenarian."

"There *is* a reason, and a very definite one indeed. It is the whole reason for this colony of chance-sought strangers living beyond their years. We do not follow an idle experiment, a mere whimsy. We have a dream and a vision. It is a vision that first appeared to old Perrault when he lay dying in this room in the year 1789. He looked back then on his long life, as I have already told you, and it seemed to him that all the loveliest things were transient and perishable, and that war, lust, and brutality might some day crush them until there were no more left in the world. He remembered sights he had seen with his own eyes, and with his mind he pictured others; he saw the nations strengthening, not in wisdom, but in vulgar passions and the will to destroy; he saw their machine power multiplying until a single-weaponed man might have matched a whole army of the Grand Monarque. And he perceived that when they had filled the land and sea with ruin, they would take to the air. . . . Can you say that his vision was untrue?"

"True indeed."

"But that was not all. He foresaw a time when men, exultant in the technique of homicide, would rage so hotly over the world that every precious thing would be in danger, every book and picture and harmony, every treasure garnered through two millenniums, the small, the delicate, the defenseless—all would be lost like the lost books of Livy, or wrecked as the English wrecked the Summer Palace in Pekin."

"I share your opinion of that."

"Of course. But what are the opinions of reasonable men against iron and steel? Believe me, that vision of old Perrault will come true. And that, my son, is why *I* am here, and why *you* are here, and why we may pray to outlive the doom that gathers around on every side."

"To outlive it?"

"There is a chance. It will all come to pass before you are as old as I am."

"And you think that Shangri-La will escape?"

"Perhaps. We may expect no mercy, but we may faintly hope for neglect. Here we shall stay with our books and our music and our meditations, conserving the frail elegancies of a dying age, and seeking such wisdom as men will need when their passions are all spent. We have a heritage to cherish and bequeath. Let us take what pleasure we may until that time comes."

"And then?"

"Then, my son, when the strong have devoured each other, the Christian ethic may at last be fulfilled, and the meek shall inherit the earth."

A shadow of emphasis had touched the whisper, and Conway surrendered to the beauty of it; again he felt the surge of darkness around, but now symbolically, as if the world outside were already brewing for the storm. And then he saw that the High Lama of Shangri-La was actually astir, rising from his chair, standing upright like the half-embodiment of a ghost. In mere politeness Conway made to assist; but suddenly a deeper impulse seized him, and he did what he had never done to any man before; he knelt, and hardly knew why he did.

"I understand you, Father," he said.

He was not perfectly aware of how at last he took his leave; he was in a dream from which he did not emerge till long afterwards. He remembered the night air icy after the heat of those upper rooms, and Chang's presence, a silent serenity, as they crossed the starlit courtyards together. Never had Shangri-La offered more concen-

trated loveliness to his eyes; the valley lay imaged over the edge of
the cliff, and the image was of a deep unrippled pool that matched
the peace of his own thoughts. For Conway had passed beyond as-
tonishments. The long talk, with its varying phases, had left him
empty of all save a satisfaction that was as much of the mind as of
the emotions, and as much of the spirit as of either; even his doubts
were now no longer harassing, but part of a subtle harmony. Chang
did not speak, and neither did he. It was very late, and he was glad
that all the others had gone to bed.

CHAPTER NINE

In the morning he wondered if all that he could call to mind were part of a waking or a sleeping vision.

He was soon reminded. A chorus of questions greeted him when he appeared at breakfast. "You certainly had a long talk with the boss last night," began the American. "We meant to wait up for you, but we got tired. What sort of guy is he?"

"Did he say anything about the porters?" asked Mallinson eagerly.

"I hope you mentioned to him about having a missionary stationed here," said Miss Brinklow.

The bombardment served to raise in Conway his usual defensive armament. "I'm afraid I'm probably going to disappoint you all," he replied, slipping easily into the mood. "I didn't discuss with him the question of missions; he didn't mention the porters to me at all; and as for his appearance, I can only say that he's a very old man who speaks excellent English and is quite intelligent."

Mallinson cut in with irritation: "The main thing to us is whether he's to be trusted or not. Do you think he means to let us down?"

"He didn't strike me as a dishonorable person."

"Why on earth didn't you worry him about the porters?"

"It didn't occur to me."

Mallinson stared at him incredulously. "I can't understand you, Conway. You were so damned good in that Baskul affair that I can hardly believe you're the same man. You seem to have gone all to pieces."

"I'm sorry."

"No good being sorry. You ought to buck up and look as if you cared what happens."

"You misunderstand me. I meant that I was sorry to have disappointed you."

Conway's voice was curt, an intended mask to his feelings, which were, indeed, so mixed that they could hardly have been guessed by others. He had slightly surprised himself by the ease with which he had prevaricated; it was clear that he intended to observe the High Lama's suggestion and keep the secret. He was also puzzled by the naturalness with which he was accepting a position which his companions would certainly and with some justification think traitorous; as Mallinson had said, it was hardly the sort of thing to be expected of a hero. Conway felt a sudden half-pitying fondness for the youth; then he steeled himself by reflecting that people who hero-worship must be prepared for disillusionments. Mallinson at Baskul had been far too much the new boy adoring the handsome games-captain, and now the games-captain was tottering if not already fallen from the pedestal. There was always something a little pathetic in the smashing of an ideal, however false; and Mallinson's admiration might have been at least a partial solace for the strain of pretending to be what he was not. But pretense was impossible anyway. There was a quality in the air of Shangri-La—perhaps due to its altitude—that forbade one the effort of counterfeit emotion.

He said: "Look here, Mallinson, it's no use harping continually on Baskul. Of course I was different then—it was a completely different situation."

"And a much healthier one in my opinion. At least we knew what we were up against."

"Murder and rape—to be precise. You can call that healthier if you like."

The youth's voice rose in pitch as he retorted: "Well, I *do* call it healthier—in one sense. It's something I'd rather face than all this mystery business." Suddenly he added: "That Chinese girl, for instance—how did *she* get here? Did the fellow tell you?"

"No. Why should he?"

"Well, why shouldn't he? And why shouldn't you ask, if you had any interest in the matter at all? Is it usual to find a young girl living with a lot of monks?"

That way of looking at it was one that had scarcely occurred to Conway before. "This isn't an ordinary monastery," was the best reply he could give after some thought.

"My God, it isn't!"

There was a silence, for the argument had evidently reached a dead-end. To Conway the history of Lo-Tsen seemed rather far from the point; the little Manchu lay so quietly in his mind that he hardly knew she was there. But at the mere mention of her Miss Brinklow had looked up suddenly from the Tibetan grammar which she was studying even over the breakfast table (just as if, thought Conway, with secret meaning, she hadn't all her life for it). Chatter of girls and monks reminded her of those stories of Indian temples that men missionaries told their wives, and that the wives passed on to their

unmarried female colleagues. "Of course," she said between tightened lips, "the morals of this place are quite hideous—we might have
expected that." She turned to Barnard as if inviting support, but the
American only grinned. "I don't suppose you folks'd value my opinion
on a matter of morals," he remarked dryly. "But I should say myself
that quarrels are just as bad. Since we've gotter be here for some
time yet, let's keep our tempers and make ourselves comfortable."

Conway thought this good advice, but Mallinson was still unpla-
cated. "I can quite believe you find it more comfortable than Dartmoor," he said meaningly.

"Dartmoor? Oh, that's your big penitentiary?—I get you. Well, yes,
I certainly never did envy the folks in them places. And there's another thing, too—it don't hurt when you chip me about it. Thick-
skinned and tender-hearted, that's my mixture."

Conway glanced at him in appreciation, and at Mallinson with some
hint of reproof; but then abruptly he had the feeling that they were
all acting on a vast stage, of whose background only he himself was
conscious; and such knowledge, so incommunicable, made him suddenly want to be alone. He nodded to them and went out into the
courtyard. In sight of Karakal misgivings faded, and qualms about
his three companions were lost in an uncanny acceptance of the new
world that lay so far beyond their guesses. There came a time, he
realized, when the strangeness of everything made it increasingly
difficult to realize the strangeness of anything; when one took things
for granted merely because astonishment would have been as tedious
for oneself as for others. Thus far had he progressed at Shangri-La,
and he remembered that he had attained a similar though far less
pleasant equanimity during his years at the War.

He needed equanimity, if only to accommodate himself to the
double life he was compelled to lead. Thenceforward, with his fellow exiles, he lived in a world conditioned by the arrival of porters
and a return to India; at all other times the horizon lifted like a
curtain; time expanded and space contracted, and the name Blue
Moon took on a symbolic meaning, as if the future, so delicately
plausible, were of a kind that might happen once in a blue moon
only. Sometimes he wondered which of his two lives were the more
real, but the problem was not pressing; and again he was reminded
of the War, for during heavy bombardments he had had the same
comforting sensation that he had many lives, only one of which could
be claimed by death.

Chang, of course, now talked to him completely without reserve,
and they had many conversations about the rule and routine of the

lamasery. Conway learned that during his first five years he would live a normal life, without any special regimen; this was always done, as Chang said, "to enable the body to accustom itself to the altitude, and also to give time for the dispersal of mental and emotional regrets."

Conway remarked with a smile: "I suppose you're certain, then, that no human affection can outlast a five-year absence?"

"It can, undoubtedly," replied the Chinese, "but only as a fragrance whose melancholy we may enjoy."

After the probationary five years, Chang went on to explain, the process of retarding age would begin, and if successful, might give Conway half a century or so at the apparent age of forty—which was not a bad time of life at which to remain stationary.

"What about yourself?" Conway asked. "How did it work out in your case?"

"Ah, my dear sir, I was lucky enough to arrive when I was quite young—only twenty-two. I was a soldier, though you might not have thought it; I had command of troops operating against brigand tribes in the year 1855. I was making what I should have called a reconnaissance if I had ever returned to my superior officers to tell the tale, but in plain truth I had lost my way in the mountains, and of my men only seven out of over a hundred survived the rigors of the climate. When at last I was rescued and brought to Shangri-La I was so ill that extreme youth and virility alone could have saved me."

"Twenty-two," echoed Conway, performing the calculation. "So you're now ninety-seven?"

"Yes. Very soon, if the lamas give their consent, I shall receive full initiation."

"I see. You have to wait for the round figure?"

"No, we are not restricted by any definite age limit, but a century is generally considered to be an age beyond which the passions and moods of ordinary life are likely to have disappeared."

"I should certainly think so. And what happens afterwards? How long do you expect to carry on?"

"There is reason to hope that I shall enter lamahood with such prospects as Shangri-La has made possible. In years, perhaps another century or more."

Conway nodded. "I don't know whether I ought to congratulate you—you seem to have been granted the best of both worlds, a long and pleasant youth behind you, and an equally long and pleasant old age ahead. When did you begin to grow old in appearance?"

"When I was over seventy. That is often the case, though I think I may still claim to look younger than my years."

"Decidedly. And suppose you were to leave the valley now, what would happen?"

"Death, if I remained away for more than a very few days."

"The atmosphere, then, is essential?"

"There is only one valley of Blue Moon, and those who expect to find another are asking too much of nature."

"Well, what would have happened if you had left the valley, say, thirty years ago, during your prolonged youth?"

Chang answered: "Probably I should have died even then. In any case, I should have acquired very quickly the full appearance of my actual age. We had a curious example of that some years ago, though there had been several others before. One of our number had left the valley to look out for a party of travelers whom we had heard might be approaching. This man, a Russian, had arrived here originally in the prime of life, and had taken to our ways so well that at nearly eighty he did not look more than half as old. He should have been absent no longer than a week (which would not have mattered), but unfortunately he was taken prisoner by nomad tribes and carried away some distance. We suspected an accident and gave him up for lost. Three months later, however, he returned to us, having made his escape. But he was a very different man. Every year of his age was in his face and behavior, and he died shortly afterwards, as an old man dies."

Conway made no remark for some time. They were talking in the library, and during most of the narrative he had been gazing through a window towards the pass that led to the outer world; a little wisp of cloud had drifted across the ridge. "A rather grim story, Chang," he commented at length. "It gives one the feeling that Time is like some balked monster, waiting outside the valley to pounce on the slackers who have managed to evade him longer than they should."

"*Slackers?*" queried Chang. His knowledge of English was extremely good, but sometimes a colloquialism proved unfamiliar.

"'Slacker,'" explained Conway, "is a slang word meaning a lazy fellow, a good-for-nothing. I wasn't, of course, using it seriously."

Chang bowed his thanks for the information. He took a keen interest in languages, and liked to weigh a new word philosophically. "It is significant," he said after a pause, "that the English regard slackness as a vice. We, on the other hand, should vastly prefer it to tension. Is there not too much tension in the world at present, and might it not be better if more people were slackers?"

"I'm inclined to agree with you," Conway answered with solemn amusement.

During the course of a week or so after the interview with the High Lama, Conway met several others of his future colleagues. Chang was neither eager nor reluctant to make the introductions, and Conway sensed a new and to him rather attractive atmosphere in which urgency did not clamor nor postponement disappoint. "Indeed," as Chang explained, "some of the lamas may not meet you for a considerable time—perhaps years—but you must not be surprised at that. They are prepared to make your acquaintance when it may so happen, and their avoidance of hurry does not imply any degree of unwillingness." Conway, who had often had similar feelings when calling on new arrivals at foreign consulates, thought it a very intelligible attitude.

The meetings he did have, however, were quite successful, and conversation with men thrice his age held none of the social embarrassments that might have obtruded in London or Delhi. His first encounter was with a genial German named Meister, who had entered the lamasery during the 'eighties, as the survivor of an exploring party. He spoke English well, though with an accent. A day or two later a second introduction took place, and Conway enjoyed his first talk with the man whom the High Lama had particularly mentioned—Alphonse Briac, a wiry, small-statured Frenchman who did not look especially old, though he announced himself as a pupil of Chopin. Conway thought that both he and the German would prove agreeable company. Already he was subconsciously analyzing, and after a few further meetings he reached one or two general conclusions; he perceived that though the lamas he met had individual differences, they all possessed that quality for which agelessness was not an outstandingly good name, but the only one he could think of. Moreover, they were all endowed with a calm intelligence which pleasantly overflowed into measured and well-balanced opinions. Conway could give an exact response to that kind of approach, and he was aware that they realized it and were gratified. He found them quite as easy to get on with as any other group of cultured people he might have met, though there was often a sense of oddity in hearing reminiscences so distant and apparently so casual. One white-haired and benevolent-looking person, for instance, asked Conway, after a little conversation, if he were interested in the Brontës. Conway said he was, to some extent, and the other replied: "You see, when I was a curate in the West Riding during the 'forties, I once visited Haworth and stayed at the Parsonage. Since coming here I've made a study of the whole Brontë problem—indeed, I'm writing a book on the subject. Perhaps you might care to go over it with me sometime?"

Conway responded cordially, and afterwards, when he and Chang were left together, commented on the vividness with which the lamas appeared to recollect their pre-Tibetan lives. Chang answered that it was all part of the training. "You see, my dear sir, one of the first steps towards the clarifying of the mind is to obtain a panorama of one's own past, and that, like any other view, is more accurate in perspective. When you have been among us long enough you will find your old life slipping gradually into focus as through a telescope when the lens is adjusted. Everything will stand out still and clear, duly proportioned and with its correct significance. Your new acquaintance, for instance, discerns that the really big moment of his entire life occurred when he was a young man visiting a house in which there lived an old parson and his three daughters."

"So I suppose I shall have to set to work to remember my own big moments?"

"It will not be an effort. They will come to you."

"I don't know that I shall give them much of a welcome," answered Conway moodily.

But whatever the past might yield, he was discovering happiness in the present. When he sat reading in the library, or playing Mozart in the music room, he often felt the invasion of a deep spiritual emotion, as if Shangri-La were indeed a living essence, distilled from the magic of the ages and miraculously preserved against time and death. His talk with the High Lama recurred memorably at such moments; he sensed a calm intelligence brooding gently over every diversion, giving a thousand whispered reassurances to ear and eye. Thus he would listen while Lo-Tsen marshaled some intricate fugue rhythm, and wonder what lay behind the faint impersonal smile that stirred her lips into the likeness of an opening flower. She talked very little, even though she now knew that Conway could speak her language; to Mallinson, who liked to visit the music room sometimes, she was almost dumb. But Conway discerned a charm that was perfectly expressed by her silences.

Once he asked Chang her history, and learned that she came of royal Manchu stock. "She was betrothed to a prince of Turkestan, and was traveling to Kashgar to meet him when her carriers lost

their way in the mountains. The whole party would doubtless have
perished but for the customary meeting with our emissaries."

"When did this happen?"

"In 1884. She was eighteen."

"Eighteen *then?*"

Chang bowed. "Yes, we are succeeding very well with her, as you
may judge for yourself. Her progress has been consistently excellent."

"How did she take things when she first came?"

"She was, perhaps, a little more than averagely reluctant to accept
the situation—she made no protest, but we were aware that she was
troubled for a time. It was, of course, an unusual occurrence—to intercept a young girl on the way to her wedding. . . . We were all
particularly anxious that she should be happy here." Chang smiled
blandly. "I am afraid the excitement of love does not make for an
easy surrender, though the first five years proved ample for their
purpose."

"She was deeply attached, I suppose, to the man she was to have
married?"

"Hardly that, my dear sir, since she had never seen him. It was
the old custom, you know. The excitement of her affections was entirely impersonal."

Conway nodded, and thought a little tenderly of Lo-Tsen. He pictured her as she might have been half a century before, statuesque
in her decorated chair as the carriers toiled over the plateau, her
eyes searching the wind-swept horizons that must have seemed so
harsh after the gardens and lotus-pools of the East. "Poor child!"
he said, thinking of such elegance held captive over the years. Knowledge of her past increased rather than lessened his content with her
stillness and silence; she was like a lovely cold vase, unadorned save
by an escaping ray.

He was also content, though less ecstatically, when Briac talked
to him of Chopin, and played the familiar melodies with much brilliance. It appeared that the Frenchman knew several Chopin compositions that had never been published, and as he had written them
down, Conway devoted pleasant hours to memorizing them himself.
He found a certain piquancy in the reflection that neither Cortot
nor Pachmann had been so fortunate. Nor were Briac's recollections
at an end; his memory continually refreshed him with some little
scrap of tune that the composer had thrown off or improvised on
some occasion; he took them all down on paper as they came into
his head, and some were very delightful fragments. "Briac," Chang
explained, "has not long been initiated, so you must make allowances

if he talks a great deal about Chopin. The younger lamas are naturally preoccupied with the past; it is a necessary step to envisaging
the future."

"Which is, I take it, the job of the older ones?"

"Yes. The High Lama, for instance, spends almost his entire life
in clairvoyant meditation."

Conway pondered a moment and then said: "By the way, when
do you suppose I shall see him again?"

"Doubtless at the end of the first five years, my dear sir."

But in that confident prophecy Chang was wrong, for less than a
month after his arrival at Shangri-La Conway received a second summons to that torrid upper room. Chang had told him that the High
Lama never left his apartments, and that their heated atmosphere
was necessary for his bodily existence; and Conway, being thus prepared, found the change less disconcerting than before. Indeed, he
breathed easily as soon as he had made his bow and been granted
the faintest answering liveliness of the sunken eyes. He felt kinship
with the mind beyond them, and though he knew that this second
interview following so soon upon the first was an unprecedented
honor, he was not in the least nervous or weighed down with solemnity. Age was to him no more an obsessing factor than rank or color;
he had never felt debarred from liking people because they were too
young or too old. He held the High Lama in most cordial respect,
but he did not see why their social relations should be anything less
than urbane.

They exchanged the usual courtesies, and Conway answered many
polite questions. He said he was finding the life very agreeable and
had already made friendships.

"And you have kept our secrets from your three companions?"

"Yes, up to now. It has proved awkward for me at times, but probably less so than if I had told them."

"Just as I surmised; you have acted as you thought best. And the
awkwardness, after all, is only temporary. Chang tells me he thinks
that two of them will give little trouble."

"I dare say that is so."

"And the third?"

Conway replied: "Mallinson is an excitable youth—he's pretty keen
to get back."

"You like him?"

"Yes, I like him very much."

At this point the tea-bowls were brought in, and talk became less
serious between sips of the scented liquid. It was an apt convention,

enabling the verbal flow to acquire a touch of that almost frivolous fragrance, and Conway was responsive. When the High Lama asked him whether Shangri-La was not unique in his experience, and if the Western world could offer anything in the least like it, he answered with a smile: "Well, yes—to be quite frank, it reminds me very slightly of Oxford, where I used to lecture. The scenery there is not so good, but the subjects of study are often just as impractical, and though even the oldest of the dons is not quite so old, they appear to age in a somewhat similar way."

"You have a sense of humor, my dear Conway," replied the High Lama, "for which we shall all be grateful during the years to come."

CHAPTER TEN

"Extraordinary," Chang said, when he heard that Conway had
seen the High Lama again. And from one so reluctant to employ superlatives, the word was significant. It had never happened before,
he emphasized, since the routine of the lamasery became established; never had the High Lama desired a second meeting until the
five years' probation had effected a purge of all the exile's likely emotions. "Because, you see, it is a great strain on him to talk to the
average new-comer. The mere presence of human passions is an un-
welcome and, at his age, an almost unendurable unpleasantness. Not
that I doubt his entire wisdom in the matter. It teaches us, I believe,
a lesson of great value—that even the fixed rules of our community
are only moderately fixed. But it is extraordinary, all the same."

To Conway, of course, it was no more extraordinary than anything
else, and after he had visited the High Lama on a third and fourth
occasion, he began to feel that it was not very extraordinary at all.
There seemed, indeed, something almost preordained in the ease
with which their two minds approached each other; it was as if in
Conway all secret tensions were relaxed, giving him, when he came
away, a sumptuous tranquillity. At times he had the sensation of
being completely bewitched by the mastery of that central intelligence, and then, over the little pale blue tea-bowls, the cerebration
would contract into a liveliness so gentle and miniature that he had
an impression of a theorem dissolving limpidly into a sonnet.

Their talks ranged far and fearlessly; entire philosophies were unfolded; the long avenues of history surrendered themselves for inspection and were given new plausibility. To Conway it was an
entrancing experience, but he did not suspend the critical attitude,
and once, when he had argued a point, the High Lama replied: "My
son, you are young in years, but I perceive that your wisdom has the
ripeness of age. Surely some unusual thing has happened to you?"

Conway smiled. "No more unusual than has happened to many
others of my generation."

"I have never met your like before."

Conway answered after an interval: "There's not a great deal of
mystery about it. That part of me which seems old to you was worn

out by intense and premature experience. My years from nineteen
to twenty-two were a supreme education, no doubt, but rather exhausting."

"You were very unhappy at the War?"

"Not particularly so. I was excited and suicidal and scared and
reckless and sometimes in a tearing rage—like a few million others,
in fact. I got mad-drunk and killed and lechered in great style. It
was the self-abuse of all one's emotions, and one came through it,
if one did at all, with a sense of almighty boredom and fretfulness.
That's what made the years afterwards so difficult. Don't think I'm
posing myself too tragically—I've had pretty fair luck since, on the
whole. But it's been rather like being in a school where there's a bad
headmaster—plenty of fun to be got if you feel like it, but nerve-
racking off and on, and not really very satisfactory. I think I found
that out rather more than most people."

"And your education thus continued?"

Conway gave a shrug. "Perhaps the exhaustion of the passions
is the beginning of wisdom, if you care to alter the proverb."

"That also, my son, is the doctrine of Shangri-La."

"I know. It makes me feel quite at home."

He had spoken no less than the truth. As the days and weeks
passed he began to feel an ache of contentment uniting mind and
body; like Perrault and Henschell and the others, he was falling under the spell. Blue Moon had taken him, and there was no escape.
The mountains gleamed around in a hedge of inaccessible purity,
from which his eyes fell dazzled to the green depths of the valley;
the whole picture was incomparable, and when he heard the harpsichord's silver monotony across the lotus-pool, he felt that it
threaded the perfect pattern of sight and sound.

He was, and he knew it, very quietly in love with the little Manchu.
His love demanded nothing, not even reply; it was a tribute of the
mind, to which his senses added only a flavor. She stood for him as
a symbol of all that was delicate and fragile; her stylized courtesies
and the touch of her fingers on the keyboard yielded a completely
satisfying intimacy. Sometimes he would address her in a way that
might, if she had cared, have led to less formal conversation; but her
replies never broke through the exquisite privacy of her thoughts,
and in a sense he did not wish them to. He had suddenly come to
realize a single facet of the promised jewel; he had Time, Time for
everything that he wished to happen, such Time that desire itself
was quenched in the certainty of fulfillment. A year, a decade hence,

there would still be Time. The vision grew on him, and he was happy with it.

Then, at intervals, he stepped into the other life to encounter Mallinson's impatience, Barnard's heartiness, and Miss Brinklow's robust intention. He felt he would be glad when they all knew as much as he; and, like Chang, he could imagine that neither the American nor the missionary would prove difficult cases. He was even amused when Barnard once said: "You know, Conway, I'm not sure that this wouldn't be a nice little place to settle down in. I thought at first I'd miss the newspapers and the movies, but I guess one can get used to anything."

"I guess one can," agreed Conway.

He learned afterwards that Chang had taken Barnard down to the valley, at his own request, to enjoy everything in the way of a "night out" that the resources of the locality could provide. Mallinson, when he heard of this, was rather scornful. "Getting tight, I suppose," he remarked to Conway, and to Barnard himself he commented: "Of course it's none of my business, but you'll want to keep yourself pretty fit for the journey, you know. The porters are due in a fort-night's time, and from what I gather, the return trip won't be exactly a joy ride."

Barnard nodded equably. "I never figgered it would," he answered. "And as for keeping fit, I guess I'm fitter than I've been for years. I get exercise daily, I don't have any worries, and the speak-easies down in the valley don't let you go too far. Moderation, y'know —the motto of the firm."

"Yes, I've no doubt you've been managing to have a moderately good time," said Mallinson acidly.

"Certainly I have. This establishment caters for all tastes—some people like little Chink gels who play the pi-anno, isn't that so? You can't blame anybody for what they fancy."

Conway was not at all put out, but Mallinson flushed like a schoolboy. "You can send them to jail, though, when they fancy other people's property," he snapped, stung to fury that set a raw edge to his wits.

"Sure, if you can catch 'em." The American grinned affably. "And that leads me to something I may as well tell you folks right away, now we're on the subject. I've decided to give those porters a miss. They come here pretty regular, and I'll wait for the next trip, or maybe the next but one. That is, if the monks'll take my word that I'm still good for my hotel expenses."

"You mean you're not coming with us?"

"That's it. I've decided to stop over for a while. It's all very fine for you—you'll have the band playing when *you* get home, but all the welcome I'll get is from a row of cops. And the more I think about it, the more it don't seem good enough."

"In other words, you're just afraid to face the music?"

"Well, I never did like music, anyhow."

Mallinson said with cold scorn: "I suppose it's your own affair. Nobody can prevent you from stopping here all your life if you feel inclined." Nevertheless he looked round with a flash of appeal. "It's not what everybody would choose to do, but ideas differ. What do you say, Conway?"

"I agree. Ideas *do* differ."

Mallinson turned to Miss Brinklow, who suddenly put down her book and remarked: "As a matter of fact, I think I shall stay too."

"*What?*" they all cried together.

She continued, with a bright smile that seemed more an attachment to her face than an illumination of it: "You see, I've been thinking over the way things happened to bring us all here, and there's only one conclusion I can come to. There's a mysterious power working behind the scenes. Don't you think so, Mr. Conway?"

Conway might have found it hard to reply, but Miss Brinklow went on in a gathering hurry: "Who am I to question the dictates of Providence? I was sent here for a purpose, and I shall stay."

"Do you mean you're hoping to start a mission here?" Mallinson asked.

"Not only hoping, but fully intending. I know just how to deal with these people—I shall get my own way, never fear. There's no real grit in any of them."

"And you intend to introduce some?"

"Yes, I do, Mr. Mallinson. I'm strongly opposed to that idea of moderation that we hear so much about. You can call it broadmindedness if you like, but in my opinion it leads to the worst kinds of laxity. The whole trouble with the people here is their so-called broadmindedness, and I intend to fight it with all my powers."

"And they're so broadminded that they're going to let you?" said Conway, smiling.

"Or else she's so strong-minded that they can't stop her," put in Barnard. He added with a chuckle: "It's just what I said—this establishment caters for all tastes."

"Possibly, if you happen to *like* prison," Mallinson snapped.

"Well, there's two ways of looking even at that. My goodness, if you think of all the folks in the world who'd give all they've got to be out of the racket and in a place like this, only they can't *get* out! Are *we* in the prison or are *they?*"

"A comforting speculation for a monkey in a cage," retorted Mallinson; he was still furious.

Afterwards he spoke to Conway alone. "That man still gets on my nerves," he said, pacing the courtyard. "I'm not sorry we shan't have him with us when we go back. You may think me touchy, but being chipped about that Chinese girl didn't appeal to my sense of humor."

Conway took Mallinson's arm. It was becoming increasingly clear to him that he was very fond of the youth, and that their recent weeks in company had deepened the feeling, despite jarring moods. He answered: "I rather took it that *I* was being ragged about her, not you."

"No, I think he intended it for me. He knows I'm interested in her. I am, Conway. I can't make out why she's here, and whether she really likes being here. My God, if I spoke her language as you do, I'd soon have it out with her."

"I wonder if you would. She doesn't say a great deal to any one, you know."

"It puzzles me that you don't badger her with all sorts of questions."

"I don't know that I care for badgering people."

He wished he could have said more, and then suddenly the sense of pity and irony floated over him in a filmy haze; this youth, so eager and ardent, would take things very hardly. "I shouldn't worry about Lo-Tsen if I were you," he added. "She's happy enough."

The decision of Barnard and Miss Brinklow to remain behind seemed to Conway all to the good, though it threw Mallinson and himself into an apparently opposite camp for the time being. It was an extraordinary situation, and he had no definite plans for tackling it.

Fortunately there was no apparent need to tackle it at all. Until the two months were past, nothing much could happen; and afterwards there would be a crisis no less acute for his having tried to prepare himself for it. For this and other reasons he was disinclined to worry over the inevitable, though he did once say: "You know, Chang, I'm bothered about young Mallinson. I'm afraid he'll take things very badly when he finds out."

Chang nodded with some sympathy. "Yes, it will not be easy to persuade him of his good fortune. But the difficulty is, after all, only a temporary one. In twenty years from now our friend will be quite reconciled."

Conway felt that this was looking at the matter almost too philosophically. "I'm wondering," he said, "just how the truth's going to be broached to him. He's counting the days to the arrival of the porters, and if they don't come—"

"But they *will* come."

"Oh? I rather imagined that all your talk about them was just a pleasant fable to let us down lightly."

"By no means. Although we have no bigotry on the point, it is our custom at Shangri-La to be moderately truthful, and I can assure you that my statements about the porters were almost correct. At any rate, we are expecting the men at or about the time I said."

"Then you'll find it hard to stop Mallinson from joining them."

"But we should never attempt to do so. He will merely discover— no doubt by personal experiment—that the porters are reluctantly unable to take any one back with them."

"I see. So that's the method? And what do you expect to happen afterwards?"

"Then, my dear sir, after a period of disappointment, he will— since he is young and optimistic—begin to hope that the next convoy of porters, due in nine or ten months' time, will prove more amenable to his suggestions. And this is a hope which, if we are wise, we shall not at first discourage."

Conway said sharply: "I'm not so sure that he'll do that at all. I should think he's far more likely to try an escape on his own."

"*Escape?* Is that *really* the word that should be used? After all, the pass is open to any one at any time. We have no jailers, save those that Nature herself has provided."

Conway smiled. "Well, you must admit that she's done her job pretty well. But I don't suppose you rely on her in every case, all the same. What about the various exploring parties that have arrived here? Was the pass always equally open to *them* when they wanted to get away?"

It was Chang's turn now to smile. "Special circumstances, my dear sir, have sometimes required special consideration."

"Excellent. So you only allow people the chance of escape when you know they'd be fools to take it? Even so, I expect some of them do."

"Well, it has happened very occasionally, but as a rule the absentees are glad to return after the experience of a single night on the plateau."

"Without shelter and proper clothing? If so, I can quite under-stand that your mild methods are as effective as stern ones. But what about the less usual cases that don't return?"

"You have yourself answered the question," replied Chang. "They do *not* return." But he made haste to add: "I can assure you, however, that there are few indeed who have been so unfortunate, and I trust your friend will not be rash enough to increase the num-ber."

Conway did not find these responses entirely reassuring, and Mal-linson's future remained a preoccupation. He wished it were possible for the youth to return by consent, and this would not be unprece-dented, for there was the recent case of Talu, the airman. Chang admitted that the authorities were fully empowered to do anything that they considered wise. "But *should* we be wise, my dear sir, in trusting ourselves and our future entirely to your friend's feelings of gratitude?"

Conway felt that the question was pertinent, for Mallinson's at-titude left little doubt as to what he would do as soon as he reached India. It was his favorite theme, and he had often enlarged upon it.

But all that, of course, was in the mundane world that was gradu-ally being pushed out of his mind by the rich, pervasive world of Shangri-La. Except when he thought about Mallinson he was ex-traordinarily content; the slowly revealed fabric of this new environ-ment continued to astonish him by its intricate suitability to his own needs and tastes.

Once he said to Chang: "By the way, how do you people here fit love into your scheme of things? I suppose it does sometimes hap-pen that those who come here develop attachments?"

"Quite often," replied Chang with a broad smile. "The lamas, of course, are immune, and so are most of us when we reach the riper years, but until then we are as other men, except that I think we can claim to behave more reasonably. And this gives me the oppor-tunity, Mr. Conway, of assuring you that the hospitality of Shangri-La is of a comprehensive kind. Your friend Mr. Barnard has already availed himself of it."

Conway returned the smile. "Thanks," he answered dryly. "I've no doubt he has, but my own inclinations are not—at the moment —so assertive. It was the emotional more than the physical aspect that I was curious about."

"You find it easy to separate the two? Is it possible that you are falling in love with Lo-Tsen?"

Conway was somewhat taken aback, though he hoped he did not show it. "What makes you ask that?"

"Because, my dear sir, it would be quite suitable if you were to do so—always, of course, in moderation. Lo-Tsen would not respond with any degree of passion—that is more than you could expect—but the experience would be very delightful, I assure you. And I speak with some authority, for I was in love with her myself when I was much younger."

"Were you indeed? And did she respond then?"

"Only by the most charming appreciation of the compliment I paid her, and by a friendship which has grown more precious with the years."

"In other words, she didn't respond?"

"If you prefer it so." Chang added, a little sententiously: "It has always been her way to spare her lovers the moment of satiety that goes with all absolute attainment."

Conway laughed. "That's all very well in your case, and perhaps in mine too—but what about the attitude of a hot-blooded young fellow like Mallinson?"

"My dear sir, it would be the best possible thing that could happen! Not for the first time, I assure you, would Lo-Tsen comfort the sorrowful exile when he learns that there is to be no return."

"*Comfort?*"

"Yes, though you must not misunderstand my use of the term. Lo-Tsen gives no caresses, except such as touch the stricken heart from her very presence. What does your Shakespeare say of Cleopatra?—'She makes hungry where she most satisfies.' A popular type, doubtless, among the passion-driven races, but such a woman, I assure you, would be altogether out of place at Shangri-La. Lo-Tsen, if I might amend the quotation, *removes* hunger where she *least* satisfies. It is a more delicate and lasting accomplishment."

"And one, I assume, which she has much skill in performing?"

"Oh, decidedly—we have had many examples of it. It is her way to calm the throb of desire to a murmur that is no less pleasant when left unanswered."

"In that sense, then, you could regard her as a part of the training equipment of the establishment?"

"*You* could regard her as that, if you wished," replied Chang with deprecating blandness. "But it would be more graceful, and just as true, to liken her to the rainbow reflected in a glass bowl or to the dewdrops on the blossom of the fruit tree."

"I entirely agree with you, Chang. That would be *much* more graceful." Conway enjoyed the measured yet agile repartees which his good-humored ragging of the Chinese very often elicited.

But the next time he was alone with the little Manchu he felt that Chang's remarks had had a great deal of shrewdness in them. There was a fragrance about her that communicated itself to his own emotions, kindling the embers to a glow that did not burn, but merely warmed. And suddenly then he realized that Shangri-La and Lo-Tsen were quite perfect, and that he did not wish for more than to stir a faint and eventual response in all that stillness. For years his passions had been like a nerve that the world jarred on; now at last the aching was soothed, and he could yield himself to love that was neither a torment nor a bore. As he passed by the lotus-pool at night he sometimes pictured her in his arms, but the sense of time washed over the vision, calming him to an infinite and tender reluctance.

He did not think he had ever been so happy, even in the years of his life before the great barrier of the War. He liked the serene world that Shangri-La offered him, pacified rather than dominated by its single tremendous idea. He liked the prevalent mood in which feelings were sheathed in thoughts, and thoughts softened into felicity by their transference into language. Conway, whom experience had taught that rudeness is by no means a guarantee of good faith, was even less inclined to regard a well-turned phrase as a proof of insincerity. He liked the mannered, leisurely atmosphere in which talk was an accomplishment, not a mere habit. And he liked to realize that the idlest things could now be freed from the curse of time-wasting, and the frailest dreams receive the welcome of the mind. Shangri-La was always tranquil, yet always a hive of unpursuing occupations; the lamas lived as if indeed they had time on their hands, but time that was scarcely a feather-weight. Conway met no more of them, but he came gradually to realize the extent and variety of their employments; besides their knowledge of languages, some, it appeared, took to the full seas of learning in a manner that would have yielded big surprises to the Western world. Many were engaged in writing manuscript books of various kinds; one (Chang said) had made valuable researches into pure mathematics; another was co-ordinating Gibbon and Spengler into a vast thesis on the history of European civilization. But this kind of thing was not for them all, nor for any of them always; there were many tideless channels in which they dived in mere waywardness, retrieving, like Briac, fragments of old tunes, or like the English ex-curate, a new theory

about *Wuthering Heights*. And there were even fainter impractical-
ities than these. Once, when Conway made some remark in this connection, the High Lama replied with a story of a Chinese artist in
the third century B.C. who, having spent many years in carving dragons, birds, and horses upon a cherry-stone, offered his finished work
to a royal prince. The prince could see nothing in it at first except
a mere stone, but the artist bade him "have a wall built, and make a
window in it, and observe the stone through the window in the glory
of the dawn." The prince did so, and then perceived that the stone
was indeed very beautiful. "Is not that a charming story, my dear
Conway, and do you not think it teaches a very valuable lesson?"

Conway agreed; he found it pleasant to realize that the serene
purpose of Shangri-La could embrace an infinitude of odd and apparently trivial employments, for he had always had a taste for such
things himself. In fact, when he regarded his past, he saw it strewn
with images of tasks too vagrant or too taxing ever to have been
accomplished; but now they were all possible, even in a mood of
idleness. It was delightful to contemplate, and he was not disposed
to sneer when Barnard confided in him that he too envisaged an
interesting future at Shangri-La.

It seemed that Barnard's excursions to the valley, which had been
growing more frequent of late, were not entirely devoted to drink
and women. "You see, Conway, I'm telling you this because you're
different from Mallinson—he's got his knife into me, as probably
you've gathered. But I feel you'll be better at understanding the
position. It's a funny thing—you British officials are so darned stiff
and starchy at first, but you're the sort a fellow can put his trust in,
when all's said and done."

"I wouldn't be too sure," replied Conway, smiling. "And anyhow,
Mallinson's just as much a British official as I am."

"Yes, but he's a mere boy. He don't look at things reasonably. You
and me are men of the world—we take things as we find them. This
joint here, for instance—we still can't understand all the ins and outs
of it, and why we've been landed here, but then, isn't that the usual
way of things? Do we know why we're in the world at all, for that
matter?"

"Perhaps some of us don't, but what's all this leading up to?"

Barnard dropped his voice to a rather husky whisper. "Gold, my
lad," he answered with a certain ecstasy. "Just that, and nothing
less. There's tons of it—literally—in the valley. I was a mining engineer in my young days and I haven't forgotten what a reef looks
like. Believe me, it's as rich as the Rand, and ten times easier to get

at. I guess you thought I was on the loose whenever I went down
there in my little armchair. Not a bit of it. I knew what I was doing.
I'd figgered it out all along, you know, that these guys here couldn't
get all their stuff sent in from outside without paying mighty high
for it, and what else could they pay with except gold or silver or
diamonds or something? Only logic, after all. And when I began to
scout round, it didn't take me long to discover the whole bag of
tricks."

"You found it out on your own?" asked Conway.

"Well, I won't say that, but I made my guess, and then I put the
matter to Chang—straight, mind you, as man to man. And believe
me, Conway, that Chink's not as bad a fellow as we might have
thought."

"Personally, I never thought him a bad fellow at all."

"Of course, I know you always took to him, so you won't be surprised at the way we got on together. We certainly did hit it fa-
mously. He showed me all over the workings, and it may interest you
to know that I've got the full permission of the authorities to prospect
in the valley as much as I like and make a comprehensive report.
What d'you think of that, my lad? They seemed quite glad to have
the services of an expert, especially when I said I could probably
give 'em tips how to increase output."

"I can see you're going to be altogether at home here," said Conway.

"Well, I must say I've found a job, and that's something. And you
never know how a thing'll turn out in the end. Maybe the folks at
home won't be so keen to jail me when they know I can show 'em
the way to a new gold mine. The only difficulty is—would they take
my word about it?"

"They might. It's extraordinary what people *will* believe."

Barnard nodded with enthusiasm. "Glad you get the point, Conway. And that's where you and I can make a deal. We'll go fifty-
fifty in everything, of course. All you've gotter do is to put your name
to my report—British Consul, you know, and all that. It'll carry
weight."

Conway laughed. "We'll have to see about it. Make your report
first."

It amused him to contemplate a possibility so unlikely to happen,
and at the same time he was glad that Barnard had found something
that yielded such immediate comfort.

So also was the High Lama, whom Conway began to see more

and more frequently. He often visited him in the late evening and
stayed for many hours, long after the servants had taken away the
last bowls of tea and had been dismissed for the night. The High
Lama never failed to ask him about the progress and welfare of his
three companions, and once he enquired particularly as to the kind
of careers that their arrival at Shangri-La had so inevitably interrupted.

Conway answered reflectively: "Mallinson might have done quite
well in his own line—he's energetic and has ambitions. The two others—" He shrugged his shoulders. "As a matter of fact, it happens
to suit them both to stay here—for a while, at any rate."

He noticed a flicker of light at the curtained window; there had
been mutterings of thunder as he crossed the courtyards on his way
to the now familiar room. No sound could be heard, and the heavy
tapestries subdued the lightning into mere sparks of pallor.

"Yes," came the reply, "we have done our best to make both of
them feel at home. Miss Brinklow wishes to convert us, and Mr.
Barnard would also like to convert us—into a limited liability company. Harmless projects—they will pass the time quite pleasantly
for them. But your young friend, to whom neither gold nor religion
can offer solace, how about *him?*"

"Yes, he's going to be the problem."

"I am afraid he is going to be *your* problem."

"Why mine?"

There was no immediate answer, for the tea-bowls were introduced at that moment, and with their appearance the High Lama
rallied a faint and desiccated hospitality. "Karakal sends us storms
at this time of the year," he remarked, feathering the conversation
according to ritual. "The people of Blue Moon believe they are
caused by demons raging in the great space beyond the pass. The
'outside,' they call it—perhaps you are aware that in their patois the
word is used for the entire rest of the world. Of course they know
nothing of such countries as France or England or even India—they
imagine the dread altiplano stretching, as it almost does, illimitably.
To them, so snug at their warm and windless levels, it appears unthinkable that any one inside the valley should ever wish to leave it;
indeed, they picture all unfortunate 'outsiders' as passionately desir-
ing to enter. It is just a question of viewpoint, is it not?"

Conway was reminded of Barnard's somewhat similar remarks,
and quoted them. "How very sensible!" was the High Lama's comment. "And he is our first American, too—we are truly fortunate."

Conway found it piquant to reflect that the lamasery's fortune

was to have acquired a man for whom the police of a dozen countries
were actively searching; and he would have liked to share the
piquancy but for feeling that Barnard had better be left to tell his
own story in due course. He said: "Doubtless he's quite right, and
there are many people in the world nowadays who would be glad
enough to be here."

"*Too* many, my dear Conway. We are a single lifeboat riding the
seas in a gale; we can take a few chance survivors, but if all the
shipwrecked were to reach us and clamber aboard we should go
down ourselves. . . . But let us not think of it just now. I hear that
you have been associating with our excellent Briac. A delightful
fellow countryman of mine, though I do not share his opinion that
Chopin is the greatest of all composers. For myself, as you know,
I prefer Mozart. . . ."

Not till the tea-bowls were removed and the servant had been
finally dismissed, did Conway venture to recall the unanswered
question. "We were discussing Mallinson, and you said he was going
to be *my* problem. Why mine, particularly?"

Then the High Lama replied very simply: "Because, my son, I
am going to die."

It seemed an extraordinary statement, and for a time Conway was
speechless after it. Eventually the High Lama continued: "You are
surprised? But surely, my friend, we are all mortal—even at Shangri-
La. And it is possible that I may still have a few moments left to me
—or even, for that matter, a few years. All I announce is the simple
truth that already I see the end. It is charming of you to appear
so concerned, and I will not pretend that there is not a touch of
wistfulness, even at my age, in contemplating death. Fortunately
little is left of me that can die physically, and as for the rest, all
our religions display a pleasant unanimity of optimism. I am quite
content, but I must accustom myself to a strange sensation during
the hours that remain—I must realize that I have time for only one
thing more. Can you imagine what that is?"

Conway was silent.

"It concerns you, my son."

"You do me a great honor."

"I have in mind to do much more than that."

Conway bowed slightly, but did not speak, and the High Lama,
after waiting awhile, resumed: "You know, perhaps, that the fre-
quency of these talks has been unusual here. But it is our tradition,
if I may permit myself the paradox, that we are never slaves to
tradition. We have no rigidities, no inexorable rules. We do as

we think fit, guided a little by the example of the past, but still more by our present wisdom, and by our clairvoyance of the future. And thus it is that I am encouraged to do this final thing."

Conway was still silent.

"I place in your hands, my son, the heritage and destiny of Shangri-La."

At last the tension broke, and Conway felt beyond it the power of a bland and benign persuasion; the echoes swam into silence, till all that was left was his own heartbeat, pounding like a gong. And then, intercepting the rhythm, came the words:

"I have waited for you, my son, for quite a long time. I have sat in this room and seen the faces of new-comers, I have looked into their eyes and heard their voices, and always in hope that some day I might find you. My colleagues have grown old and wise, but you who are still young in years are as wise already. My friend, it is not an arduous task that I bequeath, for our order knows only silken bonds. To be gentle and patient, to care for the riches of the mind, to preside in wisdom and secrecy while the storm rages without—it will all be very pleasantly simple for you, and you will doubtless find great happiness."

Again Conway sought to reply, but could not, till at length a vivid lightning-flash paled the shadows and stirred him to exclaim: "The storm . . . this storm you talk of. . . ."

"It will be such a one, my son, as the world has not seen before. There will be no safety by arms, no help from authority, no answer in science. It will rage till every flower of culture is trampled, and all human things are leveled in a vast chaos. Such was my vision when Napoleon was still a name unknown; and I see it now, more clearly with each hour. Do you say I am mistaken?"

Conway answered: "No, I think you may be right. A similar crash came once before, and then there were the Dark Ages lasting five hundred years."

"The parallel is not quite exact. For those Dark Ages were not really so very dark—they were full of flickering lanterns, and even if the light had gone out of Europe altogether, there were other rays, literally from China to Peru, at which it could have been rekindled. But the Dark Ages that are to come will cover the whole world in a single pall; there will be neither escape nor sanctuary, save such as are too secret to be found or too humble to be noticed. And Shangri-La may hope to be both of these. The airman bearing loads of death to the great cities will not pass our way, and if by chance he should, he may not consider us worth a bomb."

"And you think all this will come in my time?"

"I believe that you will live through the storm. And after, through the long age of desolation, you may still live, growing older and wiser and more patient. You will conserve the fragrance of our history and add to it the touch of your own mind. You will welcome the stranger, and teach him the rule of age and wisdom; and one of these strangers, it may be, will succeed you when you are yourself very old. Beyond that, my vision weakens, but I see, at a great distance, a new world stirring in the ruins, stirring clumsily but in hopefulness, seeking its lost and legendary treasures. And they will all be here, my son, hidden behind the mountains in the valley of Blue Moon, preserved as by miracle for a new Renaissance. . . ."

The speaking finished, and Conway saw the face before him full of a remote and drenching beauty; then the glow faded and there was nothing left but a mask, dark-shadowed, and crumbling like old wood. It was quite motionless, and the eyes were closed. He watched for a while, and presently, as part of a dream, it came to him that the High Lama was dead.

It seemed necessary to rivet the situation to some kind of actuality, lest it become too strange to be believed in; and with instinctive mechanism of hand and eye, Conway glanced at his wrist-watch. It was a quarter past midnight. Suddenly, when he crossed the room to the door, it occurred to him that he did not in the least know how or whence to summon help. The Tibetans, he knew, had all been sent away for the night, and he had no idea where to find Chang or any one else. He stood uncertainly on the threshold of the dark corridor; through a window he could see that the sky was clear, though the mountains still blazed in lightning like a silver fresco. And then, in the midst of the still encompassing dream, he felt himself master of Shangri-La. These were his beloved things, all around him, the things of that inner mind in which he lived increasingly, away from the fret of the world. His eyes strayed into the shadows and were caught by golden pin-points sparkling in rich, undulating lacquers; and the scent of tuberose, so faint that it expired on the very brink of sensation, lured him from room to room. At last he stumbled into the courtyards and by the fringe of the pool; a full moon sailed behind Karakal. It was twenty minutes to two.

Later, he was aware that Mallinson was near him, holding his arm and leading him away in a great hurry. He did not gather what it was all about, but he could hear that the boy was chattering excitedly.

CHAPTER ELEVEN

They reached the balconied room where they had meals, Mallinson still clutching his arm and half dragging him along. "Come on, Conway, we've till dawn to pack what we can and get away. Great news, man—I wonder what old Barnard and Miss Brinklow will think in the morning when they find us gone . . . still, it's their own choice to stay, and we'll probably get on far better without them. . . . The porters are about five miles beyond the pass—they came yesterday with loads of books and things . . . to-morrow they begin the journey back. . . . It just shows how these fellows here intended to let us down—they never told us—we should have been stranded here for God knows how much longer. . . . I say, what's the matter? Are you ill?"

Conway had sunk into a chair, and was leaning forward with elbows on the table. He passed his hand across his eyes. "Ill? No, I don't think so. Just—rather—tired."

"Probably the storm. Where were you all the while? I'd been waiting for you for hours."

"I—I was visiting the High Lama."

"Oh, *him!* Well, *that's* for the last time, anyhow, thank God."

"Yes, Mallinson, for the last time."

Something in Conway's voice, and still more in his succeeding silence, roused the youth to irascibility. "Well, I wish you wouldn't sound so deuced leisurely about it—we've got to get a considerable move on, you know."

Conway stiffened for the effort of emerging into keener consciousness. "I'm sorry," he said. Partly to test his nerve and the reality of his sensations he lit a cigarette. He found that both hands and lips were unsteady. "I'm afraid I don't quite follow . . . you say the porters . . ."

"Yes, the porters, man—do pull yourself together."

"You're thinking of going out to them?"

"*Thinking* of it? I'm damn well certain—they're only just over the ridge. And we've got to start immediately."

"*Immediately?*"

"Yes, yes—why not?"

Conway made a second attempt to transfer himself from the one world into the other. He said at length, having partly succeeded: "I suppose you realize that it mayn't be quite as simple as it sounds?"

Mallinson was lacing a pair of knee-high Tibetan mountain-boots as he answered jerkily: "I realize everything, but it's something we've got to do, and we shall do it, with luck, if we don't delay."

"I don't see how—"

"Oh, Lord, Conway, must you fight shy of everything? Haven't you any guts left in you at all?"

The appeal, half passionate and half derisive, helped Conway to collect himself. "Whether I have or haven't isn't the point, but if you want me to explain myself, I will. It's a question of a few rather important details. Suppose you *do* get beyond the pass and find the porters there, how do you know they'll take you with them? What inducement can you offer? Hasn't it struck you that they mayn't be quite so willing as you'd like them to be? You can't just present yourself and demand to be escorted. It all needs arrangement, negotiations beforehand—"

"Or anything else to cause a delay," exclaimed Mallinson bitterly. "God, what a fellow you are! Fortunately I haven't you to rely on for arranging things. Because they *have* been arranged—the porters have been paid in advance, and they've agreed to take us. And here are clothes and equipment for the journey, all ready. So your last excuse disappears. Come on, let's *do* something."

"But—I don't understand. . . ."

"I don't suppose you do, but it doesn't matter."

"Who's been making all these plans?"

Mallinson answered brusquely: "Lo-Tsen, if you're really keen to know. She's with the porters now. She's waiting."

"*Waiting?*"

"Yes. She's coming with us. I assume you've no objection?"

At the mention of Lo-Tsen the two worlds touched and fused suddenly in Conway's mind. He cried sharply, almost contemptuously: "That's nonsense. It's impossible."

Mallinson was equally on edge. "Why is it impossible?"

"Because . . . well, it is. There are all sorts of reasons. Take my word for it; it won't do. It's incredible enough that she should be out there now—I'm astonished at what you say has happened—but the idea of her going any further is just preposterous."

"I don't see that it's preposterous at all. It's as natural for her to want to leave here as for me."

"But she doesn't want to leave. That's where you make the mistake."

Mallinson smiled tensely. "You think you know a good deal more about her than I do, I dare say," he remarked. "But perhaps you don't, for all that."

"What do you mean?"

"There are other ways of getting to understand people without learning heaps of languages."

"For Heaven's sake, what *are* you driving at?" Then Conway added more quietly: "This is absurd. We mustn't wrangle. Tell me, Mallinson, what's it all about? I still don't understand."

"Then why are you making such an almighty fuss?"

"Tell me the truth, *please* tell me the truth."

"Well, it's simple enough. A kid of her age, shut up here with a lot of queer old men—naturally she'll get away if she's given a chance. She hasn't had one up to now."

"Don't you think you may be imagining her position in the light of your own? As I've always told you, she's perfectly happy."

"Then why did she say she'd come?"

"She said that? How could she? She doesn't speak English."

"I asked her—in Tibetan—Miss Brinklow worked out the words. It wasn't a very fluent conversation, but it was quite enough to—to lead to an understanding." Mallinson flushed a little. "Damn it, Conway, don't stare at me like that—any one would think I'd been poaching on *your* preserves."

Conway answered: "No one would think so at all, I hope, but the remark tells me more than you were perhaps intending me to know. I can only say that I'm very sorry."

"And why the devil should you be?"

Conway let the cigarette fall from his fingers. He felt tired, bothered, and full of deep conflicting tendernesses that he would rather not have had aroused. He said gently: "I wish we weren't always at such cross-purposes. Lo-Tsen is very charming, I know, but why should we quarrel about it?"

"*Charming?*" Mallinson echoed the word with scorn. "She's a good bit more than that. You mustn't think everybody's as cold-blooded about these things as you are yourself. Admiring her as if she were an exhibit in a museum may be your idea of what she deserves, but mine's more practical, and when I see some one I like in a rotten position I try and *do* something."

"But surely there's such a thing as being too impetuous? Where do you think she'll go to if she does leave?"

"I suppose she must have friends in China or somewhere. Anyhow, she'll be better off than here."

"How can you possibly be so sure of that?"

"Well, I'll see that she's looked after myself, if nobody else will. After all, if you're rescuing people from something quite hellish, you don't usually stop to enquire if they've anywhere else to go to."

"And you think Shangri-La is hellish?"

"Definitely, I do. There's something dark and evil about it. The whole business has been like that, from the beginning—the way we were brought here, without reason at all, by some madman—and the way we've been detained since, on one excuse or another. But the most frightful thing of all—to me—is the effect it's had on you."

"On *me?*"

"Yes, on you. You've just mooned about as if nothing mattered and you were content to stay here for ever. Why, you even admitted you liked the place. . . . Conway, what *has* happened to you? Can't you manage to be your real self again? We got on so well together at Baskul—you were absolutely different in those days."

"My *dear* boy!"

Conway reached his hand towards Mallinson's, and the answering grip was hot and eagerly affectionate. Mallinson went on: "I don't suppose you realize it, but I've been terribly alone these last few weeks. Nobody seemed to be caring a damn about the only thing that was really important—Barnard and Miss Brinklow had reasons of a kind, but it was pretty awful when I found *you* against me."

"I'm sorry."

"You keep on saying that, but it doesn't help."

Conway replied on sudden impulse: "Then let me help, if I can, by telling you something. When you've heard it, you'll understand, I hope, a great deal of what now seems very curious and difficult. At any rate, you'll realize why Lo-Tsen can't possibly go back with you."

"I don't think anything would make me see that. And do cut it as short as you can, because we really haven't time to spare."

Conway then gave, as briefly as he could, the whole story of Shangri-La, as told him by the High Lama, and as amplified by conversation both with the latter and with Chang. It was the last thing he had ever intended to do, but he felt that in the circumstances it was justified and even necessary; it was true enough that Mallinson *was* his problem, to solve as he thought fit. He narrated rapidly and easily, and in doing so came again under the spell of that strange, timeless world; its beauty overwhelmed him as he spoke of it, and more than once he felt himself reading from a page of memory, so clearly had ideas and phrases impressed themselves. Only one thing he withheld—and that to spare himself an emotion he could not yet grapple with—the fact of the High Lama's death that night and of his own succession.

When he approached the end he felt comforted; he was glad to have got it over, and it was the only solution, after all. He looked up calmly when he had finished, confident that he had done well.

But Mallinson merely tapped his fingers on the table-top and said, after a long wait: "I really don't know what to say, Conway . . . except that you must be completely mad. . . ."

There followed a long silence, during which the two men stared at each other in far differing moods—Conway withdrawn and disappointed, Mallinson in hot, fidgeting discomfort. "So you think I'm mad?" said Conway at length.

Mallinson broke into a nervous laugh. "Well, I should damn well say so, after a tale like that. I mean . . . well, really . . . such utter nonsense . . . it seems to me rather beyond arguing about."

Conway looked and sounded immensely astonished. "You think it's nonsense?"

"Well . . . how else can I look at it? I'm sorry, Conway—it's a pretty strong statement—but I don't see how any sane person could be in any doubt about it."

"So you still hold that we were brought here by blind accident— by some lunatic who made careful plans to run off with an aeroplane and fly it a thousand miles just for the fun of the thing?"

Conway offered a cigarette, and the other took it. The pause was one for which they both seemed grateful. Mallinson answered eventually: "Look here, it's no good arguing the thing point by point. As a matter of fact, your theory that the people here sent some one vaguely into the world to decoy strangers, and that this fellow deliberately learned flying and bided his time until it happened that a suitable machine was due to leave Baskul with four passengers . . . well, I won't say that it's literally impossible, though it does seem to me ridiculously far-fetched. If it stood by itself, it might just be worth considering, but when you tack it on to all sorts of other things that are *absolutely* impossible—all this about the lamas being hundreds of years old, and having discovered a sort of elixir of youth, or whatever you'd call it . . . well, it just makes me wonder what kind of microbe has bitten you, that's all."

Conway smiled. "Yes, I dare say you find it hard to believe. Perhaps I did myself at first—I scarcely remember. Of course it *is* an extraordinary story, but I should think your own eyes have had enough evidence that this is an extraordinary place. Think of all that we've actually seen, both of us—a lost valley in the midst of unexplored mountains, a monastery with a library of European books—"

"Oh, yes, and a central heating plant, and modern plumbing, and afternoon tea, and everything else—it's all very marvelous, I know."

"Well, then, what do you make of it?"

"Damn little, I admit. It's a complete mystery. But that's no reason for accepting tales that are physically impossible. Believing in hot baths because you've had them is different from believing in people hundreds of years old just because they've told you they are." He laughed again, still uneasily. "Look here, Conway, it's got on your nerves, this place, and I really don't wonder at it. Pack up your things and let's quit. We'll finish this argument a month or two hence after a jolly little dinner at Maiden's."

Conway answered quietly: "I've no desire to go back to that life at all."

"What life?"

"The life you're thinking of . . . dinners . . . dances . . . polo . . . all that. . . ."

"But I never said anything about dances and polo! Anyhow, what's wrong with them? D'you mean that you're not coming with me? You're going to stay here like the other two? Then at least you shan't stop *me* from clearing out of it!" Mallinson threw down his cigarette and sprang towards the door with eyes blazing. "You're off your head!" he cried wildly. "You're mad, Conway, that's what's the matter with you! I know you're always calm, and I'm always excited, but I'm sane, at any rate, and you're not! They warned me about it before I joined you at Baskul, and I thought they were wrong, but now I can see they weren't—"

"What did they warn you of?"

"They said you'd been blown up in the War, and you'd been queer at times ever since. I'm not reproaching you—I know it was nothing you could help—and Heaven knows I hate talking like this. . . . Oh, I'll go. It's all frightful and sickening, but I must go. I gave my word."

"To Lo-Tsen?"

"Yes, if you want to know."

Conway got up and held out his hand. "Good-by, Mallinson."

"For the last time, you're not coming?"

"I can't."

"Good-by, then."

They shook hands, and Mallinson left.

Conway sat alone in the lantern-light. It seemed to him, in a phrase engraved on memory, that all the loveliest things were transient and perishable, that the two worlds were finally beyond reconciliation, and that one of them hung, as always, by a thread. After he had pondered for some time he looked at his watch; it was ten minutes to three.

He was still at the table, smoking the last of his cigarettes, when Mallinson returned. The youth entered with some commotion, and on seeing him, stood back in the shadows as if to gather his wits. He was silent, and Conway began, after waiting a moment: "Hullo, what's happened? Why are you back?"

The complete naturalness of the question fetched Mallinson forward; he pulled off his heavy sheepskins and sat down. His face was ashen and his whole body trembled. "I hadn't the nerve," he cried, half sobbing. "That place where we were all roped—you remember? I got as far as that. . . . I couldn't manage it. I've no head for heights, and in moonlight it looked fearful. Silly, isn't it?" He broke down completely and was hysterical until Conway pacified him. Then he added: "They needn't worry, these fellows here—nobody will ever threaten them by land. But, my God, I'd give a good deal to fly over with a load of bombs!"

"Why would you like to do that, Mallinson?"

"Because the place wants smashing up, whatever it is. It's unhealthy and unclean—and for that matter, if your impossible yarn were true, it would be more hateful still! A lot of wizened old men crouching here like spiders for any one who comes near . . . it's filthy . . . who'd want to live to an age like that, anyhow? And as for your precious High Lama, if he's half as old as you say he is, it's time some one put him out of his misery. . . . Oh, why *won't* you come away with me, Conway? I hate imploring you for my own sake, but damn it all, I'm young and we've been pretty good friends together—does my whole life mean nothing to you compared with the lies of these awful creatures? And Lo-Tsen, too—*she's* young—doesn't *she* count at all?"

"Lo-Tsen is not young," said Conway.

Mallinson looked up and began to titter hysterically. "Oh, no, not young—not young at all, of course. She looks about seventeen, but I suppose you'll tell me she's really a well-preserved ninety."

"Mallinson, she came here in 1884."

"You're raving, man!"

"Her beauty, Mallinson, like all other beauty in the world, lies at the mercy of those who do not know how to value it. It is a fragile thing that can only live where fragile things are loved. Take it away from this valley and you will see it fade like an echo."

Mallinson laughed harshly, as if his own thoughts gave him confidence. "I'm not afraid of that. It's here that she's only an echo, if she's one anywhere at all." He added after a pause: "Not that this sort of talk gets us anywhere. We'd better cut out all the poetic stuff and come down to realities. Conway, I want to help you—it's all the sheerest nonsense, I know, but I'll argue it out if it'll do you any good. I'll pretend it's something possible that you've told me, and that it really does need examining. Now tell me, seriously, what evidence have you for this story of yours?"

Conway was silent.

"Merely that some one spun you a fantastic rigmarole. Even from a thoroughly reliable person whom you'd known all your life, you wouldn't accept that sort of thing without proof. And what proofs have you in this case? None at all, so far as I can see. Has Lo-Tsen ever told you her history?"

"No, but—"

"Then why believe it from some one else? And all this longevity business—can you point to a single outside fact in support of it?"

Conway thought a moment and then mentioned the unknown Chopin works that Briac had played.

"Well, that's a matter that means nothing to me—I'm not a musician. But even if they're genuine, isn't it possible that he could have got hold of them in some way without his story being true?"

"Quite possible, no doubt."

"And then this method that you say exists—of preserving youth and so on. What is it? You say it's a sort of drug—well, I want to know *what* drug? Have you ever seen it or tried it? Did any one ever give you any positive facts about the thing at all?"

"Not in detail, I admit."

"And you never asked for details? It didn't strike you that such a story needed any confirmation at all? You just swallowed it whole?" Pressing his advantage, he continued: "How much do you actually know of this place, apart from what you've been told? You've seen a few old men—that's all it amounts to. Apart from that, we can only say that the place is well fitted up, and seems to be run on rather highbrow lines. How and why it came into existence we've no idea, and why they want to keep us here, if they do, is equally a mystery, but surely all that's hardly an excuse for believing any old legend that comes along! After all, man, you're a critical sort of person—you'd hesitate to believe all you were told even in an English monastery—I really can't see why you should jump at everything just because you're in Tibet!"

Conway nodded. Even in the midst of far keener perceptions he could not restrain approval of a point well made. "That's an acute remark, Mallinson. I suppose the truth is that when it comes to believing things without actual evidence, we all incline to what we find most attractive."

"Well, I'm dashed if I can see anything attractive about living till you're half dead. Give me a short life and a gay one, for choice. And this stuff about a future war—it all sounds pretty thin to me. How does any one know when the next war's going to be or what it'll be like? Weren't all the prophets wrong about the last war?" He added, when Conway did not reply: "Anyhow, I don't believe in saying things are inevitable. And even if they were, there's no need to get into a funk about them. Heaven knows I'd most likely be scared stiff if I had to fight in a war, but I'd rather face up to it than bury myself here."

Conway smiled. "Mallinson, you have a superb knack of misunderstanding me. When we were at Baskul you thought I was a hero —now you take me for a coward. In point of fact, I'm neither—though of course it doesn't matter. When you get back to India you can tell people, if you like, that I decided to stay in a Tibetan monastery because I was afraid there'd be another war. It isn't my reason at all, but I've no doubt it'll be believed by the people who already think me mad."

Mallinson answered rather sadly: "It's silly, you know, to talk like that. Whatever happens, I'd never say a word against you. You can count on that. I don't understand you—I admit that—but—but—I wish I did. Oh, I wish I did. Conway, can't I possibly help you? Isn't there anything I can say or do?"

There was a long silence after that, which Conway broke at last by saying: "There's just a question I'd like to ask—if you'll forgive me for being terribly personal."

"Yes?"

"Are you in love with Lo-Tsen?"

The youth's pallor changed quickly to a flush. "I dare say I am. I know you'll say it's absurd and unthinkable, and probably it is, but I can't help my feelings."

"I don't think it's absurd at all."

The argument seemed to have sailed into a harbor after many buffetings, and Conway added: "I can't help *my* feelings either. You and that girl happen to be the two people in the world I care most about . . . though you may think it odd of me." Abruptly he got up and paced the room. "We've said all we *can* say, haven't we?"

"Yes, I suppose we have." But Mallinson went on, in a sudden rush of eagerness: "Oh, what stupid nonsense it all is—about her not being young! And foul and horrible nonsense, too. Conway, you *can't* believe it! It's just too ridiculous. How can it really mean anything?"

"How can you really know that she's young?"

Mallinson half turned away, his face lit with a grave shyness. "Because I *do* know. . . . Perhaps you'll think less of me for it . . . but I *do* know. I'm afraid you never properly understood her, Conway. She was cold on the surface, but that was the result of living here—it had frozen all the warmth. But the warmth was there."

"To be unfrozen?"

"Yes . . . that would be one way of putting it."

"And she's *young*, Mallinson—you are so *sure* of that?"

Mallinson answered softly: "God, yes—she's just a girl. I was terribly sorry for her, and we were both attracted, I suppose. I don't see that it's anything to be ashamed of. In fact in a place like this I should think it's about the decentest thing that's ever happened. . . ."

Conway went to the balcony and gazed at the dazzling plume of Karakal; the moon was riding high in a waveless ocean. It came to him that a dream had dissolved, like all too lovely things, at the first touch of reality; that the whole world's future, weighed in the balance against youth and love, would be light as air. And he knew, too, that his mind dwelt in a world of its own, Shangri-La in microcosm, and that this world also was in peril. For even as he nerved himself, he saw the corridors of his imagination twist and strain under impact; the pavilions were toppling; all was about to be in ruins. He was only partly unhappy, but he was infinitely and rather sadly perplexed. He did not know whether he had been mad and was now sane, or had been sane for a time and was now mad again.

When he turned, there was a difference in him; his voice was keener, almost brusque, and his face twitched a little; he looked much more the Conway who had been a hero at Baskul. Clenched for action, he faced Mallinson with a suddenly new alertness. "Do you think you could manage that tricky bit with a rope if I were with you?" he asked.

Mallinson sprang forward. "*Conway!*" he cried chokingly. "You mean you'll *come?* You've made up your mind at last?"

They left as soon as Conway had prepared himself for the journey. It was surprisingly simple to leave—a departure rather than an escape; there were no incidents as they crossed the bars of moonlight and shadow in the courtyards. One might have thought there was no one there at all, Conway reflected; and immediately the idea of such emptiness became an emptiness in himself; while all the time, though he hardly heard him, Mallinson was chattering about the journey. How strange that their long argument should have ended thus in action, that this secret sanctuary should be forsaken by one who had found in it such happiness! For indeed, less than an hour later, they halted breathlessly at a curve of the track and saw the last of Shangri-La. Deep below them the valley of Blue Moon was like a cloud, and to Conway the scattered roofs had a look of floating after him through the haze. Now, at that moment, it was farewell. Mallinson, whom the steep ascent had kept silent for a time, gasped out: "Good man, we're doing fine—carry on!"

Conway smiled, but did not reply; he was already preparing the rope for the knife-edge traverse. It was true, as the youth had said, that he had made up his mind; but it was only what was left of his mind. That small and active fragment now dominated; the rest comprised an absence hardly to be endured. He was a wanderer between two worlds and must ever wander; but for the present, in a deepening inward void, all he felt was that he liked Mallinson and must help him; he was doomed, like millions, to flee from wisdom and be a hero.

Mallinson was nervous at the precipice, but Conway got him over in traditional mountaineering fashion, and when the trial was past, they leaned together over Mallinson's cigarettes. "Conway, I must say it's damned good of you. . . . Perhaps you guess how I feel. . . . I can't tell you how glad I am. . . ."

"I wouldn't try, then, if I were you."

After a long pause, and before they resumed the journey, Mallinson added: "But I *am* glad—not only for my own sake, but for yours as well. . . . It's fine that you can realize now that all that stuff was sheer nonsense . . . it's just wonderful to see you your real self again. . . ."

"Not at all," responded Conway with a wryness that was for his own private comforting.

Towards dawn they crossed the divide, unchallenged by sentinels, even if there were any; though it occurred to Conway that the route, in the true spirit, might only be moderately well watched. Presently they reached the plateau, picked clean as a bone by roaring winds, and after a gradual descent the encampment of porters came in sight. Then all was as Mallinson had foretold; they found the men ready for them, sturdy fellows in furs and sheepskins, crouching under the gale and eager to begin the journey to Tatsien-Fu—eleven hundred miles eastward on the China border.

"He's coming with us!" Mallinson cried excitedly when they met Lo-Tsen. He forgot that she knew no English; but Conway translated.

It seemed to him that the little Manchu had never looked so radiant. She gave him a most charming smile, but her eyes were all for the boy.

EPILOGUE

It was in Delhi that I met Rutherford again. We had been guests at a Viceregal dinner-party, but distance and ceremonial kept us apart until the turbanned flunkeys handed us our hats afterwards. "Come back to my hotel and have a drink," he invited.

We shared a cab along the arid miles between the Lutyens still-life and the warm, palpitating motion picture of Old Delhi. I knew from the newspapers that he had just returned from Kashgar. His was one of those well-groomed reputations that get the most out of everything; any unusual holiday acquires the character of an exploration, and though the explorer takes care to do nothing really original, the public does not know this, and he capitalizes the full value of a hasty impression. It had not seemed to me, for instance, that Rutherford's journey, as reported in the press, had been particularly epoch-making; the buried cities of Khotan were old stuff, if any one remembered Stein and Sven Hedin. I knew Rutherford well enough to chaff him about this, and he laughed. "Yes, the truth would have made a better story," he admitted cryptically.

We went to his hotel room and drank whisky. "So you *did* search for Conway?" I suggested when the moment seemed propitious.

"Search is much too strong a word," he answered. "You can't search a country half as big as Europe for one man. All I can say is that I visited places where I was prepared to come across him or to get news of him. His last message, you remember, was that he had left Bangkok for the northwest. There were traces of him up-country for a little way, and my own opinion is that he probably made for the tribal districts on the Chinese border. I don't think he'd have cared to enter Burma, where he might have run up against British officials. Anyhow, the definite trail, you may say, peters out somewhere in Upper Siam, but of course I never expected to follow it far that end."

"You thought it might be easier to look for the valley of Blue Moon?"

"Well, it did seem as if it might be a more fixed proposition. I suppose you glanced at that manuscript of mine?"

"Much more than glanced at it. I should have returned it, by the way, but you left no address."

Rutherford nodded. "I wonder what you made of it?"

"I thought it very remarkable—assuming, of course, that it's all quite genuinely based on what Conway told you."

"I give you my solemn word for that. I invented nothing at all—indeed, there's even less of my own language in it than you might think. I've a good memory, and Conway always had a way of describing things. Don't forget that we had about twenty-four hours of practically continuous talk."

"Well, as I said, it's all very remarkable."

He leaned back and smiled. "If that's all you're going to say, I can see I shall have to speak for myself. I suppose you consider me a rather credulous person. I don't really think I am. People make mistakes in life through believing too much, but they have a damned dull time if they believe too little. I was certainly taken with Conway's story—in more ways than one—and that was why I felt interested enough to put as many tabs on it as I could—apart from the chance of running up against the man himself."

He went on, after lighting a cigar: "It meant a good deal of odd journeying, but I like that sort of thing, and my publishers can't object to a travel book once in a while. Altogether I must have done some thousands of miles—Baskul, Bangkok, Chung-Kiang, Kashgar—I visited them all, and somewhere inside the area between them the mystery lies. But it's a pretty big area, you know, and all my investigations didn't touch more than the fringe of it—or of the mystery either, for that matter. Indeed, if you want the actual downright facts about Conway's adventures, so far as I've been able to verify them, all I can tell you is that he left Baskul on the twentieth of May and arrived in Chung-Kiang on the fifth of October. And the last we know of him is that he left Bangkok again on the third of February. All the rest is probability, possibility, guesswork, myth, legend, whatever you like to call it."

"So you didn't find anything in Tibet?"

"My dear fellow, I never got into Tibet at all. The people up at Government House wouldn't hear of it; it's as much as they'll do to sanction an Everest expedition, and when I said I thought of wandering about the Kuen-Luns on my own, they looked at me rather as if I'd suggested writing a life of Gandhi. As a matter of fact, they knew more than I did. Strolling about Tibet isn't a one-man job; it needs an expedition properly fitted out and run by some one who knows at least a word or two of the language. I remember when

Conway was telling me his story I kept wondering why there was
all that fuss about waiting for porters—why didn't they all simply
walk off? I wasn't very long in discovering. The Government people
were quite right—all the passports in the world couldn't have got
me over the Kuen-Luns. I actually went as far as seeing them in
the distance, on a very clear day—perhaps fifty miles off. Not many
Europeans can claim even that."

"Are they so very forbidding?"

"They looked just like a white frieze on the horizon, that was all.
At Yarkand and Kashgar I questioned every one I met about them,
but it was extraordinary how little I could discover. I should think
they must be the least-explored range in the world. I had the luck
to meet an American traveler who had once tried to cross them, but
he'd been unable to find a pass. There *are* passes, he said, but they're
terrifically high and unmapped. I asked him if he thought it possible
for a valley to exist of the kind Conway described, and he said he
wouldn't call it impossible, but he thought it not very likely—on
geological grounds, at any rate. Then I asked if he had ever heard
of a cone-shaped mountain almost as high as the highest of the Hi-
malayas, and his answer to that was rather intriguing. There was a
legend, he said, about such a mountain, but he thought himself there
could be no foundation for it. There were even rumors, he added,
about mountains actually higher than Everest, but he didn't himself
give credit to them. 'I doubt if any peak in the Kuen-Luns is more
than twenty-five thousand feet, if that,' he said. But he admitted
that they had never been properly surveyed.

"Then I asked him what he knew about Tibetan lamaseries—he'd
been in the country several times—and he gave me just the usual
accounts that one can read in all the books. They weren't beautiful
places, he assured me, and the monks in them were generally corrupt
and dirty. 'Do they live long?' I asked, and he said, yes, they often
did, if they didn't die of some filthy disease. Then I went boldly to
the point and asked if he'd ever heard legends of extreme longevity
among the lamas. 'Heaps of them,' he answered; 'it's one of the stock
yarns you hear everywhere, but you can't verify them. You're told
that some foul-looking creature has been walled up in a cell for a
hundred years, and he certainly looks as if he might have been, but
of course you can't demand his birth certificate.' I asked him if he
thought they had any occult or medicinal way of prolonging life or
preserving youth, and he said they were supposed to have a great
deal of very curious knowledge about such things, but he suspected
that if you came to look into it, it was rather like the Indian rope

trick—always something that somebody else had seen. He did say, however, that the lamas appeared to have odd powers of bodily control. 'I've watched them,' he said, 'sitting by the edge of a frozen lake, stark naked, with a temperature below zero and in a tearing wind, while their servants break the ice and wrap sheets round them that have been dipped in the water. They do this a dozen times or more, and the lamas dry the sheets on their own bodies. Keeping warm by will-power, so one imagines, though that's a poor sort of explanation.'"

Rutherford helped himself to more drink. "But of course, as my American friend admitted, all that had nothing much to do with longevity. It merely showed that the lamas had somber tastes in self-discipline. . . . So there we were, and probably you'll agree with me that all the evidence, so far, was less than you'd hang a dog on."

I said it was certainly inconclusive, and asked if the names "Karakal" and "Shangri-La" had meant anything to the American.

"Not a thing—I tried him with them. After I'd gone on questioning him for a time, he said: 'Frankly, I'm not keen on monasteries—indeed, I once told a fellow I met in Tibet that if I went out of my way at all, it would be to avoid them, not pay them a visit.' That chance remark of his gave me a curious idea, and I asked him when this meeting in Tibet had taken place. 'Oh, a long time ago,' he answered, 'before the War—in nineteen-eleven, I think it was.' I badgered him for further details, and he gave them, as well as he could remember. It seemed that he'd been traveling then for some American geographical society, with several colleagues, porters, and so on— in fact, a pukka expedition. Somewhere near the Kuen-Luns he met this other man, a Chinese who was being carried in a chair by native bearers. The fellow turned out to speak English quite well, and strongly recommended them to visit a certain lamasery in the neighborhood—he even offered to be the guide there. The American said they hadn't time and weren't interested, and that was that."

Rutherford went on, after an interval: "I don't suggest that it means a great deal. When a man tries to remember a casual incident that happened twenty years ago, you can't build *too* much on it. But it offers an attractive speculation."

"Yes, though if a well-equipped expedition had accepted the invitation, I don't see how they could have been detained at the lamasery against their will."

"Oh, quite. And perhaps it wasn't Shangri-La at all."

We thought it over, but it seemed too hazy for argument, and I went on to ask if there had been any discoveries at Baskul.

"Baskul was hopeless, and Peshawur was worse. Nobody could tell me anything, except that the kidnaping of the aeroplane did undoubtedly take place. They weren't keen even to admit that—it's an episode they're not proud of."

"And nothing was heard of the plane afterwards?"

"Not a word or a rumor, or of its four passengers either. I verified, however, that it was capable of climbing high enough to cross the ranges. I also tried to trace that fellow Barnard, but I found his past history so mysterious that I wouldn't be at all surprised if he really were Chalmers Bryant, as Conway said. After all, Bryant's complete disappearance in the midst of the big hue and cry was rather amazing."

"Did you try to find anything about the actual kidnaper?"

"I did, but again it was hopeless. The Air Force man whom the fellow had knocked out and impersonated had since been killed, so one promising line of enquiry was closed. I even wrote to a friend of mine in America who runs an aviation school, asking if he had had any Tibetan pupils lately, but his reply was prompt and disappointing. He said he couldn't differentiate Tibetans from Chinese, and he had had about fifty of the latter—all training to fight the Japs. Not much chance there, you see. But I did make one rather quaint discovery—and which I could have made just as easily without leaving London. There was a German professor at Jena about the middle of the last century who took to globe-trotting and visited Tibet in 1887. He never came back, and there was some story about him having been drowned in fording a river. His name was Friedrich Meister."

"Good heavens—one of the names Conway mentioned!"

"Yes—though it may only have been coincidence. It doesn't prove the whole story, by any means, because the Jena fellow was born in 1845. Nothing very exciting about that."

"But it's odd," I said.

"Oh, yes, it's odd enough."

"Did you succeed in tracing any of the others?"

"No. It's a pity I hadn't a longer list to work on. I couldn't find any record of a pupil of Chopin's called Briac, though of course that doesn't prove that there wasn't one. Conway was pretty sparing with his names, when you come to think about it—out of fifty odd lamas supposed to be on the premises he only gave us one or two. Perrault and Henschell, by the way, proved equally impossible to trace."

"How about Mallinson?" I asked. "Did you try to find out what had happened to him? And that girl—the Chinese girl?"

"My dear fellow, of course I did. The awkward part was, as you perhaps gathered from the manuscript, that Conway's story ended at the moment of leaving the valley with the porters. After that he either couldn't or wouldn't tell me what happened—perhaps he might have done, mind you, if there'd been more time. I feel that we can guess at some sort of tragedy. The hardships of the journey would be perfectly appalling, apart from the risk of brigandage or even treachery among their own escorting party. Probably we shall never know exactly what did occur, but it seems tolerably certain that Mallinson never reached China. I made all sorts of enquiries, you know. First of all I tried to trace details of books, et cetera, sent in large consignments across the Tibetan frontier, but at all the likely places, such as Shanghai and Pekin, I drew complete blanks. That, of course, doesn't count for much, since the lamas would doubtless see that their methods of importation were kept secret. Then I tried at Tatsien-Fu. It's a weird place, a sort of world's-end market town, deuced difficult to get at, where the Chinese coolies from Yunnan transfer their loads of tea to the Tibetans. You can read about it in my new book when it comes out. Europeans don't often get as far. I found the people quite civil and courteous, but there was absolutely no record of Conway's party arriving at all."

"So how Conway himself reached Chung-Kiang is still unexplained?"

"The only conclusion is that he wandered there, just as he might have wandered anywhere else. Anyhow, we're back in the realm of hard facts when we get to Chung-Kiang, that's something. The nuns at the mission hospital were genuine enough, and so, for that matter, was Sieveking's excitement on the ship when Conway played that pseudo-Chopin." Rutherford paused and then added reflectively: "It's really an exercise in the balancing of probabilities, and I must say the scales don't bump very emphatically either way. Of course if you don't accept Conway's story, it means that you doubt either his veracity or his sanity—one may as well be frank."

He paused again, as if inviting a comment, and I said: "As you know, I never saw him after the War, but people said he was a good deal changed by it."

Rutherford answered: "Yes, and he was, there's no denying the fact. You can't subject a mere boy to three years of intense physical and emotional stress without tearing something to tatters. People would say, I suppose, that he came through without a scratch. But the scratches were there—on the inside."

We talked for a little time about the War and its effects on various

people, and at length he went on: "But there's just one more point
that I must mention—and perhaps in some ways the oddest of all.
It came out during my enquiries at the mission. They all did their
best for me there, as you can guess, but they couldn't recollect much,
especially as they'd been so busy with a fever epidemic at the time.
One of the questions I put was about the manner Conway had
reached the hospital first of all—whether he had presented himself
alone, or had been found ill and been taken there by some one
else. They couldn't exactly remember—after all, it was a long while
back—but suddenly, when I was on the point of giving up the cross-
examination, one of the nuns remarked quite casually, 'I think the
doctor said he was brought here by a woman.' That was all she could
tell me, and as the doctor himself had left the mission, there was no
confirmation to be had on the spot.

"But having got so far, I wasn't in any mood to give up. It appeared that the doctor had gone to a bigger hospital in Shanghai, so
I took the trouble to get his address and call on him there. It was
just after the Jap air-raiding, and things were pretty grim. I'd met
the man before during my first visit to Chung-Kiang, and he was
very polite, though terribly overworked—yes, terribly's the word, for,
believe me, the air-raids on London by the Germans were just nothing to what the Japs did to the native parts of Shanghai. Oh, yes,
he said instantly, he remembered the case of the Englishman who
had lost his memory. Was it true he had been brought to the mission
hospital by a woman? I asked. Oh, yes, certainly, by a woman, a
Chinese woman. Did he remember anything about her? Nothing, he
answered, except that she had been ill of the fever herself, and had
died almost immediately. . . . Just then there was an interruption—
a batch of wounded were carried in and packed on stretchers in the
corridors—the wards were all full—and I didn't care to go on taking
up the man's time, especially as the thudding of the guns at Woosung
was a reminder that he would still have plenty to do. When he came
back to me, looking quite cheerful even amidst such ghastliness, I
just asked him one final question, and I dare say you can guess what
it was. 'About that Chinese woman,' I said. 'Was she young?'"

Rutherford flicked his cigar as if the narration had excited him
quite as much as he hoped it had me. Continuing, he said: "The
little fellow looked at me solemnly for a moment, and then answered
in that funny clipped English that the educated Chinese have—
'Oh, no, she was most old—most old of any one I have ever seen.'"

We sat for a long time in silence, and then talked again of Conway as I remembered him, boyish and gifted and full of charm, and of the War that had altered him, and of so many mysteries of time and age and of the mind, and of the little Manchu who had been "most old," and of the strange ultimate dream of Blue Moon. "Do you think he will ever find it?" I asked.

WOODFORD GREEN
April, 1933

Good-bye, Mr. Chips

PREFACE

Good-bye, Mr. Chips was written in London during a foggy week of November, 1933. I am chary of using the word "inspiration," which is too often something nonexistent that a writer waits for when he is lazy; but, as a matter of record, *Good-bye, Mr. Chips* was written more quickly, more easily, and with fewer subsequent alterations than anything I had ever written before, or have ever written since.

It was first published in the Christmas number of the *British Weekly*, in December 1933; after which, with a certain wild abandon, I had it sent to the *Atlantic Monthly*—a magazine which I had long held as a secret pinnacle of ambition. The *Atlantic* printed the story in its issue of April 1934, and about the same time proposed its publication as a book. This publication took place on June 8. Four months later *Good-bye, Mr. Chips* first appeared as a book in England, from Messrs. Hodder and Stoughton. Thus one may summarize that, having been written and first printed in its native land, it was discovered by America, and later came back to England with the success that America had given it. And now, again in America, it appears in this new and sumptuous dress.

If I recount these details with pride, I do so also with modesty, for I know how few are the writers to whom such romances happen, and that, with no matter how much or little merit, a portion of luck must be distilled. But I do take pride in the reception that America has given to my very English book; certainly no author could ever have enjoyed his correspondence more than I have during the past year. One feature has been the discovery of the original Mr. Chips in so many different parts of the world; and I believe those letters from readers have told the whole truth, and that my tribute to a great profession has fitted a great many members of it everywhere.

J. H.

Wanstead, London
March, 1935

CHAPTER ONE

When you are getting on in years (but not ill, of course), you get very sleepy at times, and the hours seem to pass like lazy cattle moving across a landscape. It was like that for Chips as the autumn term progressed and the days shortened till it was actually dark enough to light the gas before call-over. For Chips, like some old sea captain, still measured time by the signals of the past; and well he might, for he lived at Mrs. Wickett's, just across the road from the School. He had been there more than a decade, ever since he finally gave up his mastership; and it was Brookfield far more than Greenwich time that both he and his landlady kept. "Mrs. Wickett," Chips would sing out, in that jerky, high-pitched voice that had still a good deal of sprightliness in it, "you might bring me a cup of tea before prep, will you?"

When you are getting on in years it is nice to sit by the fire and drink a cup of tea and listen to the school bell sounding dinner, call-over, prep, and lights-out. Chips always wound up the clock after that last bell; then he put the wire guard in front of the fire, turned out the gas, and carried a detective novel to bed. Rarely did he read more than a page of it before sleep came swiftly and peacefully, more like a mystic intensifying of perception than any changeful entrance into another world. For his days and nights were equally full of dreaming.

He was getting on in years (but not ill, of course); indeed, as Doctor Merivale said, there was really nothing the matter with him. "My dear fellow, you 're fitter than I am," Merivale would say, sipping a glass of sherry when he called every fortnight or so. "You 're past the age when people get these horrible diseases; you 're one of the few lucky ones who 're going to die a really natural death. That is, of course, if you die at all. You 're such a remarkable old boy that one never knows." But when Chips had a cold or when east winds roared over the fenlands, Merivale would sometimes take Mrs. Wickett aside in the lobby and whisper: "Look after him, you know. His chest . . . it puts a strain on his heart. Nothing really wrong with him—only anno domini, but that's the most fatal complaint of all, in the end."

Anno domini . . . by Jove, yes. Born in 1848, and taken to the Great Exhibition as a toddling child—not many people still alive could boast a thing like that. Besides, Chips could even remember Brookfield in Wetherby's time. A phenomenon, that was. Wetherby had been an old man in those days—1870—easy to remember because of the Franco-Prussian War. Chips had put in for Brookfield after a year at Melbury, which he had n't liked, because he had been ragged there a good deal. But Brookfield he *had* liked, almost from the beginning. He remembered that day of his preliminary interview —sunny June, with the air full of flower scents and the plick-plock of cricket on the pitch. Brookfield was playing Barnhurst, and one of the Barnhurst boys, a chubby little fellow, made a brilliant century. Queer that a thing like that should stay in the memory so clearly. Wetherby himself was very fatherly and courteous; he must have been ill then, poor chap, for he died during the summer vacation, before Chips began his first term. But the two had seen and spoken to each other, anyway.

Chips often thought, as he sat by the fire at Mrs. Wickett's: I am probably the only man in the world who has a vivid recollection of old Wetherby. . . . Vivid, yes; it was a frequent picture in his mind, that summer day with the sunlight filtering through the dust in Wetherby's study. "You are a young man, Mr. Chipping, and Brookfield is an old foundation. Youth and age often combine well. Give your enthusiasm to Brookfield, and Brookfield will give you something in return. And don't let anyone play tricks with you. I—er— gather that discipline was not always your strong point at Melbury?"

"Well, no, perhaps not, sir."

"Never mind; you 're full young; it 's largely a matter of experience. You have another chance here. Take up a firm attitude from the beginning—that 's the secret of it."

Perhaps it was. He remembered that first tremendous ordeal of taking prep; a September sunset more than half a century ago; Big Hall full of lusty barbarians ready to pounce on him as their legitimate prey. His youth, fresh-complexioned, high-collared, and side-whiskered (odd fashions people followed in those days), at the mercy of five hundred unprincipled ruffians to whom the baiting of new masters was a fine art, an exciting sport, and something of a tradition. Decent little beggars individually, but, as a mob, just pitiless and implacable. The sudden hush as he took his place at the desk on the dais; the scowl he assumed to cover his inward nervousness; the tall clock ticking behind him, and the smells of ink and varnish; the last blood-red rays slanting in slabs through the stained-glass windows. Someone dropped a desk lid. Quickly, he must take everyone by surprise; he must show that there was no nonsense about him. "You there in the fifth row—you with the red hair—what's your name?" "Colley, sir." "Very well, Colley, you have a hundred lines." No trouble at all after that. He had won his first round.

And years later, when Colley was an alderman of the City of London and a baronet and various other things, he sent his son (also red-haired) to Brookfield, and Chips would say: "Colley, your father was the first boy I ever punished when I came here twenty-five years ago. He deserved it then, and you deserve it now." How they all laughed; and how Sir Richard laughed when his son wrote home the story in next Sunday's letter!

And again, years after that, many years after that, there was an even better joke. For another Colley had just arrived—son of the Colley who was a son of the first Colley. And Chips would say, punctuating his remarks with that little "umph-um" that had by then become a habit with him: "Colley, you are—umph—a splendid example of—umph—inherited traditions. I remember your grandfather —umph—he could never grasp the Ablative Absolute. A stupid fellow, your grandfather. And your father, too—umph—I remember him —he used to sit at that far desk by the wall—he was n't much better, either. But I do believe—my dear Colley—that you are—umph—the biggest fool of the lot!" Roars of laughter.

A great joke, this growing old—but a sad joke, too, in a way. And as Chips sat by his fire with autumn gales rattling the windows, the waves of humor and sadness swept over him very often until tears fell, so that when Mrs. Wickett came in with his cup of tea she did not know whether he had been laughing or crying. And neither did Chips himself.

CHAPTER TWO

Across the road behind a rampart of ancient elms lay Brookfield, russet under its autumn mantle of creeper. A group of eighteenth-century buildings centred upon a quadrangle, and there were acres of playing fields beyond; then came the small dependent village and the open fen country. Brookfield, as Wetherby had said, was an old foundation; established in the reign of Elizabeth, as a grammar school, it might, with better luck, have become as famous as Harrow. Its luck, however, had been not so good; the School went up and down, dwindling almost to nonexistence at one time, becoming almost illustrious at another. It was during one of these latter periods, in the reign of the first George, that the main structure had been rebuilt and large additions made. Later, after the Napoleonic Wars and until mid-Victorian days, the School declined again, both in numbers and in repute. Wetherby, who came in 1840, restored its fortunes somewhat; but its subsequent history never raised it to front-rank status. It was, nevertheless, a good school of the second rank. Several notable families supported it; it supplied fair samples of the history-making men of the age—judges, members of parliament, colonial administrators, a few peers and bishops. Mostly, however, it turned out merchants, manufacturers, and professional men, with a good sprinkling of country squires and parsons. It was the sort of school which, when mentioned, would sometimes make snobbish people confess that they rather thought they had heard of it.

But if it had not been this sort of school it would probably not have taken Chips. For Chips, in any social or academic sense, was just as respectable, but no more brilliant, than Brookfield itself.

It had taken him some time to realize this, at the beginning. Not that he was boastful or conceited, but he had been, in his early twenties, as ambitious as most other young men at such an age. His dream had been to get a headship eventually, or at any rate a senior mastership in a really first-class school; it was only gradually, after repeated trials and failures, that he realized the inadequacy of his qualifications. His degree, for instance, was not particularly good, and his discipline, though good enough and improving, was not absolutely reliable under all conditions. He had no private means and no family connections of any importance. About 1880, after he had been at Brookfield a decade, he began to recognize that the odds were heavily against his being able to better himself by moving elsewhere; but about that time, also, the possibility of staying where he was began to fill a comfortable niche in his mind. At forty, he was rooted, settled, and quite happy. At fifty, he was the doyen of the staff. At sixty, under a new and youthful Head, he *was* Brookfield—the guest of honor at Old Brookfeldian dinners, the court of appeal in all matters affecting Brookfield history and traditions. And in 1913, when he turned sixty-five, he retired, was presented with a check and a writing desk and a clock, and went across the road to live at Mrs. Wickett's. A decent career, decently closed; three cheers for old Chips, they all shouted, at that uproarious end-of-term dinner.

Three cheers, indeed; but there was more to come, an unguessed epilogue, an encore played to a tragic audience.

CHAPTER THREE

It was a small but very comfortable and sunny room that Mrs. Wickett let to him. The house itself was ugly and pretentious; but that did n't matter. It was convenient—that was the main thing. For he liked, if the weather were mild enough, to stroll across to the playing fields in an afternoon and watch the games. He liked to smile and exchange a few words with the boys when they touched their caps to him. He made a special point of getting to know all the new boys and having them to tea with him during their first term. He always ordered a walnut cake with pink icing from Reddaway's, in the village, and during the winter term there were crumpets, too—a little pile of them in front of the fire, soaked in butter so that the bottom one lay in a little shallow pool. His guests found it fun to watch him make tea—mixing careful spoonfuls from different caddies. And he would ask the new boys where they lived, and if they had family connections at Brookfield. He kept watch to see that their plates were never empty, and punctually at five, after the session had lasted an hour, he would glance at the clock and say: "Well—umph—it 's been very delightful—umph—meeting you like this—I 'm sorry—umph—you can't stay. . . ." And he would smile and shake hands with them in the porch, leaving them to race across the road to the School with their comments. "Decent old boy, Chips. Gives you a jolly good tea, anyhow, and you *do* know when he wants you to push off. . . ."

And Chips also would be making his comments—to Mrs. Wickett when she entered his room to clear away the remains of the party. "A most—umph—interesting time, Mrs. Wickett. Young Branksome tells me—umph—that his uncle was Major Collingwood—the Collingwood we had here in—umph—nought-two, I think it was. Dear me, I remember Collingwood very well. I once thrashed him—umph—for climbing on to the gymnasium roof—to get a ball out of the gutter. Might have—umph—broken his neck, the young fool. Do you remember him, Mrs. Wickett? He must have been in your time."

Mrs. Wickett, before she saved money, had been in charge of the linen room at the School.

"Yes, I knew 'im, sir. Cheeky, 'e was to me, gener'ly. But we never 'ad no bad words between us. Just cheeky-like. 'E never meant no harm. That kind never does, sir. Was n't it 'im that got the medal, sir?"

"Yes, a D.S.O."

"Will you be wanting anything else, sir?"

"Nothing more now—umph—till chapel time. He was killed—in Egypt, I think. . . . Yes—umph—you can bring my supper about then."

"Very good, sir."

A pleasant, placid life, at Mrs. Wickett's. He had no worries; his pension was adequate, and there was a little money saved up besides. He could afford everything and anything he wanted. His room was furnished simply and with schoolmasterly taste: a few bookshelves and sporting trophies; a mantelpiece crowded with fixture cards and signed photographs of boys and men; a worn Turkey carpet; big easy-chairs; pictures on the wall of the Acropolis and the Forum. Nearly everything had come out of his old housemaster's room in School House. The books were chiefly classical, the classics having been his subject; there was, however, a seasoning of history and belles-lettres. There was also a bottom shelf piled up with cheap editions of detective novels. Chips enjoyed these. Sometimes he took down Vergil or Xenophon and read for a few moments, but he was soon back again with Doctor Thorndyke or Inspector French. He was not, despite his long years of assiduous teaching, a very profound classical scholar; indeed, he thought of Latin and Greek far more as dead languages from which English gentlemen ought to know a few quotations than as living tongues that had ever been spoken by living people. He liked those short leading articles in the *Times* that introduced a few tags that he recognized. To be among the dwindling number of people who understood such things was to him a kind of secret and valued freemasonry; it represented, he felt, one of the chief benefits to be derived from a classical education.

So there he lived, at Mrs. Wickett's, with his quiet enjoyments of reading and talking and remembering; an old man, white-haired and only a little bald, still fairly active for his years, drinking tea, receiving callers, busying himself with corrections for the next edition of the Brookfeldian Directory, writing his occasional letters in thin, spidery, but very legible script. He had new masters to tea, as well as new boys. There were two of them that autumn term, and as they were leaving after their visit one of them commented: "Quite a character, the old boy, is n't he? All that fuss about mixing the tea—a typical bachelor, if ever there was one."

Which was oddly incorrect; because Chips was not a bachelor at all. He had married; though it was so long ago that none of the staff at Brookfield could remember his wife.

CHAPTER FOUR

There came to him, stirred by the warmth of the fire and the gentle aroma of tea, a thousand tangled recollections of old times. Spring—the spring of 1896. He was forty-eight—an age at which a permanence of habits begins to be predictable. He had just been appointed housemaster; with this and his classical forms, he had made for himself a warm and busy corner of life. During the summer vacation he went up to the Lake District with Rowden, a colleague; they walked and climbed for a week, until Rowden had to leave suddenly on some family business. Chips stayed on alone at Wasdale Head, where he boarded in a small farmhouse.

One day, climbing on Great Gable, he noticed a girl waving excitedly from a dangerous-looking ledge. Thinking she was in difficulties, he hastened toward her, but in doing so slipped himself and wrenched his ankle. As it turned out, she was not in difficulties at all, but was merely signaling to a friend farther down the mountain; she was an expert climber, better even than Chips, who was pretty good. Thus he found himself the rescued instead of the rescuer; and neither rôle was one for which he had much relish. For he did not, he would have said, care for women; he never felt at home or at ease with them; and that monstrous creature beginning to be talked about, the New Woman of the nineties, filled him with horror. He was a quiet, conventional person, and the world, viewed from the haven of Brookfield, seemed to him full of distasteful innovations; there was a fellow named Bernard Shaw who had the strangest and most reprehensible opinions; there was Ibsen, too, with his disturbing plays; and there was this new craze for bicycling which was being taken up by women equally with men. Chips did not hold with all this modern newness and freedom. He had a vague notion, if he ever formulated it, that nice women were weak, timid, and delicate, and that nice men treated them with a polite but rather distant chivalry. He had not, therefore, expected to find a woman on Great Gable; but, having encountered one who seemed to need masculine help, it was even more terrifying that she should turn the tables by helping him. For she did. She and her friend had to. He could scarcely walk, and it was a hard job getting him down the steep track to Wasdale.

Her name was Katherine Bridges; she was twenty-five—young enough to be Chips's daughter. She had blue, flashing eyes and freckled cheeks and smooth straw-colored hair. She too was staying at a farm, on holiday with a girl friend, and as she considered herself responsible for Chips's accident, she used to bicycle along the side of the lake to the house in which the quiet, middle-aged, serious-looking man lay resting.

That was how she thought of him at first. And he, because she rode a bicycle and was unafraid to visit a man alone in a farmhouse sitting room, wondered vaguely what the world was coming to. His sprain put him at her mercy, and it was soon revealed to him how much he might need that mercy. She was a governess out of a job, with a little money saved up; she read and admired Ibsen; she believed that women ought to be admitted to the universities; she even thought they ought to have a vote. In politics she was a radical, with leanings toward the views of people like Bernard Shaw and William Morris. All her ideas and opinions she poured out to Chips during those summer afternoons at Wasdale Head; and he, because he was not very articulate, did not at first think it worth while to contradict them. Her friend went away, but she stayed; what *could* you do with such a person, Chips thought. He used to hobble with sticks along a footpath leading to the tiny church; there was a stone slab on the wall, and it was comfortable to sit down, facing the sunlight and the green-brown majesty of the Gable and listening to the chatter of—well, yes, Chips had to admit it—a very beautiful girl.

He had never met anyone like her. He had always thought that the modern type, this "new woman" business, would repel him; and here she was, making him positively look forward to the glimpse of her safety bicycle careering along the lakeside road. And she, too, had never met anyone like *him*. She had always thought that middle-aged men who read the *Times* and disapproved of modernity were terrible bores; yet here he was, claiming her interest and attention far more than youths of her own age. She liked him, initially, because he was so hard to get to know, because he had gentle and quiet manners, because his opinions dated from those utterly impossible seventies and eighties and even earlier—yet were, for all that, so thoroughly honest; and because—because his eyes were brown and he looked charming when he smiled. "Of course, *I* shall call you Chips, too," she said, when she learned that was his nickname at school.

Within a week they were head over heels in love; before Chips could walk without a stick, they considered themselves engaged; and they were married in London a week before the beginning of the autumn term.

CHAPTER FIVE

When Chips, dreaming through the hours at Mrs. Wickett's, recollected those days, he used to look down at his feet and wonder which one it was that had performed so signal a service. That, the trivial cause of so many momentous happenings, was the one thing of which details evaded him. But he resaw the glorious hump of the Gable (he had never visited the Lake District since), and the mouse-gray depths of Wastwater under the Screes; he could resmell the washed air after heavy rain, and refollow the ribbon of the pass across to Sty Head. So clearly it lingered, that time of dizzy happiness, those evening strolls by the waterside, her cool voice and her gay laughter. She had been a very happy person, always.

They had both been so eager, planning a future together; but he had been rather serious about it, even a little awed. It would be all right, of course, her coming to Brookfield; other housemasters were married. And she liked boys, she told him, and would enjoy living among them. "Oh, Chips, I'm so glad you are what you are. I was afraid you were a solicitor or a stockbroker or a dentist or a man with a big cotton business in Manchester. When I first met you, I mean. Schoolmastering 's so different, so important, don't you think? To be influencing those who are going to grow up and matter to the world . . ."

Chips said he had n't thought of it like that—or, at least, not often. He did his best; that was all anyone could do in any job.

"Yes, of course, Chips. I do love you for saying simple things like that."

And one morning—another memory gem-clear when he turned to it—he had for some reason been afflicted with an acute desire to depreciate himself and all his attainments. He had told her of his only mediocre degree, of his occasional difficulties of discipline, of the certainty that he would never get a promotion, and of his complete ineligibility to marry a young and ambitious girl. And at the end of it all she had laughed in answer.

She had no parents and was married from the house of an aunt in Ealing. On the night before the wedding, when Chips left the house to return to his hotel, she said, with mock gravity: "This is an occasion, you know—this last farewell of ours. I feel rather like a new boy beginning his first term with you. Not scared, mind you—but just, for once, in a thoroughly respectful mood. Shall I call you 'sir'— or would 'Mr. Chips' be the right thing? 'Mr. Chips,' I think. Good-bye, then—good-bye, Mr. Chips. . . ."

(A hansom clop-clopping in the roadway; green-pale gas lamps flickering on a wet pavement; newsboys shouting something about South Africa; Sherlock Holmes in Baker Street.)

"Good-bye, Mr. Chips. . . ."

CHAPTER SIX

There had followed then a time of such happiness that Chips, remembering it long afterward, hardly believed it could ever have happened before or since in the world. For his marriage was a triumphant success. Katherine conquered Brookfield as she had conquered Chips; she was immensely popular with boys and masters alike. Even the wives of the masters, tempted at first to be jealous of one so young and lovely, could not long resist her charms.

But most remarkable of all was the change she made in Chips. Till his marriage he had been a dry and rather neutral sort of person; liked and thought well of by Brookfield in general, but not of the stuff that makes for great popularity or that stirs great affection. He had been at Brookfield for over a quarter of a century, long enough to have established himself as a decent fellow and a hard worker; but just too long for anyone to believe him capable of ever being much more. He had, in fact, already begun to sink into that creeping dry rot of pedagogy which is the worst and ultimate pitfall of the profession; giving the same lessons year after year had formed a groove into which the other affairs of his life adjusted themselves with insidious ease. He worked well; he was conscientious; he was a fixture that gave service, satisfaction, confidence, everything except inspiration.

And then came this astonishing girl-wife whom nobody had expected—least of all Chips himself. She made him, to all appearances, a new man; though most of the newness was really a warming to life of things that were old, imprisoned, and unguessed. His eyes gained sparkle; his mind, which was adequately if not brilliantly equipped, began to move more adventurously. The one thing he had always had, a sense of humor, blossomed into a sudden richness to which his years lent maturity. He began to feel a greater sureness; his discipline improved to a point at which it could become, in a sense, less rigid; he became more popular. When he had first come to Brookfield he had aimed to be loved, honored, and obeyed—but obeyed, at any rate. Obedience he had secured, and honor had been granted him; but only now came love, the sudden love of boys for a man who was kind without being soft, who understood them well enough, but not too much, and whose private happiness linked them with their own. He began to make little jokes, the sort that schoolboys like—mnemonics and puns that raised laughs and at the same time imprinted something in the mind. There was one that never failed to please, though it was only a sample of many others. Whenever his Roman History forms came to deal with the Lex Canuleia, the law that permitted patricians to marry plebeians, Chips used to add: "So that, you see, if Miss Plebs wanted Mr. Patrician to marry her, and he said he could n't, she probably replied: 'Oh yes, you can, you liar!'" Roars of laughter.

And Kathie broadened his views and opinions, also, giving him an outlook far beyond the roofs and turrets of Brookfield, so that he saw his country as something deep and gracious to which Brookfield was but one of many feeding streams. She had a cleverer brain than his, and he could not confute her ideas even if and when he disagreed with them; he remained, for instance, a Conservative in politics, despite all her radical-socialist talk. But even where he did not accept, he absorbed; her young idealism worked upon his maturity to produce an amalgam very gentle and wise.

Sometimes she persuaded him completely. Brookfield, for example, ran a mission in East London, to which boys and parents contributed generously with money but rarely with personal contact. It was Katherine who suggested that a team from the mission should come up to Brookfield and play one of the School's elevens at soccer. The idea was so revolutionary that from anyone but Katherine it could not have survived its first frosty reception. To introduce a group of slum boys to the serene pleasances of better-class youngsters seemed at first a wanton stirring of all kinds of things that had better be left untouched. The whole staff was against it, and the School, if its opinion could have been taken, was probably against it too. Everyone was certain that the East End lads would be hooligans, or else that they would be made to feel uncomfortable; anyhow, there would be "incidents," and everyone would be confused and upset. Yet Katherine persisted.

"Chips," she said, "they 're wrong, you know, and I 'm right. I 'm looking ahead to the future, they and you are looking back to the past. England is n't always going to be divided into officers and 'other ranks.' And those Poplar boys are just as important—to England—as Brookfield is. You 've got to have them here, Chips. You can't satisfy your conscience by writing a check for a few guineas and keeping them at arm's length. Besides, they 're proud of Brookfield—just as you are. Years hence, maybe, boys of that sort will be coming here—a few of them, at any rate. Why not? Why ever not? Chips, dear, remember this is eighteen-ninety-seven—not sixty-seven, when you were up at Cambridge. You got your ideas well stuck in those days, and good ideas they were too, a lot of them. But a few—just a few, Chips—want unsticking. . . ."

Rather to her surprise, he gave way and suddenly became a keen advocate of the proposal, and the *volte-face* was so complete that the authorities were taken unawares and found themselves consenting to the dangerous experiment. The boys from Poplar arrived at Brookfield one Saturday afternoon, played soccer with the School's second team, were honorably defeated by seven goals to five, and later had high tea with the School team in the Dining Hall. They then met the Head and were shown over the School, and Chips saw them off at the railway station in the evening. Everything had passed without the slightest hitch of any kind, and it was clear that the visitors were taking away with them as fine an impression as they had left behind.

They took back with them also the memory of a charming woman who had met them and talked to them; for once, years later, during the War, a private stationed at a big military camp near Brookfield called on Chips and said he had been one of that first visiting team. Chips gave him tea and chatted with him, till at length, shaking hands, the man said: "And 'ow 's the missus, sir? I remember her very well."

"Do you?" Chips answered, eagerly. "Do you remember her?"

"Rather. I should think anyone would."

And Chips replied: "They don't, you know. At least, not here. Boys come and go; new faces all the time; memories don't last. Even masters don't stay forever. Since last year—when old Gribble retired —he 's—um—the School butler—there has n't been anyone here who ever saw my wife. She died, you know, less than a year after your visit. In ninety-eight."

"I 'm real sorry to 'ear that, sir. There 's two or three o' my pals, anyhow, who remember 'er clear as anything, though we did only see 'er that wunst. Yes, we remember 'er, all right."

"I 'm very glad. . . . That was a grand day we all had—and a fine game, too."

"One o' the best days aht I ever 'ad in me life. Wish it was then and not nah—straight, I do. I 'm off to Frawnce to-morrer."

A month or so later Chips heard that he had been killed at Passchendaele.

CHAPTER SEVEN

And so it stood, a warm and vivid patch in his life, casting a radiance that glowed in a thousand recollections. Twilight at Mrs. Wickett's, when the School bell clanged for call-over, brought them back to him in a cloud—Katherine scampering along the stone corridors, laughing beside him at some "howler" in an essay he was marking, taking the cello part in a Mozart trio for the School concert, her creamy arm sweeping over the brown sheen of the instrument. She had been a good player and a fine musician. And Katherine furred and muffed for the December house matches, Katherine at the Garden Party that followed Speech Day Prize-giving, Katherine tendering her advice in any little problem that arose. Good advice, too—which he did not always take, but which always influenced him.

"Chips, dear, I 'd let them off if I were you. After all, it 's nothing very serious."

"I know. I 'd like to let them off, but if I do I 'm afraid they 'll do it again."

"Try telling them that, frankly, and give them the chance."

"I might."

And there were other things, occasionally, that *were* serious.

"You know, Chips, having all these hundreds of boys cooped up here is really an unnatural arrangement, when you come to think about it. So that when anything does occur that ought n't to, don't you think it 's a bit unfair to come down on them as if it were their own fault for being here?"

"Don't know about that, Kathie, but I do know that for everybody's sake we have to be pretty strict about this sort of thing. One black sheep can contaminate others."

"After he himself has been contaminated to begin with. After all, that 's what probably *did* happen, is n't it?"

"Maybe. We can't help it. Anyhow, I believe Brookfield is better than a lot of other schools. All the more reason to keep it so."

"But this boy, Chips . . . you 're going to sack him?"

"The Head probably will, when I tell him."

"And you 're going to tell the Head?"

"It 's a duty, I 'm afraid."

"Could n't you think about it a bit . . . talk to the boy again . . . find out how it began . . . After all—apart from this business—is n't he rather a nice boy?"

"Oh, he 's all right."

"Then, Chips dear, don't you think there *ought* to be some other way . . ."

And so on. About once in ten times he was adamant and would n't be persuaded. In about half of these exceptional cases he afterward rather wished he had taken her advice. And years later, whenever he had trouble with a boy, he was always at the mercy of a softening wave of reminiscence; the boy would stand there, waiting to be told his punishment, and would see, if he were observant, the brown eyes twinkle into a shine that told him all was well. But he did not guess that at such a moment Chips was remembering something that had happened long before he was born; that Chips was thinking: Young ruffian, I 'm hanged if *I* can think of any reason to let him off, but I 'll bet *she* would have done!

But she had not always pleaded for leniency. On rather rare occasions she urged severity where Chips was inclined to be forgiving. "I don't like his type, Chips. He 's too cocksure of himself. If he 's looking for trouble I should certainly let him have it."

What a host of little incidents, all deep-buried in the past—problems that had once been urgent, arguments that had once been keen, anecdotes that were funny only because one remembered the fun. Did any emotion really matter when the last trace of it had vanished from human memory; and if that were so, what a crowd of emotions clung to him as to their last home before annihilation! He must be kind to them, must treasure them in his mind before their long sleep. That affair of Archer's resignation, for instance—a queer business, that was. And that affair about the rat that Dunster put in the organ loft while old Ogilvie was taking choir practice. Ogilvie was dead and Dunster drowned at Jutland; of others who had witnessed or heard of the incident, probably most had forgotten. And it had been like that, with other incidents, for centuries. He had a sudden vision of thousands and thousands of boys, from the age of Elizabeth onward; dynasty upon dynasty of masters; long epochs of Brookfield history that had left not even a ghostly record. Who knew why the old fifth-form room was called "the Pit"? There was probably a reason, to begin with; but it had since been lost—lost like the lost books of Livy. And what happened at Brookfield when Cromwell fought at Naseby, near by? How did Brookfield react to the great scare of the "Forty-Five"? Was there a whole holiday when news came of Waterloo? And so on, up to the earliest time that he himself could remember—1870, and Wetherby saying, by way of small talk after their first and only interview: "Looks as if we shall have to settle with the Prussians ourselves one of these fine days, eh?"

When Chips remembered things like this he often felt that he would write them down and make a book of them; and during his years at Mrs. Wickett's he sometimes went even so far as to make desultory notes in an exercise book. But he was soon brought up against difficulties—the chief one being that writing tired him, both mentally and physically. Somehow, too, his recollections lost much of their flavor when they were written down; that story about Rushton and the sack of potatoes, for instance—it would seem quite tame in print, but Lord, how funny it had been at the time! It was funny, too, to remember it; though perhaps if you did n't remember Rushton . . . and who would, anyway, after all those years? It was such a long time ago . . . Mrs. Wickett, did you ever know a fellow named Rushton? Before your time, I dare say . . . went to Burma in some government job . . . or was it Borneo? . . . Very funny fellow, Rushton. . . .

And there he was, dreaming again before the fire, dreaming of times and incidents in which he alone could take secret interest. Funny and sad, comic and tragic, they all mixed up in his mind, and some day, however hard it proved, he *would* sort them out and make a book of them. . . .

CHAPTER EIGHT

And there was always in his mind that spring day in ninety-eight when he had paced through Brookfield village as in some horrifying nightmare, half struggling to escape into an outside world where the sun still shone and where everything had happened differently. Young Faulkner had met him there in the lane outside the School. "Please, sir, may I have the afternoon off? My people are coming up."

"Eh? What 's that? Oh yes, yes. . . ."

"Can I miss Chapel, too, sir?"

"Yes . . . yes . . ."

"And may I go to the station to meet them?"

He nearly answered: "You can go to blazes for all I care. My wife is dead and my child is dead, and I wish I were dead myself."

Actually he nodded and stumbled on. He did not want to talk to anybody or to receive condolences; he wanted to get used to things, if he could, before facing the kind words of others. He took his fourth form as usual after call-over, setting them grammar to learn by heart while he himself stayed at his desk in a cold, continuing trance. Suddenly someone said: "Please, sir, there are a lot of letters for you."

So there were; he had been leaning his elbows on them; they were all addressed to him by name. He tore them open one after the other, but each contained nothing but a blank sheet of paper. He thought in a distant way that it was rather peculiar, but he made no comment; the incident gave hardly an impact upon his vastly greater preoccupations. Not till days afterward did he realize that it had been a piece of April foolery.

They had died on the same day, the mother and the child just born; on April 1, 1898.

CHAPTER NINE

Chips changed his more commodious apartments in School House for his old original bachelor quarters. He thought at first he would give up his housemastership, but the Head persuaded him otherwise; and later he was glad. The work gave him something to do, filled up an emptiness in his mind and heart. He was different; everyone noticed it. Just as marriage had added something, so did bereavement; after the first stupor of grief he became suddenly the kind of man whom boys, at any rate, unhesitatingly classed as "old." It was not that he was less active; he could still knock up a half century on the cricket field; nor was it that he had lost any interest or keenness in his work. Actually, too, his hair had been graying for years; yet now, for the first time, people seemed to notice it. He was fifty. Once, after some energetic fives, during which he had played as well as many a fellow half his age, he overheard a boy saying: "Not half bad for an old chap like him."

Chips, when he was over eighty, used to recount that incident with many chuckles. "Old at fifty, eh? Umph—it was Naylor who said that, and Naylor can't be far short of fifty himself by now! I wonder if he still thinks that fifty's such an age? Last I heard of him, he was lawyering, and lawyers live long—look at Halsbury—umph—Chancellor at eighty-two, and died at ninety-nine. There's an—umph—age for you! Too old at fifty—why, fellows like that are too *young* at fifty. . . . I was myself . . . a mere infant. . . ."

And there was a sense in which it was true. For with the new century there settled upon Chips a mellowness that gathered all his developing mannerisms and his oft-repeated jokes into a single harmony. No longer did he have those slight and occasional disciplinary troubles, or feel diffident about his own work and worth. He found that his pride in Brookfield reflected back, giving him cause for pride in himself and his position. It was a service that gave him freedom to be supremely and completely himself. He had won, by seniority and ripeness, an uncharted no-man's-land of privilege; he had acquired the right to those gentle eccentricities that so often attack schoolmasters and parsons. He wore his gown till it was almost too tattered to hold together; and when he stood on the wooden bench by Big Hall steps to take call-over, it was with an air of mystic abandonment to ritual. He held the School List, a long sheet curling over a board; and each boy, as he passed, spoke his own name for Chips to verify and then tick off on the list. That verifying glance was an easy and favorite subject of mimicry throughout the School—steel-rimmed spectacles slipping down the nose, eyebrows lifted, one a little higher than the other, a gaze half rapt, half quizzical. And on windy days, with gown and white hair and School List fluttering in uproarious confusion, the whole thing became a comic turn sandwiched between afternoon games and the return to classes.

Some of those names, in little snatches of a chorus, recurred to him ever afterward without any effort of memory. . . . Ainsworth, Attwood, Avonmore, Babcock, Baggs, Barnard, Bassenthwaite, Battersby, Beccles, Bedford-Marshall, Bentley, Best . . .

Another one:—

. . . Unsley, Vailes, Wadham, Wagstaff, Wallington, Waters Primus, Waters Secundus, Watling, Waveney, Webb . . .

And yet another that comprised, as he used to tell his fourth-form Latinists, an excellent example of a hexameter:—

. . . Lancaster, Latton, Lemare, Lytton-Bosworth, MacGonigall, Mansfield . . .

Where had they all gone to, he often pondered; those threads he had once held together, how far had they scattered, some to break, others to weave into unknown patterns? The strange randomness of the world beguiled him, that randomness which never would, so long as the world lasted, give meaning to those choruses again.

And behind Brookfield, as one may glimpse a mountain behind another mountain when the mist clears, he saw the world of change and conflict; and he saw it, more than he realized, with the remembered eyes of Kathie. She had not been able to bequeath him all her mind, still less the brilliance of it; but she had left him with a calmness and a poise that accorded well with his own inward emotions. It was typical of him that he did not share the general jingo bitterness against the Boers. Not that he was a pro-Boer—he was far too traditional for that, and he disliked the kind of people who *were* pro-Boers; but still, it did cross his mind at times that the Boers were engaged in a struggle that had a curious similarity to those of certain English history-book heroes—Hereward the Wake, for instance, or Caractacus. He once tried to shock his fifth form by suggesting this, but they only thought it was one of his little jokes.

However heretical he might be about the Boers, he was orthodox about Mr. Lloyd George and the famous Budget. He did not care for either of them. And when, years later, L. G. came as the guest of honor to a Brookfield Speech Day, Chips said, on being presented to him: "Mr. Lloyd George, I am nearly old enough—umph—to remember you as a young man, and—umph—I confess that you seem to me—umph—to have improved—umph—a great deal." The Head, standing with them, was rather aghast; but L. G. laughed heartily and talked to Chips more than to anyone else during the ceremonial that followed.

"Just like Chips," was commented afterward. "He gets away with it. I suppose at that age anything you say to anybody is all right. . . ."

CHAPTER TEN

In 1900 old Meldrum, who had succeeded Wetherby as Head and had held office for three decades, died suddenly from pneumonia; and in the interval before the appointment of a successor, Chips became Acting Head of Brookfield. There was just the faintest chance that the Governors might make the appointment a permanent one; but Chips was not really disappointed when they brought in a youngster of thirty-seven, glittering with Firsts and Blues and with the kind of personality that could reduce Big Hall to silence by the mere lifting of an eyebrow. Chips was not in the running with that kind of person; he never had been and never would be, and he knew it. He was an altogether milder and less ferocious animal.

Those years before his retirement in 1913 were studded with sharply remembered pictures.

A May morning; the clang of the School bell at an unaccustomed time; everyone summoned to assemble in Big Hall. Ralston, the new Head, very pontifical and aware of himself, fixing the multitude with a cold, presaging severity. "You will all be deeply grieved to hear that His Majesty King Edward the Seventh died this morning. . . . There will be no school this afternoon, but a service will be held in the Chapel at four-thirty."

A summer morning on the railway line near Brookfield. The railwaymen were on strike, soldiers were driving the engines, stones had been thrown at trains. Brookfield boys were patrolling the line, thinking the whole business great fun. Chips, who was in charge, stood a little way off, talking to a man at the gate of a cottage. Young Cricklade approached. "Please, sir, what shall we do if we meet any strikers?"

"Would you like to meet one?"

"I—I don't know, sir."

God bless the boy—he talked of them as if they were queer animals out of a zoo! "Well, here you are, then—umph—you can meet Mr. Jones—he 's a striker. When he 's on duty he has charge of the signal box at the station. You 've put your life in his hands many a time."

Afterward the story went round the School: There was Chips,

talking to a striker. Talking to a striker. Might have been quite friendly, the way they were talking together.

Chips, thinking it over a good many times, always added to himself that Kathie would have approved, and would also have been amused.

Because always, whatever happened and however the avenues of politics twisted and curved, he had faith in England, in English flesh and blood, and in Brookfield as a place whose ultimate worth depended on whether she fitted herself into the English scene with dignity and without disproportion. He had been left a vision that grew clearer with each year—of an England for which days of ease were nearly over, of a nation steering into channels where a hair's breadth of error might be catastrophic. He remembered the Diamond Jubilee; there had been a whole holiday at Brookfield, and he had taken Kathie to London to see the procession. That old and legendary lady, sitting in her carriage like some crumbling wooden doll, had symbolized impressively so many things that, like herself, were nearing an end. Was it only the century, or was it an epoch?

And then that frenzied Edwardian decade, like an electric lamp that goes brighter and whiter just before it burns itself out.

Strikes and lockouts, champagne suppers and unemployed marchers, Chinese labor, tariff reform, *H.M.S. Dreadnought,* Marconi, Home Rule for Ireland, Doctor Crippen, suffragettes, the lines of Chatalja. . . .

An April evening, windy and rainy; the fourth form construing Vergil, not very intelligently, for there was exciting news in the papers; young Grayson, in particular, was careless and preoccupied. A quiet, nervous boy.

"Grayson, stay behind—umph—after the rest."

Then:—

"Grayson, I don't want to be—umph—severe, because you are generally pretty good—umph—in your work, but to-day—you don't seem —umph—to have been trying at all. Is anything the matter?"

"N-no, sir."

"Well—umph—we 'll say no more about it, but—umph—I shall expect better things next time."

Next morning it was noised around the School that Grayson's father had sailed on the *Titanic,* and that no news had yet come through as to his fate.

Grayson was excused lessons; for a whole day the School centred emotionally upon his anxieties. Then came news that his father had been among those rescued.

Chips shook hands with the boy. "Well, umph—I 'm delighted, Grayson. A happy ending. You must be feeling pretty pleased with life."

"Y-yes, sir."

A quiet, nervous boy. And it was Grayson Senior, not Junior, with whom Chips was destined later to condole.

CHAPTER ELEVEN

And then the row with Ralston. Funny thing, Chips had never liked him; he was efficient, ruthless, ambitious, but not, somehow, very likable. He had, admittedly, raised the status of Brookfield as a school, and for the first time in memory there was a longish waiting list. Ralston was a live wire; a fine power transmitter, but you had to beware of him.

Chips had never bothered to beware of him; he was not attracted by the man, but he served him willingly enough and quite loyally. Or, rather, he served Brookfield. He knew that Ralston did not like him, either; but that did n't seem to matter. He felt himself sufficiently protected by age and seniority from the fate of other masters whom Ralston had failed to like.

Then suddenly, in 1908, when he had just turned sixty, came Ralston's urbane ultimatum. "Mr. Chipping, have you ever thought you would like to retire?"

Chips stared about him in that book-lined study, startled by the question, wondering why Ralston should have asked it. He said, at length: "No—umph—I can't say that—umph—I have thought much about it—umph—yet."

"Well, Mr. Chipping, the suggestion is there for you to consider. The Governors would, of course, agree to your being adequately pensioned."

Abruptly Chips flamed up. "But—umph—I don't want—to retire. I don't—umph—need to consider it."

"Nevertheless, I suggest that you do."

"But—umph—I don't see—why—I should!"

"In that case, things are going to be a little difficult."

"Difficult? Why—difficult?".

And then they set to, Ralston getting cooler and harder, Chips getting warmer and more passionate, till at last Ralston said, icily: "Since you force me to use plain words, Mr. Chipping, you shall have them. For some time past, you have n't been pulling your weight here. Your methods of teaching are slack and old-fashioned; your personal habits are slovenly; and you ignore my instructions in a way which, in a younger man, I should regard as rank insubordination. It won't do, Mr. Chipping, and you must ascribe it to my forbearance that I have put up with it so long."

"But—" Chips began, in sheer bewilderment; and then he took up isolated words out of that extraordinary indictment. "*Slovenly*—umph —you said—?"

"Yes, look at the gown you 're wearing. I happen to know that that gown of yours is a subject of continual amusement throughout the School."

Chips knew it, too, but it had never seemed to him a very regrettable matter.

He went on: "And—you also said—umph—something about—*insubordination*—?"

"No, I did n't. I said that in a younger man I should have regarded it as that. In your case it 's probably a mixture of slackness and obstinacy. This question of Latin pronunciation, for instance—I think I told you years ago that I wanted the new style used throughout the School. The other masters obeyed me; you prefer to stick to your old methods, and the result is simply chaos and inefficiency."

At last Chips had something tangible that he could tackle. "Oh, *that!*" he answered scornfully. "Well, I—umph—I admit that I don't agree with the new pronunciation. I never did. Umph—a lot of nonsense, in my opinion. Making boys say 'Kickero' at school when— umph—for the rest of their lives they 'll say 'Cicero'—if they ever— umph—say it at all. And instead of 'vicissim'—God bless my soul— you 'd make them say, 'We kiss 'im'! Umph—umph!" And he chuckled momentarily, forgetting that he was in Ralston's study and not in his own friendly form room.

"Well, there you are, Mr. Chipping—that 's just an example of what I complain of. You hold one opinion and I hold another, and, since you decline to give way, there can't very well be any alternative. I aim to make Brookfield a thoroughly up-to-date school. I 'm a science man myself, but for all that I have no objection to the classics—provided that they are taught efficiently. Because they are dead languages is no reason why they should be dealt with in a dead educational technique. I understand, Mr. Chipping, that your Latin and Greek lessons are exactly the same as they were when I began here ten years ago?"

Chips answered, slowly and with pride: "For that matter—umph —they are the same as when your predecessor—Mr. Meldrum—came here, and that—umph—was thirty-eight years ago. We began here, Mr. Meldrum and I—in—umph—in 1870. And it was—um—Mr. Mel-

drum's predecessor, Mr. Wetherby—who first approved my syllabus.
'You 'll take the Cicero for the fourth,' he said to me. Cicero, too—not
Kickero!"

"Very interesting, Mr. Chipping, but once again it proves my point
—you live too much in the past, and not enough in the present and
future. Times are changing, whether you realize it or not. Modern
parents are beginning to demand something more for their three
years' school fees than a few scraps of languages that nobody speaks.
Besides, your boys don't learn even what they 're supposed to learn.
None of them last year got through the Lower Certificate."

And suddenly, in a torrent of thoughts too pressing to be put into
words, Chips made answer to himself. These examinations and certificates and so on—what did they matter? And all this efficiency
and up-to-dateness—what did *that* matter, either? Ralston was trying
to run Brookfield like a factory—a factory for turning out a snob culture based on money and machines. The old gentlemanly traditions
of family and broad acres were changing, as doubtless they were
bound to; but instead of widening them to form a genuine inclusive
democracy of duke and dustman, Ralston was narrowing them upon
the single issue of a fat banking account. There never had been so
many rich men's sons at Brookfield. The Speech Day Garden Party
was like Ascot. Ralston met these wealthy fellows in London clubs
and persuaded them that Brookfield was *the* coming school, and,
since they could n't buy their way into Eton or Harrow, they greed-
ily swallowed the bait. Awful fellows, some of them—though others
were decent enough. Financiers, company promoters, pill manufacturers. One of them gave his son five pounds a week pocket money.
Vulgar . . . ostentatious . . . all the hectic rotten-ripeness of the age.
. . . And once Chips had got into trouble because of some joke he
had made about a boy's name. The boy wrote home about it, and his
father sent an angry letter to Ralston. Touchy, no sense of humor,
no sense of proportion—that was the matter with them, these new
fellows. . . . No sense of proportion. And it was a sense of proportion, above all things, that Brookfield ought to teach—not so much
Latin or Greek or Chemistry or Mechanics. And you could n't expect
to test that sense of proportion by setting papers and granting
certificates. . . .

All this flashed through his mind in an instant of protest and indignation, but he did not say a word of it. He merely gathered his
tattered gown together and with an "umph—umph" walked a few
paces away. He had had enough of the argument. At the door he

turned and said: "I don't—umph—intend to resign—and you can—umph—do what you like about it!"

Looking back upon that scene in the calm perspective of a quarter of a century, Chips could find it in his heart to feel a little sorry for Ralston. Particularly when, as it happened, Ralston had been in such complete ignorance of the forces he was dealing with. So, for that matter, had Chips himself. Neither had correctly estimated the toughness of Brookfield tradition, and its readiness to defend itself and its defenders. For it had so chanced that a small boy, waiting to see Ralston that morning, had been listening outside the door during the whole of the interview; he had been thrilled by it, naturally, and had told his friends. Some of these, in a surprisingly short time, had told their parents; so that very soon it was common knowledge that Ralston had insulted Chips and had demanded his resignation. The amazing result was a spontaneous outburst of sympathy and partisanship such as Chips, in his wildest dreams, had never envisaged. He found, rather to his astonishment, that Ralston was thoroughly unpopular; he was feared and respected, but not liked; and in this issue of Chips the dislike rose to a point where it conquered fear and demolished even respect. There was talk of having some kind of public riot in the School if Ralston succeeded in banishing Chips. The masters, many of them young men who agreed that Chips was hopelessly old-fashioned, rallied round him nevertheless because they hated Ralston's slave driving and saw in the old veteran a likely champion. And one day the Chairman of the Governors, Sir John Rivers, visited Brookfield, ignored Ralston, and went direct to Chips. "A fine fellow, Rivers," Chips would say, telling the story to Mrs. Wickett for the dozenth time. "Not—umph—a very brilliant boy in class. I remember he could never—umph—master his verbs. And now—umph—I see in the papers—they 've made him—umph—a baronet. It just shows you—umph—it just shows you."

Sir John had said, on that morning in 1908, taking Chips by the arm as they walked round the deserted cricket pitches: "Chips, old boy, I hear you 've been having the deuce of a row with Ralston. Sorry to hear about it, for your sake—but I want you to know that the Governors are with you to a man. We don't like the fellow a great deal. Very clever and all that, but a bit too clever, if you ask me. Claims to have doubled the School's endowment funds by some monkeying on the Stock Exchange. Dare say he has, but a chap like that wants watching. So if he starts chucking his weight about with you, tell him very politely he can go to the devil. The Governors don't want you to resign. Brookfield would n't be the same without you, and they know it. We all know it. You can stay here till you 're a hundred if you feel like it—indeed, it 's our hope that you will."

And at that—both then and often when he recounted it afterward —Chips broke down.

CHAPTER TWELVE

So he stayed on at Brookfield, having as little to do with Ralston as possible. And in 1911 Ralston left, "to better himself"; he was offered the headship of one of the greater public schools. His successor was a man named Chatteris, whom Chips liked; he was even younger than Ralston had been—thirty-four. He was supposed to be very brilliant; at any rate, he was modern (Natural Sciences Tripos), friendly, and sympathetic. Recognizing in Chips a Brookfield institution, he courteously and wisely accepted the situation.

In 1913 Chips had had bronchitis and was off duty for nearly the whole of the winter term. It was that which made him decide to resign that summer, when he was sixty-five. After all, it was a good, ripe age; and Ralston's straight words had, in some ways, had an effect. He felt that it would not be fair to hang on if he could not decently do his job. Besides, he would not sever himself completely. He would take rooms across the road, with the excellent Mrs. Wickett who had once been linen-room maid; he could visit the School whenever he wanted, and could still, in a sense, remain a part of it.

At that final end-of-term dinner, in July 1913, Chips received his farewell presentations and made a speech. It was not a very long speech, but it had a good many jokes in it, and was made twice as long, perhaps, by the laughter that impeded its progress. There were several Latin quotations in it, as well as a reference to the Captain of the School, who, Chips said, had been guilty of exaggeration in speaking of his (Chips's) services to Brookfield. "But then—umph —he comes of an—umph—exaggerating family. I—um—remember— once—having to thrash his father—for it. [Laughter] I gave him one mark—umph—for a Latin translation, and he—umph—exaggerated the one into a seven! Umph—umph!" Roars of laughter and tumultuous cheers! A typical Chips remark, everyone thought.

And then he mentioned that he had been at Brookfield for forty-two years, and that he had been very happy there. "It has been my life," he said, simply. "*O mihi praeteritos referat si Jupiter annos.* . . . Umph—I need not—of course—translate. . . ." Much laughter.

"I remember lots of changes at Brookfield. I remember the—um—the first bicycle. I remember when there was no gas or electric light and we used to have a member of the domestic staff called a lamp-boy—he did nothing else but clean and trim and light lamps throughout the School. I remember when there was a hard frost that lasted for seven weeks in the winter term—there were no games, and the whole School learned to skate on the fens. Eighteen-eighty-something, that was. I remember when two thirds of the School went down with German measles and Big Hall was turned into a hospital ward. I remember the great bonfire we had on Mafeking night. It was lit too near the pavilion and we had to send for the fire brigade to put it out. And the firemen were having their own celebrations and most of them were—um—in a regrettable condition. [Laughter] I remember Mrs. Brool, whose photograph is still in the tuckshop; she served there until an uncle in Australia left her a lot of money. In fact, I remember so much that I often think I ought to write a book. Now what should I call it? 'Memories of Rod and Lines'—eh? [Cheers and laughter. That was a good one, people thought—one of Chips's best.] Well, well, perhaps I shall write it, some day. But I 'd rather tell you about it, really. I remember . . . I remember . . . but chiefly I remember all your faces. I never forget them. I have thousands of faces in my mind—the faces of boys. If you come and see me again in years to come—as I hope you all will—I shall try to remember those older faces of yours, but it 's just possible I shan't be able to—and then some day you 'll see me somewhere and I shan't recognize you and you 'll say to yourself, 'The old boy does n't remember me.' [Laughter] But I *do* remember you—as you are *now*. That 's the point. In my mind you never grow up at all. Never. Sometimes, for instance, when people talk to me about our respected Chairman of the Governors, I think to myself, 'Ah yes, a jolly little chap with hair that sticks up on top—and absolutely no idea whatever about the difference between a Gerund and a Gerundive.' [Loud laughter] Well, well I must n't go on—umph—all night. Think of me sometimes as I shall certainly think of you. *Haec olim meminisse juvabit* . . . again I need not translate." Much laughter and shouting and prolonged cheers.

August 1913. Chips went for a cure to Wiesbaden, where he lodged at the home of the German master at Brookfield, Herr Staefel, with whom he had become friendly. Staefel was thirty years his junior, but the two men got on excellently. In September, when term began, Chips returned and took up residence at Mrs. Wickett's. He felt a great deal stronger and fitter after his holiday, and almost wished he had not retired. Nevertheless, he found plenty to do. He had all the new boys to tea. He watched all the important matches on the Brookfield ground. Once a term he dined with the Head, and once also with the masters. He took on the preparation and editing of a new Brookfeldian Directory. He accepted presidency of the Old Boys' Club and went to dinners in London. He wrote occasional articles, full of jokes and Latin quotations, for the Brookfield terminal magazine. He read his *Times* every morning—very thoroughly; and he also began to read detective stories—he had been keen on them ever since the first thrills of Sherlock. Yes, he was quite busy, and quite happy, too.

A year later, in 1914, he again attended the end-of-term dinner. There was a lot of war talk—civil war in Ulster, and trouble between Austria and Serbia. Herr Staefel, who was leaving for Germany the next day, told Chips he thought the Balkan business would n't come to anything.

CHAPTER THIRTEEN

The War years.

The first shock, and then the first optimism. The Battle of the Marne, the Russian steam-roller, Kitchener.

"Do you think it will last long, sir?"

Chips, questioned as he watched the first trial game of the season, gave quite a cheery answer. He was, like thousands of others, hopelessly wrong; but, unlike thousands of others, he did not afterward conceal the fact. "We ought to have—um—finished it—um—by Christmas. The Germans are already beaten. But why? Are you thinking of—um—joining up, Forrester?"

Joke—because Forrester was the smallest new boy Brookfield had ever had—about four feet high above his muddy football boots. (But not so much a joke, when you came to think of it afterward; for he was killed in 1918—shot down in flames over Cambrai.) But one did n't guess what lay ahead. It seemed tragically sensational when the first Old Brookfeldian was killed in action—in September. Chips thought, when that news came: A hundred years ago boys from the school were fighting *against* the French. Strange, in a way, that the sacrifices of one generation should so cancel out those of another. He tried to express this to Blades, the Head of School House; but Blades, eighteen years old and already in training for a cadetship, only laughed. What had all that history stuff to do with it, anyhow? Just old Chips with one of his queer ideas, that 's all.

1915. Armies clenched in deadlock from the sea to Switzerland. The Dardanelles. Gallipoli. Military camps springing up quite near Brookfield; soldiers using the playing fields for sports and training; swift developments of Brookfield O.T.C. Most of the younger masters gone or in uniform. Every Sunday night, in the Chapel after evening service, Chatteris read out the names of old boys killed, together with short biographies. Very moving; but Chips, in the back pew under the gallery, thought: They are only names to him; he does n't see their faces as I do. . . .

1916. . . . The Somme Battle. Twenty-three names read out one Sunday evening.

Toward the close of that catastrophic July, Chatteris talked to Chips one afternoon at Mrs. Wickett's. He was overworked and over-worried and looked very ill. "To tell you the truth, Chipping, I 'm not having too easy a time here. I 'm thirty-nine, you know, and un-married, and lots of people seem to think they know what I ought to do. Also, I happen to be diabetic, and could n't pass the blindest M.O., but I don't see why I should pin a medical certificate on my front door."

Chips had n't known anything about this; it was a shock to him, for he liked Chatteris.

The latter continued: "You see how it is. Ralston filled the place up with young men—all very good, of course—but now most of them have joined up and the substitutes are pretty dreadful, on the whole. They poured ink down a man's neck in prep one night last week—silly fool—got hysterical. I have to take classes myself, take prep for fools like that, work till midnight every night, and get cold-shoul-dered as a slacker on top of everything. I can't stand it much longer. If things don't improve next term I shall have a breakdown."

"I do sympathize with you," Chips said.

"I hoped you would. And that brings me to what I came here to ask you. Briefly, my suggestion is that—if you felt equal to it and would care to—how about coming back here for a while? You look pretty fit, and, of course, you know all the ropes. I don't mean a lot of hard work for you—you need n't take anything strenuously—just a few odd jobs here and there, as you choose. What I 'd like you for more than anything else is not for the actual work you 'd do—though that, naturally, would be very valuable—but for your help in other ways—in just *belonging* here. There 's nobody ever been more popu-lar than you were, and are still—you 'd help to hold things together if there were any danger of them flying to bits. And perhaps there *is* that danger. . . ."

Chips answered, breathlessly and with a holy joy in his heart: "I 'll come. . . ."

CHAPTER FOURTEEN

He still kept on his rooms with Mrs. Wickett; indeed, he still lived there; but every morning, about half-past ten, he put on his coat and muffler and crossed the road to the School. He felt very fit, and the actual work was not taxing. Just a few forms in Latin and Roman History—the old lessons—even the old pronunciation. The same joke about the Lex Canuleia—there was a new generation that had not heard it, and he was absurdly gratified by the success it achieved. He felt a little like a music-hall favorite returning to the boards after a positively last appearance.

They all said how marvelous it was that he knew every boy's name and face so quickly. They did not guess how closely he had kept in touch from across the road.

He was a grand success altogether. In some strange way he did, and they all knew and felt it, help things. For the first time in his life he felt *necessary*—and necessary to something that was nearest his heart. There is no sublimer feeling in the world, and it was his at last.

He made new jokes, too—about the O.T.C. and the food-rationing system and the anti-air-raid blinds that had to be fitted on all the windows. There was a mysterious kind of rissole that began to appear on the School menu on Mondays, and Chips called it *abhorrendum*— "meat to be abhorred." The story went round—heard Chips's latest?

Chatteris fell ill during the winter of '17, and again, for the second time in his life, Chips became Acting Head of Brookfield. Then in April Chatteris died, and the Governors asked Chips if he would carry on "for the duration." He said he would, if they would refrain from appointing him officially. From that last honor, within his reach at last, he shrank instinctively, feeling himself in so many ways unequal to it. He said to Rivers: "You see, I 'm not a young man and I don't want people to—um—expect a lot from me. I 'm like all these new colonels and majors you see everywhere—just a war-time fluke. A ranker—that 's all I am really."

1917. 1918. Chips lived through it all. He sat in the headmaster's study every morning, handling problems, dealing with plaints and requests. Out of vast experience had emerged a kindly, gentle confidence in himself. To keep a sense of proportion, that was the main thing. So much of the world was losing it; as well keep it where it had, or ought to have, a congenial home.

On Sundays in Chapel it was he who now read out the tragic list, and sometimes it was seen and heard that he was in tears over it. Well, why not, the School said; he was an old man; they might have despised anyone else for the weakness.

One day he got a letter from Switzerland, from friends there; it was heavily censored, but conveyed some news. On the following Sunday, after the names and biographies of old boys, he paused a moment and then added:—

"Those few of you who were here before the War will remember Max Staefel, the German master. He was in Germany, visiting his home, when war broke out. He was popular while he was here, and made many friends. Those who knew him will be sorry to hear that he was killed last week, on the Western Front."

He was a little pale when he sat down afterward, aware that he had done something unusual. He had consulted nobody about it, anyhow; no one else could be blamed. Later, outside the Chapel, he heard an argument:—

"On the Western Front, Chips said. Does that mean he was fighting for the Germans?"

"I suppose it does."

"Seems funny, then, to read his name out with all the others. After all, he was an *enemy*."

"Oh, just one of Chips's ideas, I expect. The old boy still has 'em."

Chips, in his room again, was not displeased by the comment. Yes, he still had 'em—those ideas of dignity and generosity that were becoming increasingly rare in a frantic world. And he thought: Brookfield will take them, too, from me; but it would n't from anyone else.

Once, asked for his opinion of bayonet practice being carried on near the cricket pavilion, he answered, with that lazy, slightly asthmatic intonation that had been so often and so extravagantly imitated: "It seems—to me—umph—a very vulgar way of killing people."

The yarn was passsed on and joyously appreciated—how Chips had told some big brass hat from the War Office that bayonet fighting was vulgar. Just like Chips. And they found an adjective for him—an adjective just beginning to be used: he was pre-War.

CHAPTER FIFTEEN

And once, on a night of full moonlight, the air-raid warning was given while Chips was taking his lower fourth in Latin. The guns began almost instantly, and, as there was plenty of shrapnel falling about outside, it seemed to Chips that they might just as well stay where they were, on the ground floor of School House. It was pretty solidly built and made as good a dugout as Brookfield could offer; and as for a direct hit, well, they could not expect to survive that, wherever they were.

So he went on with his Latin, speaking a little louder amid the reverberating crashes of the guns and the shrill whine of anti-aircraft shells. Some of the boys were nervous; few were able to be attentive. He said, gently: "It may possibly seem to you, Robertson—at this particular moment in the world's history—umph—that the affairs of Cæsar in Gaul some two thousand years ago—are—umph—of somewhat secondary importance—and that—umph—the irregular conjugation of the verb *tollo* is—umph—even less important still. But believe me—umph—my dear Robertson—that is not really the case." Just then there came a particularly loud explosion—quite near. "You cannot—umph—judge the importance of things—umph—by the noise they make. Oh dear me, no." A little chuckle. "And these things—umph—that have mattered—for thousands of years—are not going to be—snuffed out—because some stink merchant—in his laboratory—invents a new kind of mischief." Titters of nervous laughter; for Buffles, the pale, lean, and medically unfit science master, was nicknamed the Stink Merchant. Another explosion—nearer still. "Let us—um—resume our work. If it is fate that we are soon to be—umph—interrupted, let us be found employing ourselves in something—umph—really appropriate. Is there anyone who will volunteer to construe?"

Maynard, chubby, dauntless, clever, and impudent, said: "I will, sir."

"Very good. Turn to page forty and begin at the bottom line."

The explosions still continued deafeningly; the whole building shook as if it were being lifted off its foundations. Maynard found the page, which was some way ahead, and began, shrilly:—

"*Genus hoc erat pugnae*—this was the kind of fight—*quo se Germani exercuerant*—in which the Germans busied themselves. Oh, sir, that's good—that's really very funny indeed, sir—one of your very best—"

Laughing began, and Chips added: "Well—umph—you can see —now—that these dead languages—umph—can come to life again —sometimes—eh? Eh?"

Afterward they learned that five bombs had fallen in and around Brookfield, the nearest of them just outside the School grounds. Nine persons had been killed.

The story was told, retold, embellished. "The dear old boy never turned a hair. Even found some old tag to illustrate what was going on. Something in Cæsar about the way the Germans fought. You wouldn't think there were things like that in Cæsar, would you? And the way Chips laughed . . . you know the way he *does* laugh . . . the tears all running down his face . . . never seen him laugh so much. . . ."

He was a legend.

With his old and tattered gown, his walk that was just beginning to break into a stumble, his mild eyes peering over the steel-rimmed spectacles, and his quaintly humorous sayings, Brookfield would not have had an atom of him different.

November 11, 1918.

News came through in the morning; a whole holiday was decreed for the School, and the kitchen staff were implored to provide as cheerful a spread as war-time rationing permitted. There was much cheering and singing, and a bread fight across the Dining Hall. When Chips entered in the midst of the uproar there was an instant hush, and then wave upon wave of cheering; everyone gazed on him with eager, shining eyes, as on a symbol of victory. He walked to the dais, seeming as if he wished to speak; they made silence for him, but he shook his head after a moment, smiled, and walked away again.

It had been a damp, foggy day, and the walk across the quadrangle to the Dining Hall had given him a chill. The next day he was in bed with bronchitis, and stayed there till after Christmas. But already, on that night of November 11, after his visit to the Dining Hall, he had sent in his resignation to the Board of Governors.

When school reassembled after the holidays he was back at Mrs. Wickett's. At his own request there were no more farewells or presentations, nothing but a handshake with his successor and the word "acting" crossed out on official stationery. The "duration" was over.

CHAPTER SIXTEEN

And now, fifteen years after that, he could look back upon it all with a deep and sumptuous tranquillity. He was not ill, of course—only a little tired at times, and bad with his breathing during the winter months. He would not go abroad—he had once tried it, but had chanced to strike the Riviera during one of its carefully unadvertised cold spells. "I prefer—um—to get my chills—umph—in my own country," he used to say, after that. He had to take care of himself when there were east winds, but autumn and winter were not really so bad; there were warm fires, and books, and you could look forward to the summer. It was the summer that he liked best, of course; apart from the weather, which suited him, there were the continual visits of old boys. Every week-end some of them motored up to Brookfield and called at his house. Sometimes they tired him, if too many came at once; but he did not really mind; he could always rest and sleep afterward. And he enjoyed their visits—more than anything else in the world that was still to be enjoyed. "Well, Gregson—umph—I remember you—umph—always late for everything—eh—eh? Perhaps you'll be late in growing old—umph—like me—umph—eh?" And later, when he was alone again and Mrs. Wickett came in to clear away the tea things: "Mrs. Wickett, young Gregson called—umph—you remember him, do you? Tall boy with spectacles. Always late. Umph. Got a job with the—umph—League of Nations—where—I suppose—his—um—dilatoriness—won't be noticeable—eh?"

And sometimes, when the bell rang for call-over, he would go to the window and look across the road and over the School fence and see, in the distance, the thin line of boys filing past the bench. New times, new names . . . but the old ones still remained . . . Jefferson, Jennings, Jolyon, Jupp, Kingsley Primus, Kingsley Secundus, Kingsley Tertius, Kingston . . . where are you all, where have you all gone to? . . . Mrs. Wickett, bring me a cup of tea just before prep, will you, please?

The post-War decade swept through with a clatter of change and maladjustments; Chips, as he lived through it, was profoundly disappointed when he looked abroad. The Ruhr, Chanak, Corfu; there was enough to be uneasy about in the world. But near him, at Brookfield, and even, in a wider sense, in England, there was something that charmed his heart because it was old—and had survived. More and more he saw the rest of the world as a vast disarrangement for which England had sacrificed enough—and perhaps too much. But he was satisfied with Brookfield. It was rooted in things that had stood the test of time and change and war. Curious, in this deeper sense, how little it *had* changed. Boys were a politer race; bullying was nonexistent; there was more swearing and cheating. There was a more genuine friendliness between master and boy—less pomposity on the one side, less unctuousness on the other. One of the new masters, fresh from Oxford, even let the Sixth call him by his Christian name. Chips didn't hold with that; indeed, he was just a little bit shocked. "He might as well—umph—sign his terminal reports—umph —'yours affectionately'—eh—eh?" he told somebody.

During the General Strike of 1926, Brookfield boys loaded motor vans with foodstuffs. When it was all over, Chips felt stirred emotionally as he had not been since the War. Something had happened, something whose ultimate significance had yet to be reckoned. But one thing was clear: England had burned her fire in her own grate again. And when, at a Speech Day function that year, an American visitor laid stress on the vast sums that the strike had cost the country, Chips answered: "Yes, but—umph—advertisement—always *is* costly."

"Advertisement?"

"Well, was n't it—umph—advertisement—and very fine advertisement—too? A whole week of it—umph—and not a life lost—not a shot fired! Your country would have—umph—spilt more blood in—umph— raiding a single liquor saloon!"

Laughter . . . laughter . . . wherever he went and whatever he said, there was laughter. He had earned the reputation of being a great jester, and jests were expected of him. Whenever he rose to speak at a meeting, or even when he talked across a table, people prepared their minds and faces for the joke. They listened in a mood to be amused and it was easy to satisfy them. They laughed sometimes before he came to the point. "Old Chips was in fine form," they would say, afterward. "Marvelous the way he can always see the funny side of things. . . ."

After 1929, Chips did not leave Brookfield—even for Old Boys' dinners in London. He was afraid of chills, and late nights began to tire him too much. He came across to the School, however, on fine days; and he still kept up a wide and continual hospitality in his room. His faculties were all unimpaired, and he had no personal worries of any kind. His income was more than he needed to spend, and his small capital, invested in gilt-edged stocks, did not suffer when the slump set in. He gave a lot of money away—to people who called on him with a hard-luck story, to various School funds, and also to the Brookfield mission. In 1930 he made his will. Except for legacies to the mission and to Mrs. Wickett, he left all he had to found an open scholarship to the school.

1931. . . . 1932. . . .

"What do you think of Hoover, sir?"

"Do you think we shall ever go back to gold?"

"How d'you feel about things in general, sir? See any break in the clouds?"

"When's the tide going to turn, Chips, old boy? You ought to know, with all your experience of things."

They all asked him questions, as if he were some kind of prophet and encyclopædia combined—more even than that, for they liked their answer dished up as a joke. He would say:—

"Well, Henderson, when I was—umph—a much younger man—there used to be someone who—um—promised people ninepence for four-pence. I don't know that anybody—umph—ever got it, but—umph—our present rulers seem—um—to have solved the problem how to give —umph—fourpence for ninepence."

Laughter.

Sometimes, when he was strolling about the School, small boys of the cheekier kind would ask him questions, merely for the fun of getting Chips's "latest" to retail.

"Please, sir, what about the Five-Year Plan?"

"Sir, do you think Germany wants to fight another war?"

"Have you been to the new cinema, sir? I went with my people the other day. Quite a grand affair for a small place like Brookfield. They 've got a Wurlitzer."

"And what—umph—on earth—is a Wurlitzer?"

"It 's an organ, sir—a cinema organ."

"Dear me. . . . I 've seen the name on the hoardings, but I always —umph—imagined—it must be some kind of—umph—sausage."

Laughter. . . . Oh, there 's a new Chips joke, you fellows, a per-fectly lovely one. I was gassing to the old boy about the new cinema, and . . .

CHAPTER SEVENTEEN

He sat in his front parlor at Mrs. Wickett's on a November afternoon in thirty-three. It was cold and foggy, and he dared not go out. He had not felt too well since Armistice Day; he fancied he might have caught a slight chill during the Chapel service. Merivale had been that morning for his usual fortnightly chat. "Everything all right? Feeling hearty? That's the style—keep indoors this weather—there's a lot of flu about. Wish I could have your life for a day or two."

His life . . . and what a life it had been! The whole pageant of it swung before him as he sat by the fire that afternoon. The things he had done and seen: Cambridge in the sixties; Great Gable on an August morning; Brookfield at all times and seasons throughout the years. And, for that matter, the things he had *not* done, and would never do now that he had left them too late—he had never traveled by air, for instance, and he had never been to a talkie-show. So that he was both more and less experienced than the youngest new boy at the School might well be; and that, that paradox of age and youth, was what the world called progress.

Mrs. Wickett had gone out, visiting relatives in a neighboring village; she had left the tea things ready on the table, with bread and butter and extra cups laid out in case anybody called. On such a day, however, visitors were not very likely; with the fog thickening hourly outside, he would probably be alone.

But no. About a quarter to four a ring came, and Chips, answering the front door himself (which he ought n't to have done), encountered a rather small boy wearing a Brookfield cap and an expression of anxious timidity. "Please, sir," he began, "does Mr. Chips live here?"

"Umph—you'd better come inside," Chips answered. And in his room a moment later he added: "I am—umph—the person you want. Now what can I—umph—do for you?"

"I was told you wanted me, sir."

Chips smiled. An old joke—an old leg-pull, and he, of all people, having made so many old jokes in his time, ought not to complain. And it amused him to cap their joke, as it were, with one of his own; to let them see that he could keep his end up, even yet. So he said, with eyes twinkling: "Quite right, my boy. I wanted you to take tea with me. Will you—umph—sit down by the fire? Umph— I don't think I have seen your face before. How is that?"

"I 've only just come out of the sanatorium, sir—I 've been there since the beginning of term with measles."

"Ah, that accounts for it."

Chips began his usual ritualistic blending of tea from the different caddies; luckily there was half a walnut cake with pink icing in the cupboard. He found out that the boy's name was Linford, that he lived in Shropshire, and that he was the first of his family at Brookfield.

"You know—umph—Linford—you 'll like Brookfield—when you get used to it. It 's not half such an awful place—as you imagine. You 're a bit afraid of it—um, yes—eh? So was I, my dear boy—at first. But that was—um—a long time ago. Sixty-three years ago—umph—to be precise. When I—um—first went into Big Hall and—um—I saw all those boys—I tell you—I was quite scared. Indeed—umph—I don't think I 've ever been so scared in my life. Not even when—umph—the Germans bombed us—during the War. But—umph—it did n't last long —the scared feeling, I mean. I soon made myself—um—at home."

"Were there a lot of other new boys that term, sir?" asked Linford shyly.

"Eh? But—God bless my soul—I was n't a boy at all—I was a man— a young man of twenty-two! And the next time you see a young man—a new master—taking his first prep in Big Hall—umph—just think—what it feels like!"

"But if you were twenty-two then, sir—"

"Yes? Eh?"

"You must be—very old—now, sir."

Chips laughed quietly and steadily to himself. It was a good joke.

"Well—umph—I 'm certainly—umph—no chicken."

He laughed quietly to himself for a long time.

Then he talked of other matters, of Shropshire, of schools and school life in general, of the news in that day's papers. "You 're growing up into—umph—a very cross sort of world, Linford. Maybe it will have got over some of its—umph—crossness—by the time you 're ready for it. Let 's hope so—umph—at any rate. . . . Well . . ." And with a glance at the clock he delivered himself of his old familiar formula. "I 'm—umph—sorry—you can't stay . . ."

At the front door he shook hands.

"Good-bye, my boy."

And the answer came, in a shrill treble: "Good-bye, Mr. Chips. . . ."

Chips sat by the fire again, with those words echoing along the corridors of his mind. "Good-bye, Mr. Chips. . . ." An old leg-pull, to make new boys think that his name was really Chips; the joke was almost traditional. He did not mind. "Good-bye, Mr. Chips. . . ." He remembered that on the eve of his wedding day Kathie had used that same phrase, mocking him gently for the seriousness he had had in those days. He thought: Nobody would call me serious to-day, that 's very certain. . . .

Suddenly the tears began to roll down his cheeks—an old man's failing; silly, perhaps, but he could n't help it. He felt very tired; talking to Linford like that had quite exhausted him. But he was glad he had met Linford. Nice boy. Would do well.

Over the fog-laden air came the bell for call-over, tremulous and muffled. Chips looked at the window, graying into twilight; it was time to light up. But as soon as he began to move he felt that he could n't; he was too tired; and, anyhow, it did n't matter. He leaned back in his chair. No chicken—eh, well—that was true enough. And it had been amusing about Linford. A neat score off the jokers who had sent the boy over. Good-bye, Mr. Chips . . . odd, though, that he should have said it just like that. . . .

CHAPTER EIGHTEEN

When he awoke, for he seemed to have been asleep, he found himself in bed; and Merivale was there, stooping over him and smiling. "Well, you old ruffian—feeling all right? That was a fine shock you gave us!"

Chips murmured, after a pause, and in a voice that surprised him by its weakness: "Why—um—what—what has happened?"

"Merely that you threw a faint. Mrs. Wickett came in and found you—lucky she did. You 're all right now. Take it easy. Sleep again if you feel inclined."

He was glad someone had suggested such a good idea. He felt so weak that he was n't even puzzled by the details of the business—how they had got him upstairs, what Mrs. Wickett had said, and so on. But then, suddenly, at the other side of the bed, he saw Mrs. Wickett. She was smiling. He thought: God bless my soul, what 's she doing up here? And then, in the shadows behind Merivale, he saw Cartwright, the new Head (he thought of him as "new," even though he had been at Brookfield since 1919), and old Buffles, commonly called "Roddy." Funny, the way they were all here. He felt: Anyhow, I can't be bothered to wonder why about anything. I 'm going to go to sleep.

But it was n't sleep, and it was n't quite wakefulness, either; it was a sort of in-between state, full of dreams and faces and voices. Old scenes and old scraps of tunes: a Mozart trio that Kathie had once played in—cheers and laughter and the sound of guns—and, over it all, Brookfield bells, Brookfield bells. "So you see, if Miss Plebs wanted Mr. Patrician to marry her . . . yes, you can, you liar. . . ." Joke . . . Meat to be abhorred. . . . Joke . . . That you, Max? Yes, come in. What 's the news from the Fatherland? . . . *O mihi praeteritos* . . . Ralston said I was slack and inefficient—but they could n't manage without me. . . . *Obile heres ago fortibus es in aro* . . . Can you translate that, any of you? . . . It 's a joke. . . .

Once he heard them talking about him in the room.

Cartwright was whispering to Merivale. "Poor old chap—must have lived a lonely sort of life, all by himself."

Merivale answered: "Not always by himself. He married, you know."

"Oh, did he? I never knew about that."

"She died. It must have been—oh, quite thirty years ago. More, possibly."

"Pity. Pity he never had any children."

And at that, Chips opened his eyes as wide as he could and sought to attract their attention. It was hard for him to speak out loud, but he managed to murmur something, and they all looked round and came nearer to him.

He struggled, slowly, with his words. "What—was that—um—you were saying—about me—just now?"

Old Buffles smiled and said: "Nothing at all, old chap—nothing at all—we were just wondering when you were going to wake out of your beauty sleep."

"But—umph—I heard you—you *were* talking about me—"

"Absolutely nothing of any consequence, my dear fellow—really, I give you my word. . . ."

"I thought I heard you—one of you—saying it was a pity—umph —a pity I never had—any children . . . eh? . . . But I have, you know . . . I have . . ."

The others smiled without answering, and after a pause Chips began a faint and palpitating chuckle.

"Yes—umph—I have," he added, with quavering merriment. "Thousands of 'em . . . thousands of 'em . . . and all boys."

And then the chorus sang in his ears in final harmony, more grandly and sweetly than he had ever heard it before, and more comfortingly too. . . . Pettifer, Pollett, Porson, Potts, Pullman, Purvis, Pym-Wilson, Radlett, Rapson, Reade, Reaper, Reddy Primus . . . come round me now, all of you, for a last word and a joke. . . . Harper, Haslett, Hatfield, Hatherley . . . my last joke . . . did you hear it? . . . Did it make you laugh? . . . Bone, Boston, Bovey, Bradford, Bradley, Bramhall-Anderson . . . wherever you are, whatever has happened, give me this moment with you . . . this last moment . . . my boys . . .

And soon Chips was asleep.

He seemed so peaceful that they did not disturb him to say goodnight; but in the morning, as the School bell sounded for breakfast, Brookfield had the news. "Brookfield will never forget his lovableness," said Cartwright, in a speech to the School. Which was absurd, because all things are forgotten in the end. But Linford, at any rate, will remember and tell the tale: "I said good-bye to Chips the night before he died. . . ."

Random Harvest

"According to a British Official Report, bombs fell at Random."

—GERMAN OFFICIAL REPORT

PART ONE

On the morning of the eleventh of November, 1937, precisely at
eleven o'clock, some well-meaning busybody consulted his watch
and loudly announced the hour, with the result that all of us in
the dining car felt constrained to put aside drinks and newspapers
and spend the two minutes' silence in rather embarrassed stares at
one another or out of the window. Not that anyone had intended
disrespect—merely that in a fast-moving train we knew no rules for
correct behavior and would therefore rather not have behaved at
all. Anyhow, it was during those tense uneasy seconds that I first
took notice of the man opposite. Dark-haired, slim, and austerely
good-looking, he was perhaps in his early or middle forties; he wore
an air of prosperous distinction that fitted well with his neat but
quiet standardized clothes. I could not guess whether he had originally moved in from a third- or a first-class compartment. Half a
million Englishmen are like that. Their inconspicuous correctness
makes almost a display of concealment.

As he looked out of the window I saw something happen to his
eyes—a change from a glance to a gaze and then from a gaze to a
glare, a sudden sharpening of focus, as when a person thinks he rec-
ognizes someone fleetingly in a crowd. Meanwhile a lurch of the train
spilt coffee on the table between us, providing an excuse for apologies
as soon as the two minutes were over; I got in with mine first, but
by the time he turned to reply the focus was lost, his look of recognition unsure. Only the embarrassment remained, and to ease it
I made some comment on the moorland scenery, which was indeed
somberly beautiful that morning, for overnight snow lay on the summits, and there was one of them, twin-domed, that seemed to keep
pace with the train, moving over the intervening valley like a ghostly
dromedary. "That's Mickle," I said, pointing to it.

Surprisingly he answered: "Do you know if there's a lake—quite
a small lake—between the peaks?"

Two men at the table across the aisle then intervened with the
instant garrulousness of those who overhear a question put to someone else. They were also, I think, moved by a common desire to

talk down an emotional crisis, for the entire dining car seemed suddenly full of chatter. One said there *was* such a lake, if you called it a lake, but it was really more of a swamp; and the other said there wasn't any kind of lake at all, though after heavy rain it might be "a bit soggy" up there, and then the first man agreed that maybe that was so, and presently it turned out that though they were both Derbyshire men, neither had actually climbed Mickle since boyhood.

We listened politely to all this and thanked them, glad to let the matter drop. Nothing more was said till they left the train at Leicester; then I leaned across the table and said: "It doesn't pay to argue with local inhabitants, otherwise I'd have answered your question myself—because I was on top of Mickle yesterday."

A gleam reappeared in his eyes. "*You* were?"

"Yes, I'm one of those eccentric people who climb mountains for fun all the year round."

"So you saw the lake?"

"There wasn't a lake or a swamp or a sign of either."

"Ah. . . ." And the gleam faded.

"You sound disappointed?"

"Well no—hardly that. Maybe I was thinking of somewhere else. I'm afraid I've a bad memory."

"For mountains?"

"For names too. *Mickle,* did you say it was?" He spoke the word as if he were trying the sound of it.

"That's the local name. It isn't important enough to be on maps."

He nodded and then, rather deliberately, held up a newspaper throughout a couple of English counties. The sight of soldiers marching along a Bedfordshire lane gave us our next exchange of remarks—something about Hitler, the European situation, chances of war, and so on. It led to my asking if he had served in the last war.

"Yes."

"Then there must be things you wish you *had* forgotten?"

"But I have—even *them*—to some extent." He added as if to deflect the subject from himself: "I imagine you were too young?"

"Too young for the last, but not for the next, the way things are going."

"Nobody will be either too young or too old for the next."

Meanwhile men's voices were uprising further along the car in talk of Ypres and Gallipoli; I called his attention and commented that thousands of other Englishmen were doubtless at that moment reminiscing about their war experiences. "If you've already forgotten yours, you're probably lucky."

"I didn't say I'd forgotten *everything*."

He then told me a story which I shall summarize as follows: During the desperate months of trench warfare in France an English staff officer reasoned that if some spy whom the Germans had learned to trust were to give them false details about a big attack, it might have a better chance of success. The first step was to establish the good faith of such a spy, and this seemed only possible by allowing him, over a considerable period, to supply true information. Accordingly, during several weeks before the planned offensive, small raiding parties crawled across no man's land at night while German machine gunners, having been duly tipped off as to time and place, slaughtered them with much precision. One of these doomed detachments was in charge of a youth who, after enlisting at the beginning of the war, had just begun his first spell in the front line. Quixotically eager to lead his men to storybook victory, he soon found that his less-inspiring task was to accompany a few wounded and dying survivors into a shell hole so close to the enemy trenches that he could pick up snatches of German conversation. Knowing the language fairly well, he connected something he heard with something he had previously overheard in his commanding officer's dugout; so that presently he was able to deduce the whole intrigue of plot and counterplot. It came to him as an additional shock as he lay there, half drowned in mud, delirious with the pain of a smashed leg, and sick with watching the far greater miseries of his companions. Before dawn a shell screamed over and burst a few yards away, killing the others and wounding him in the head so that he saw, heard, and could think no more.

"What happened to him afterwards?"

"Oh, he recovered pretty well—except for partial loss of memory. . . . He's still alive. Of course, when you come to think about it logically, the whole thing was as justifiable as any other piece of wartime strategy. The primary aim is to frustrate the enemy's knavish tricks. Anything that does so is the thing to do, even if it seems a bit knavish itself."

"You say that defensively, as if you had to keep on convincing yourself about it."

"I wonder if you're right."

"I wonder if you're the survivor who's still alive."

He hesitated a moment, then answered with an oblique smile: "I don't suppose you'd believe me even if I said no." I let it go at that, and after a pause he went on: "It's curious to reflect that one's death was planned by *both* sides—it gives an extra flavor to the life one

managed to sneak away with, as well as a certain irony to the mood
in which one wears a decoration."

"So I should imagine."

I waited for him to make some further comment but he broke a
long silence only to summon the waiter and order a whiskey and
soda. "You'll have one with me?"

"No thanks."

"You don't drink?"

"Not very often in the morning."

"Neither do I, as a rule. Matter of fact, I don't drink much at all."

I felt that these trivial exchanges were to cover an inner stress
of mind he was trying to master. "Coming back to what you were
saying," I coaxed, eventually, but he interrupted: "No, let's *not* come
back to it—no use raking over these things. Besides, everybody's so
bored with the last war and so scared of the next that it's almost
become a social *gaffe* to bring up the matter at all."

"Except on one day of the year—which happens to be today. Then
the taboos are lifted."

"Thanks to the rather theatrical device of the two minutes' silence?"

"Yes, and 'thanks' is right. Surely we English need some release
from the tyranny of the stiff upper lip."

He smiled into his drink as the waiter set it before him. "So you
think it does no harm—once a year?"

"On the contrary, I think it makes a very healthy purge of our
normal—which is to say, our *abnormal*—national inhibitions."

Another smile. "Maybe—if you like psychoanalysts' jargon."

"Evidently *you* don't."

"Sorry. If you're one of them, I apologize."

"No, I'm just interested in the subject, that's all."

"Ever studied it—seriously?"

I said I had, which was true, for I had written several papers
on it for the Philosophical Society. He nodded, then read again for
a few score miles. The train was traveling fast, and when next he
looked up it was as if he realized that anything he still had to say
must be hurried; we were already streaking past the long rows of
suburban back gardens. He suddenly resumed, with a touch of his
earlier eagerness: "All right then—listen to this—and don't laugh . . .
it may be up your street. . . . Sometimes I have a feeling of being—
if it isn't too absurd to say such a thing—of being *half somebody else*.
Some casual little thing—a tune or a scent or a name in a newspaper
or a look of something or somebody will remind me, just for a second

—and yet I haven't time to get any grip of what it *does* remind me of—it's a sort of wisp of memory that can't be trapped before it fades away. . . . For instance, when I saw that mountain this morning I felt I'd been there—I almost *knew* I'd been there. . . . I could see that lake between the summits—why, I'd *bathed* in it—there was a slab of rock jutting out like a diving board—and the day I was there I fell asleep in the shade and woke up in the sun . . . but I suppose I've got to believe the whole thing never happened, just because you say there isn't a lake there at all. . . . Does all this strike you as the most utter nonsense?"

"By no means. It's not an uncommon experience."

"Oh, it *isn't?*" He looked slightly dismayed, perhaps robbed of some comfort in finding himself not unique.

"Dunne says it's due to a half-remembered dream. You should read his book *An Experiment with Time*. He says—this, of course, is condensing his theory very crudely—that dreams *do* foretell the future, only by the time they come true, we've forgotten them—all except your elusive wisp of memory."

"So I once dreamed about that mountain?"

"Perhaps. It's an interesting theory even if it can't be proved. Anyhow, the feeling you have is quite a normal one."

"I don't feel that it *is* altogether normal, the way I have it."

"You mean it's beginning to worry you?"

"Perhaps sometimes—in a way—yes." He added with a nervous smile: "But that's no reason why I should worry *you*. I can only plead this one-day-a-year excuse—the purging of the inhibitions, didn't you call it? Let's talk about something else—cricket—the Test Match. . . . Wonder what will happen to England . . . ?"

"Somehow today that doesn't sound like cricket talk."

"I know. After the silence there *are* overtones . . . but all I really wanted to prove was that I'm not a complete lunatic."

"Most people have a spot of lunacy in them somewhere. It's excusable."

"Provided they don't inflict it on strangers."

"Why not, if you feel you want to?"

"I don't want to—not consciously."

"Unconsciously then. Which makes it worst of all. Not that in your case it sounds very serious."

"You don't think so? You don't think these—er—peculiarities of memory—are—er—anything to worry about?"

"Since you ask me, may I be perfectly frank?"

"Of course."

"I don't know what your work is, but isn't it possible you've been overdoing things lately—not enough rest—relaxation?"

"I don't need a psychoanalyst to tell me that. My doctor does— every time I see him." ·

"Then why not take his advice?"

"*This* is why." He pulled a small notebook from his vest pocket. "I happen to be in what is vaguely called public life—which means I'm on a sort of treadmill I can't get off until it stops—and it won't stop." He turned over the pages. "Just to show you—a sample day of my existence. . . . Here, you can read it—it's typed." He added, as I took the book: "My secretary—very neat. *She* wouldn't let me forget anything."

"But she can't spell 'archaeological.' "

"Why does she have to?" He snatched the book back for scrutiny and I had the feeling he was glad of the excuse to do so and keep it. "Calderbury Archaeological and Historical Society? . . . Oh, they're my constituents—I have to show them round the House— guidebook stuff—an awful bore . . . that's this afternoon. This evening I have an Embassy reception; then tomorrow there's a board meeting, a lunch party, and in the evening I'm guest speaker at a dinner in Cambridge."

"Doesn't look as if there's anything you could cut except possibly tomorrow's lunch."

"I expect I'll do that, anyway—even though it's at my own house. There'll be a crowd of novelists and actors and titled people who'd think me surly because I wouldn't talk to them half as freely as I'm talking to you now."

I could believe it. So far he had made no move towards an exchange of names between us, and I guessed that on his side, the anonymity had been not only an encouragement to talk, but a temptation to reveal himself almost to the point of self-exhibition. And there had been a certain impish exhilaration in the way he had allowed me to glance at his engagement book for just those few seconds, as if teasing me with clues to an identity he had neither wish nor intention to disclose. Men in whom reticence is a part of good form have fantastic ways of occasional escape, and I should have been the last to embarrass an interesting fellow traveler had he not added, as the train began braking into St. Pancras: "Well, it's been a pleasant chat. Some day—who knows?—we might run into each other again."

Spoken as if he sincerely half meant it, the remark merely emphasized the other half sense in which he did not mean it at all;

and this, because I already liked him, irked me to the reply: "If it's the Swithin's Dinner tomorrow night we may as well introduce ourselves now as then, because I'll be there too. My name's Harrison. I'm on the Reception Committee."

"Oh, really?"

"And I don't know what your plans are, but after the show I'd be delighted if you'd come up to my rooms and have some coffee."

"Thanks," he muttered with sudden glumness, gathering up his newspapers and brief case. Then I suppose he realized it would be pointless, as well as discourteous, to refuse the name which I should inevitably discover so soon. He saved it for a last unsmiling afterthought as he jumped to the platform. "My name's Rainier . . . Charles Rainier."

*   *   *

Rainier nodded rather coldly when I met him again the following day. In his evening clothes and with an impressive array of decorations he looked what he was—a guest of honor about to perform his duties with the touch of apathy that so effectively disguises the British technique of authority. Not necessarily an aristocratic technique. I had already looked him up in reference books and found that he was the son of a longish line of manufacturers—no blue blood, no title (I wondered how he had evaded that), a public school of the second rank, Parliamentary membership for a safe Conservative county. I had also mentioned his name to a few people I knew; the general impression was that he was rich and influential, and that I was lucky to have made such a chance encounter. He did not, however, belong to the small group of well-known personalities recognizable by the man-in-the-street either in the flesh or in Low cartoons. On the contrary he seemed neither to seek nor to attract the popular sort of publicity, nor yet to repel it so markedly as to get in reverse; it was as if he deliberately aimed at being nondescript. A journalist told me he would be difficult to build up as a newspaper hero because his personality was "centripetal" instead of "centrifugal"; I was not quite certain what this meant, but Who's Who was less subtle in confiding that his recreations were mountaineering and music.

On the whole I secured a fair amount of information without much real enlightenment; I hoped for more from a second meeting and traveled to Cambridge in a mood of considerable anticipation. It was the custom of the secretary and committee of the Swithin's Society to receive guests informally before dining in the College Hall; so we gathered first in the Combination Room, where we made introduc-

tions, drank sherry, and exchanged small talk. It is really hard to
know what to say to distinguished people when you first meet them—
that is, it is hard to think of talk small enough to be free from pre-
sumption. Rainier, for instance, had lately been in the financial news
in connection with a proposed merger of cement companies, a
difficult achievement for which negotiations were still proceeding;
but it was impossible to say "How is your merger getting on?" as
one might say "How are your chrysanthemums?" to a man whom
you knew to be an enthusiastic gardener. Presently, to my relief,
some other guests arrived whom I had to attend to, and it was perhaps a quarter of an hour before I saw him edging to me through
the crowd. "Sorry," he began, "but I've got to let you down—awful
toothache—where's the nearest dentist?" I hustled him out as inconspicuously as possible and at the door of the taxi received his promise
to return to the dinner if he felt equal to it. Then I went back and
explained to the company what had happened. Somehow it did not
sound very convincing, and none of us really expected to see him
again. But we did. An hour later he took the vacant place we had
left at the High Table and was just in time to reply to the toast with
one of the best after-dinner speeches I had ever heard. Maybe the
escape from physical pain plus the Cambridge atmosphere, with its
mingling of time-honored formality and youthful high spirits, suited
a mood in which he began with badinage about toothache and ended
with a few graceful compliments to the College and University.
Among other things I remember him recalling that during his undergraduate days he had had an ambition to live at Cambridge all his
life, as a don of some sort (laughter), but exactly what sort he hadn't
stayed long enough to decide (laughter), because fate had called
him instead to be some sort of businessman politician, but even what
sort of *that* he hadn't yet entirely made up his mind (more laughter).
. . . "So because of this fundamental indecision, I still hope that some
day I shall throw off the cares of too many enterprises and seek the
tranquillity of a room overlooking a quadrangle and an oak that can
be sported against the world." (Prolonged laughter in which the
speaker joined.) After he had finished, we all cheered uproariously
and then, relaxing, drank and argued and made a night of it in the
best Swithin's tradition; when eventually the affair broke up, it was
Rainier himself who asked if my invitation to coffee still held good.

"Why, of course—only I thought maybe after the dentist you'd
feel—"

"My dear boy, don't ever try to imagine what my feelings are."

But he smiled in saying it, and I gathered he had forgiven not so much me as himself for having taken part in our train conversation. A few friends adjourned to my rooms near by, where we sat around and continued discussions informally. Again he charmed us by his talk, but even more by his easy manners and willingness to laugh and listen; long after most of the good-nights he still lingered chatting, listening, and smoking cigarette after cigarette. I didn't know then that he slept badly and liked to stay up late, that he enjoyed young company and jokes and midnight argument, that he had no snobbisms, and that public speaking left him either very dull and listless or very excitable and talkative, according to the audience. Towards three in the morning, when we found ourselves sole survivors, I suggested more coffee, and at that he sank into an armchair with a sigh of content and put his feet against the mantelpiece as if the place belonged to him—which, in a sense, it did, as to any Swithin's man since the reign of Elizabeth the Foundress. "I've been in these rooms before—often. Fellow with the disarming name of Pal had them in my time—'native of Asia or Africa not of European parentage,' as the University regulations so tactfully specify. High-caste Hindoo. Mathematician—genius in his own line—wonder what he's doing now?—probably distilling salt out of sea water or lying down in front of trains or some other blind-alley behavior. Used to say he felt algebra emotionally—told me once he couldn't read through the Binomial Theorem without tears coming into his eyes—the whole concept, he said, was so shatteringly beautiful. . . . Wish I could have got into his world, somehow or other. And there are other worlds, too—wish sometimes I could get into any of them—out of my own."

"What's so wrong about your own?"

He laughed defensively. "Now there you've got me. . . . Maybe, as you hinted yesterday, just a matter of overwork. But it's true enough that talking to all you young fellows tonight made me feel terribly ancient and envious."

"Not *envious*, surely? It's we who are envious of you—because you've made a success of life. We're a pretty disillusioned crowd when we stop laughing—we know there won't be decent jobs for more than a minority of us unless a war comes to give all of us the kind of job we don't want."

He mused over his coffee for a moment and then continued: "Yes, that's true—and that's probably why I feel how different everything is here instead of how much the same—because my Cambridge days *were* different. The war was just over then, and our side had won, and we all of us thought that winning a great war ought to mean something, either towards making our lives a sort of well-deserved happy-ever-after—a long golden afternoon of declining effort and increasing reward—or else to give us chances to rebuild the world this way or that. It all depended whether one were tired or eager after the strain. Most of us were both—tired of the war and everything connected with it, eager to push ahead into something new. We soon stopped hating the Germans, and just as soon we began to laugh at the idea of anyone caring enough about the horrid past to ask us that famous question on the recruiting posters—'What did you do in the Great War?' But even the most cynical of us couldn't see ahead to a time when the only logical answer to that question would be another one—'*Which* Great War?'

"There was a room over a fish shop in Petty Cury where some of us met once a week to talk our heads off—we called ourselves the Heretics, but I can't remember anything said at those meetings half so well as I can remember the smell of fish coming up from the shop below. And J. M. Keynes was lecturing in the Art School, politely suggesting that Germany mightn't be able to pay off so many millions in reparations, or was it billions?—in those days one just thought of a number and stuck as many naughts as one fancied after it. And there were Holland Rose on Napoleon and Pigou on Diminishing Returns, and Bury still explaining the Decline and Fall of the Roman Empire, and one evening Pal and I—sounds sentimental, doesn't it, Pal and I?—lined up in a queue that stretched halfway round Trinity Great Court to hear a lecture by a fellow named Eddington about some new German fellow named Einstein who had a theory about light bending in the middle—that brought the house down, of course—roars of laughter—just as you heard tonight only more so—good clean undergraduate fun at its best. And behind us on the wall the portrait of Catholic Mary scowled down on this modern audience that scoffed at science no less than at religion. Heretics indeed—and laughing heretics! But my pal Pal didn't laugh—he was transfixed with a sort of ecstasy about the whole thing.

"I did a good deal of reading on the river, and also at the Orchard at Grantchester—you remember Rupert Brooke's poem? Brooke would be fifty today, if he'd lived—think of that. . . . Still stands the clock at ten to three, but Rupert Brooke is late for tea—confined to his bed with rheumatism or something—that's what poets get for not dying young. The woman at the Orchard who served the teas remembered Brooke—she was a grand old chatterbox and once I got to know her she'd talk endlessly about undergraduates and professors past and present—many a yarn, I daresay, that I've forgotten since and that nobody else remembered even then. . . . Trivial talk—just as trivial as the way I'm talking to you now. Nineteen-twenty, that was—Cambridge full of demobilized old-young men still wearing dyed officers' overcoats—British warms sent up to Perth and returned chocolate-brown—full of men still apt to go suddenly berserk in the middle of a rag and turn it into a riot, or start whimpering during a thunderstorm—aftereffects of shell shock, you know. Plenty of us had had that—including myself."

"As a result of the head injury you mentioned yesterday?"

"I suppose so."

"You had a pretty bad time?"

"No, I was one of the lucky ones—comparatively, that is. But when you're blown up, even if you're not physically smashed to bits . . ." He broke off awkwardly. "I'm sorry. It isn't Armistice Day any more. These confessions are out of place."

"Not at all. I'm interested. It's so hard for my generation to imagine what it was like."

"Don't worry—you'll learn soon enough."

"How long was it before you were rescued?"

"Haven't the faintest idea. I suppose I was unconscious."

"But you must have recovered consciousness later?"

"Presumably. I don't remember when or where or any of the details. But I've some reason to believe I was taken prisoner."

"Reason to believe? That's a guarded way of putting it."

"I know—but it happens to be just about all I can say. You see, I literally don't remember. From that moment of being knocked out my memory's a complete blank till years later when I found myself lying on a park seat in Liverpool."

"*Years* later?"

"Getting on for three years, but of course I didn't know that at first. And it was a wet day, as luck would have it." He smiled. "You don't find my story very plausible?"

"I might if you'd tell me the whole of it—without gaps."

"But there *are* gaps—that's just the trouble."

"What were you doing in Liverpool?"

"Once again, I haven't the faintest idea. I didn't even know it was Liverpool at first. The main thing was to know *who* I was—where and when were easy enough to find out later."

"Do you mean you'd been going by some other name until then?"

"Maybe. I suppose so. That's another of the things I don't know. It's as if . . . well, I've sometimes worked it out this way—there were different rooms in my mind, and as soon as the light came on in one it had to go out in the other."

"Well, what did you do when you realized who you were?"

"What anybody else would do. I went home. I felt in my pockets and found I had a small sum in cash, so I bought a new outfit of clothes, took a bath at a hotel, and then went to the railway station. It was as simple as that, because along with knowing my own name it had come to me without apparent effort that I lived at Stourton, that my father owned the Rainier Steelworks and all the other concerns, that we had a butler named Sheldon, and any other details I cared to recall. In fact I knew all about myself in a perfectly normal way up to the moment of that shell burst near Arras in 1917."

"Your father must have got a very pleasant shock."

"He was too ill to be allowed it, but the family got one all right. Of course, since I'd been reported missing in the casualty lists, they'd long since given me up for dead."

"It's a very remarkable story."

"Remarkable's a well-chosen word. It doesn't give you away."

I thought for a moment; then I said: "But the Army authorities must have had some record of your coming back to England?"

"None—not under the name of Rainier."

"But wasn't there a disc or something you had to wear all the time on active service?"

"There was, but if you'd ever experienced levitation by high explosive you wouldn't put much faith in a bit of metal tied round your neck. It's quite possible there was nothing the Germans could identify me by when they took me prisoner."

"What makes you think you were ever in Germany at all?"

"Surely if I'd been dragged in by my own men they'd have known who I was?"

"H'm, yes, I suppose so."

He went on, after a pause: "I don't blame you at all if you don't believe a word of all this. And it's just as well you're the first person I've confided in for years—just as well for my reputation as a sober citizen." He laughed with self-protective cynicism. "It's been a conspiracy of events to make me talk like this—Armistice Day—our meeting on the train—and then something the dentist said tonight when I came out of his nitrous oxide."

"The dentist? What's he got to do with it?"

"He was making polite conversation while I spat blood. One of the things he said was, 'So you were a prisoner in Germany?' I asked him what gave him that idea, and he answered, 'Because I notice you have a tooth filled with a substitute metal German dentists were having to use during the latter part of the war'—apparently he'd come across other instances of it."

We were silent for a moment. I could hear the first stir of early morning traffic beginning along King's Parade. Rainier heard it too, and as at a signal rose to go. "A strange business, the war. The English told the Germans exactly where I was, so that the Germans could kill me . . . then the Germans did half kill me, patched me up, and saw that my teeth were properly cared for . . . after which the English gave me a medal for having displayed what they called 'conspicuous gallantry in the field.'" He fingered it on his lapel, adding: "I wear it at shows like this, along with the Most Noble Order of Something-or-Other which the Greeks gave me for arranging a loan on their currant crop in 1928." He began putting on his overcoat, heedless of my assurance that there was no hurry and that I often sat up till dawn myself. "Please don't bother to see me out—I'll take a bath at my hotel and be in time for the first train."

On his way across the room he paused at my shelves of books and asked what tripos I was taking.

"Economics. I took the first part of the History last year."

"Really? I did the same when I was here. But where does the psychoanalysis come in?"

"Oh, that's only a side line."

"I see. Made any plans for when you go down?"

"I'd like to be a journalist."

He nodded, shaking hands at the door. "Well, I've got a few contacts in Fleet Street. Write to me when you're ready for a job—I might be able to do something for you."

*   *   *

Early the following year I took a Ph.D. and began looking around for the post which, it seemed to me then, ought to drop snugly into the lap of any bright young man who had written a two-hundred-page thesis on "The Influence of Voltaire on the English Laissez-Faire Economists." Cambridge had deemed this worthy of a doctorate; nobody in Fleet Street, however, held it worth a regular job. I had a very small private income and could therefore afford to cadge snippets of highbrow reviewing from some of the more illustrious and penurious weeklies, reckoning myself well-paid if the books themselves were expensive and could be sold for more cash to Mr. Reeves of the Strand; but the newspaper world at that time was full of journalists out of work through amalgamations, and the chance of getting on the staffs of any of the big dailies was not encouraging.

Of course I remembered Rainier's offer, but apart from my reluctance to bother him, he was abroad—in South America on some financial business. But by the time he returned I had been disappointed often enough to feel I should take him at his word. He replied instantly to my note, asking me to lunch the next day.

Thus I made my first trip to Kenmore. "Near the World's End pub," Rainier used to say, and it was the fashion among certain guests to pretend it was at some actual world's end if not beyond it—the world in this super-sophisticated sense being that part of London within normal taxi range. I went by bus, which puts you down at the corner of the road with only a hundred yards or so to walk. I had no idea how notable, not to say notorious, those Kenmore lunches were; indeed, since the invitation had come so promptly, I had beguiled myself with visions of an intimate foursome composed of host and hostess with perhaps a press magnate summoned especially to meet me. I did not know then that Mrs. Rainier gave lunches for ten or twelve people two or three times a week, enticing every temporary or permanent celebrity to meet other temporary or permanent celebrities at her house, and that these affairs were as frequently joked about as they were infrequently declined. She functioned, in fact, as a kind of liaison officer between Society and Bohemia, with a Maecenas glance at moneyless but personable young men; and though there is no kind of social service I would less willingly undertake myself, there are few that I respect more when competently performed by someone else.

Searching my memory for impressions of that first arrival, I find I cannot put Mrs. Rainier into the picture at all. She was there, she must have been; but she was so busy making introductions that she could not have given me more than a few words, and those completely unimportant. I came a little late and found myself ushered into a drawing room full of initiates, all talking with great gusto, and all—so it seemed to me (quite baselessly, of course)—resentful of intrusion by a stranger who had neither written a banned novel nor flown somewhere and back in an incredibly short time. I say this because one of the guests *had* written such a novel, and another *had* made such a flight, and it was my fate to be seated between them while they talked either to their outside neighbors or across me to each other. There was an empty place at the head of the table, and presently I gathered from general conversation that Rainier often arrived late and sometimes not at all, so that he was never on any account waited for. I had already written off the whole affair as a rather profitless bore when the guests rose, murmured hasty goodbyes, and dashed out to waiting cars and taxis. (Mrs. Rainier's lunches were always like that—one-fifteen sharp to two-fifteen sharp and not too much to drink, so that you did not kill your afternoon.) Just as I was following the crowd, a touch on my arm accompanied the whisper: "Stay a moment if you aren't in a hurry."

Mrs. Rainier led me a few paces back along the hall after the others had gone. "I didn't quite catch your name—"

"Harrison."

"Oh yes. . . . You're a friend of Charles's—it's too bad he couldn't get here—he's so busy nowadays."

I murmured something vague, polite, and intended to be reassuring.

"It's a pity people who can fly halfway round the world haven't any manners," she went on, and I answered: "Well, I suppose there are quite a number of people who have manners and couldn't fly halfway round the world."

"But having manners is so much more important," she countered. "Tell me . . . what . . . er . . . I mean, are you a . . . let me see . . . *Harrison* . . ."

I smiled—suddenly and rather incomprehensibly at ease with her. "You're trying to recall a Harrison who's written something, married somebody, or been somewhere," I said. "But it's a waste of time— I'm not *that* Harrison, even if he exists. I'm just—if I call myself anything—a journalist."

"Oh . . . then you must come again when we have really *literary* parties," she replied, with an eagerness I thought charming though probably insincere. I promised I would, with equal eagerness, and every intention of avoiding her really *literary* parties like the plague. Then I shook hands, left the house, and on the bus back to Fleet Street suddenly realized that it had been a very good lunch from one point of view. I had never tasted better eggs Mornay.

The next afternoon Rainier telephoned, profuse in apologies for his absence from the lunch, and though the matter could hardly have been important to him, I thought I detected a note of sincerity. "I gather you didn't have a very good time," he said, and before I could reply went on: "I'm not keen on the mob, either, but Helen's a born hostess—almost as good as an American—she can take in twenty new names all in a row and never make a mistake."

"She didn't take in mine. In fact it was pretty clear she didn't know me from Adam."

"My fault, I expect. Must have forgotten to tell her."

"So a perfect stranger could walk into your house and get a free lunch?"

"They're doing that all the time—though most of 'em have invitations. . . . Look here, if you're not busy just now, why not come over to the House for tea?"

I said I would, and took the bus again to Chelsea. But at Kenmore the maid told me that Rainier hadn't been in since morning and never by any chance took tea at home; and just then, while we were arguing on the doorstep (I insisting I had been invited less than twenty minutes ago), Mrs. Rainier came up behind me and began to laugh. "He meant the House of Commons," she said, passing into the hall. "You'd better let my car take you there."

Extraordinary how stupid one can be when one would prefer to impress by being knowledgeable. I knew quite well that the House of Commons, along with the Stock Exchange and Christchurch, Oxford, was called "the House," yet somehow, when Rainier had used the phrase over the telephone, I could only think of Kenmore. Most of the way to Westminster in the almost aggressively unostentatious Daimler (so impersonal you could believe it part of an undertaker's fleet), I cursed my mistake as a poor recommendation for any kind of job. I had feared Rainier might be waiting for me, and was relieved when, after sending in my name, I had to kill time for half an hour before a policeman led me through devious passages to the Terrace, where Rainier greeted me warmly. But his appearance was slightly disconcerting; there was a twitch about his mouth and eyes as he spoke, and a general impression of intense nervous energy in desperate need of relaxation. During tea he talked about his South American trip, assuming far too modestly that I had read nothing about it in the papers. Presently the division bell rang and only as we hurried across the Smoke Room did he broach the matter I had really come about. "I inquired from a good many people after I got your letter, Harrison, but there doesn't seem to be a thing doing in Fleet Street just now."

"That was my own experience too."

"So I wondered if you'd care for a secretary's job until something else turns up?"

I hadn't really thought about such a thing, and maybe hesitation revealed my disappointment.

He said, patting my arm: "Well, think it over, anyway. I've had a girl up to now, but she's due to get married in a few weeks—time enough to show you the ropes . . . that is, of course, if you feel you'd like the job at all. . . ."

*   *   *

So I became Rainier's secretary, and Miss Hobbs showed me the ropes. It had been flattery to call her a girl. She was thin, red-faced, middle-aged, and so worshipful of Rainier that no husband could hope to get more than a remnant of any emotion she was capable of; indeed, I felt that the chance of marriage was tempting her more because she feared it might be her last than because she was certain she wanted it. She hinted this much during our first meeting. "I almost feel I'm deserting *him*," she said, and the stress on "him" was revealing. Presently, showing me how she filed his correspondence, she added: "I'm so relieved he isn't going to have another *lady* secretary. I'd be afraid of some awful kind of person coming here and—perhaps—*influencing* him."

I said I didn't imagine Rainier was the type to be influenced by that kind of woman.

"Oh, but you never know what kind of woman will influence a man."

We went on inspecting the filing system. "The main thing is to see he doesn't forget his appointments. He doesn't do much of his correspondence here—he has another secretary at his City office. So it won't matter a great deal if you don't know shorthand and typewriting."

I said I did know shorthand and typewriting.

"Well, so much the better, of course. You'll find him wonderful to work with—at least *I* always have, though of course we're more like old friends than employer and secretary. I call him Charles, you know, when we're alone together. And he always calls me Elsie, whether we're alone or not. We've been together now for nearly fifteen years, so it's really quite natural, don't you think?"

During the next few hours she gave me her own version of the entire Rainier ménage. "Of course the marriage never has been all it should be—I daresay you can imagine that. Mrs. Rainier isn't the right kind of wife for a man like Charles. He's so tired of all those parties she gives, especially the house-parties at Stourton—that's their big place in the country, you know . . . they have no children—that's another thing, because he'd love children, and I don't know why they don't have them, maybe there's a reason. When you've worked with him for a time you'll feel how restless he is—I do blame her for *that*—she doesn't give him a proper home—Kenmore's just a hotel with different guests every day. I do believe there's only one room he feels really comfortable in, and that's this one—with his poor little secretary slaving away while he smokes—and he shouldn't smoke either, so he's been told. . . . D'you know, he often locks himself in when he wants to work, because the rest of the house is so full of Goyas and Epsteins and whatnot that people wander in and out of all the rooms as if it were a museum. Of course there really are priceless things in it—why not?—he gives her the money to spend, and I suppose she has taste—that is if you *like* a house that's like a museum. I sometimes wonder if Charles does."

After a pause during which I made no comment she turned to the writing desk. "Charles gets hundreds of letters from complete strangers—about one thing and another, you know. If they're abusive we take no notice—in fact, whatever they are, *he* doesn't bother much about them, but I'll let you into a secret—something he doesn't suspect and never will unless you tell him, and I'm sure you won't—I always write a little note of thanks to anyone who sends a *nice* letter . . . of course I write as if he'd dictated it. . . . I really think a good secretary *should* do little things like that on her own, don't you?"

I said nothing.

"Really, if he were to ask me to stay, I believe I would, marriage or no marriage—I mean, it would be so hard to refuse him anything—but then, he's too fine and generous to ask—as soon as he knew about it he urged me not to delay my happiness on his account—just as if his own marriage had brought *him* happiness. . . . Not that Charles would be an easy man to *make* happy, even if he *had* got the right woman. But he isn't happy *now*—that I *do* know—there's always a look in his eyes as if he were searching for something and couldn't find it."

For two or three days Miss Hobbs continued to show me the ropes; Rainier was away in Lancashire. During this time Mrs. Rainier gave several lunch parties to which I was not invited, though I was in the house at the time and was even privileged to give assistance to a foreign plenipotentiary who spoke little English and had strayed into the study in search of a humbler apartment. I could better understand after that why Rainier sometimes locked the door.

Then he returned, having wired me to meet his train at Euston. As soon as we had found a taxi and were driving out of the station he asked me how I'd been getting on, and added without waiting for an answer: "I don't suppose you'll find it hard to be as good as your predecessor."

I said I should certainly hope to be.

"Then you've already found out a few of the things I've been putting up with?"

"Yes, but not why you *have* put up with them, for so many years."

"Pure sentiment, plus the fact that I've always had a submerged sympathy with crazy people, and Elsie's crazy enough. She used to work at Stourton in my father's time, then she worked for my brother, and when he naturally wanted to get rid of her there was no one fool enough to take her but me. I made her my social secretary—because in those days I had no social life and it didn't matter. But after I married there were social things for her to do and she did them with a peculiar and fascinating idiocy. D'you know I've found out she writes long letters to people I've never heard of and signs my name to them? . . . And by the way, did she tell you I'm not happy with my wife?"

"Well—er—"

"Don't believe it. My wife and I are the best of friends. I suppose she also hinted it was a marriage of convenience?"

I felt this was incriminating Miss Hobbs too much and was beginning a noncommittal answer when he interrupted: "Well, *that* happens to be true. I married her because it seemed to me she'd be just the person to turn a tired businessman into a thumping success. She *was* and she *did*. . . . Can you think of a better reason?"

"There's generally considered to be *one* better reason."

He switched the subject suddenly, pointing out of the window to a news placard that proclaimed, in letters a foot high: "Collapse of England." At that moment I felt that one thing Miss Hobbs had said about him *was* true—that look in his eyes as if he were searching for something and couldn't find it. He began to talk rapidly and nervously, apropos of the placard: "Odd to think of some foreigner translating without knowing it's only about cricket . . . it was something you said about that on a train that first made me want to know you better—but really, in a sense, it doesn't refer to cricket at all, but to how God-damned sure we are of ourselves—you can't imagine the same phrase in the streets of Paris or Berlin—it would begin panic or riots or something. . . . Just think of it—'*Débâcle de France*' or '*Untergang Deutschlands.*' . . . Impossible . . . but here it means nothing because we don't believe it could ever happen—and that's not wishful thinking—it's neither wishing nor thinking, but a kind of inbreathed illusion. . . . Reminds me of that last plenary session of the London Conference when it was quite clear there was to be no effective disarmament by anybody and we were all hard at work covering up the failure of civilization's last hope with a mess of smeary platitudes . . . Lord, how tired I was, listening to strings of words that meant nothing in any language and even less when you

had to wait for an interpreter to turn 'em into two others . . . and
all the time the dusty sunlight fell in slabs over the pink bald heads
—godheads from the power entrusted to them and gargoyles from
the way I hated 'em . . . and during all that morning, full of the
trapped sunlight and the distant drone of traffic past the Cenotaph,
there was only one clean eager thing that happened—young Drexel
whispering to me during a tepid outburst of applause: 'See the old
boy in the third row—fifth from the end—Armenia or Irak or some
place . . . but did you ever see anybody more like Harry Tate?'
. . . And by Jove, he *was* like Harry Tate, and Drexel and I lived on
it for the rest of the session—lived on it and on our own pathetic
fancy that foreigners were strange and at best amusing creatures,
rather like music-hall comedians or one's French master at school—
tolerable if they happen to be musicians or dancers or ice-cream
sellers—but definitely to be snubbed if they venture on the really
serious business of governing the world. . . . Look—there's another!"
It was a later placard, proclaiming in letters equally large, "England
Now without Hope." Rainier laughed. "Maybe some fussy archae-
ologist of the twenty-fifth century—a relative of Macaulay's sketching
New Zealander—will dig this up from a rubbish heap and say it es-
tablishes definite proof that we'd all been well warned in advance!
. . . Has my wife got a party tonight?"

"Yes."

"What sort of a crowd?"

"Mostly sporting and dramatic, I think."

"Then I'll dine and sleep at the Club. Borotra's the only dramatic
sportsman I care about, and he probably won't come."

He put his head out of the cab window, giving the change of address, and also telling the man to drive more slowly. I could see he
was nervously excited, and I was beginning to know by now that
when he was in such a mood he talked a good deal in an attempt
to race his thoughts—an attempt which usually failed, leaving a litter
of unfinished sentences, mixed metaphors, and unpolished epigrams,
with here and there some phrase worthy of one of his speeches, but
flung off so carelessly that if the hearer did not catch it at the time
Rainier himself could never recall it afterwards. I have tried to give
an impression of this kind of talk, but even the most faithful reportage would miss a curious excitement of voice and gesture, the or-
chestration of some inner emotion turbulent under the surface. Nor,
one felt, would such emotion wear out in fatigue, but rather increase
to some extinguishing climax as an electric globe burns brighter be-

fore the final snapping of the filament. It was of this I felt suddenly afraid, and he noticed the anxious look I gave him.

"Sorry to be a chatterer like this, Harrison, but it's after a bout of public speech-making—I always feel I have to use up the words left over, or perhaps the words I couldn't use. . . . I suppose you'd call me a rather good speaker?"

I said I certainly should.

"And you'd guess that it comes easily to me?"

"It always sounds like it."

He laughed. "That's what practice can do. I *loathe* speaking in public—I'm always secretly afraid I'm going to break down or stammer or something. Stammering especially . . . of course I never do. . . . By the way, you remember that mountain in Derbyshire I thought I recognized?"

"Yes."

"The same sort of thing happened in Lancashire, only it wasn't quite so romantic. Just a house in a row. I was helping Nixon in the Browdley by-election—we held meetings at street corners, then Nixon dragged me round doing the shake-hands and baby-kissing stuff—that's the way his father got into the Gladstone Parliaments, so Nixon still does it. I admit I'm pretty cynical about elections—the very look of the voting results, with two rows of figures adding neatly up to a third one, gives me the same itch as a company balance sheet, exact to the last penny . . . whose penny? Was there ever a penny? . . . My own majority in Lythamshire, for instance—precisely twelve—but who *were* the twelve? Twelve good men and true, maybe, or twelve drunken illiterates . . . ? Don't you sometimes feel how *false* it all is, and how falsely reassuring—this nineteenth-century gloss of statistical accuracy, as if the flood tide of history could run in rivulets tidy enough for garden irrigation, safe enough for a million taps in suburban bathrooms . . . but when the storm does come, who'll give a damn if the rows of little figures still add up—who'll care if the sums are all wrong provided one man knows a right answer?"

"You were talking about a house."

"Oh yes. . . . Just an ordinary four-room workingman's house—tens of thousands like it. A cold day, and as we stood waiting at the door I could see a great yellow glow of firelight behind the lace curtains of the parlor window. Nothing extraordinary in that, either, and yet . . . it's hard to describe the feelings I had, as if that house were waiting for me—a welcome—out of the wintry dusk and into the warm firelight . . . a welcome home."

His eyes were full of eagerness, and I said, trying to hasten his story before we reached the end of the journey: "Did the feeling disappear when a stranger answered the door?"

"I'm coming to that. . . . There were three of us, Nixon, myself, and Ransome, the local party secretary, nice little man. We knocked and knocked and nobody came. Then I saw Ransome fumbling in his pocket. 'Can't think where she is,' he said, 'but I expect she'll be back in a jiffy.' I realized then that it was *his* house, and that we were being invited in. He found a key, unlocked the door, and we entered. No lobby or hall—straight into the warmth and firelight. There was a kettle steaming on the hob, cups and saucers set out, plates of bread and butter. Everything spotlessly neat, furniture that shone, a clock ticking loudly somewhere. It was all so beautiful, this warm small room. The man kept talking about his wife—how proud she'd been at the thought of having two such men as Nixon and myself to tea in her home—such an honor—she'd never forget it—and how embarrassed she'd be when she came back and found us already there. 'I'll bet she's gone round the corner for a Dundee cake,' he laughed. But as time passed he began to be a bit embarrassed himself, and presently suggested having tea ourselves without waiting for his wife. So we did—I sat in a rocking chair by the fireside, and the flames were still leaping up so brightly we didn't need any other light, even though it was quite dark outside by the time we left."

"So you never saw his wife at all?"

"No, she didn't come back in time. . . . But that room—the feeling I had in it—of comfort, of being *wanted* there. . . . It's just another thing of the same kind. That part of my life—well, you remember what I told you at Cambridge."

"Why do you worry about it so much?"

"I wouldn't if it would leave me alone. But it keeps on teasing me —with clues. So what can I do?"

"I still say—more rest and less work."

He patted my arm. "It's good to know I can talk to you whenever I'm in this mood. Watson to my Sherlock, eh? Or perhaps that's not much of a compliment?"

"Not to yourself, anyhow. Watson was at least an *honest* idiot."

He smiled. "That must be the Higher Criticism. Of course you were born too late to feel as I did—Sherlock's in Baker Street, all's right with the world."

"Since we now realize that most things are wrong with the world—"

"I know—that was part of the illusion. I remember Sheldon taking me on a trip to London when I was six or seven years old . . . the first place I asked to see was Baker Street, and being a sympathetic fellow he didn't tell me that the stories were just stories. We walked gravely along the pavement one afternoon early in the century—a small boy and his father's butler—looking up at the tall houses with respectful hero worship. Distant thrones might totter, anarchists might throw bombs, a few lesser breeds might behave provokingly in odd corners of the world, but when all was said and done, there was nothing to fear while the stately Holmes of England, doped and dressing-gowned for action, readied his wits for the final count with Moriarty! And who the deuce *was* this Moriarty? Why, just a big-shot crook whom the honest idiot romanticized in order to build up his hero's reputation! Nothing but a middle-aged stoop-shouldered Raffles! And that, mind you, was the worst our fathers' world could imagine when it talked about Underground Forces and Powers of Evil! . . . Ah well, happy days. You'd better keep the cab to go home in. Good night!"

*   *   *

I hadn't taken Rainier's problem very seriously till then. For one thing, loss of memory is normal. We all forget things, and are equally likely to be reminded of them long after we think they have been forgotten for good. Often, too, the reminder is faint enough to be no more than a clue which we fail to follow up because the matter does not seem important. The unusual part of Rainier's experience was that he *did* think it important, so that from something merely puzzling it was already on the way to becoming an obsession.

Some part of his story could doubtless be verified, and I already felt enough curiosity to make the attempt. I said nothing to him, but the next time the chance occurred I led Miss Hobbs to talk in a general way about her employer's early life and career. She was more than willing—except for a continual tendency to drift into later and somewhat disparaging gossip about Mrs. Rainier. "Wasn't he in the war?" I began, putting the leading question that anyone might have asked.

"Oh yes. He got a medal—didn't you know that? And the strange thing was—they thought he was dead. So it was given post—post—"

"Posthumously."

"Yes, that's it. But you couldn't blame them, because after the attack he was reported missing and nothing was heard about him till—oh, it was years later when he suddenly arrived home without any warning. And then it turned out he'd lost his memory."

"Seems to me the sort of story for headlines."

"You mean in the papers? Oh no, it was kept out—the family didn't want any publicity."

"That wouldn't have been enough reason for most of the journalists I know."

"Ah, but Sheldon arranged it."

"Sheldon?"

"He's the butler at Stourton. You haven't been to Stourton yet, have you?"

"No."

"It's really a marvelous place."

"Sheldon sounds a marvelous butler if he knows how to stop journalists from getting a good story and editors from printing it."

"Well, he *is* rather marvelous, and I don't suppose there's much he doesn't know—not about the family, anyhow. He really rules Stourton—lives there all the year round, even during the winter when the family never go out of town. I really owe him a good deal—I was only just a local girl in those days, I used to do bookkeeping and secretarial work at the house, and that brought me into contact with Sheldon constantly." She added, rather coyly: "You know—perhaps you don't know—how difficult it can be for a girl employed in a big house if the butler isn't all he should be."

I said I could imagine it.

"Sheldon was always a gentleman. Never a word—or a gesture—that anyone could object to."

I said nothing.

"And later, when Mr. Charles took over Stourton, Sheldon personally asked him if he could do anything for me, otherwise I don't suppose I'd be here."

"I see. . . . But coming back to the time when Mr. Rainier—*our* Mr. Rainier, I mean—suddenly returned to Stourton. Were you working there then?"

"Not *just* then. It was Christmas and as old Mr. Rainier was ill they canceled the usual parties and gave me a holiday. It was parties that always kept me busy—writing out invitations and place cards and things."

"What was Mr. Rainier like when he returned?"

"I didn't see him till a good while afterwards, but I do know there was a lot of trouble about it, one way and another—Sheldon would never tell us half that went on."

So there the trail ended; she didn't know much of what had actually happened; and since then a great many years had passed, old Mr. Rainier was dead, and probably the same fate had overtaken most of the personnel from whom any elucidating inquiries might have been made at the time. Perhaps there were traces somewhere, a dossier preserved in forgotten files, memoranda hidden away in official archives; but there seemed small chance of unearthing them, or even of finding if they existed at all.

"Quite a mystery," I commented. "Didn't Mr. Rainier himself ever try to solve it?"

"You mean, did he try to remember things?"

"Well, more than that—didn't he ever consult anybody—specialists, psychoanalysts, or anyone?"

"You don't know him, or you wouldn't ask that. The last thing he'd ever do is to go to anybody and tell them things about himself. The only person he ever did talk to was someone he'd known at Cambridge, some professor—Freeman, I think his name was."

"You mean *Dr.* Freeman—*the* Dr. Freeman?"

"Maybe he was a doctor."

"A tall white-haired man with a stoop?"

"Yes, that was him—he used to visit Charles a good deal before the marriage. You know him?"

"Slightly. Why not since the marriage?"

"He didn't like parties, and I don't think he liked Mrs. Rainier for beginning all that sort of life for Charles. She's very ambitious, you know. People say she'll make him Prime Minister before she's finished."

I laughed—having heard similar remarks myself, followed as a rule by some ribald comment on her party-giving technique. Miss Hobbs added: "Not that she isn't a good hostess—that I *will* say."

Since the point was raised, it seemed to me that Mrs. Rainier was *too* good, and that for this reason she might miss the secret English bull's-eye that can only be hit by guns sighted to a 97 or 98 per cent degree of accuracy. Anything more than that, even if achievable, is dangerous in England, because English people mistrust perfection, regarding it in manners as the stigma of foreigners, just as they suspect it in teeth to be the product of dentistry. All this, of course, I did not discuss with Miss Hobbs.

I saw Freeman a few days later. He had been a rather impressive figure at Cambridge, in my time as well as Rainier's, but had recently retired to live at Richmond with an unmarried sister. It was probably a lonely life, and he seemed glad to hear my voice on the telephone and to accept an invitation to dinner. I had known him fairly well, since he had long been president of the Philosophical Society and I in my last year its vice president, and though he had written several

standard works on psychology he was not psychologist enough to
suspect an ulterior motive behind my apparent eagerness to look
him up and talk over old times.

We met at Boulestin's that same evening.

After waiting patiently till the inevitable question as to what I
was doing with myself nowadays, I said that I had become Rainier's
secretary.

"Ah, Rainier—yes," he muttered, as if raking over memories. And
he added, with a thin cackle: "Well, history won't repeat itself."

"How do you mean?"

"He married one of them."

"You mean *Mrs.* Rainier? You mean she was his secretary before
Miss Hobbs?"

"Oh, the Hobbs woman was with him all the time—a family heir-
loom. Must be forty now, if she's a day. What did she do at last—
retire?"

"She's leaving to get married."

"Heavens—I never thought her turn would come. Who's the lucky
man? . . . But I can answer that myself—Rainier is, to get rid of her."

"You know her then?"

"Hardly at all, I'm glad to say. But she used to write me the most
ridiculous notes whenever Rainier made an appointment to see me.
They were supposed to be from him, but I found out quite casually
afterwards that she forged his name to 'em. . . . *Absurd* notes—it
interested me, as a psychologist, that she should have thought them
appropriate."

"But to come back to Mrs. Rainier—"

"Oh, she worked in his *City* office, I think. A different dynasty.
These great magnates have platoons of secretaries."

"Queer Miss Hobbs never mentioned it. I should have thought it
was something she'd have liked to drive home."

"On a point of psychology I think you're wrong. She'd prefer to
conceal the fact though they were both, so to say, equal at the start-
ing post, the other woman won."

"Maybe. I gather you know Rainier rather well?"

"I used to. You see, I began with the initial advantage of meeting him anonymously."

"I'm not quite clear what you mean."

He expanded over a further glass of brandy. "Rainier's a peculiar
fellow. He has a curious fear of his own identity. He lets you get to
know him best when he doesn't think you know who he is. . . . It's
an interesting kink, psychologically. I first met him through Werneth,

who was his tutor at St. Swithin's. Apparently he told Werneth about —er—well, perhaps I ought not to discuss it, but it was something interesting to me—as a psychologist—but not particularly to Werneth, who was a mere historian." Again the cackle. "Anyhow, Werneth could only get his permission to pass it on to me by promising not to divulge his name, and on hearing what it was all about I was so interested that we actually arranged a meeting—again anonymously —I wasn't supposed to know who he was. . . . But I'll let you into a secret—Werneth *had* told me, privately, beforehand—unscrupulous fellow, Werneth. And then one morning several months later I couldn't find my bicycle outside the college gate after a lecture, but in its place was a similar model with the name 'Charles Rainier' on it. I make his mistake an excuse to call on him—and I must say—after the opening embarrassment—we very soon became friends." He added: "And now, of course, I know what you're going to ask me, but being less unscrupulous than Werneth I can't tell you."

"I don't think you need, because I already know about Rainier's— er—peculiarity. I suppose it *was* that."

"Suppose you tell me first of all what *that* is."

"The blank patch in his life that he can't remember."

"A rather inexact description."

"No doubt, and that's why I'd very much like to hear your own."

He smiled. "It was an unusual case—but I've heard of several similar ones. They're recorded, you know, in technical journals. Rainier had—if one might so put it—certain threads of recollection about the blank period, though they were so faint as to be almost nonexistent at first. After he left Cambridge we didn't meet again for ten years— by that time the threads had become a little less faint. It was my aim, when I came to know Rainier again after the ten-year interval, to sort out those threads, to disentangle them—to expand them, as it were, into a complete corpus of memory."

"I understand. But you didn't succeed."

"Are you asking me that or telling me?"

"Both, in a way."

He said, smiling: "My expectation all along had been that his full memory would eventually return—a little bit here, a little bit there —till finally, like a key turning in a lock, or like the last few pieces of a jigsaw puzzle, the whole thing would slip into position. But I gather that it hasn't yet happened?"

"The bits are still being assembled, but nowhere near to completion."

"Tell me, Harrison, if I may ask the question—why are you taking such a keen interest in this matter? Hardly within the scope of secretarial duties. . . . Or *is* it?"

"I like him and I hate to see him bothered by it as he still is. That's the only reason."

"A good one."

"Now *you* tell *me* something—have you any theories about the blank patch?"

"Theories? I can only guess it was a pretty bad time. He was injured, if I remember rightly, just above the left parietal bone of the . . ." He went off into a medical survey that conveyed nothing to me. "It was an injury that would require operative treatment—perhaps a series of operations. That's why it's perhaps a pity that he still bothers, as you say he does. Even if complete recollection were to return to him now, it would probably be only of pain, unhappiness, boredom."

"On the other hand, even such memories might be better than an increasing obsession about the loss of them?"

"Possibly."

We were silent for a time after that. Presently I said: "You know he was taken prisoner by the Germans?"

"Oh yes. But German or English—all hospitals are unhappy places, especially for a man who can't tell anyone who he is. I imagine the Germans treated him namelessly or by error under someone else's name, and eventually returned him to England under the same condition. Then there would be other hospitals in England, full of experiences nobody would wish to remember. There were a great many shell-shock and loss-of-memory cases that took years—some of them are still taking years, God help them. The whole thing happened so long ago I don't see how we can ever expect to know all the details. Tell me *your* theory, if you have one."

"That's the trouble, I haven't."

"The real trouble, of course, is Mrs. Rainier."

Curious, the way people sooner or later led the talk to her. Freeman, reticent at first about a former friend, saw no reason now to conceal his opinion of a former friend's wife. "She's an unusual sort of woman, Harrison."

"Well, he's not so usual, either."

"They get on well together? Is that your impression?"

I answered guardedly: "I think she makes a good politician's wife."

"And I suppose, by the same token, you think he makes a good politician?"

"He has some of the attributes. Clever speaker and a good way with people."

"When he's in the mood. He isn't always. . . . Did you ever hear about the Bridgelow Antiquarian Dinner?"

I shook my head.

"It was—oh, several years ago. He was supposed to be helping the candidate, and during the campaign we asked him to our annual beano—strictly non-party—just a semi-learned society, with the accent on the semi. I was president at the time, and Rainier was next to me at the table. Halfway through his speech, which began pretty well, there was a bit of a disturbance caused by old General Wych-Furlough fumbling in late and apologizing—his car had broken down or something. He talked rather loudly, like most deaf people, and of course it *was* annoying to a speaker, but the whole incident was over in a minute, most people would have passed it off. Rainier, however, seemed to freeze up suddenly, couldn't conceal the way he felt about it, finished his speech almost immediately and left the table rather sooner than he decently could. I went out with him for a moment, told him frankly I thought his behavior had been rather childish—surely age and infirmity entitled people to some latitude—it wasn't as if there'd been any intentional discourtesy. He said then, in a rather panicky way: 'It wasn't that—it was something in the fellow himself—something chemical, maybe, in the way we react to each other.' I thought his explanation even more peculiar than his behavior."

I checked myself from commenting, and Freeman, noticing it, said: "Go on—what was it you were going to ask?"

"I was just wondering—is it possible he had one of those submerged memories—of having met the General before?"

"I thought of that later on, but it didn't seem likely they could ever have met. He didn't even know the General's name. And if they *had* met before, I still can't think of any reason for antagonism—the old boy was just a fussy, simple-minded, stupid fellow with a distinguished military career and a repertoire of exceptionally dull stories about hunting."

"Was Mrs. Rainier at the dinner?"

"No, she wouldn't come to anything *I* was president of—that's very certain." He added, as if glad to get back to the subject: "A strange woman. I'm not sure I altogether trust her—and that isn't because I don't particularly like her. It's something deeper. She always seems to me to be hiding something. I suppose it's part of my job to have

these psychic feelings about people. . . . You know about her famous parties?"

"Who doesn't? I've sampled them."

"Mind you, let's be fair. She's not a snob in the ordinary sense—I
mean about birth or money. Of course it would be too ridiculous
if she were—since she began with neither herself. But what exactly *is*
it that she goes for? Brains? Celebrity? Notoriety? I went to Kenmore
once, and I must admit she plays the game loathsomely well. But all
this relentless celebrity-hunting and party-giving doesn't make a
home—and I'm damned if I know what it *does* make."

"Some people say it's made Rainier's career."

"I've heard that too—from people who don't like him. The people
who don't like *her* will tell you her methods have actually held him
back. Still, I don't deny she's a good mate for a man of affairs. The
real point is whether Rainier's life ought to be cluttered up with
business and politics at all."

"What do you mean?"

"Simply that I've always considered him—abstractly—one of the
rare spirits of our time, so that success of the kind he has attained
and may yet attain becomes a detestable self-betrayal."

"So you think the marriage was a mistake?"

"Not at all, if he felt he had to have that sort of life."

"What other sort of life *could* he have had?"

"Out of my province to say. I'm talking about the *quality* of the
man, not his opportunities. I suppose it wasn't his fault his father left
him a small industrial empire to look after—steelworkers and newspapers and interlocking holding companies and whatnot—all more
or less bankrupt, though people didn't know it at the time. Even the
seat in Parliament was a sort of family inheritance he had to take
over."

"Like Miss Hobbs?"

"Yes, like *her*—just as idiotic but not so loyal. He only scraped in
by twelve votes last time. . . . But since you mention the Hobbs
woman, let me assure you she's a modernistic jewel compared with
the old butler they keep at Stourton . . . Sheldon, I think his name
is."

"You don't like him either?"

Freeman shrugged. "It isn't that I mind his eccentric impertinences
—Scottish servants are like that and one takes it from them—even
Queen Victoria had to. What makes me really uncomfortable is the
same feeling I have about Mrs. Rainier—that he's hiding something."

"Maybe they're hiding something together?"

His smile was of another kind and did not answer mine. "You haven't been to Stourton yet, have you? It's an amazing hiding place for anything they've got to hide."

*   *   *

Miss Hobbs left during the week that followed and I settled down to the task of becoming her successor. It was not quite as simple as she had led me to believe. Rainier's interests were manifold; besides holding directorships of important companies he was a member of many societies and organizations—all this, of course, on top of his political work. I had plenty to do, and he expected it done quickly and efficiently. We had little chance to talk on other than business matters, and for the time he seemed to have dropped completely the preoccupation that had begun to interest me. One thing happened that I had not after Freeman's remarks anticipated: Mrs. Rainier invited me to another of her lunch parties. This time it was really *literary*, as she had promised (Maurice Baring, Charles Morgan, Louis Bromfield, Henry Bernstein, Mrs. Belloc Lowndes, H. G. Wells, and a pale young man whose name I have forgotten who wrote highbrow detective novels whose names I have also forgotten), and despite initial misgivings I found the whole affair quite pleasant. Once more there was the empty chair for Rainier, if he should turn up, but he failed to, and nobody seemed surprised. Again also Mrs. Rainier asked me to stay a moment after the others had gone, but now the request was less remarkable, since I had work in the same house. "Can you spare time to look at my garden?" she said, leading me to the back of the hall where the French windows were open.

We sauntered across the lawn to a door in the high surrounding wall; unlocking it, she watched my face as I showed surprise, for within was a second garden, not much bigger than a large room, but so enclosed by trees and carpeted with flowers that one could hardly have believed it to exist in the middle of a London borough. "It's a secret," she confided. "I only show it to close friends—or to those who I hope are going to be."

I murmured something polite that might equally have referred to her last remark or to the garden itself.

"You see," she went on, "I never cared for Miss Hobbs. I don't think Charles did, either, but he was too kind to get rid of her. If she told you things against me, and I'm sure she did, just suspend judgment till you know me better."

I went on saying polite things.

"You and Charles first met on a train, didn't you?" She stooped to a vase. "One of those chance meetings—I've had them myself—when you tell all your secrets to a perfect stranger because you're certain you'll never meet him again. . . . Something like that?"

I said guardedly: "I don't know about secrets, but we certainly found it easy to talk."

"And you like your work here?"

"Very much."

"I'm glad. It will be wonderful if you can really help Charles—apart from just office work. He needs the right sort of companionship sometimes—he has difficult moods, you know. Or perhaps you don't know—*yet*. Anyhow, the thing to do is not to take him too seriously when he has them." I waited for her to continue, knowing that she too was waiting for me; even if I were willing to suspend judgment I was also, like Freeman, unwilling to trust her completely. She suddenly smiled. "Well, now you know *my* secret. Keep it for me." And she added, leading me back through the doorway: "*This*, I mean. It used to be the place where the gardener threw all the rubbish. I planned it myself—I do most of the work here still. Charles never looks in—hasn't time. Hasn't time for my lunches either—not that I mind that so much, but I do wish—sometimes—I'd find him sitting here—quietly—alone—like men you sometimes see outside their cottages in the country—at peace. He never is, you know."

I felt she would like to tell me something if I already knew enough to make it advisable, but she wasn't certain I did know, so she hesitated. I asked her why she thought he was never at peace.

"For one thing, he's so terribly overworked."

"Yes, I know, but apart from that?"

"Oh, well, it's hard for anyone to feel at peace these days. Don't you think so?"

"What about the men you sometimes see outside their cottages in the country?"

She smiled, suddenly on the defensive, sure now that I didn't know as much as she had half suspected, and for that reason anxious not to give me any further opening. "They're probably not really at peace at all—just too old and tired to worry about things any more." As we entered the house the social manner closed about her like the fall of a curtain. "Now that we're becoming friends you must come to Stourton for week ends as soon as we open it up. There's a *real* secret garden there—I mean one that everybody knows about."

* * *

I hadn't expected Stourton to be quite so overwhelming. We drove there a few weeks later in four Daimlers—"like a high-speed funeral," said Rainier, who was in a macabre mood altogether; three of them packed with luggage and servants from Kenmore, the first one containing ourselves and an elegant young man named Woburn, who was coming to catalogue the Stourton library. Most guests would arrive the following day—perhaps twenty-odd: politicians, peers, actors, novelists, crack tennis players, celebrities of all kinds. It was a warm morning and as we drove through Reading and Newbury the sun broke through the haze and kindled the full splendor of an English summer, with its ever-changing greens under a dappled sky.

Presently we turned off the main road and curved for a mile between high hedges; then suddenly, in a distant fold of the downs, a vision in cream-colored stone broke through heavy parkland trees. Woburn, who had not seen it before, joined me in a little gasp of admiration. "You were intended to do that," said Rainier. "In fact the architect and roadbuilder conspired about it two hundred years ago. My brother Julian, who fancied himself as a phrase maker, once called it 'a stucco prima donna making a stage entrance.' Now, you see, it goes out of sight." Intervening upland obscured the house for another mile or so until, at a new turn of the road, it reappeared so much more intimately that one could only give it a nod of respectful recognition. "But here we are again, and for the rest of the way we simply have to give it all the stars in Baedeker." We swooped into the final half-mile stretch that ended in a wide Palladian portico. "A house like this is like some kinds of women—too expensive even to cast off. Of course what you really pay for isn't the thing itself, but the illusion—the sense of ownership, the intangible Great I Am. Nowadays a bankrupt illusion—the farms don't pay, the hills that belong to me are just as free for anyone else to roam over, the whole idea of *possessing* this place is just a legal fiction entitling me to pay bills. I think it would sooner possess me, if I'd let it. . . . Hello, Sheldon."

Sheldon was waiting on the top step to welcome us. Neither plump nor cadaverous, obsequious nor pompous, he shook the hand that Rainier offered him, bowed to Mrs. Rainier, and gave Woburn and myself a faintly appraising scrutiny until Rainier made the introductions. Then he said: "Well, Mr. Harrison, if this is your first visit to Stourton it probably won't be your last. Mr. Rainier keeps his secretaries a long time." The remark struck me as rather offhandedly familiar as well as a somewhat gauche reminder of Mrs. Rainier's former position, but there was a general laugh, from which I gathered that Sheldon enjoyed privileges of this kind, perhaps on account

of age. He was certainly a well-preserved antiquity, with an air of
serene yet somehow guarded responsibility; in different clothes he
might have looked a cabinet minister, in contradistinction to those
cabinet ministers who, even in their own clothes, look like butlers.

By the time I had been shown to my room in the East Wing
(Stourton, like every grand house of its period, had to have wings)
the sun was almost down over the rim of the hills and the slow magic
of a summer twilight was beginning to unfold; through my window
the vista of formal gardens and distant skyline was entrancingly
beautiful. I was admiring it as Rainier entered with Woburn, whom
he had been showing round the library. "I hope you don't object to
views," he said. "I know it's the latest artistic fad to consider them
rather vulgar. I put in these large windows myself, against all the
advice of architects who said this sort of house shouldn't have them.
Otherwise, except for a few extra bathrooms, I haven't touched the
place."

Behind the two of them stood Sheldon, announcing that our baths
were ready; Rainier turned then and led us across the corridor into
an extraordinary room of Moorish design embellished with fluted
columns and Arabic gargoyles and a high domed ceiling. He watched
our faces and seemed to derive a certain satisfaction. "My father
built this," he explained, "as what he called an extra billiard room.
He made the bulk of his fortune during the Edwardian era, when
the social hallmark was to have a billiard room, and during the last
year of the war, when money was coming in so fast he didn't know
what to do with it, he conceived the idea of an *extra* billiard room
as a symbol of utter superfluity. . . . At least, that's the only theory
I can imagine. I don't think a single game of billiards was ever played
in it, and I turned it into a bathhouse without any feeling of impiety."
We passed through the room, which was furnished with divans and
sun-ray lamps, into a further apartment containing a row of small
but quite modern cubicle bathrooms, three of which Sheldon was
already preparing for our use. "There were only four bathrooms in
the entire house before I made these," Rainier continued. "One was
in the servants' quarters and Sheldon had actually paid for it out of
his own pocket. That gives you some idea of the times, even as late
as 1919." He added, after a pause and another glance at our faces:
"And of my father too—I know that's what you're thinking. But it
wasn't really niggardliness. He gave a great deal during his lifetime
to the more orthodox charities. What he mostly suffered from was a
few strikingly wrong notions. One of them was doubtless that servants
didn't need bathrooms. Another was that he was really an English

gentleman. And another was that the remaining saga of mankind would be largely a matter of tidying up the jungle and making the whole earth a well-administered English colony under a Liberal government. I think when the war ended he assumed that's what was going to be done to Germany."

"Maybe it should have been," said Woburn quietly. He had done little but smile until then, and I noticed Rainier give him a look of sharpened interest. Then we went into our respective cubicles, but the walls were only neck-high and conversation rose easily with the steam. I could hear Rainier and Woburn veering onto a political argument, while in my own cubicle Sheldon, arranging towels, saw me notice the slightly brown color of the water as it filled the tub. "Won't harm you," he remarked. "We tell some of our guests it's due to mineral springs that are good for rheumatism, but as you're one of the family I'll let you into a family secret—*it's just the rust in the pipes.*"

He was going out chuckling when I retorted, quite without secondary meaning: "I hope all the family secrets are as innocent."

The chuckle ended sharply as he turned on me a look that evidently reassured him, for his mouth slanted into a slow smile as he resumed his exit. "I trust you will find them so, Mr. Harrison."

Meanwhile Rainier had come back to the subject of Stourton, and I heard him saying to Woburn: "My father bought it after it had bankrupted the Westondales, and the Westondales inherited it from ancestors who had built it out of profits from the African slave trade. This made my father's purchase almost appropriate, since my great-great-grandfather made his pile out of the first steam-driven cotton mills in Lancashire. You may imagine Stourton, therefore, peopled with the ghosts of Negroes and little children."

A short while later we dressed and dined in the vast room that would have seated fifty with ease, instead of our four selves. Mrs. Rainier, I noticed, was particularly gracious to Woburn, whom she probably felt to be shy in surroundings of such unaccustomed grandeur. There was talk of how he would set about the library-cataloguing job; most of the books, it appeared, had been taken over from the Westondales along with the house. "My father was not a great reader, but he had a curious knack of reading the right things. One day he read that some pine forests in Hampshire were supposed to be healthy to live amongst, so he promptly bought several hundred acres of them—on which part of Bournemouth now stands. Quite an interesting man, my father. He played the cornet, and he also cried

over all Dickens's deathbed scenes—Little Nell and Paul Dombey
especially. He liked to have them read to him, for preference, and
his favorite reader was an old governess of mine named Miss
Ponsonby, who hated him and used to come out of one of those tear-
ful séances muttering 'The old humbug!' But he *wasn't* altogether a
humbug—at least no more than most of us are. I'm not quite certain
what he was. . . . Somebody ought to write a really good biography
of him some day. He did have one written just before he died, but
it was a commissioned job and made him into a not very convincing
plaster saint—and, of course, it would be easy to write the other sort,
showing him as a sinister capitalistic villain. . . . But in between,
somewhere, is probably the truth—if anyone thought it worth while
to make the search."

"Why shouldn't Mr. Woburn try?" asked Mrs. Rainier.

"Not a bad idea, if he wants to. But let him finish the cataloguing
first. Ever write anything, Woburn?"

"A few stories, Mr. Rainier. You read one of them—probably you've
forgotten it—"

"Ah yes, of course. The one about the unfortunate Russian?"

Woburn nodded, and the somewhat mysterious reference was not
explained. After coffee Mrs. Rainier said she was tired and would
go to bed; Rainier mentioned letters he had to write; so there seemed
nothing left for Woburn and me but to pass the evening together,
somehow or other.

Sheldon suggested the library, ushering us into the fine somber
room with a touch of evident pride, and obligingly switching on a
radio in time for the news summary of a Hitler speech delivered in
Berlin earlier that day. We listened awhile, then Woburn snapped
off the machine with a gesture—the meager residuum of protest to
which modern man has been reduced. "I hope there isn't a war this
year," he remarked, as one hoping the weather would stay fine. "You
see, as soon as I finish this job I have another with the Kurtzmayers—
they have a big collection at Nice and I daresay I shall spend all
the autumn there—unless," he added with a half-smile, "Mr. Hitler's
plans interfere with mine." I smiled back with a touch of the uncom-
fortableness that afflicts me when some facetious travel-film com-
mentator refers to "Mr. and Mrs. Hippopotamus" and waits for the
laugh. I was thinking of this, and also wondering how a youngster
like Woburn (at least ten years my junior) had managed to establish
this cataloguing racket amongst the rich and eminent, when he dis-
armingly told me all about it. "It was the Rainiers who gave me an

introduction to the Kurtzmayers—they've been rather good at putting things in my way."

I asked him how long he had known the Rainiers.

"Only a few months. And you?"

"About two years. I met him first—quite by accident—in a train."

"I met him first in a public library."

"By accident?"

"No, I had a job there and he came to see me. Mrs. Rainier sent him."

"*Mrs.* Rainier?"

"Yes, I met her before him. It was her idea I should do the Stourton job—that's why she sent him to see me."

"I should have thought she'd have asked you to see him."

"So should I, but it seems he had a queer idea he wanted to see me first without either of us knowing who the other was, so that if he didn't like me the whole thing could be dropped."

"I see."

"Haven't you ever noticed that for all his glib speech and ease of manner he's really shy of meeting new people—in a rather odd way?"

I said perhaps I had, and asked him how his own meeting had happened.

"He didn't have far to come—the library was only just across the river in Lambeth. Of course I took him for just an ordinary visitor. He first of all asked at the counter if we had any illustrated books on English villages. It's the sort of vague request you fairly often get from people, so I picked a few books off the shelves and left him at a table with them. Presently he handed them back with a few words of thanks, and out of politeness I then asked if he'd found what he'd been looking for. He said, well no, not exactly—he'd just thought the pictures and photographs in some illustrated book might happen to include one of a place he'd once seen but had forgotten the name of. They hadn't though, and it didn't matter."

"You must have thought it curious."

"Yes, but the really curious thing was that I'd just written a short story based on a similar idea. He seemed quite interested when I told him this and we talked on for a while—then finally he stared round rather vaguely and said, 'I'm supposed to see a man who works here called Woburn.' I said I was Woburn and he pretended to be surprised and pleased, but somehow I felt he had known all the time, though his pleasure seemed genuine. He then said his wife had talked about me and thought I might do some cataloguing, and of course he had to say then who he was. I told him I'd be very glad, and he said that was fine, he'd let me know; then he shook hands hurriedly and left."

"Did he let you know?"

"Not immediately. After a few weeks I wrote to him, because I really wanted the job if I could get it—I was only earning three pounds a week. Of course I'd found out all about him in the interval —about his Fleet Street interests—that's really why I sent him that short story I'd written, because I thought maybe he'd pass it on to one of his editors." Woburn smiled. "He returned it a few days later, without comment, but said I could begin the cataloguing any time I liked."

"Tell me about the story."

"Oh, it was nothing much—just a rather feeble yarn about a Russian soldier returning from the front after the Revolution."

"What happened to him?"

"Nothing exciting. He just roamed about the country trying to find where he lived."

"Had he—had he lost his memory?"

"No, he was just a simple fellow—couldn't read and write—all he could give was the name of the village and a description of it that might equally have applied to ten thousand other Russian villages. The government officials wouldn't bother with him, because he couldn't fill out the proper forms, so he just had to go on wandering vaguely about trying to find the place."

"And did he—eventually?"

"He was run over by a train and carried to a neighboring village where he died without knowing that it actually was the one he'd been looking for . . . of course you might have guessed that."

"Having read Gogol and Chekhov, I think I might."

"I know, it was just an imitation. I haven't any real originality— only a technique. I suppose Rainier realized that. So I'd better stick to the catalogues."

It seemed to me a courageous, but also a rather desolate thing for a young writer to admit.

"Why not try the biography, if they give you the chance?"

"I might, but I doubt if it would work out. You can't be sure they'd really *want* anyone to be impartial. That's why it's an affectation of Rainier's to run down his ancestors. A sort of inverted snobbery put on to impress people because the direct kind isn't fashionable any more. . . . Mind you, I like him *immensely*."

"And her?"

"Oh, she's marvelous, isn't she? The way she can remember dozens of names when she introduces people. . . ." I remembered Rainier had once commented on that too. But Woburn added: "Rather a mistake, though, in English life—never to make a mistake. Like knowing too much—such as the names of all the states in America. Stamps one as a bit of an outsider."

"You seem to have sized things up pretty well."

"Probably because I *am* an outsider."

"So am I. So are most of the people who come here. So are half the names in Debrett. Come to think about it, that's one healthy symptom of English so-called society—its inside is full of outsiders."

"I suppose the Rainiers are outsiders—in a sense."

"Well, they haven't a title, but that makes no difference. Owning Stourton's almost a title in itself."

"Yes, it's a wonderful place. There's an odd atmosphere here, though, don't you think?"

"Do *you* think so?"

"You don't know everything, you don't know everything—that's what the place seems to say."

"Maybe those ghosts of Negroes and little children?"

"They haven't got any children, have they?"

"No."

"Did they ever have?"

"I don't know. One somehow doesn't get to know things like that."

"Do you think they're happy?"

Before I could attempt an answer we both turned sharply to see Sheldon carrying in a tray with siphon, glasses, and whiskey decanter. "I thought perhaps you two gentlemen might like to help yourselves, either now or later." Without offering to serve us he placed the tray on a table and walked out of the room, pausing at the door to deliver a quizzical good night.

We returned the salutation and then, as soon as the door closed, looked at each other rather uneasily. "I didn't hear him come in," said Woburn, after a pause. "He didn't knock."

"Good servants don't—except at bedroom doors."

"Oh? I don't know things like that. My mother never had a servant."

"Now who's being an inverted snob? My mother had *one* servant, whom we called the skivvy. That sets us both pretty equal so far as Stourton's concerned."

"You probably went to a good school, though."

I mentioned the name of my school and agreed that it was generally considered fairly good. "As good as Netherton, which is where

Rainier went. Anyhow, from a social angle, the main thing is the accent—which you and I both seem to have. Nobody's going to ask us where we picked it up."

"I don't mind if they do. I was at a board school up to the age of twelve—then I won a scholarship to a suburban grammar school. I took a London degree last year, working in the evenings. I never try to conceal the truth."

"*Conceal* it? I should think you'd boast about it."

"I suppose that's really what I *am* doing. Will you have a drink?"

"Yes, please."

He began to mix them and presently, while working off a certain embarrassment, added: "How does that fellow Sheldon strike you?"

I said I thought he was the kind of person one could avoid a decision about by calling him a character. "Maybe the keeper of the family skeleton," I added.

"No—because if there were one, Rainier would take a perverse delight in dragging it out of the cupboard for everyone to stare at."

We laughed and agreed that that might well be so.

It was past eleven before we yawned our way upstairs. When I reached my room I found it full of cool air and moonlight; in the vagrant play of moving curtain shadows I did not at first see Rainier sitting by the window in an armchair. He spoke as I approached: "Don't let me scare you—I'm only admiring your view. It's exactly the same as mine, so that isn't much of an excuse. . . . How did you and Woburn get along?"

"Quite well. I like him. An intelligent young fellow."

"Spoken with all the superiority of thirty to twenty?"

"No, I don't think so. I *do* like him, anyhow."

"He's my wife's protégé. She wants to see him get on in the world— made me root him out of a municipal library to do this card-indexing job. . . . Yes, he might go far, as they say, if there's anywhere far to go these days."

"That's the trouble, and he probably realizes it as much as we do."

"Well, we can't change the world for him, but it's nice to have him around—company for Helen, if nothing else. I like him too, for that matter. I like most boys of his age—and of your age. Wish I had an army of 'em."

"What would you do with an army of them?"

"Something better, I hope, than have them catalogue books or write biographies of my ancestors." He read my thoughts enough to continue: "I daresay you're rather surprised at my lack of enthusiasm for the family tree. That may be because I didn't have a very satis-

factory home life. When I was a small boy my father was just something distant and booming and Olympian—a bit of a bully in the
house, or at least a bit of a Bultitude (if you remember your *Vice-
Versa*)—all of which made it fortunate for the family that he wasn't
much in the home at all. My mother died when I was ten."

"But you liked *her?*"

"I loved her very dearly. She was a delicate, soft-voiced, kind-
hearted, sunny-minded, but rather helpless woman—but then most
women would have been helpless against my father. *He* loved her,
I've no doubt, in his own possessive way. Perhaps a less loving and
more thoughtful husband would have sent her to a warmer climate
during the winters, but my father wasn't thoughtful—at best his
thoughtlessness became comradely, as when he insisted on taking her
for brisk walks over the hills on January days. It was a cherished
saying of his that fresh air would blow the cobwebs out of your lungs.
It also blew the life out of my mother's lungs, for it was after one
of those terrible walks, during which she gasped and panted while
my father shouted Whitmanesque encouragement, that she called
in Sanderstead, our local doctor, who diagnosed t.b. My father was
appalled from that moment and spent a small fortune on all kinds of
cures, but it was too late—she died within the year, and my father,
I have since felt, promptly did something about her in his mind that
corresponded to winding up or writing off or some other operation
that happens even in the best financial circles."

He suddenly stood up and moved to the open window, staring out
as if facing something that challenged him. "Those are the hills where
he made her walk. You can see the line of them against the sky."
Then he turned abruptly and said he was sure I was tired and would
want to go to bed.

I assured him I wasn't sleepy at all.

"But you came in yawning."

"Maybe, but I'm wide-awake now. The breeze is so fresh. . . . You
must have hated your father."

He answered slowly: "Yes, I suppose I did. Freud would say so,
anyhow. But of course when I was a boy and even up to my undergraduate days people only admitted the politer emotions."

"The war changed all that."

"Yes, indeed, and so many other things too."

He was silent for a moment; then I went on: "You once told me
about a certain day, sometime after the war ended, when you found
yourself on a park seat in Liverpool."

"When did I tell you that?" He controlled a momentary alarm, then added with a smile: "Ah, yes, I remember—in your rooms at St. Swithin's. I'm always garrulous after public speeches. . . . Well, if I told you, you know. That's how it was. And don't ask me about anything *before* the park seat because I can't answer."

"But how about *after* the park seat?"

He seemed relieved. "*After?* Oh, I can stand any amount of cross-examination there—I'm on safe ground from about noon on December 27, 1919."

"I wish you'd begin your story there, then, and bring it up to date."

"But there *is* no story—except my life story."

"That's what I'd like to hear."

"How I Made Good? From Park Seat to Parliament?"

"If you like to call it that."

He laughed. "It's mostly a lot of sordid business details and family squabbles. You don't know the family, either."

"All the same, I wish you'd tell me. The effort of setting it all out might even help you towards the other memory—if you're still anxious for it."

I could see the response to that in his eyes as he entered the light again.

"So you really think memory's like an athlete—keep it in training—take it for cross-country runs? H'm, might be something in the idea. When do we start?"

"Now, if you're not too sleepy. I'm not. . . . Go back to that park seat in Liverpool."

"But I told you about that once."

"Tell me again. And then go on."

So he began, and as it makes a fairly long story, it goes better in the third person.

PART TWO

He found himself lying on that park seat. He had opened his eyes to see clouds and drenched trees, and to feel the drops splashing on his face. After a while his position began to seem more and more odd, so he raised himself to a sitting angle, and was immediately aware of sodden clothes, stiff limbs, a terrific headache, and a man stooping over him. His first thought was that he must have been drunk the night before, but he soon rejected it, partly because he could not remember the night before at all, partly because he somehow did not think he was the sort of young man to have had that sort of night, but chiefly because of a growing interest in what the man stooping over him was saying. It was a kind of muttered chorus—"That's right, mister—take it easy. Didn't 'ardly touch yer—it was the wet roadway, you sort o' slipped. Cheer up, mister, no bones broke—you'll be all right—wouldn't leave you 'ere, I wouldn't, if I didn't know you'd be all right. . . ."

Presently, suggested by the muttered chorus and supported by the fact that his clothes were not only sopping wet but also muddied and torn, another hypothesis occurred to him—that he had been run down by a car whose driver had brought him into the park and was now leaving him there.

But *where?* His brain refused an answer, and when pressed offered a jumble of memories connected only with war—shellfire for headaches, a smashed leg for stiffness, no man's land for all the mud and rain in the world.

He stood up, feeling dizzy, swayed and almost fell. The man had gone, was now nowhere to be seen. Then he noticed he had been lying down on sheets of newspaper. He stooped to peel one off the seat, hoping it might afford some clue, but the top of the page that would have contained a name and date was an unreadable mush, and the rest was rapidly softening under the heavy rain. He peered at it, nevertheless, searching for some helpful word or phrase before the final disintegration. Most of the letterpress seemed to be news about floods and flood damage—rescues from swollen rivers, people stranded in upper floors, rowboats in streets, and so on.

Then suddenly his eyes caught a paragraph headed "Rainier Still in Germany"—one of those mock-cheerful items that tired sub-editors put in to fill an odd corner—something about soaked holiday crowds taking comfort from the thought that somebody somewhere was faring even worse.

Now it is curious how one's own name, or the name of one's home, or a word like "cancer," will sometimes leap out of a page as if it were printed in red ink. It was like that for the young man as he staggered through the deserted park towards a gate he could see in the distance. *Rainier Still in Germany—Rainier Still in Germany*. It was a challenge, something he had to answer; and the answer came. "*Impossible*—I'm *here*, reading a newspaper, and the newspaper's in English—therefore this can't be Germany."

Presently he passed through the park gate into a busy thoroughfare. A tram came along, mud-splashed to its upper windows and sluicing swathes of water from the rails to the gutters. It was difficult to see through the spray of mud and rain, but on the side of the tram as it passed by he could just read the inscription—"Liverpool City Corporation."

He walked along by the high railings till the park came to an end and shops began. Meanwhile he had been feeling in his pockets, finding money—coins and several treasury notes, amounting in all to over four pounds. Reaching a news agent's shop he went inside and asked for a paper.

"*Post* or *Courier*, sir?"

"Doesn't matter."

A paper was handed over. "Looks like you've had a fall, sir? Terribly slippery after all this rain. . . . Like me to give you a bit of a brush?"

"Er . . . thanks."

"Why, you're wet through—if I was you I'd get home and to bed as quick as I could. Like me to get you a cab?"

"No, that wouldn't help. I don't live here. But if there's a tailor nearabouts—"

"Two doors ahead, sir. He'll fix you up. Say I sent you."

"Thanks."

He walked out, glancing at the paper as he did so. He saw that the date was December 27, 1919.

So now he knew three important things: *Who*, *Where*, and *When*.

Two hours later Charles Rainier was in a train to London. He had had a hot bath and a meal; his clothes did not fit well, but were dry;

and after a lightning headache-cure across a chemist's counter he felt somewhat drowsily relieved.

Beside him were several more newspapers and magazines. As it was the end of December, some contained résumés of the events of 1919; and these at first he had found very astonishing. Biggest of all surprises was to find that the war had been over for more than a year and had ended in complete victory for the Allies; this was surprising because his last recollected idea on the subject had been that the Allies were just as likely to lose. But that dated back to a certain night in 1917 when he lay in a shell hole near Arras, half delirious with the pain of a smashed leg, watching shell after shell dig other holes round about him, until finally one came that seemed to connect by a long dark throbbing corridor with his headache that morning.

Charles arrived in London towards dusk, in time to catch the last train that would get him to Stourton that night. The train was late in reaching Fiveoaks, which is the station for Stourton, and three miles away from it, as anyone knows who has ever received a letter on Stourton notepaper. From Fiveoaks he walked, because all the cabs were taken before he reached the station yard, and also because he hoped the cold air might clear that still-surviving headache. He was glad they were putting out the lamps as he gave up his ticket at the barrier, so that the collector did not recognize him.

He realized that his return was bound to come as a shock, and he hardly knew what reason he could give anyone for his long and peculiar absence; he hardly knew yet what reason he could give himself. He was puzzled, too, by an absence of joy in his heart at the prospect of home and familiar faces; more than by any excitement he was possessed by a deep and unutterable numbness of spirit, a numbness so far without pain yet full of the hint of pain withdrawn and waiting.

Presently he turned off the main road. He remembered that turn, and the curve of the secondary road over the hill to the point where suddenly, in daylight, the visitor caught his first glimpse of the house. Often, as a boy, he had met such visitors at Fiveoaks, hoping that when they reached that particular point of the drive they would not be so immersed in conversation as to miss the view.

Now when he came to the view there was nothing to see, nothing to hear but an owl hooting, nothing to feel but the raw air blowing from the uplands.

He was glad he had sent no wire to tell them of his arrival. He had refrained because he felt the shock might be greater that way than if he were to see Sheldon first, and also because he hardly knew how

much or how little to say in a wire; but now he perceived another
advantage in not having sent any message—it preserved for a few
extra minutes the curious halfway comfortableness of being alive
only in the first person singular.

Towards midnight he reached the wrought-iron gates of the main
entrance; they were closed and locked, of course, but there was a
glow in one of the adjacent windows, and as he approached the small
square-built lodge a gap in a curtain revealed a lighted Christmas
tree. Odd, because he remembered Parsloe as a tight-fisted bachelor
unlikely to spend money on that sort of thing—unless, of course, he
had married in the interval; but that was odder still to contemplate—
Parsloe married!

It was not Parsloe, however, who opened the door to his persistent
ringing, but a half-dressed stranger—middle-aged, suspicious, challenging.

"Well, young man?"

"I'd like to go up to the house, if you'll let me through."

"We don't admit anyone, not without you give your name and
business."

"I know, but you see . . ." He hesitated, realizing the difficulties
ahead—his story, told cold with no corroborations, would sound
sheerly incredible. Eventually he added, rather weakly: "If Parsloe
were here, he'd know me."

"Maybe he would, but he ain't here—having been dead these fifteen months. You'd better be off, sir, dragging people out of bed at
this hour."

The "sir" was some progress anyway; a social acknowledgment
that, drunk or sober, honest or fraudulent, at least one had the right
accent.

"Perhaps I could see Sheldon, then—"

"You can't disturb Mr. Sheldon either—especially now."

"You mean there's a party?" (Of course there would be—there
were always big parties at Stourton through Christmas and New
Year.)

Suddenly the question: "You wouldn't be Dr. Astley, by any
chance?"

Charles was about to ask who Dr. Astley was when he thought
better of it and replied hastily, perhaps too hastily: "Yes, that's who
I am."

But the lodgekeeper was still suspicious. Moving over to a telephone just inside the door, he wound up the instrument, listened,
then began muttering something inaudible. Afterwards he turned to

beckon Charles inside. "Mr. Sheldon says he'd like a word with you first, sir."

"Certainly. I'll be glad of one with him, too."

Good old Sheldon—taking no chances. The voice at the other end was impersonally wary. "Dr. Astley? Have you come alone?"

No need to say anything but: "Sheldon, it isn't Dr. Astley—whoever he is. It's Charles—you know, *Charles*."

"*Charles?*"

"Charles who was. . . . Oh, God, I don't want to have to go into all that, but remember the Left-Handed Room? . . . *That* Charles."

"Mr. Charles?"

"Yes—Yes!"

Long pause. Then: "I'll—I'll come along—immediately—if—if you'll wait there—for me."

"Good—but first of all say something to this fellow—he thinks I'm a fake. Don't tell him anything—just say it's all right."

He handed the receiver to the lodgekeeper, who took it, listened a moment, then hung up with more puzzlement than satisfaction. "Well, sir, you'd better wait here, seeing as how Mr. Sheldon says so."

"Thanks. And please understand that I don't blame you in the least. One can't be too careful."

Somewhat mollified, the man brought forward a chair, then accepted a cigarette that Charles proffered. "Marsh is my name, sir. If you're a friend of the family, you'll know of course there's no parties this year on account of old Mr. Rainier being ill."

"*Ill?* No, I—er—I didn't know that."

"That's why I thought you might be Dr. Astley. He's a London doctor they're expecting."

"But what about Sanderstead?"

"Dr. Sanderstead wanted to consult with Dr. Astley, sir."

"Sounds serious."

"Yes, sir, I'm afraid so. Of course he's an old man, getting to be. It's his heart."

"Where's the family?"

"They're all here, sir, except Mrs. Jill and Mr. Julian."

"Where are they?"

"On their way back from abroad, I think, sir."

Strange to be edging one's way into such realizations. The sick man was his father, and yet, somehow, the springs of his emotion were dried up, could offer nothing in response to the news but an intensification of that feeling of numbness. He went on smoking thoughtfully. Really, when he came to think of it, Sheldon was the person he came nearest to any warm desire to see. . . . Marsh continued after a pause: "I could get you a nip of something, sir, if you wanted. It'll take Mr. Sheldon twenty minutes at least to come down —all the cars are locked up, and it's a good mile to walk."

(As if he didn't know it was a good mile to walk!) He answered: "That's not a bad idea."

Marsh went to an adjoining room and came back with two stiff drinks. "Thought you looked a bit pale, sir, that's why I suggested it."

"*Do* I look pale?"

"Just a bit, sir. Or maybe it's the light."

Charles walked over to a near-by mirror and stood for a moment examining himself. Yes—there was a queer look; one could call it pallor, for want of an exacter word. Actually, he felt overwhelmingly tired, tired after the long and troubled journey, tired after that knock on the head in the early morning, tired after something else that was difficult—impossible—to analyze. He sipped the whiskey and relaxed as he felt it warming him. "By the way, Marsh—it's some time since I was here last . . . any particular changes? You told me of one of them just now, for instance—Parsloe dead. Anything else?"

"You mean among the staff, sir? I've only been here fifteen months."

"Well, the staff or—oh, anything." He hardly liked to ask direct questions.

"There's been a few changes in the house, sir—maybe you'll notice. Mr. Rainier pulled down the old billiard room and built two new ones."

"*Two* new billiard rooms? Good God!"

"Well, one of them isn't much used. There's just a table in it, in case anyone wants to play. And of course since Mr. Rainier took ill—"

"He's been ill a long time?"

"Six months, sir, just about. Sort of gradual, it's been . . ."

And so on; so that when, eventually, the knock came at the door and Marsh opened it, recognition was silent, tight-lipped, almost wordless till they were alone together. Just "Hello, Sheldon"—and "Good evening!"

Leaving Marsh more puzzled than before, they turned into the darkness of the long curving drive. Out of earshot Charles stopped a moment, feeling for the other's hand and shaking it rather clumsily.

"Sorry to be sentimental, Sheldon, but that's how glad I am to see you. Matter of fact, it's too dark to see you, but I've a feeling you look exactly the same."

"I—I can't quite collect myself yet, Mr. Charles—but—I—I'd like to be the first to—to congratulate you!"

"Thanks—though I don't know whether congratulation's quite the word."

"It's so—extraordinary—to have you back with us. I can hardly believe it—"

"Neither can I, Sheldon, so don't press me for details. All I can tell you is that I was in Liverpool this morning—and don't ask why Liverpool, because I don't know any more than you. But I had some money as well as the devil of a headache from having been run down by a car, maybe . . . that's all the evidence, so help me God. Before that I can't remember a thing since—since all sorts of things I don't *want* to remember—the war—lying between the lines with shells bursting . . . years ago, I realize. There's a sort of dark corridor between then and this morning—don't ask me about that, either. What you and I've got to decide now is how to go about the job of reintroducing me, as it were. . . . Any ideas?"

"If you'll give me a little time, Mr. Charles—I'm still rather—"

"I know—bumfoozled is the word old Sarah used to use."

"Fancy you remembering that."

"What's happened to her?"

"She's still living in the village. Of course she's very feeble."

"Poor old girl. . . . And too bad about Parsloe—how did that happen?"

"Pneumonia after the flu. Very sudden. We had quite an epidemic about a year ago."

"The new man seems all right."

"Marsh? Oh yes. Used to be one of the gardeners."

"Don't remember him. . . . God, what are we gossiping like this for?"

"Just what I was thinking, sir, because there *are* more important things I must tell you about. I'm afraid you'll find the house in a rather disturbed condition—"

"I know. I realize I couldn't have turned up at a more awkward moment—in some ways. Much rather have come when it's quiet—nobody here—"

"You mean the family?"

"Well yes—bit of a problem, how to let them know."

"We have to face it, sir."

"*They* have to face it, you mean."

"Naturally they'll be delighted to see you once they get over the—the surprise."

"The surprise of finding I'm still alive?"

"Well, after such an interval, and with no news—"

"I know. For God's sake don't think I'm blaming anybody."

"May I say, sir, speaking for myself—"

"I know, I know, and I'm grateful—think it was marvelous the way you kept your head in front of Marsh. Of course he'll have to know soon, like everybody else, but I was glad you postponed the—er—the sensation. Funny . . . when I wanted to say something over the telephone that would make you know I was genuine and yet wouldn't mean a thing to him, the only thing I could think of was the Left-Handed Room—remember how we used to call it that because the door opened the other way?"

"You remember those days very clearly, sir."

"So clearly it's like—like headlamps along a road on a dark night. *Too* clearly, that is—everything a bit out of focus. It'll all come right, I daresay."

"I hope so, sir."

"Well, let's not talk about it. . . . We've got this other problem to settle, and my suggestion is what we always used to say when we were kids—leave it to Sheldon."

"I was about to suggest that too."

"Well, go ahead—any way you like. And in the meantime if you'll find me a bedroom that's a bit off the map I'll get a good night's sleep before making my bow at the breakfast table."

"I'm afraid—er—Mr. Rainier doesn't come down to breakfast nowadays."

"I know, Marsh said he was ill. I'm sorry. You'd better go easy when you tell him—the shock, I mean." He caught Sheldon's glance and interpreted it. "Don't worry about me, Sheldon—I know you're thinking I'm not behaving according to formula, but I can't help it— I'm too dead tired to face any reunions tonight."

After a pause Sheldon answered: "I doubt if there *is* any formula for what you must be feeling, Mr. Charles. I could give you a bed in my own apartments if that would suit."

"Excellent. . . . Thank heaven something's settled. . . . Been having decent weather here lately?"

"Fairly, sir, for the time of the year. I noticed the barometer's rising."

"Good. It was raining in Liverpool this morning."

He slept a heavy troubled sleep, full of dreams he could not clarify, but which left him vaguely restless, unsatisfied. December sunlight waked him by pouring onto his bed; he stared round, wondering where he was, then remembering. But he could not recognize the room—somewhere in the servants' wing, he supposed, and he confirmed this by leaning up to the window. The central block of Stourton faced him grandly across the courtyard—there was the terrace, the big curving windows of the dining room, the East Wing with its corner turret. The spectacle found and fitted into a groove of his mind—somehow like seeing a well-known place and deciding it was reasonably like its picture postcards. . . . He was still musing when Sheldon came in with a tray.

"Good morning, Mr. Charles. I brought you some tea."

"Thanks."

"The barometer's still rising. Did you sleep well?"

"Pretty well. What time is it?"

"Eight o'clock. The family usually begin to come down about nine, but perhaps this morning—we stayed up rather late, you see . . . on the other hand, they may be anxious. . . ."

"I understand. You can't ever be certain how people will react, can you?"

"No, sir."

"You should have brought an extra cup for yourself. Sit down and tell me all about it. What time did *you* go to bed? You look fagged out."

"To tell you the truth, I haven't been to bed at all. There were so many things to do—I had to talk to Dr. Sanderstead—and then your clothes—you'd hardly wish to wear them again, I think."

"No?"

"I took the liberty of borrowing a suit from Mr. Chetwynd—"

"Look here, never mind about all that—let's have first things first. You told them all?"

"Not your father, sir—but I told the others."

"How did they take it?"

"They were naturally surprised—in fact they could hardly believe me at first."

"And then?"

"Well, I suppose they *did* believe me—eventually. They expect to see you at breakfast."

"Good . . . but you say you haven't yet told my father?"

"That was why I went to see Dr. Sanderstead—to ask his advice."

"Ah yes, of course. You always think of the sensible things, Sheldon."

"He was rather troubled about the danger of giving the old gen-

tleman a shock—he says he'd like to have a talk with you about it
first."

"All right, if he says so."

"I also took the liberty of telephoning to Mr. Truslove."

"Truslove?"

"It seemed to me that—er—he ought to be informed also, as soon
as possible."

"Well, maybe that's sensible too, though it hadn't occurred to me.
. . . How about a bath?"

"Already waiting for you—if you'll follow me."

"What about the servants, if I meet any of them?"

"They don't know yet, except Wilson and Lucas—I shall call the
others together during the morning and tell them. And Mr. Truslove
will be here for lunch—along with Dr. Sanderstead and Dr. Astley
from London."

By that time they were at the door of the bathroom. "Quite elegant, Sheldon—new since I was here, isn't it?"

"Yes, sir."

"From which I gather the family income remains—er—not so bad?"

A wrinkled smile. "Like the barometer, sir—still rising. . . ."

He bathed, smoked a cigarette, and put on the clothes Sheldon
had laid out for him. Brown tweeds—Chet had always favored them,
and they fitted pretty well—as children he and Chet could generally
wear each other's suits. And a Netherton tie—trust Sheldon to think
of details. *Netherton;* and a whole cloud of memories assailed him
suddenly: strapping on cricket pads in front of the pavilion; strawberries and cream in the tuckshop; the sunlight slanting into the
chapel during Sunday services; hot cocoa steaming over the study
gas ring in wintertime; the smell of mud and human bodies in a
Rugby scrum. . . . Netherton. And then Cambridge. And then the
cadet school. And then France. And then . . . the full stop. . . . He
controlled himself, leading his thoughts back from the barrier, gently
insinuating them into the immediate future. He found he could best
do this by adopting a note of sardonic self-urging: come along—
trousers, waistcoat, tie, shoes, coat—button up for the great family
reunion. "All aboard for the Skylark"—which set him recollecting holidays with his mother as a small boy—never with his father; his father
had always been too busy. They used to rent a house at Brighton, in
Regency Square, taking servants with them—Miss Ponsonby and a
maid named Florrie, and every morning they would walk along the
front not quite as far as Portslade, turning back so inevitably that
Portslade became for him a sort of mysterious place beyond human

access—until, one afternoon while his mother was having a nap, he escaped from the house and reached Portslade a dauntless but somewhat disappointed explorer.

"I hope the clothes will do for the time being, Mr. Charles."

"Fine—just a bit loose in front. Chet must be putting on weight."

"I'll have a talk with Mr. Masters sometime today. He has your old measurements, but it might be safer to have him visit you again."

"Much safer, I'm sure. You think I've changed a lot, Sheldon?"

"Not in appearance, sir. You look very fit."

"And yet there *is* a difference?"

"In your manner, perhaps. But that's natural. It's a nervous strain one can well understand after all you've been through."

"I'd understand it better if I knew what I *have* been through. But never mind that. Time for breakfast."

He walked across the courtyard, entering the house from the terrace. No one had yet appeared; the usual new-lit fire was burning, the usual blue flames distilling a whiff of methylated spirit from under the copper dishes. The *Morning Post* and *Times* on the little table. A cat on the hearthrug—a new cat, who looked up indifferently and then resumed a comprehensive toilet. Wilson was standing by the dishes, trying hard to behave as if the return of a long-lost son were one of the ordinary events of an English household.

"Good morning, Mr. Charles."

"Morning, Wilson."

"What can I get you, sir? Some kedgeree—or ham and eggs—kipper —kidneys—"

"Suppose I have a look."

He eased a little of his embarrassment by the act of serving himself. He knew Wilson must be staring at him all the time. As he carried his plate back to the table he said: "Well, it's good to be back." It was a remark without meaning—a tribute to a convention that did not perfectly fit, like Chetwynd's clothes, but would do for the time being.

"Yes, indeed, sir. Very glad to see you again."

"Thanks." And he opened the *Times,* the dry and crinkly pages engaging another memory. "You still warm the paper in front of the fire, Wilson?"

"Yes, sir. I always had to when Mr. Rainier used to come down— it's got to be a sort of habit, I suppose."

"Queer how one always associates big things with little things. I get the whole picture of my childhood from the smell of toasted printers' ink."

"Yes, sir."

He ate his ham and eggs, scanning the inside news page. Trouble in Europe—the usual Balkan mix-up. Trouble in Ireland, and that was usual too—British officers assassinated. Not much of a paper after the holiday—never was. The usual chatty leader about Christmas, full of Latin quotations and schoolmasterly facetiousness—dear old *Times*. A long letter from somebody advocating simplified spelling —God, were they still at that? Now that the war was over, it seemed both reassuring and somehow disappointing that England had picked up so many old threads and was weaving them into the same pattern.

Then Chetwynd, eldest of the brothers, began the procession.

"Hello, old chap, how are you?"

(What a thing to say! But still, what else?)

(Miss Ponsonby, his old governess, had once adjured him: When people say "How are you?" the correct answer is "How are *you*?" If you tell them how you are, you show yourself a person of inferior breeding. . . . "But suppose, Miss Ponsonby," he had once asked, "you really *want* to know how somebody else is, mustn't they ever tell you?")

However, he answered: "Hello, Chet. How are *you*?"

"Want you to meet my wife, Lydia. . . . Lydia . . . this is Charlie."

An oversized good-looking woman with small, rather hostile eyes.

And then Julia, plumper than when he had seen her last, but still the same leathery scarecrow—red-complexioned, full of stiff outdoor heartiness.

"Hel*lo*, Charles! Sheldon told us *all* about it, and it's just too *won*-derful. I can't *tell* you how—"

But then, as he kissed her, the fire went out like a damp match and they neither of them knew what to say to each other. He and Chet almost collided in their eagerness to serve her with food; Chet beat him to it; he slipped back into his chair.

"Kidneys, Julia?"

"Only scrambled eggs, please, Chet."

"Not even a little piece of bacon?"

"No, really, Chet."

"Any news of Father this morning?"

"I saw one of the nurses as I came down—she said he'd had a fairly good night and was about the same."

"Oh good. . . . Quite sure about the bacon, Julia?"

"Quite sure."

"Charles, what about you while I'm here? You don't seem to have much on your plate."

"Nothing more for me, thanks."

"Well, must be my turn then, and I don't mind admitting I'm hungry. Thrilling events always take me that way. . . . Too bad Father's ill—we'd have had a party or something to celebrate."

"I'm sorry he's ill, but not for that reason, I assure you."

"No? Well . . ." Chet came to the table with his plate, having deliberately delayed at the sideboard till he heard the voices of others approaching. Now he looked up as if in surprise. "Morning, George. . . . Morning, Bridget. . . ."

George, a nervous smile on his plump mustached face; Bridget, the youngest of the family, sweet and shy, always ready to smile if you looked at her or she thought you were likely to look at her. George's wife Vera, and Julia's husband . . . an introduction necessary here—"Charles, this is Dick Fontwell"—"Ahdedoo, ahdedoo"—a tall, long-nosed fellow who threw all his embarrassment into a fierce handshake.

Breakfast at Stourton was a hard meal at the best of times, only mitigated by ramparts of newspapers and unwritten permission to be as morose as one wished. But this morning they all felt that such normal behavior must be reversed—everybody had to talk and go on talking. Charles guessed that they were all feeling as uncomfortable as he, with the additional drawback of having had less sleep. During the interchange of meaningless remarks about the weather, the news in the paper, Christmas, and so on, he meditated a little speech which he presently made to them when Wilson had left to bring in more coffee.

He began, clearing his throat to secure an audience: "Er . . . I really do feel I owe you all sorts of explanations, but the fact is, this whole business of coming back here is in many ways as big a mystery to me as it must be to you—I suppose loss of memory's like that—but what I *do* want to tell you is that in spite of all the mystery I'm a perfectly normal person so far as everyday things are concerned—I'm not ill, you don't have to be afraid of me or treat me with any special consideration. . . . So just carry on here as usual—I'm anxious not to cause any additional upset at a moment when we're all of us bound to be upset anyhow."

He hoped that was a helpful thing to have said, but for a moment after he had finished speaking he caught some of their eyes and wondered if it had been wise to say anything at all. Then Bridget leaned over and touched his hand.

"That's all right, Charles."

Chet called out huskily from the far end of the table: "Quite understand, old chap. We're all more pleased than we can say, God bless. Of course with the old man being ill we can't exactly kill the fatted calf, but—but—"

"I'll consider it killed," he interrupted, just as Wilson arrived with more coffee. They all smiled or laughed, and the situation seemed eased.

Dr. Sanderstead had been expected for lunch, but he arrived a good deal earlier, along with Dr. Astley. Sanderstead was a wordy, elderly, fairly efficient general practitioner who could still make a good living out of his private patients, leaving a more efficient junior partner to take care of the rest. He had been the Stourton doctor ever since the family were children. Accompanied by the London heart specialist, whose herringbone tweeds for a country visit were almost too formally informal, he spent over an hour in the sickroom, after which Astley left and gave him a chance to talk to Charles alone.

They shook hands gravely, then at the doctor's suggestion began walking in the garden. Five minutes were occupied by a seesaw of congratulations, expressions of pleasure, thanks, and acknowledgments. Charles became more and more silent as these proceeded, eventually leading to a blank pause which Sanderstead broke by exclaiming: "Don't be afraid I'm going to ask you questions—none of my business, anyhow. Sheldon told me all that you told him—it's a very peculiar case, and I know very little about such things. There are some who claim to, and if you wished to consult—"

"At the moment, no."

"Well, I don't blame you—get settled down first, not a bad idea. All the same, though, if ever you want—"

"That's very kind of you, but I'd rather you tell me something about my father."

"I was coming to that. I'm afraid he's quite ill."

They walked on a little way in silence; then Sanderstead continued: "I'm sure the first thing you wished to do on coming back to us in this—er—remarkable way was to see him, and for that reason I'm grateful to you for deferring the matter at my request."

Charles did not think there was any particular cause for gratitude. He said: "Tell me frankly how things are."

"That's what I want to talk to you about. In a man of his age, and suffering from his complaint, complete recovery can't exactly be counted on—but we can all hope for some partial improvement that will enable him to—to—face a situation which will undoubtedly give him a great deal of pleasure once the initial shock has been—er —overcome."

Charles was beginning to feel irritated. "You don't have to break things gently with *me*, Sanderstead. What you're hinting at, I take it, is that my father shouldn't learn of my existence till he's a good deal better than he is at present."

"Well—er—perhaps—"

"To save you the trouble of arguing the point, I may as well tell you I entirely agree and I'm willing to wait as long as you think fit."

"I don't know how to express my appreciation—"

"You don't have to. Naturally I'd like to see my father, but if you say he's not well enough, that settles it. After all this time I daresay we can both wait a bit longer."

They did not talk much after that. Charles was aware he had rumpled the doctor's feelings by not living up to the conventional pattern of a dutiful son; but he began to feel increasingly that he could not live up to any conventional pattern, still less could he be "himself," whatever that was; all he could do was to cover his inner numbness with a façade of slightly cynical objectivity. It was the only attitude that didn't seem a complete misfit.

A further problem arose later in the morning, but Sheldon broached it, and somehow he found it easier to talk to *him*.

"Dr. Sanderstead tells me you've agreed to his suggestion that for the time being—"

"Yes, I agreed."

"I'm afraid that opens up another matter, sir. Now that the servants know—which of course is inevitable—I don't see how we can prevent the story from leaking out."

"I don't suppose you can, nor do I see why you should. I'm not breaking any local bylaws by being alive, am I?"

"It isn't that, Mr. Charles, but your father sometimes asks to see a paper, and I'm afraid that once the story gets around it'll attract quite a considerable amount of attention."

"Headlines, you mean?"

"Yes, sir."

"I wouldn't like that for my own sake, let alone my father's."

"It would doubtless be very unpleasant. A young man from the *Daily Post* was on the telephone just now."

"*Already?* Well, if they think they're going to make a national hero of me, they're damn well mistaken. I won't see *anybody*."

"I'm afraid that might not help, sir. It's their job to get the news and they usually manage it somehow or other."

"Well, what do you suggest?"

"I was thinking that if somebody were to explain the matter personally on the telephone, giving the facts and using Mr. Rainier's state of health as ground for the request—"

"You mean get in touch with all the editors?"

"No, not the editors, sir—the owners. You see Mr. Rainier has a large newspaper interest himself, and that makes for a certain—"

"Owns a paper, does he? I never knew that."

"It was acquired since your time, sir. The *Evening Record*."

"Well, if you think it'll do any good, let's try. Who do you think should do the talking—George or Chet? Better Chet, I'd say."

"Well yes, Mr. Chetwynd would perhaps explain it more convincingly than Mr. George. But what I really had in mind—"

"Yes?"

"Lord Borrell has stayed here several times, sir—bringing his valet, a very intelligent man named Jackson. So I thought perhaps if I were to telephone Jackson—"

An hour later Chet came up to Charles with a beaming smile.

"Everything fixed, old boy. Sheldon wangled it through Borrell of the International Press—there won't be a word anywhere. Censorship at source. Borrell was puzzled at first, but eventually he said he'd pass the word round. All of which saves me a job, God bless."

So the story, which became one for curious gossip throughout the local countryside as well as in many a London club, was never hinted at by Fleet Street. The only real difficulty was with the editor of the *Stourton and District Advertiser*, a man of independent mind who did not see why he should not offer as news an item of local interest that was undoubtedly true and did not libel anybody. A personal visit by Chetwynd to the landlord of the premises in which the *Advertiser* housed its printing plant was necessary before the whole matter could be satisfactorily cleared up.

Charles spent the morning in a wearying and, he knew, rather foolish attempt to play down the congratulations. Every servant who had known him from earlier days sought him out to say a few halting, but demonstrably sincere words. It rather surprised as well as pleased him to realize that he had been remembered so well; but the continual smiling and handshaking became a bore. There were new faces too, recent additions to the Stourton staff, whom he caught staring at him round corners and from doorways. They all knew his story by now and wished to see the hero of it; the whole thing was doubtless more exciting than a novel because more personal in their lives, something to save up for relatives when they wrote the weekly letter or took their next day off.

Once, on his way through the house, he passed the room on the first floor where his father lay ill. It was closed, of course, but the door of an adjoining room was open, and through it he could see two young nurses chatting volubly over cups of tea. They stared as he went by, and from that he knew that they too had heard and were excited over the news.

When he appeared at lunch, he found Sanderstead and Truslove in the midst of what was evidently a sharp argument. Truslove was the family solicitor, a sallow sharp-faced man in his late fifties. During the little hiatus of deferential how-d'ye-dos and handshaking, the doctor and the lawyer continued to glare at each other as if eager to make an end of the truce. It came as soon as Charles said: "Don't let me interrupt your talk."

"What I was saying, Mr. Charles," resumed Truslove, eager for an ally, "is that the problem has a legal as well as a medical side. Naturally one would prefer to spare your father any kind of shock, but can we be certain that he himself would wish to be spared—when the alternatives are what they are?"

"All I can say," Sanderstead growled, "is that in his present state a shock might kill him."

"But we have Mr. Charles to think about," urged Truslove; which made Charles interject: "Oh, for heaven's sake don't bother about *me*."

"Very natural of you to say that, Mr. Charles, but as a lawyer I'm bound to take a somewhat stricter viewpoint. There's the question of the *Will*." He spoke the word reverentially, allowing it to sink in before continuing: "None of us should forget that we're dealing with an estate of very considerable value. We should bear in mind what would be your father's wishes if he were to know that you were so—so happily restored to us."

"We should also bear in mind that he's a very sick man," retorted Sanderstead.

"Precisely—and all the more reason that his desire, which I am sure would be to make certain adjustment necessary for the fair and equal division—"

Charles drummed his fingers on the table. "I get your point, Truslove, but I'm really not interested in that side of it."

"But it's my duty, Mr. Charles—my duty to your father and to the family quite as much as to you. If I feel morally sure that a client of mine—"

Sanderstead interrupted: "If changing his will is what you're thinking about, he could no more do that than address a board meeting! And that's apart from the question of shock!"

"Isn't it possible that a shock caused by good news might give him sudden strength—just enough to do what he would feel at once to be necessary?"

"Thanks for the interesting theory, Truslove. When you want any advice about law, just come to *me*."

Charles intervened with a slightly acid smile. "I don't know why you two should quarrel. You may be right, either of you—but suppose I claim the casting vote? I don't want to see my father if there's any chance the shock might be bad for him, and I don't give a damn whether I'm in or out of his will. . . . Now are you both satisfied?"

But of course they were not, and throughout lunch, which was a heavy affair with nobody quite knowing what to talk about, he was aware that the two men were engrossed in meditations of further argument.

During the afternoon he tried for a little quiet in the library, but Chet found him there and seemed anxious to express *his* point of view. "You see, old chap, I can understand how Truslove feels. Legally you're—well, I won't say *dead* exactly—but not normally alive. He's bound to look at things from that angle. What I mean is, if anything were to happen to the old man—let's hope it won't, but you never can tell—you wouldn't get a look in. Now that's not fair to you, especially as there's plenty for everybody, God bless. That's why I think Truslove's right—surely there must be a way of breaking good news gently—Sheldon, for instance—"

"Yes, we all think of Sheldon in emergencies. But I do hope, Chet, you won't press the matter. Truslove tells me there'll be no difficulty about my resuming the income we all had from Mother—"

"But good God, man, you can't live on five hundred a year!"

"Oh, I don't know. Quite a number of people seem to manage on it."

"But—my dear chap—*where?* What would you *do?*"

"Don't know exactly. But I daresay I should find something."

"Of course if you fancied a salaried job in one of the firms—"

"I rather feel that most jobs in firms wouldn't appeal to me."

"You wouldn't have to take it very seriously."

"Then it would probably appeal to me even less. . . . But we don't have to decide it now, do we?"

"No, of course not. Have a drink?"

"No, thanks."

"I think I will. Tell you the truth, all this is just about wearing me down. Gave me an appetite at first, but now I feel sort of—"

"You mean all the fuss connected with my return?"

"Oh, not *your* fault, old chap. After all, what else could you do? But you know what families are like—and wives. Argue a man off his head."

"But what could there have been any argument about?"

"Well, Truslove and Sanderstead—like cat and dog all day. Personally, as I told you, I back Truslove—but Lydia—well, she's never seen you before—she can't help feeling there's something a bit fishy about it—and of course, old chap, you must admit you haven't explained everything down to the last detail."

"I'm aware of that. If the last detail were available, I should be very glad to know it myself."

"Don't misunderstand me, though. Far more things in heaven and earth than—than something or other—know what I mean? I accept your statement *absolutely*."

"But I haven't made any statement."

"Well, at breakfast you did—you said you were all right—*normal*, I mean. And I'm prepared to take your word for it whatever anyone else thinks."

"Meaning that your wife believes I'm a fake?"

"A fake or else. . . . Well, if she does, she's wrong, that's all I can tell her."

"I hope you won't bother to."

"Nice of you to put it that way, but still. . . . Sure you won't have a drink?"

"No thanks."

"Cheerio, then. God bless. . . ."

By evening he had decided to leave. It was not that anyone had been unkind to him—quite the contrary, but he felt that he was causing a disturbance, and the disturbance disturbed him just as much as the others. He had given Truslove and Sanderstead his decision; it merely irritated him that they continued to wrangle. "The fact is, Sheldon, my remaining here is just an added complication at the moment, affording no pleasure either to myself or anyone else—so I'll just fold my tent and silently steal away. But I won't go far and I'll leave you my address so that you can get in touch with me if there's any need—if, for instance, Sanderstead decides my father's well

enough to see me. Don't tell Truslove where I am—I don't want
any messages from *him*—and as for what you say to the others, I
simply leave it to you, except that I'd rather they didn't take my
departure as a sign of either disgust or—er—abdication. . . . Perhaps
you could think of something casual enough? And while I'm in
Brighton I'll warm your heart by buying a few good suits of clothes."

"*Brighton*, sir?"

"Yes, I always did like Brighton. I'll be all right alone—don't worry.
If you could pack a bag for me, and get hold of a little pocket money
from the family vault or archives or wherever it's kept—I suppose
the hardest thing is to find any spare cash in a rich man's house. . . ."

"I can advance it, sir, with pleasure."

"Good . . . and put a few books in the bag, some of my old college
books if you can find them."

"Maybe you oughtn't to overtax your mind, sir?"

"On the contrary, I feel rather inclined to treat my mind as one
does a clock when it won't go—give it a shake-up and see what happens. . . . Oh, and one other thing—I'd prefer to have the car drive
me to Scoresby for the train. I'm so tired of shaking hands with people, and most of the station staff at Fiveoaks—"

"I understand." Sheldon hesitated a moment and then said: "You
really *are* going to Brighton? I mean, you're not—er—thinking of—
er—"

Charles laughed. "Not a bit of it, Sheldon. Put detectives on me if
you like. And to show you it's all open and aboveboard, you can
send a wire booking a room for me at the Berners Hotel."

"*Berners?* I don't think that's one of the—"

"I know, but I looked it up in the back of the railway guide and
it's in Regency Square—where my mother and Miss Ponsonby used
to rent a house for the summer when I was a small boy."

So much for sentiment; actually when he got there he found the
Berners Hotel in Regency Square not quite comfortable enough, and
moved to a better one the next day, notifying Sheldon of the
change. It teased him to realize that though he did not care for
grandeur and did not insist on luxury, he yet inclined to a certain
standard in hotels—a standard above that of the clothes in which he
had arrived at Stourton. He wished he hadn't told the Liverpool tailor
to throw away his original torn and rain-sodden suit; it might have
afforded some clue to the mystery. He pondered over it intermittently, but the effort merely tired him and brought nearer to the
surface an always submerged sadness, that sense of bewildering,

pain-drenched loss. He was afraid of that, and found relief in recollecting earlier clear-seen days of childhood and boyhood, the prewar years during which he had grown up to be—as Miss Ponsonby would have said (only a governess could say such a thing outright) —an English gentleman.

Sheldon had packed a few books, chosen almost at random; a further selection, more carefully made, arrived from Stourton two days later. They included several he remembered studying in preparation for Cambridge—Stubbs's *Constitutional History of England,* Bryce's *Holy Roman Empire,* Gibbon's *Decline and Fall.* Good meaty reading, a little tough in places, suitable for whole mornings on the Promenade in one of the glass shelters; equally suitable for wet days in the hotel lounge. One morning, walking along the cliffs towards Rottingdean, he met an elderly man with a dog; interest in a wreck on the beach below drew them into a conversation which presently veered to books and politics. For three successive mornings afterwards he took the same walk, met the same man, and continued the same conversation, each time more interestingly; but on the fourth morning the man didn't appear, nor on any subsequent morning when Charles took the same walk. He didn't particularly mind; indeed, it almost comforted him to think of such mutual contacts as possible without the foolish establishment of names and identities.

Sheldon wrote to him regularly, giving him news of Stourton, but there wasn't much to relate: Mr. Rainier kept about the same; Sanderstead and Truslove were still quarreling; while the family chafed more restively, finding Stourton rather dull to do nothing in, and wondering how long they must wait before they could decently decide to return to their respective homes. Not, of course, that they wanted the old man to die, but they clearly felt they shouldn't have been sent for so soon; on top of which Charles's return had somehow disturbed their equilibrium, for if there is one thing more mentally upsetting to a family than death, it must be (on account of its rarity) resurrection. All of which Charles either deduced from or read between the lines of Sheldon's direct reportage of facts—such as that Truslove had had an unsatisfactory interview with Dr. Astley, that Chet's wife was no longer on speaking terms with Bridget, that Chet had taken to spending most of his time practising shots in the billiard room, that the local vicar had paid a discreet visit hoping to see Charles, and that the weather was still fine, but the barometer beginning to fall.

One morning at breakfast, while he was in the midst of reading Sheldon's latest assurance that things were still about the same, a page boy brought a wire informing him at a glance that things were no longer the same at all. His father had died suddenly a few hours before.

He packed his bag and left for Stourton by the next train, arriving at Fiveoaks towards late afternoon. There he acknowledged the greetings of several of the station staff (noting with relief that the sensation value of his own existence had considerably diminished), and hurried into the waiting car. This time the skies were darkening as the moment of the "view" appeared, but the great house still made its bow impressively.

Sheldon was waiting at the open door to receive him; within the house, in the deliberately half-lit hall, Chet stood holding a whiskey and soda.

"Hello, old chap. Had a good time? Sheldon says you've been dosing yourself with sea air—don't blame you. . . . Turned chilly these last few hours—what about a drink?"

Charles said he would have one, so Chet marched him into the dining room, where the liquor was kept. "You know, I once went to see a man in London—somewhere in Campden Hill, I think it was—sort of artist's studio—but the chap had built a regular bar, like a pub, at one end of his dining room—awfully good idea, don't you think? . . . Well, God bless."

Charles asked for details of his father's death and received them; then, alone, he went upstairs and entered the room where the old man lay. The numbness in his heart almost stirred; he touched the dead hand, feeling a little dead himself as he did so. Then he went downstairs to meet the others of the family, among them three recent arrivals, Jill with Kitty, and Julian. Jill was a heavily built, smartly dressed woman in her late forties, the eldest of the family and the widow of a civil servant who had left her with a daughter by an earlier marriage of his own. Kitty was fourteen and generally described, even by those who did not dislike her, as "a bit of a handful." Julian, back from Cannes, where he had been spending the winter, gave Charles a languid salutation and a remark evidently well prepared in advance. "How charming to see you again, Charles! I understand that when you regained your memory you found yourself in Liverpool on a wet day! Your only consolation must have been that it wasn't Manchester!"

Epigrams of this kind had established Julian's reputation as the family wit, but they lacked spontaneity and his opening remark in any conversation was generally on a level, however disputable, to which he did not afterwards attain. In appearance he was tall, lean, and handsome in a rather saturnine, over-elegant way; he lived most of his life in fashionable resorts where he played a little tennis, indulged in little friendships, and painted little pictures of scenery which his friends said were "not so bad."

So now they were all gathered together, the Rainier family, in descending order of age, as follows: Jill, Chetwynd, George, Julia, Charles, Julian, and Bridget. It was a stale family joke to say that they were seven. Like many families who have dispersed, they found conversation hard except in exchanges of news about their own affairs—troubles with servants, new houses, business squabbles, and so on. During the difficult interval between death and the funeral it was Sheldon who took control like some well-built machine slipping into a particularly silent but effective gear. Charles was grateful for this, and especially, too, that Sheldon had arranged a quiet room for him, his old turret room, in which he could rest and read a good deal of the time. He was aware that all the family viewed him with curiosity and some with suspicion, and that intimacy with any of them would probably lead to questions about himself that he could not answer.

A minor but on the whole welcome diversion was caused by the revelation that during the last twelve months of his life old Mr. Rainier had been having his biography written. The author was a young and unknown man named Seabury, who had apparently made a business of persuading rich men that posterity would regret the absence of any definitive story of their lives. Rainier, usually a shrewd detector of flattery, had in this case succumbed, so that the book had been commissioned, a sum paid to Seabury there and then, and a further sum promised "on completion" and "if approved." When the old man's state of health became serious, Seabury had evidently begun to fear for the balance of his payment, and so had hurried his manuscript into final shape, hoping perhaps to impress the assembled relatives by a certain fulsomeness of treatment that might be considered additionally appropriate in the circumstances.

The manuscript, neatly typed and with a covering letter, was brought to Stourton by special messenger on the evening before the funeral; Sheldon accepted it and placed it on the hall table; Charles, passing by an hour later, opened it at random. He happened to light on a description of Cowderton, where the Rainier steelworks were situated, and read:—

But what has been sacrificed in the sylvan peace of its surroundings has been gained in the town's prevalent atmosphere of optimism and prosperity; and for these gifts, connected so visibly with the firm of Rainier, Cowderton must thank the dreams of a lad who was himself born in the heart of rural England.

Charles smiled slightly and did not read any more. He felt that the book, if it were all in such a vein, would probably have pleased his father, while at the same time affording him the additional pleasure of not being taken in by it.

Others of the family, however, got hold of the manuscript and read enough of it to decide it was rather good, though of course they had to be a little patronizing about a mere writer, especially an unknown one, while at the same time nourishing the secret wonderment of all healthy-minded Philistines that the act of writing can be protracted throughout three hundred pages. But the manuscript's chief value lay in its usefulness as a subject for conversation during the rather hard-going lunch party that assembled towards half-past two the following afternoon. Those who had just seen old Mr. Rainier's remains lowered into their final resting place in Stourton Churchyard were relaxing after the strain of the ordeal while steeling themselves for another—the reading of the will; and there, at the table, with all the secrets in his pocket, sat Truslove, somehow larger now than life, munching saddle of mutton in full awareness that his moment was about to arrive, and striking the exact professional balance between serious-mindedness and good humor—prepared to respond to a joke if one were offered, or to commiserate with a tear if one were let fall.

It seemed to be a family convention—unwritten, unspoken, even in a sense not consciously thought about—that Sheldon was one of them at such moments, and that as soon as the other servants had left the dining room his own remaining presence need impose no censorship. Chetwynd had been talking business optimism with Truslove. "What we've got to do now, old chap, is to plan for peace as efficiently as we planned for war, because there's going to be no limit to what British industry can do in the future—why, only during the last few weeks one of our war factories turned to making motorcycles—we're snowed under with orders already, simply can't cope with them." This was vaguely pleasant news to the family, though business was always tiresome—and yet, what else was there to talk about? Then somebody thought of the biography, and George asked Sheldon his opinion of it.

"I looked it over, sir, and it seemed quite respectably written."

"Respectably—or respectfully?" put in Julian, staking out his epigram rather faster than usual.

"Both, I think, sir."

Sheldon smiled, and then all of them, except Charles, began to laugh, as if suddenly realizing that there was no reason why they shouldn't. In the midst of the laughter Chetwynd glanced across the table and caught a ready eye. "How about an adjournment to the library, Truslove?"

Half an hour later the secrets were known, and there was nothing very startling about them. The bulk of Henry Rainier's fortune, amounting after payment of death duties to over one million eight hundred thousand pounds, was divided equally between six of the children enumerated by name, except that Chetwynd, because of seniority and closer contacts with the industrial firms, took over a few additional controlling interests. Stourton was also left to him, as well as the town house in London. A few heirlooms went to various members of the family; there were bequests to servants and a few small gifts to charity. Charles, of course, was not mentioned.

The whole revelation was so unspectacular that when Truslove had folded up the will and replaced it in his pocket there was a general feeling of relief and anticlimax. Any faint fears the family might have entertained (and there always are such faint fears where money is concerned) could now be disbanded; they were all going to stay comfortably rich for the rest of their lives—even richer than most of them had anticipated.

Sheldon had not been present during the actual will reading, but when he next entered Chetwynd was the first to address him, almost jauntily: "Well, Sheldon, he remembered you. You get a thousand."

"That was very generous of Mr. Rainier."

"And if you take my advice you'll put it back in the firm—wonderful chance to double or treble it. . . . However, we can discuss that later. By the way, I'm taking it for granted you'll stay with me here?"

"I shall be very pleased to do so, Mr. Chetwynd."

Chet, it was clear, was already seeing himself an Industrial Magnate, Master of Stourton, and Supreme Arbiter of Family Affairs. There was a touch of childishness in his attitude that prevented it from being wholly unpleasant. Having made his gesture, he now turned to Truslove, whose eye still watchfully waited. "Now, old chap, before we close the meeting, I think you've something else to say."

Truslove rose, cleared his throat, and began by remarking that it was perhaps appropriate at such a moment to turn from a sad event to one which, by being almost contemporaneous, had undoubtedly served to balance pleasure against pain, gain against loss. Indeed, had the late Mr. Rainier been permitted to learn of it, who knows but what. . . . However, they knew his views about *that,* and the differences that had arisen between himself and Dr. Sanderstead; death had put an end to them, so it was perhaps unnecessary to refer to them again. What he did feel was undoubtedly what they all felt— a desire to welcome Mr. Charles to their midst and to assure him of their unbounded joy at the extraordinary good fortune that had befallen him. "We don't pretend to understand exactly how it happened, Mr. Charles, but a very famous hymn informs us that God moves in a mysterious way." A little titter all around the room. "And if our congratulations may have seemed either belated or lacking in expression, I am sure you will make allowances at this troubled time."

Charles bowed slightly. He did not think their congratulations either belated or lacking in expression—indeed, his chief complaint was that there had been so many of them so many times repeated.

The lawyer continued: "Now I come to a matter nearer to my own province, and one that I must deal with directly and briefly. It has seemed both to Mr. Chetwynd, as the future head of the family concerns, and to myself, as representing in some sense the wishes which I feel would have been those of the late Mr. Rainier, a man whom it was my privilege to know for over forty years, and whose probable intentions I can therefore speak of with some justification . . ."

And so on. What had happened, clearly, was that Truslove, having lost his battle with the doctors, had talked the family into an equity settlement—each of them agreeing to sacrifice a seventh part of his or her bequest in order that Charles should acquire an equal share. Dressed up in legal jargon, and with a good deal of smooth talk about "justice" and "common fairness," the matter took ten minutes to enunciate, during which time Charles sat back in his chair, glancing first at one face and then at another, feeling that nothing could have been less enthusiastic than (except for Chet's and Bridget's) their occasional smiles of approval. Chet was expansive, like Santa Claus basking in an expected popularity; Bridget was sweet and ready with a smile, as always. But the others were grimly resigned to doing their duty in the most trying possible circumstances —each of them saying good-bye to forty thousand pounds with a glassy determination and a stiff upper lip. They were like boys at a good English school curbing their natural inclinations in favor of what had been successfully represented to them as "the thing to do." Truslove must have given them a headmasterly pi-jaw, explaining just where their duty lay and how inevitably they must make up their minds to perform it; Chet had probably backed him up out of sheer grandiloquence—"Damn it all, we *must* give the fellow a square deal"; begun under such auspices the campaign could not have failed. But when Charles looked at George, and Julia, and Jill, and Julian, and Lydia, he knew they were all desperately compelling themselves to swallow something unpleasant and get it over; which gave him a key to the mood in which he felt most of them regarded him: he was just a piece of bad luck, like the income tax or a horse that comes in last.

Suddenly he found himself on his feet and addressing them; it was almost as if he heard his own voice, spoken by another person. "I'm sure I thank you all very much, and you too, Truslove. The proposal you've outlined is extremely generous—*too* generous, in fact. I'm a person of simple tastes—I need very little to live comfortably on—in fact the small income I already have is ample. So I'm afraid I can't accept your offer, though I do once again thank you for making it."

He looked round their faces again, noting the sudden amazement and relief in the eyes of some of them—especially Chet's wife, Lydia. Clearly they had never contemplated the possibility of his refusing. That began to amuse him, and then he wondered whether his refusal had not been partly motivated by a curiosity to see how they would take it. He really hadn't any definite inclination, either to have the money or not; but his lack of desire for it himself was certainly not balanced by any particular wish that they should be enriched.

Truslove and Chetwynd were on their feet with an instant chorus of objections. Truslove's were doubtless sincere—after all, he had nothing to lose. But Chet—was it possible that *his* protests were waging sham war against an imperceptible hope that had dawned in him, a hope quite shamelessly reflected in the eyes of his wife? Was he seeking to employ just a featherweight too little persuasion to succeed? Charles did not believe that Chet would have attempted this balancing act if left to himself, but there was Lydia by his side, and he was undoubtedly afraid of her. Nevertheless he kept up the protesting, and Charles kept up the refusal; the whole family then began to argue about it, with more vehement generosity now that they felt the issue was already decided; but they made the mistake of keeping it up too long, for Charles suddenly grew tired and exclaimed: "All right then, if you all insist, I'll agree to take it."

Truslove beamed on what he imagined to be his own victory; Chet, after a second's hesitation, came across the room and shook Charles by the hand. "Fine, old chap. . . . Now we're all set and Truslove can do the rest." But the others could only stare in renewed astonishment as they forced deadly smiles into the supervening silence.

There were papers they all had to sign; then Charles escaped upstairs. His room was the one he had slept in as a boy, though it had since been refurnished more opulently; it expanded at one corner into a sort of turret, windowed for three fourths of the circle, and from this viewpoint the vista of gardens and skyline was beautiful even towards dusk on a gray day. He was staring at it when Kitty entered. "Oh, Uncle Charles, I *must* show you this—it's in today's *Times*. . . ." She held out the paper, folded at the column of obituary appreciations. The item she pointed to ended as follows:—

A lifelong individualist, there was never any wavering in his political and economic outlook, while his contributions to the cause of Free Trade, both financially and by utterance, were continual and ungrudging. A man whose character more easily won him the respect of his foes than the applause of the multitude, he rightly concentrated on an industrial rather than a political career, and though his representation of West Lythamshire in the Conservative interest had been in the strictest sense uneventful, his influence behind the political scene was never entirely withdrawn, nor did his advice go long unsought.

"Uncle Charles, what does it mean?"

"It's just something—that somebody's written."

"But I can't understand it—at least, I can understand some of the words, but they don't seem to mean anything. It's about *him*, isn't it?"

He answered then, forgetting whom he was addressing: "It's a charming letter about my father from a man who probably knew him slightly and disliked him intensely."

"Why did he dislike him?"

He tried to undo the remark. "Stupid of me to say that—maybe he didn't dislike him at all. . . . Run along—haven't you had tea?"

When he had been her age there had been a schoolroom high tea, with Miss Ponsonby dispensing bread and jam and cakes.

"They're serving it now on the terrace. Aren't you coming down?"

Self-possessed little thing; not quite spoilt yet.

"I'll probably miss tea today."

"Don't you feel well?"

"Oh, I'm all right."

"Did it upset you, going to the funeral?"

"Funerals are always rather upsetting."

She still stood by, as if she wanted to be friendly. Suddenly she said: "Julian's very funny, isn't he?"

"Yes, he's quite the humorist of the family."

"He's going back to Cannes tonight."

"Oh, is he?"

"Do you mind if I smoke a cigarette?"

"A *cigarette?* Well—"

"I do smoke, you know—most of the girls at Kirby do as soon as they get into the sixth." She had taken a cigarette out of her bag and was already lighting it. "You don't mind, do you?"

"Not particularly."

"I knew you wouldn't. You don't give a damn about anything."

"Do they also say 'damn' in the sixth?"

"No—that's what Mother said to Uncle Chet about you."

"I see. . . . Well . . ."

"But I've got to stay here now till I finish it. . . . Don't you think Sheldon's rather marvelous?"

"Not only rather, but quite."

"I think he's the one who really ought to write a book about Grandfather."

"Not a bad idea—why don't you tell him?"

"I did, but he only smiled. He's so nice to everybody, isn't he? We had a wonderful Christmas party here last year, before Grandfather was ill—we had charades and one of them was his name—*Shell,* you know, and then *done*—but of course everybody guessed it—it was far too easy. Then we had Buffalo—*buff,* the color, and then a Frenchman answering the telephone—and then the whole word *Buffalo* in America. . . . No, it wasn't Christmas, it was New Year, because Bridget and I had an argument about who had the darkest hair to let the New Year in with . . . but I did it."

"You would, I'm sure."

"Will Uncle Chet have any New Year's party this year?"

"I shouldn't think so. . . . Here's an ashtray."

"What I really came for was to say good-bye. Mother wants to get away this evening." She held out her hand.

"Good-bye, Kitty—nice of you to come up."

He led her to the door. Then:—

"Uncle Charles, is it true you don't remember a thing that's happened to you for over two years?"

"Perfectly true."

"But how marvelous. Then *anything* might have happened to you?"

He laughed at that and patted her on the shoulder. "Yes, and for-getfulness may have its points. For instance, I daresay you'd rather I forgot that you smoked a cigarette—or don't you mind?"

"Perhaps I'm like you—I don't give a damn," she answered, scam-pering out of the room. "Good-bye, Uncle Charles!"

When she had gone he decided he had behaved pretty badly, encouraging her to smoke and swear; there was some imp of mischief in him that drove him to such things, except that "imp" and "mis-chief" were far too cheerful words for it.

Dinner, a little later, proved another difficult meal. Julian, Jill, and Kitty had already left; others were planning a departure the following day. Julia and her husband had agreed to stay over the New Year, "helping" Chet and Lydia. Lydia said: "Jill and Julian were anxious to say good-bye to you, Charles, but they felt you mightn't want to be disturbed, especially as Kitty said you weren't coming down for tea."

He smiled and said he perfectly understood. Chet talked business again with Truslove, who was staying the night; Chet also drank too much and said that British business was headed for the biggest boom in history, by Jove, always provided the government would keep off their backs. Which led to politics and the family constitu-ency of West Lythamshire: "I'm no politician, old chap, but still if the local association were to make the suggestion . . . of course it's too early yet even to think of it."

But Chet evidently *was* thinking of it, readying himself for the doing of his duty, wherever it might lead him.

The following morning, when George and his wife had left im-mediately after breakfast, taking Bridget with them, Charles sud-denly decided to return to London with Truslove, who had a car. They drove away together, amidst noisy farewells from Chet and a few quiet words from Sheldon as the latter stowed away the bags.

"Do you propose to stay in London, Mr. Charles?"

"I'll let you know, Sheldon. I'll be all right, anyway."

"I hope so."

During the journey through Reading and Maidenhead he told Truslove he had been quite sincere in his original refusal of the equity settlement, and had only agreed to it because it was what the family said they wanted, so if they now cared to go back on the decision, it would still be all right with him.

Truslove, of course, replied that that was out of the question. "In fact, Mr. Charles, you seem to have given this matter far too little thought. A quarter of a million pounds is not to be treated lightly."

"That's just the point. I don't know *how* to treat it."

Truslove assured him, entirely without irony, that there would be no trouble attaching to the inheritance. "The bulk of it's invested in shares of the company—you'll merely receive the regular dividends."

"That leads me to what I wanted to say. I'd rather not be connected with the family business at all. I'm not a businessman. If I *have* to have the money, I'd like to sell the shares immediately and invest the proceeds in government stock."

"But, Mr. Charles, I—I really don't advise—"

"Why not? Isn't it possible to do that?"

"*Possible*, of course—the shares command a very ready market. But I couldn't *advise* it—not as things are."

"That's odd—I always thought you lawyers had a passion for government stocks. Aren't they supposed to be safer than anything else? What about consols?"

Truslove seemed disturbed at the prospect of having to assess the relative merits of consols and Rainier ordinaries. "Naturally I've nothing against government securities—no one *can* have, and I should be the first to advise such prudence in investment, but for . . . well, perhaps I may let you into a secret—of course the whole matter's very technical and hasn't been settled yet, but it was on the cards when your father passed away and I think events will go forward a little quicker now . . . it's a question of refloating the entire group of Rainier companies on terms that would of course be very favorable to present holders. I can't give you any details, but you'll realize why it would be unwise to dispose of anything at the present moment."

"Still, I'd rather you sell. I'm not interested in speculation and share movements. I really mean what I say, so don't wait for me to change my mind."

"Of course if you give me direct instructions, I can't refuse. But you realize that, in addition to any question of capital value, the income from government stocks will be very much less?"

"I don't mind that, either. I'll probably live very well on a fraction of it. Matter of fact, you might as well know my plans. I'm going to Cambridge."

"Cambridge?"

"I was going to go there, you know, when war broke out—I'd really taken the entrance examination. Not a bad idea to go on where you left off, especially if you can't think of anything else to do."

*   *   *

His rooms at St. Swithin's overlooked the river and the Backs, and from the first January day when he settled in, he felt peace surrounding him. It was not that he himself was at peace—often the contrary; but he always felt the rooms and the college weighing *with* him, as it were, in the silent pressures of his mind. His rooms were rather austerely furnished when he took possession; he made them less so by books, pictures, and a couple of easy chairs, yet they still remained—as Herring, his gyp, remarked—a *reading* gentleman's rooms. After half a century of experience as a college servant, Herring counted himself fortunate whenever a newcomer to his staircase entered that category.

Charles had visited Cambridge for a week during his last term at Netherton; he had then put up in back-street lodgings while taking the Littlego, which had left him no time to make acquaintances or get much impression of the place except that he thought he was going to like it. He was glad of this now, for it meant that no one remembered him and that his past life was neither known nor inquired about. To be a younger son of a rich industrialist counted for nothing among dons and fellow undergraduates; that he had served in the war merely placed him among the vast majority; and that he made few friends and liked to be left alone was, after all, the not unusual characteristic of reading gentlemen.

He told his Senior Tutor, a harassed little man named Bragg, that he would like to take history; and a further interview with Werneth, the history don, decided him to try for the tripos instead of an ordinary degree. So he acquired the necessary books, began to attend recommended lectures, and dined in Hall for the required nights each week—which is about all a Cambridge life need consist of structurally, until the scaffolding is removed later and one sees how much else there must have been.

Sheldon sent him news from Stourton fairly often, generally to say there wasn't any news. Still reading, however, between the lines, Charles gathered that Chet and Lydia were failing to evolve a well-controlled household, and that Sheldon was less comfortable than in the earlier days of despotism. Truslove also wrote, reporting progress in his own sphere; transfers of property took time, and it was March before the lawyer could notify him that he no longer possessed any financial interest in the Rainier enterprises. The shares had been sold for seventy shillings (fifteen more than the price at Christmas), and the purchaser had been none other than Chetwynd, who had apparently been glad to add to his own already large holding. Truslove added that he regarded the price as satisfactory, though he still thought the sale unwise in view of a probably much higher price eventually.

Charles wrote back that he was perfectly satisfied, and that if his "unwise" action had been the means of obliging Chet, so much the better. Just about then came the Easter vacation; he did not visit Stourton or see any of the family, but spent the three weeks in an unplanned trip around northern France, visiting Chartres, Lisieux, Caen, and Rouen. Returning to London the day before the Cambridge summer term began, he bought an evening paper at Victoria Station and glanced through what had come to be the almost usual news of famine and revolution somewhere or other on the Continent; not till late at night, in his hotel room, did he happen to notice a headline on the financial page—"Rainier's Still Soaring: Reported Terms of Bonus." He read that the shares had topped five pounds and that there was talk of an issue of new stock to existing shareholders in the proportion of two for one. It wasn't all very clear to him, for he never studied the financial columns and did not understand their jargon; but he realized that from the point of view of immediate profit, Truslove and Chet had been right, and he himself wrong; which didn't trouble him at all. He was almost glad for his own sake, as well as Chet's, for he would have had no use for the extra money, whereas Chet enjoyed both spending and the chance to say "I told you so, old chap." In fact he felt so entirely unregretful about what had happened that he sent both Chet and Truslove short notes of congratulation.

The next day he went to Cambridge and completely lost track of financial news amidst the many more interesting pursuits of term time. He still did not make friends easily, but he joined the "Heretics" and sometimes attended the weekly debating sessions over the fish shop in Petty Cury; he also came to know the occupant of the rooms next to his on the same staircase—a high-caste Hindoo named Pal who was a mathematician and perhaps also a genius. Pal claimed to feel numerals emotionally and to find them as recognizable as human faces; Charles took him first as an oddity, then as a personality, later as a friend. He formed a habit of having coffee in Pal's rooms once or twice a week.

As summer came, he did most of his reading on the river, generally on the Upper Cam at Grantchester, and sometimes he would

portage the canoe across the roadway to the deep tranquil reach
beyond the Old Mill. One morning, having done this, he turned to
the right, along a tributary; the going was difficult, for he had to
slide over sunken logs and push away branches that trailed in the
water, but after an arduous yard-by-yard struggle he was suddenly
able to paddle into a dark pool overhung with willows; and there,
as he rested, a feeling of discovery came over him, as if it were the
Congo or the Amazon instead of a little English stream; he felt
strangely happy and stayed there all day till it was time to return
for tea at the Orchard, which was the Grantchester resort patronized
by undergraduates. He was on friendly terms with the old lady there
who served strawberries and cream under the apple trees, and when
he showed his scratched arms and said where he had been, she
answered very casually: "Oh, you must have been up the Bourne—
Rupert Brooke used to say how beautiful it was there—*he* got his
arms scratched too." Somehow the whole incident, with its hint of
something seen by no human eye between Brooke's and his own
(highly unlikely, but tempting to contemplate), gave him a curious
pleasure which he felt he would spoil by ever going there again; so
he never did.

He got on well with lecturers and tutors, and soon acquired one
of those intangible reputations, breathed in whispers across High
Tables, that rest on anything except past achievement; he lived retiringly and took hardly any part in University activities, yet it had
already become expected that he would do well. Werneth had even
consented to his taking the first part of the history tripos in July—
after two terms of preparation for an examination for which most
students took three, and some even six. "But you have a good background of knowledge," he told Charles, adding with a smile: "And
also a good memory."

On an impulse he could not check quickly enough, Charles answered: "It's odd you should compliment me on my memory, because—" And then he told Werneth about his war injury, and the
strange gap of years which he had christened in his own mind the
Dark Corridor.

Werneth listened with an abstract attention beyond the range of
mere inquisitiveness. After the brief account was finished, he tore a
sheet of paper from a pad on his desk and drew a large rectangle.
"Not exactly my province, as a historian, but nevertheless quite a
teasing problem, Rainier. Your life, from what you say, appears to be
divided into three parts—like Caesar's Gaul?"

"Or like Regent Street," Charles interjected, beginning to be amused.

"Or like a Victorian novel," capped Werneth, delightedly.

"Or like an artichoke," recapped Charles.

That put them both in a highly agreeable mood. "Let us call the parts A, B, and C," resumed Werneth, drawing verticals across the rectangle and lettering the segments. "A is your life before the war injury; B is your life between that injury and the moment in Liverpool last December 27 when, according to your statement, you suddenly remembered your name and identity; C is your life since then. Now it is demonstrably true that during Period C—that is to say, at the present time—you enjoy a normally clear recollection of both Period C and Period A, but not of Period B. Am I right?"

"Perfectly."

"And it must also be inferentially clear that during Period B you could not have had any recollection at all of Period A?"

"Naturally not."

"Thank you. . . . There's only one thing more I should like to ask —and that is if I might send this diagram to my friend Dr. Freeman, of St. Jude's, along with a brief résumé of the facts which it illustrates?"

When Charles hesitated before replying Werneth added: "I won't mention your name if you'd prefer not."

Charles then consented. The matter was not referred to at his next meeting with Werneth, but some weeks later the history don asked Charles to stay behind after a lecture. "As I expected, my friend Freeman found my notes on your case extremely teasing. In fact he'd very much like to meet you if you haven't any objection. You probably know his reputation as a philosopher and psychologist."

Again Charles was reluctant, and again consented on the understanding that his name was not to be divulged; so the curious meeting took place in Werneth's rooms. The eminent authority talked to Charles for over an hour in a completely detached and anonymous way, stating as his opinion that Period B would probably return, though there could be no certainty about it or prophecy as to the time required. Charles had several further interviews with Freeman, and began to take a certain pleasure in consulting an expert thus obliquely; he thought it typical of the amenities of Cambridge civilization that such a plan could have been worked out to suit him. At the same time he came to like Freeman personally, so that when his own identity became later revealed through an accident, it did not bother him much.

Charles took a First Class in the first part of the history tripos, which was quite a brilliant achievement in the circumstances. After consultations with Bragg and Werneth, he decided to switch over to economics during the following year—an effective piece of specialization, for he had already gone a certain way in economic history. He was increasingly interested in the background of knowledge and theory behind the lives of men, and the astounding clumsiness of world behavior compared with the powers of the planning mind. To use Werneth's favorite word, he found the paradox teasing.

During the Long Vacation he stayed in Cambridge, putting in mornings and evenings of study interspersed with afternoons on the river or walks to Grantchester through the meadows; he liked Cambridge during vacation time—the quieter streets, the air of perpetual Sunday, the August sunlight bleaching the blinds in many a shop that would not pull them up until term time. Most of the bookshops remained open, however, and there were a few good concerts. The two months passed very quickly.

Sheldon wrote to him every week, but with no news except of domestic trouble at Stourton—an outbreak of petty thefts due (Charles could judge) to Chet's refusal to back up Sheldon in some earlier trouble with one of the gardeners. Now that it was too late, Chet seemed to be handling the matter rather unfortunately, dealing out wholesale dismissals to servants who had given years of service, and leaving a staff both too small and too disgruntled to work well. Chet also wrote, giving his side of the question, casting doubts on Sheldon's efficiency, and asking how Charles, as one of the family, would feel about selling the place. Charles replied instantly that Chet should sell by all means; Stourton was far too big for any modern uses, and family sentiment should not weigh against common sense. Chet did not reply to that, but a few weeks later, at Cambridge, Charles heard from Truslove that Stourton was on the market, but wouldn't be easy to sell "in these days."

Then one Saturday, returning to his rooms from a lecture, he found Kitty sprawled on a sofa and Herring teetering doubtfully in the pantry. "Hello, Uncle Charles," she cried loudly, and then added in a whisper: "That's for *his* benefit. He didn't believe me—I could see that."

"But why didn't you tell me you were coming?" Charles began, trying to infuse a note of mild pleasure into his astonishment.

"Because you'd probably have told me not to," she answered promptly.

He admitted he probably would, and then asked why she *had* come.

"It's my birthday."

"Is it? But—well, many happy returns—but—"

"Uncle Chet promised me a big party at Stourton, but he canceled it at the last moment because he said Aunt Lydia wasn't very well, and as I'd already got leave of absence from Kirby I didn't feel I could *waste* the week end."

"But you're not intending to stay here for the whole week end, are you?"

"Oh yes, I've taken a room at the Bull. Surprising what a girl can do by herself these days."

"But if they find out—at Kirby—"

"That I've been visiting one uncle instead of another? Will it matter? And I don't really care if they *do* find out—I'm tired of school anyway. I'd like to go to Newnham."

"Anything wrong with Somerville at Oxford?"

"Oh, how you'd loathe to have me anywhere around, wouldn't you?"

He began to laugh and suggested taking her to lunch.

"Can't I have lunch here—in the college?"

"No."

"Well, that's better than the little German at our school who pretends to be French and gives us art lessons—he gets in an awful temper and then says, 'In one word I vill not have it.'"

They lunched at Buol's, in King's Parade, and afterwards he said: "Now, young lady, having invited yourself here, you'll have to take the consequences. My usual way of spending an afternoon is to punt up the river, and I don't care how dull you find it, it's either that or off you go on your own."

"But I don't mind at all—I can punt awfully well."

"You wouldn't get the chance—*I'll* do the punting."

But she lazed quite happily during the hour-long journey, chatting all the time about school, life, the family, herself, and himself. "It's made a great difference, you passing that examination, Uncle Charles. I believe the family had an idea you were a bit queer till you did that—now they still think you're queer, but a marvel too. You've quite pushed Uncle Julian off the shelf as the one in the family with brains."

He made no comment; the effort of digging the pole in and out of the river bed gave him an easy excuse for silence. He didn't dislike Kitty, indeed there were certain qualities in her—or perhaps there was only one quality—that definitely attracted him.

She went on: "Of course the family don't really *respect* brains—they just have a scared feeling that brains might come in handy some day."

"What makes you say that?"

"Oh, I don't know—just the general atmosphere before Mother went away. She's at Cannes, you know—staying with Uncle Julian."

They had tea at the Orchard and then returned to her hotel for dinner. "I'm glad you're showing up with me here," she said, as they entered the lobby, he in cap and gown as prescribed by University regulations for all undergraduates after dark. "It lets them know I'm respectable even if I *am* only fifteen. . . . By the way, how old are *you*?"

"Twenty-six."

"Do you *feel* twenty-six?"

"Sometimes I feel ninety-six—so I try not to bother about how I feel."

"Are you *happy*?"

"Oh, happy enough."

"Can you remember ever being *terribly* happy?"

He pondered. "Once when I was a small boy and Sheldon visited us at Brighton for some reason, and *he* took me for a walk along the Promenade instead of Miss Ponsonby." He laughed. "Such a thrill."

She laughed also. "And I was happiest once when I'd had a toothache and it began to stop. Before it *finished* stopping. I really enjoyed the last bit of the pain."

"Morbid creature."

"But pain is part of love, isn't it?"

He was studying the menu. "At the moment I'm rather more concerned with the question of steak versus lamb chops."

"You *would* say that, but you don't really mean it. . . . Oh, and another time I was happy was Armistice Night, at school. So wonderful, to think the war was all over, wasn't it? Like waking up on end-of-term morning and realizing it's really come. But somehow everything's been a bit of a letdown since, don't you think? I mean, if you stop now and say to yourself, the war's over, the war's over, it can't keep on making you happy as it did that first night, can it?"

"I've practically decided on steak. What about you?"

"Uncle Charles, are you sorry I came here to see you?"

"Well, I'm a little puzzled about what to do with you tomorrow."

"I'd like to do whatever you were going to do."

"That's well meant, but I don't think it would work. I intended to read most of the day and go to a concert in the afternoon."

"I'd love the concert."

"I don't expect you would. Beethoven Quartets make no attempt to be popular."

"Neither do you, Uncle Charles, but *I* don't mind."

He smiled, appreciating the repartee whilst resolute to make no concessions throughout the rest of the evening and the following day; he would teach her to play truant from school and fasten herself on him like that. After a long and, he hoped, exhausting walk on Sunday morning, he took her to the concert in the afternoon, and in the evening saw her off on the train with much relief and a touch of wry amusement.

"Uncle Charles, you've been so *sweet* to me."

"I haven't been aware of it."

"Would you really mind if I were to come to Newnham?"

"It isn't in my power to stop you. But don't imagine you'd see much of me—the Newnham rules wouldn't allow it, for one thing."

"Do you think Newnham would be good for me?"

"Another question is would you be good for Newnham?"

"Won't you be serious a moment? I wish you'd write to Mother and tell her it would be good for me."

"Oh, I don't know that I could do that. It's for her and you to decide."

"She says she doesn't think she can afford it these days."

"Not *afford* it? Surely—" But that, after all, wasn't his business either. If Jill thought she could afford expensive cruises and winterings abroad, and yet decided to economize on her daughter's education—well, it still remained outside his province.

The girl added, as the train came in: "It's because trade's not so good, or something. I think that's really why Uncle Chet canceled my party, not because of Aunt Lydia." She mimicked Chet as she added: "Time for economies, old chap."

"I don't think you really know anything about it. After all, a party wouldn't cost—"

"I know, but Uncle Chet wouldn't think of that. There's nobody worse than a scared optimist." She gave him a look, then added: "I suppose you think I heard somebody say that? Well, I didn't—I thought it out myself. I'm not the fool you think I am."

"I don't think you're a fool at all. But I don't see how you can know much about financial matters."

"Oh, can't I? Uncle Chet used to rave so much about Rainier shares

whenever I saw him that I and a lot of other girls at Kirby clubbed
together and bought some. We look at the price every morning."

He said sternly: "I think you're very foolish. You and your friends
should have something better to spend your time on—and perhaps
your money, too. . . . Good-bye."

The train was moving. "Good-bye, Uncle Charles."

Returning to St. Swithin's in the mellow October twilight he pondered on that phrase "in these days." Truslove had used it in connection with the possible sale of Stourton, and now Jill also, about
the expense of sending Kitty to college. Always popular as an excuse
for action or inaction, and uttered by Englishmen in 1918 and 1919
with a hint of victorious pride, it had lately—during 1920—turned
downwards from the highest notes. There was nothing gloomy yet,
nothing in the nature of a dirge; just an allegro simmering down to
andante among businessmen and stockbrokers. Trade, of course, had
been so outrageously and preposterously good that there was nothing
for the curve to do except flatten; the wild boom on the markets
could not continue indefinitely. Charles looked up Rainier shares in
the *Times* when he got back to his rooms; he found they stood at
four pounds after having been higher—which, allowing for the bonus,
really meant that the shares he had sold to Chet for seventy shillings
were now more than twice the price. Chet shouldn't worry—and yet,
according to Kitty, he *was* worrying—doubtless because there had
been a small fall from the peak. Her comment had been shrewd—
nobody like a scared optimist.

The next morning at breakfast his thoughts were enough on the
subject for him to glance at the later financial news, which informed
him by headline that Rainier's had announced an interim dividend
of 10 per cent, as against 15 the previous year. It seemed to him
good enough, and nothing for anyone to worry about, but by evening
as he walked along Petty Cury the newsboys were carrying placards,
"Slump on 'Change" and "Rainier Jolts Markets." He found that the
reduced dividend had tipped over prices rather as an extra brick on
a child's toy tower will send half of it toppling. Rainier's had fallen
thirty shillings during the day's trading, and other leading shares
proportionately. It had been something that sensational journalism
delighted to call a "Black Monday."

Still he did not think there was anything much to worry about.
The theoretical study of economics was far removed from the practical guesswork of Throgmorton Street, and his reading of Marshall
and Pigou had given him no insight into the psychology of speculation. For a week afterwards he ignored the financial pages, being

temperamentally as well as personally disinterested in them; not till
he received an alarming letter from Sheldon did he search the financial lists again to discover that in the interval Rainier ordinaries had
continued their fall from two pounds ten to seventeen shillings. And
even then his first thought was a severely logical one—that they were
either worth more than that, or else had never been worth the higher
prices at all.

Sheldon wrote that Chet was terribly worried, had been having
long consultations with bank and Stock Exchange people, and had
stayed all night in his City office on several occasions. Charles could
not understand that; what had bank or Stock Exchange people got
to do with the firm? Surely the Rainier business was principally carried on at Cowderton and other places, not in the City of London;
and as for the falling price of the shares, what did it matter what
the price of something was, if you didn't have either to buy or to
sell? He replied to Sheldon somewhat on these lines, half wishing
he could write a similar note to Chet, but as Chet had not approached him, he did not care to offer comment or advice.

But towards the beginning of December a letter from Chet did
arrive; and it was, when one reached the last page, an appeal for a
loan. He didn't say how much, but no sum, it appeared, would be
either too small or too great; he left the choice to Charles with a
touch of his vague expansiveness, assuring him that it was a merely
temporary convenience and would soon be repaid. Charles was
puzzled, unable to imagine how much Chet needed—surely it
couldn't be a small sum, a few hundreds, and if it were a matter of
thousands, what could he possibly want it for? He felt he had a right
to inquire, and did so. Back came a franker, longer, and much more
desperate appeal, again saving its pith until the last page, wherein
Chet admitted he had been speculating heavily in the shares of the
firm, borrowing from banks in order to do so. At first the result had
been highly successful; his own constant buying on a rising market
had given him huge profits, and with those (uncashed, of course)
as security he had borrowed and purchased more. Then the inevitable had happened. Chet didn't put it in this way; he seemed to think
that a conjunction of bad trade, falling share prices, and a request
by the bank for him to begin repayment of loans was some malign
coincidence instead of a series of causes and effects. If only Charles
could help him out with ten or twelve thousand—he'd pay interest,
let's call it a short-term investment, old chap, the badness of trade
could only be exceptional, Rainier shares were destined to far higher
levels eventually—hadn't they once been "talked" to twenty pounds?

And Chet added that he hated making such a request, and only did so because there was much more at stake than his own personal affairs; Rainier's was a family concern, there were Julian and Jill and Bridget and Julia and all the others to think about. If he threw his own shares on the market, it would make for a further fall in the price, and that would be bad for the firm itself and so affect the stability of the family property and livelihood.

The letter arrived on a Friday; Charles answered it that same evening, enclosing a check for as large a round figure as he happened to have on hand, and promising more in a few days. But by the following morning the affairs of Rainier's had already broken out of the financial columns and were invading the news pages of all the daily papers. Apparently the shares had crashed in the "Street" after the Stock Exchange closed the previous evening, the final price being a very nominal half-crown. Accompanying the collapse were wild rumors—some of them, according to a discreet reporter, "of a serious nature."

That sent him to Bragg to ask for leave of absence; he then wired Sheldon and left immediately for Stourton, reaching the house in the late afternoon. From the cars outside he guessed there was a family conclave before Sheldon told him who had arrived. He found them assembled in the library, already in the midst of stormy argument. Bridget, who was near the door, said "Hello, Charlie," but the others were too preoccupied to hear this, even to see him at first. It was curious to note the utter disintegration of formal manners in face of such a crisis; to watch a favored few, long accustomed to regard the family business as a rock of ages cleft for them, suddenly contemplating phenomena so normal in most people's lives—the uncertainties of the future. Charles stayed close to the door, reluctant to intervene; so far as he could make out, the family had been heckling Chet for some time, for his temper was considerably frayed, and at one question he suddenly lost it and shouted: "Look here, I'm not going to shoulder the blame for everything! You were all damned glad to leave things in my hands as long as you thought they were going well—"

"As long as we thought you knew what you were up to—we never guessed you were monkeying like this—"

"God damn it, Jill—what did *you* ever do except draw dividends and spend 'em on Riviera gigolos?"

"How *dare* you say that!"

"Well, if you can suggest there's been anything crooked in the way I've—"

Jill was on the verge of hysteria. "I know my life isn't stuffy and narrow-minded like yours—but did I have to travel all the way here just to be insulted? Julian knows what a lie it is—he *lives* there— he's been at Cannes all the season except when we went to Aix for a month—Julian, I appeal to you—are you going to stay here and allow things like this to be said—*Julian*—"

George interposed feebly: "Steady now, steady—both of you."

Julia said, with cold common sense: "I think we might as well stick to the point, which isn't Jill's morals, but our money."

Jill was still screaming: "Julian can tell you—*Julian*—"

Everybody stared at Julian, who couldn't think of a sufficiently clever remark and was consequently silent. Meanwhile Chet's anger rose to white heat. "Look at *me*—don't look at Julian! *I* haven't had a decent sleep for weeks, while you've all been gallivanting about in Cannes or Aix or God knows where! *Look* at me! I've put on ten years—that's what they say at the office!" And he added, pathetically: "To say nothing of it giving Lydia a breakdown."

It was also pathetic that he should have asked them to look at him, for his claim was a clear exaggeration; he certainly looked tired —perhaps also in need of a Turkish bath and a shave; but his hair had failed to turn white after any number of sleepless nights. He was still expansive, even in self-pity. Charles felt suddenly sorry for him, as much because as in spite of this.

Julian, having now thought of something, intervened in his sly, high-pitched voice: "I'm afraid it wasn't your looks we were all relying on, Chet . . ."

Then Julia, glancing towards the door, spotted Charles. "Ah, here's the mystery man arrived! Hello, darling! How wise you were to sell Rainier's at three pounds ten and buy War Loan, you shrewd man! Come to gloat over us?"

It was the interpretation Charles had feared. He stepped forward, nodded slightly to the general assembly. "You're quite wrong, Julia. . . . How are you, Chet?"

Chet, on the verge of tears after his outburst, put out his hand rather as a dog extends an interceding paw; he murmured abjectly: "Hello, old chap—God bless. Caught us all at a bad moment. . . . And thanks for your letter—damn nice of you, but I'm afraid it's a bit late—a sort of tide in the affairs of men, you know—"

Charles, not fully aware what Chet was talking about, answered for want of anything else to say: "I should have come earlier, but I just missed a train."

"You missed Chet's news, too," Jill cried, still half-hysterical. "Such

splendid news! I've been traveling all night to hear it—so has Julian
—would somebody mind repeating it for Charles's benefit?"

"*I'll* tell him," Julia interrupted, venomously. "We're all on the
rocks, and Chet's just the most wonderful financier in the world!"

"Except," added Julian, "a certain undergraduate who thoughtfully added a quarter of a million to Chet's bank loan by demanding
cash."

Charles swung round on him. "What on earth do you mean by
that?"

"Well, you sold your stuff to Chet, didn't you?"

"He wanted to buy—I didn't ask him to."

"But he paid you in cash."

"Naturally—what else?"

"Well, where d'you suppose he found the cash? In his pocket?"

"You mean he had to borrow from the bank to pay me?" Charles
then turned on Chet. "Is this true?"

"'Fraid it is, Charlie. After all, you *wanted* the cash."

"Well, *you* wanted the shares."

"Wasn't exactly that I wanted 'em, old chap, but I had to take
'em."

"But—I don't see that—surely I could have sold them to someone
else?"

"Not at that price. You try dumping sixty thousand on the market
and see what happens. I had to take 'em to keep the price firm.
Isn't that right, Truslove?"

Charles peered beyond the faces; Truslove was standing in the
shadows, fingering the embroidery at the back of a chair; leaning
forward he answered: "That was your motive, undoubtedly, Mr.
Chetwynd. But I think we can hardly blame Mr. Charles for—"

"Is it a matter for blaming anybody?" Charles interrupted, with
tightened lips. "I can only say that I—I—"

And then he stopped. What *could* he say? That he was sorry? That
had he known Chet was having to borrow he would have insisted
on selling in the market? That if he could have forecast a crisis like
this, he would have held on to his shares, just to be one of the family
in adversity? None of these things was true, except the first. He said,
lamely: "I feel at a disadvantage—not having known of these things
before."

"Well, whose fault was that?" Jill shouted at him.

"My own, I'm perfectly well aware. I took no interest in them."

"It doesn't cost you anything to admit it now, does it?"

There was such bitterness in her voice that he stared with astonishment. "I—I don't know what you mean, Jill."

"Oh, don't put on that Cambridge air—we're not all fools! And we haven't all got queer memories either! If you want my opinion, you can have it—you're morally liable to return that cash—"

Truslove stepped forward with unexpected sprightliness. "I must say I consider that a most unfair and prejudiced remark—"

Jill screamed on: "I said *morally*, Truslove, not *legally!* Isn't that the way you argued us all into the equity settlement with Charles after Father died? We didn't *have* to do it then! He doesn't *have* to do it now! But what he *ought* is another matter!"

Nobody said anything to that, but Julian stroked his chin thoughtfully, while Julia stared across at Jill with darkly shining eyes. It was as if the family were at last converging on a more satisfying emotion than that of blaming Chet, who, after all, was only one of themselves. But Charles was different. He took in their various glances, accepting —even had he never done so before—the position of utter outsider. His own glance hardened as he answered quietly: "I'm still rather hazy about what's happened. Can't I talk to somebody—alone, for preference, and without all this shouting? How about you, Chet? . . . Or you, Julian?" Chet shifted weakly; Julian did not stir. "Truslove, then?"

The room was silent as he and the lawyer passed through the French windows on to the terrace. They did not speak till they were well away from the house, halfway to the new expensive tennis courts that Chet had had installed just before he decided to sell Stourton if he could. Truslove began by saying how distressed he was at such a scene, as well as at the events leading up to it; in all his experience with the family, over forty years . . . Charles cut him short. "I don't think this is an occasion for sentiment, Truslove."

"But perhaps, Mr. Charles, you'll allow me to say that I warned Mr. Chetwynd a great many times during recent months, but in vain —he fancied he had the Midas touch—there was no arguing with him. . . . I only wish he had more of your own level-headedness."

"No compliments either, please. I want facts, that's all. First, is the firm bankrupt?"

"That's hard to say, Mr. Charles. Many a firm would be bankrupt if its creditors all jumped at the same moment, and that's just what often happens when things begin to go wrong. I daresay the firm's still making profits, but there are loans of various kinds and if they're called in just now, as they may be with the shares down to half a crown—"

"Is that a fair price for what they're worth?"

"Well, there again it's hard to say—always hard to separate price from worth."

"What will happen if the loans are called in?"

"The company will have to look for new money—if it can find any."

"And if it can't?"

"Then, of course, there'd be nothing for it but a receivership, or at any rate some sort of arrangement with creditors."

"May I ask you, though you needn't answer if you don't want— did Chet speculate with any of the firm's money?"

"Again, it's hard to draw a line between speculation and legitimate business practice. Mr. Chetwynd bought rather large quantities of raw materials, thinking prices would continue to rise. In that he made the same mistake as a great many very shrewd and reputable people."

"Will *he* be forced into bankruptcy?"

"A good deal depends on what happens to the firm. If it weathers the storm the bank would probably give him a chance—subject, of course, to mortgaging Stourton and cutting down personal expenses to the bone. That applies to the others also."

"I see. . . . Now may I ask you one final question? You were saying just now that the firm will need new money. You know how much I have myself. Would such a sum be any use in weathering the storm, as you put it?"

"That also is hard to say, Mr. Charles. I hardly care to advise you in—"

"I'm not asking for advice. I want to know how much the firm needs, so that I can judge whether it's even possible for me to save the situation at all."

"I—I can't say, Mr. Charles. The whole matter's very complicated. We should have to see accountants, and find out certain things from the banks—it's quite impossible for me to make an estimate offhand."

"Well, thanks for telling me all you can. Perhaps we could return by the side gate—I'd like to escape any more of the family wrangle if it's still in progress. . . ."

He drove away from Stourton an hour later, without seeing the family again; but he left a note for Chet with Sheldon, saying he would get in touch within a day or two. After a dash across London he was just in time to catch the last train from Liverpool Street and be in his rooms at St. Swithin's by midnight. He had already decided to help if his help could do any vital amount of good. He couldn't exactly say why he had come to this decision; it certainly wasn't any sense of the moral obligation that Jill had tried to thrust on him. And he didn't think it could be any sentimental feeling about the family, whom (except for Chet and Bridget) he didn't particularly like, and whose decline to the status of those who had to earn their own living would not wring from him a tear. If sentiment touched him at all it was more for Sheldon and other servants whom he knew, as well as for the thousands of Rainier employees whom he didn't know, but whom he could imagine in their little houses sleeping peacefully without knowledge that their future was being shaped by one man's decision in a Cambridge college room. That aspect of the thing was fantastic, but it was true, nevertheless. But perhaps strongest of all the arguments was the fact that the money didn't matter to him; even the income from it was more than he could ever spend; if he could put it to some act, however debatable, at least it would not be useless, as it was and always would be in his possession. For his own personal future had already begun to mold itself; he would probably stay at Cambridge after obtaining a degree. Werneth had once hinted at a fellowship, and if this should happen, he would be enabled to live frugally but quite comfortably on his own earnings.

End of term came a couple of days later; he returned to London and took a room at a hotel. Having conveyed his conditional decision to Chet and to Truslove, he had now only to discover if his money had any chance to perform the necessary miracle. This meant interviews in City offices with bank officials and chartered accountants, long scrutinies of balance sheets and many wearisome hours in the Rainier Building, demanding documents and statements that took so long to unearth and were frequently so confusing that he soon realized how far Chet's slackness had percolated downwards into all departments.

One of the accountants took him aside after an interview. "It's no business of mine, Mr. Rainier, but I know something of the situation and what you're thinking of doing, and my advice to you would be to keep out of it—don't send good money after bad!"

"Thanks for the tip," Charles answered, with no other comment.

During the next two weeks it became a matter of some absorption to him to discover exactly what Chet had been up to. So far he hadn't detected any actual crookedness—only the grossest negligence and the most preposterous—well, *expansiveness* was perhaps again the word. Chet had not only bought shares at absurd prices and in absurd quantities; he had done the same with office desks, with electric lamps, even with pen nibs. A small change, apparently fancied by him, in the firm's style of note-paper heading had condemned enormous stacks of the original kind to wastepaper. An ugly marble mantelpiece in Chet's private office had cost six hundred pounds. And so far as Charles could judge from his somewhat anomalous position of privileged outsider, every department was staffed by well-paid sycophants whose most pressing daily task was to convince their immediate superior that they were indispensable.

By Christmas Charles had almost reached the same opinion as the accountant—that it would be folly to send good money after bad. Even a total repayment of loans would not alone suffice to lift the firm from the trough of depression into which the entire trade of the country was rapidly sinking; nothing could save an enterprise of such complexity but completely centralized and economical control. Without that a cash loan could only stave off the inevitable for a few months.

On one of those oddly unbusinesslike days between Christmas and the New Year he lunched with Chet and Truslove in Chet's office and told them this. "I must be frank, Chet. I've spent a fortnight looking into every corner I could find, and I'm not much of an opti-mist as a result. It isn't only new *money* that the firm needs, it's new —well, new other things."

Chet nodded with an air of magnanimous comprehension. "You're probably right, old chap. How about a new boss? Suppose I were to swap round with George on the board?" Charles smiled gently. "I know my faults," Chet ran on. "I'm a fair-weather pilot—good when everything's on the up-and-up. Nobody can act and think bigger when times are right for it. But these days you want a chap who can act and think *small*. That's what put George in my mind."

Charles was quite willing to subscribe to a theory that left Chet holding all the laurels, but he felt he had to say more. "I'm afraid it isn't just a matter of changing the pilot. You've got to change a good deal of the ship. And you also may have to change the voyage —or perhaps even lie up in harbor for a time and make no voyages at all."

"Just a figure of speech, old chap—don't press it too far."

"All right, I won't . . . but take this lunch as an example. Although I'm a guest, you'll perhaps forgive me for saying it's a pretty bad lunch. And I know where it comes from—the canteen, as they call it, downstairs. And I've seen the prices on the menu, so I know your canteen is either badly managed or a swindle or both."

"Well, maybe—but surely it's not so important—"

"It's one thing with another. The whole place wants reorganizing from top to bottom, and I can't exactly see George as the new broom."

"Well, let's assume you're right—but the more urgent issue still remains. The banks don't give a damn whether the canteen serves good food or not. They just won't wait for their money. What do *you* say, Truslove?"

Truslove temporized as usual. "I think we owe Mr. Charles a deep debt of gratitude for devoting two weeks of his Christmas vacation to making this inquiry. I'm sure everything he has said is very valuable."

"But some of his cash would be more valuable still—don't we agree, old chap?"

"That, I understand, is why Mr. Charles has met us here—to give us his decision."

Both of them looked to Charles, who answered, rather hesitantly: "I was hoping you'd see what I'm driving at without forcing me to a direct reply. In my opinion a loan or even a gift wouldn't help unless you completely reorganize the firm. That's all I can say."

"You mean your answer's a definite 'no'?"

"If you insist on putting it that way, but you've heard my reasons."

"Well, I'm damned." Chet stared gloomily at the tablecloth for a moment, while the waitress came in with coffee. Transferring his stare to the cup, he suddenly turned on her with a vehemence that almost made her drop the tray. "Call this *coffee?* Take it back and bring something worth drinking. And what's the cause of the rotten meals we get here? Send up the canteen manager to my office afterwards . . . and let me look at your hands! Why . . . damn it, I won't have this sort of thing—get your week's wages and don't come here again!"

Throughout all this Truslove and Charles had looked on uncomfortably. As soon as the girl, too startled and upset to make any reply, had left the room, Charles said quietly: "I'm not sure that was very fair of you, Chet. She wasn't responsible."

"What more can I do? Her hands—you should have seen them."

"Yes, yes . . . I daresay."

There was a long silence. Then Chet exploded:—

"Well, have I done anything *wrong?* You talk about reorganization —what do you *mean* by it? If it isn't just a word, *tell* me. Unless it's merely that you haven't got the courage to say outright that you're not going to risk your precious cash. I'd respect you more for saying that than for hiding behind all this reorganization pi-jaw."

("Pi-jaw"—that was the word they used at Netherton for interviews with the headmaster. It stirred in him a little instant pity for Chet.)

"I'm not hiding behind anything."

"You mean you'd lend the money if we *did* reorganize?"

Charles was silent a moment; Chet went on: "That's a fair question, isn't it, Truslove? Let him answer, then we'll know where we stand. Let's have a straight 'yes' or 'no,' for God's sake."

"Very well, then . . . probably I would."

Chet beamed. "Fine, old chap. I take back any aspersions, God bless. *Now* all you've got to tell us is what you'd call reorganizing. What have I got to do? Or what's anybody got to do? And for that matter, who's got to be the fellow to do it?"

"I—I can't easily answer those questions, Chet. I'm not a business expert. It's hardly possible for me to suggest a new board, new managers, new heads of departments—all out of the blue—in a couple of minutes."

"You think we ought to have new ones—all of them?"

"I do."

"You mean you've seen enough during these last two weeks to get an idea who's not pulling his weight?"

"To some extent, yes."

Then Chet, beaming again, played his trump card. "Well, all I've got to say, old chap, is—come here and do the job yourself." He kept on beaming throughout their stare of immediate astonishment. "Why not? Lend the money, then come and look after it. What could give you a better safeguard? You say you're not a businessman, but you know enough to have found out what's wrong—that's a good deal of the way to knowing what's right. Truslove, arrange a board meeting or whatever there has to be and get it all fixed up. I'll resign, and then—"

Charles got up from the table and strode to the window, interrupting as he stared over the City roof tops. "But I don't *want* such a job—can't you understand that? I've got my work at Cambridge—"

"You could go back there afterwards—putting things straight mightn't take you more than a few weeks, once you got down to it."

"But I've no desire to get down to it!"

"Then it's damnably selfish of you! Worse than that, it's nothing but hypocrisy the way you've led us on into thinking you'd help us! First you make terms for getting us all out of a hole—then we agree to the terms—then you go back on them—"

"But I never made such terms! I never hinted at tackling a job like this myself! I don't even know that I could do it, anyhow."

Chet shrugged his shoulder, turning round to the lawyer. "Well, that's his second 'no'—I suppose we'll just have to let the little tick go back to his study books."

("Tick"—the worst term of Netherton opprobrium, and one that Charles had never used, even at school, because he had always considered it childish.)

Afterwards, walking disconsolately along Cheapside and through Paternoster Row to Ludgate Hill and his hotel in the Strand, he felt he had considerably bungled the entire interview. He should have said "no" from the first; then there would have had to be only one "no."

Charles took over control of the Rainier firm in January 1921. To do so he obtained a term's leave of absence from St. Swithin's, smiling at the tense in Bragg's remark: "You would have done very well here, you know."

"*Would* have? I still intend to."

"Well, we shall see, we shall see."

He practically lived in Chet's office in Old Broad Street—no longer Chet's, of course, but he refused to put his own name on the door. At a special board meeting he had been appointed managing director with the consent of the bank creditors, to whom he had turned over his own government securities. The bank men doubtless smiled over the arrangement, since it was one by which they could not possibly lose; while the family, faced with even a thousand-to-one chance, grabbed it gladly if not gratefully. They could not get it out of their minds that Charles was somehow taking advantage of them, instead of they of him; but if (as Kitty had said) they had ever had a scared feeling that brains might come in handy some day, this was undoubtedly the day. The scared feeling developed until they actually believed in him a little, but without reasoned conviction and certainly without affection—rather as if he were some kind of astrologer whose abracadabra might, after all, perform some miracle of market manipulation. That, of course, was their only criterion of success; and it so happened that the mere closing of bear accounts sent up the price of Rainier shares from half a crown to six shillings within a month of his taking control, a rise that considerably helped his prestige though he made no attempt to claim any. Less popular was his early insistence on economies in their personal lives, but after one or two suggestions had been badly taken, he contented himself with sending each member of the family a personal note, merely conveying advance information that the preference dividend that year would not be paid. (The preference shares were all held by the

family.) Expected protests came in the form of a personal visit from
Chet, telephone calls from Jill, Julia, and George, and a strong letter
from Julian in Cannes. He took no notice of any of them, his only
concession being an offer to Jill to pay for Kitty's college education,
if she still wanted one.

Kitty came to his office to thank him. "Sweet of you, Uncle Charles.
But of course you don't mind my going to Newnham now you're not
at St. Swithin's—isn't that it?"

"Not altogether. Besides, I hope I'll be back there soon."

"You mean you haven't taken on this as a lifework?"

"Good heavens, no!"

"I hear you're dismissing everybody."

"Not *everybody*."

"And nobody wants to buy Stourton."

"That doesn't surprise me."

"Where do you live?"

"In a little apartment near the British Museum."

"How appropriate! Can I visit you there?"

"You wouldn't find me in. I work late most evenings."

"Won't you take me to lunch?"

"I was just going to ask you. But there's no *taking*—we have it
here—on my desk. And it's pretty bad—though not so bad as it used
to be."

She chattered on about her personal affairs, the new and smaller
house Jill and she had had to move into—a little suburban villa at
Hendon, with only one maid—"and there's a house further along the
road where a little man kisses his wife on the doorstep every morning
at three minutes past eight and comes running past our house to
catch the eight-seven—just like you read about in the comic papers."

"I'm glad you live so near a station. It must be very convenient."

"I know—you think I'm a snob."

"Not exactly."

"Then what?"

"I'm not quite certain."

"You mean you haven't made up your mind?"

"That would be too flattering to your sense of importance."

"I believe you *do* think about me, sometimes."

"Obviously—that's why it occurred to me you might go to college."

"Uncle Charles . . . what's going to happen to everybody . . .
whether they go to college or not?"

"I don't think I know what you mean."

"I get terribly upset thinking about it sometimes. The little man

who runs for the train every day—I'm not really a snob about him,
I think he's wonderful, and it's beautiful the way you can always tell
the time by him, and the way he always catches the train—at least
I hope he does, in case somebody like you goes round his firm dis-
missing everyone who's late. . . . Oh, but what's going to happen,
Uncle Charles—eventually?"

"You mean will he stop running?"

"Yes, or will the train stop running, or will he stop kissing his wife,
or will you stop being able to dismiss people—I don't know, it all
seems so fragile—the least touch—"

"I've had that feeling."

"Oh, you *have?*" Then pleadingly: "Don't make a joke about too
much to drink, or lobster for supper. Please don't make a joke."

"I wasn't going to. There isn't any joke."

She said somberly: "I know that too, and I'm only seventeen."

A tap came at the door and a young man entered with a sheaf of
papers. When he had gone Charles scanned them through, then
apologized perfunctorily for having done so. "But you see, Kitty, I'm
terribly busy."

"Perhaps I'd better leave you to it then?"

"If you wouldn't mind." He smiled, escorting her to the door and
saying as she left him: "I'm really glad you're going to Newnham.
Write to me when you're there and tell me what it's like."

Then he went back to his desk. The papers included a list of names,
over a hundred, of employees who would have to go that week. He
glanced down the list, initialed his approval of it, and passed on to
another job.

(But what would happen to them? And yet, on the other hand,
what else could he do?)

By Easter he had made economies everywhere, yet the continuing
malaise of trade kept up a tragic pace. There were few positive signs
that his job could be regarded as approaching an end, and it was
small satisfaction to know that without his efforts the whole concern
would have already foundered like a waterlogged ship. As it was,
the pumps were just a few gallons ahead of the still-encroaching
ocean. Even the very energies he devoted to the task, his frequent
feelings of thanklessness and exasperation, fought for a continuance
of effort; he was giving the job so much that he had to give it more,
because "if you work hard enough at something, it begins to make
itself part of you, even though you hate it and the part isn't real."
He wrote that in a letter to Kitty, explaining why he would have to
postpone returning to Cambridge for another term. He found he

could write to her more freely than he could talk to her, and more freely than he could talk to anyone except Sheldon.

✷   ✷   ✷

He was still at his desk in the Rainier office when Kitty left Newnham in 1924. The desk was the same, one of Chet's fantastic purchases that were really more economical to keep and use than to sell in exchange; but the office was different—no longer opulent in Old Broad Street within a few yards of the Stock Exchange, but tucked away in an old shabby building off St. Mary Axe. Convenient, though—within easy reach of Mark Lane Station, and near enough to the river to get the smell of the tide and an occasional whiff of tobacco from the big bonding warehouses.

Much had happened since 1921. He had pulled Rainier's out of the depths into shallow water; there had even, during the second half of 1923 and first few months of 1924, been a few definite pointers to dry land. The preference dividend was now being paid again, while the ordinary shares, dividendless and without sign of any dividends, stood at twelve shillings and were occasionally given a run up to sixteen or seventeen. Chet had a continuing order with a broker to sell a couple of thousand at the higher figure and buy back at the lower; it was the only speculation Charles would allow, but Chet derived a good deal of pleasure from it, imagining himself a titan of finance whenever he made the price of a new car. Chet still lived at Stourton, though part of the place was closed up; it was really cheaper to live in a house one couldn't sell than rent another.

The rest of the family had had to make similar economies, but the real pressure had been relaxed by the resumption of the preference dividend, and they were all comfortably off by any standards except those of the really rich. Jill could afford once more her cruises and flirtations, with no handicaps to the latter except advancing middle age and none to the former save an increasing difficulty in finding new places to cruise to. Julia and her husband lived in Cheltenham, playing golf and breeding Sealyhams; George and Vera preferred town life and had taken a newly built *maisonnette* in Hampstead. Julian was at Cannes, doing nothing in particular with his usual slightly sinister elegance; once or twice a year he turned up in London, took Charles for lunch to the Reform Club, and worked off a few well-polished epigrams. Bridget had married an officer in an Irish regiment and lived in a suburb of Belfast. She had had one child, a boy, and was expecting another. With George's girl and Julia's boy and girl, this made a problematical five as against seven of the previous generation, unless (as Chet put it) Charles hurried up. They were not, however, at all anxious for Charles to hurry up; and as both Lydia and Jill were past the age when any amount of hurry might be expected to yield result, and as Vera was sickly and Julia (so she boasted) had nothing to do with her husband any more, the ratio really depended on Bridget—plus, of course, an outside chance from Charles. Nobody even considered Julian in such a connection.

Much more, though, had happened between 1921 and 1924. The ancient Irish problem had apparently been settled; a conference at Washington had arranged limitation of naval armaments between England, Japan, France, and the United States; someone had almost climbed Everest; the German mark had collapsed and French troops had entered the Ruhr; Mussolini was rebuilding Italy and had already bombarded Corfu; there had been an earthquake in Japan, there had almost been another war with Turkey, there was still a war in Morocco, and there was going to be an exhibition at Wembley.

By 1924 Charles also had changed a little. It was not so much that he looked older—rather that he seemed to have reached the beginnings of a certain agelessness that might last indefinitely. He kept himself fit with careful living and week ends by the sea; faithful to memories, he had bought a small house in Portslade that was not too expensive to keep up in addition to his London apartment—no longer the one near the British Museum, but a service flat in Smith Square. He worked long office hours, and had to make frequent journeys to Rainier factories throughout England; there were certain hotels where he always stayed, and to the staffs of these he was satisfyingly known as the kind of man who gave no trouble, drank little, tipped generously but not lavishly, and always appeared to be wearing the same perfectly neat but nondescript suit of clothes. The fact that he was head of the Rainier firm merely added, if it added at all, to the respect they would have felt for such a man in any case.

In 1924 Charles was thirty and Kitty nineteen. She had done well at Newnham, obtaining a second in the men's tripos examination, but of course she could not take a degree. On the day that she finally left the college she went direct from Liverpool Street Station to the Rainier offices, hoping Charles might be free for lunch; he was out, but found her still waiting in his private room on his return during the late afternoon.

"Oh, Uncle Charles, did you mind? I felt I must call—I feel so sad, I don't know what to do with my life—I've said good-bye to so many people there seems nobody left in the world but you!"

He laughed and telephoned for tea. "I'm glad I never had the experience of leaving Cambridge knowing it would be for good. It was only going to be for a term, and then two terms, and then a year . . ."

"And what now? Don't say you've given it up altogether."

"It must have given me up, anyway."

"But that's so awful to think of. You fitted Cambridge life, some-how. Remember that day I came from Kirby and waited in your rooms at St. Swithin's—just like this, except that the chair was more comfortable?"

"I don't hold with too comfortable chairs in offices."

"But you *do* remember that day?"

"Yes—and so does Herring, I'm sure."

"God, I always thought it was a shame to drag you from what you wanted to do to run a business, but I must say you've done it pretty well—even Mother admits that, but I'll tell you something that'll amuse you—just because *you've* done it she thinks it couldn't have been so very hard and probably other people could have done it just as well."

"Probably they could. Anyhow, if it releases your mother from any embarrassment of gratitude, it's a thought worth thinking. Where is she now, by the way?"

"Somewhere in mid-Mediterranean, drinking cocktails. Chet asked me down to Stourton for the week end. Why don't you come?"

"To be quite frank, because when I do go there, I'm usually bored."

"You mightn't be if I were there too."

He laughed and said he'd think about it, and after thinking about it several times during the next twenty-four hours he rang up Chet and said he was coming. Chet was delighted. Apparently Kitty was in the same room with him when the conversation took place, because he heard her excited voice in the background, then a scuffle to grab the instrument, and finally a torrent of enthusiasm which he cut short by asking to speak to Chet again.

He enjoyed himself at Stourton that week end, and his lack of boredom was not entirely due to Kitty, for there was another guest, a man who had traveled in China and was interesting to listen to if difficult to talk to—a division of labor which suited Charles; and there were also local people, agreeable enough, who played tennis in the afternoons and stayed to dinner. Actually he did not see much of Kitty, who seemed generally to be surrounded by handsome young men in white flannels, and when chances came to join her group he did not do so. He wondered why he did not, and with a touch of quizzical self-scrutiny was prepared to diagnose even a twinge of jealousy; he would really have liked to, just for the chance to laugh at himself, but honestly he could not. Naturally the girl liked people of her own age; but there was another sense in which he had to realize now how old as well as young she was; those youths treated her with such obvious worship, it would not be fair for him to come along with his usual offhand badinage as to a child, and so deflate her adult prestige. And yet that was the only way he knew *how* to treat her—casually, unsparingly, never very politely. Perhaps that made up the chief reason he kept out of her way.

As soon as the dinner guests had left on the Sunday evening, he began to make his own farewells, for he intended to drive off early in the morning to reach his office by nine. Leaving Chet, Lydia, and Kitty in the drawing room, he sidestepped into the library for something to read in bed. It was a superb July night; he did not feel sleepy, yet he knew he must sleep—he had a busy day tomorrow. One of the library windows was open to admit the warm breeze; there was a full moon, and the illumination, tricked by flapping curtains, played over the books like something alive and restless. He was fumbling along the wall for a switch when he heard a sound behind him.

"Uncle Charles—don't put on any lights."

He turned round, startled. She went on: "Why have you been avoiding me? And don't say you haven't."

"Of course I won't. I have. I know I have. And this is why. I can tell you very clearly, because I've been thinking it out myself."

He made his point about her age, and the young men, and his own offhand manner. When he had finished she said: "It's *too* clear, too *ingenious*."

"But don't you think one's subconscious mind does work ingeniously?"

"Maybe yours does. I'll bet it would."

"You see, Kitty, you're no longer a child."

"Oh God—for *you* to tell me that!"

Suddenly the wind dropped, the curtains ceased flapping, the moonlight seemed to focus in a stilled and breathless glare upon her face. It was not exactly a beautiful face, but he knew at that moment it held something for him, touched a chord somewhere, very distantly. He said, smiling: "I'll try to practise company manners for a future occasion."

"No, *never* do that. Be yourself—as you were in all those letters.

And if you'd rather have the Cambridge life than run the firm, then give it up—before it's too late!"

"*Now* what are you talking about?"

"You—*you*—because I'm always thinking about you. You're not happy—you're not *real!* But those letters you wrote were real—when you felt crushed and hopeless and things had gone wrong all day, and you used to sit in your office when everyone had gone home and type them yourself, with all the mistakes. . . . I suppose I'm being sentimental. The little college girl, treasuring letters from the beloved uncle who saved the family from ruin. . . . But haven't you *finished* that yet? Haven't you done enough for us? You pulled the firm through the worst years—now trade's improving, Chet says, so *now's* your time to get free! Don't you realize that? You still hanker after the other kind of life, don't you—study, books, all that sort of thing? When I came in just now and saw you in the moonlight peering along the shelves I could have cried."

"I don't see why. I was only looking for the lights and hoping there was a detective novel I hadn't read."

"But—but don't you want—Cambridge—any more?"

"I wonder, sometimes, if I do. . . . To grow old in a cultured groove, each year knowing more and more about less and less, as they say about those specialist dons, till at last one's mental equipment becomes an infinitely long and narrow strip leading nowhere in particular—"

"Like the Polish Corridor!"

He laughed. "How do you think of such things?"

"My subconscious—like yours—ingenious. But never mind that— what *do* you want to do?"

"You talk as if I'd been complaining. Far from it. I'm quite satisfied to go on doing what I am."

"Managing the firm, increasing the dividends, refloating the companies, a regular Knight of the Prospectus, Savior of the Mites of Widows and Orphans—"

"Now you're being sarcastic."

"Can't you think of anything you've ever wanted passionately and still—would like?"

He said after a pause: "Yes, I can, but it's rather trivial. When I was at school I had a great ambition to paddle down the Danube in a canoe, but my father didn't approve of the idea and wouldn't let me have the money for it."

"Oh, but that's not trivial—it's wonderful. And you can afford it now all right."

"The money, perhaps, but not the time."

"You ought to *make* the time."

He laughed. "If I can steal a quiet fortnight at Portslade I'll be lucky this year." He took her arm and led her towards the door. "And now, I'm afraid, since I have to leave so early in the morning—"

"I know. You want to look for a book." She suddenly took his hand and pressed it over the switch. "Good night, Uncle Charles."

As he went back to the shelves he heard her footsteps fading through the house—no longer a child, that was true, but she still scampered like one. He searched for a while without finding anything he wanted to read.

Nineteen twenty-five was another improving year, the year of Locarno, the false dawn. It was a year perhaps typical of the twenties in its wishful optimism backed by no growth of overtaking realism; another sixpence off the income tax, another attempt to harness a vague shape of things to come with the even vaguer shapes of things that had been. For the public would not yet look squarely into that evil face (publishers were still refusing "war books") and few also were those who feared the specter might return. The England hoped for by the majority of Englishmen was a harking back to certain frugalities of the past (lower and lower income tax, smaller and smaller government expenditure) in order to enjoy more and more the pleasures of the present; the Europe they dreamed of was a continent in which everybody placidly "saw reason," while cultivating summer schools, youth hostels, and peasant-costume festivals in the best tradition of Hampstead Garden Suburb; in exchange for which the City would make loans, trade would thus be encouraged, and taxes fall still further. Mixed up with this almost mystic materialism was the eager, frightened idealism of the Labour Party (both the eagerness and the fright came to a head a year later, in the General Strike); the spread of the belief that the League of Nations never would be much good but was probably better than nothing, a belief that effectively converted Geneva into a bore and anyone who talked too much about it into a nuisance. Meanwhile a vast and paralyzing absence of hostility gripped Englishmen from top to bottom of the social scale, not a toleration on principle but a muteness through indifference; they were not *against* the League of Nations, they were not *against* Russia, they were not *against* disarmament, or the Treaty of Versailles, or the revision of the Treaty of Versailles, or the working classes, or Mussolini—who had, after all, made the Italian trains run on time. Their favorite gesture was to give credit to an opponent

("You'll find a good many of those Labour chaps are quite decent fellows"); their favorite conclusion to an argument the opinion that, "Ah well, these things'll probably right themselves in time."

And amidst such gestures and opinions the postwar England took physical shape and permitted itself limited expression. By 1925 the main features were apparent: arterial roads along which the speculative builder was permitted to put up his 600-pound houses and re-create the problem the roads themselves had been designed to solve; the week-end trek to the coasts and country through the bottlenecks of Croydon and Maidenhead; the blossoming of the huge motor coach, and the mushrooming of outer suburbs until London almost began where the sprawling coast towns left off—while in book-shops and theaters the rage was for Michael Arlen and Noel Coward, two men whose deft orchestrations of nerves without emotions, cynicism without satire, achieved a success that must have increased even their own disillusionment.

In this same year 1925 Rainier's made a profit that could have paid a small dividend on the ordinary shares; but Charles chose not to do so, despite appeals and protests from the family. And in that same year Lydia died of pneumonia, and Bridget had another baby, and Kitty got herself engaged to a young man named Walter Haversham, who preached Communism at London street corners and had been to Russia. For six months she was swept by an enthusiasm which considerably shocked the family, but somehow did not especially disturb Charles. He saw her once carrying a pictorial banner with Wal (they called him Wal) in a May Day procession; when he met her some weeks later he chaffed her gently about it, saying that workmen on banners always had enormous fists, whether for fraternization or for assault and battery he could never be quite certain—maybe both. He smiled as he said it, but she suddenly flew into a rage, accusing him of being a coward who took refuge in cynicism from the serious issues of the world. "And don't tell me I've lost my sense of humor. I have—I *know* I have. There isn't any room for humor in the world as it is today. And it's that English sense of humor, which everybody boasts about, that really prevents things from being done."

"You're probably right. But think of all the things that are better left undone."

"The day will come when men may be *killed* for laughing."

"And that will also be the day when men laugh at killing."

She went out of his office, banging the door. He did not see her again for several months—till after the General Strike in 1926. One day she rang him up on the telephone. "Uncle Charles, may I come and talk to you?"

"Of course." He was about to add an invitation to lunch when the receiver was banged down at the other end. Two minutes later she came bounding into his office.

"I rang up from just outside. I thought you might not want to see me after our last meeting."

"I don't think I should ever not want to see you. What's been happening to you all this while?"

"Not much. But I've got my sense of humor back."

"Where's Wal?"

"He's gone to Russia—for good. You know I really *admire* him. He has the courage of what he believes, he's going to become a Russian citizen if they let him. He wanted me to go with him—as his wife, but I just couldn't. I'm weak—I couldn't live in a little cubicle and learn a new language and wear rough clothes—I'd die of misery, even if I really loved him—which I'm beginning to doubt, now that he's gone. I saw him off at Tilbury and felt awful, and then I went in a little pub near the docks and a fellow was standing in the doorway, playing a mandolin and singing with his mouth all crooked,—you know the way they do,—and inside the bar there was a workman sitting over a glass of beer and looking up at the other man with a funny sort of adoring expression, same as you see people looking up at the Madonna in Catholic pictures, and presently he said to me, quite casual, as if he'd known me for years—'Gawd, I wish I could do that' . . . and I wanted to laugh and cry together. I know I'll never leave England as long as I live, so here I am—and Wal's in Moscow."

Nineteen twenty-six went by, the year of the General Strike, and Germany's admission to the League of Nations; of an Imperial Conference and trouble in Shanghai; of large socialist gains in municipal pools throughout England, and of Hitler's climb towards power in Germany. Trade remained good; the stock market pushed up Rainier's to twenty-five shillings in anticipation of a dividend which Charles again declined to pay. Nineteen twenty-seven brought riots in Vienna and executions in Russia; while for once Englishmen found themselves suddenly and astonishingly *against* something—they were against the Revised Prayer Book, proposed by the Church Assembly and sent to the House of Commons to be voted on, according to the curious English custom by which a political majority decides the dogmatic beliefs of a religious minority. And during the next year,

1928, the House of Commons again turned down the Revised Prayer Book, as if it tremendously mattered. But this flurry of against-ness was soon exhausted, and Englishmen, including Members of Parliament, resumed their benevolence towards most things that continued to happen throughout the world.

And in that same year 1928 Bridget had another baby, her fourth, and Kitty got herself engaged again, to a young man named Roland Turner, who had advanced ideas about the "cinema," and was understood to be working on a scenario or something or other that he hoped to sell for a fabulous price to somebody or other, but was otherwise romantically out of a job—romantically, because he wasn't eligible for the dole yet managed to run a car.

"And I suppose if he *did* draw the dole and *couldn't* run a car, that would be prosaic?" Charles queried, when she told him.

"You still think I'm a snob, don't you? But I'm not—it isn't that at all—I'm just lost in amazement, because he always dresses well and goes to the best restaurants, and has a sweet little studio off Ebury Street—I don't know *where* he gets the money from, but I do wish you could find him something to do."

"But I don't want any scenarios today, thank you."

"Not *that,* of course, but he can do all kinds of other things—write and paint, for instance—he does marvelous frescoes, at least they say the one he did was marvelous, but most of it came off during the damp weather. . . . He can paint machinery, too."

"Unfortunately we don't paint our machinery."

"Pictures of machinery, I mean—he did one for an exhibition, symbolizing something—but I'm sure he could do a serious one, if you wanted it. Don't you ever have illustrated catalogues?"

Charles smiled. "Suppose you bring him to lunch."

They met at the Savoy Grill; Roland Turner proved to be rather tall and thin ("lissom" was almost the word); his clothes were impeccable, with just a faintly artistic note in his silk bow tie; his manners were perfect and his choices of food delicate; even his talk was sufficiently intelligent and modulated to what Charles felt to be an exactly determined mean between independence and obsequiousness in the presence of Big Business. Immediately after coffee the youth mentioned an afternoon appointment and decorously bowed himself out, leaving Kitty and Charles together.

Laughing, she said: "He's got no appointment, he's just being tactful—giving me a chance to do the Don't-you-think-he's-wonderful stuff." She paused for a few seconds, then added: "Well, *don't* you?"

"He's a very personable young man, and if you like him, that's the main thing."

"*Personable?* What exactly do you mean by that?"

"Attractive."

"Are you sure it's not something nice to say about someone you don't care for?"

"Not at all. I like him all right, and if there's anything he could do that I wanted done, I'd be glad to give him the job."

"He was wondering about Stourton—do you think I could take him down there to see Uncle Chet?"

"With what in mind?"

"You're so suspicious, aren't you? Well, he has ideas about landscape gardening. . . . Of course he knows Chet and you aren't my real uncles."

"I don't see how he knows that, unless you told him, and I don't see that it matters, anyway."

"I had to tell him—indirectly. You see, Mother discovered him first of all—in Mentone. He was staying with somebody there and they danced a lot—Mother and him, I mean. I think she rather fell for him, because when he came on to London she had him to stay at the house, with me as a sort of chaperon. We weren't attracted at all in the beginning, but I began to be awfully sorry for him when I saw how bored he was with Mother. He has nice feelings, you know— I don't think he'd have found it easy to switch over if she'd *really* been my mother."

"I'm afraid the point is too subtle for me to grasp."

"Well—like the *Vortex*, you know. . . . Of course Mother was furious."

"The whole situation must have amused you a good deal."

"Well, it had its funny side. . . . Of course his friends don't like me—they never thought he'd pick up a girl."

"Are you in love with him?"

"Yes, I think I am. . . . By the way, he's having an exhibition of paintings at the Coventry Galleries—you *will* come, won't you, and buy something?"

He promised he would, and went to the private view the following week. He didn't think much of the pictures, but his private view of Roland Turner was worth the journey—that suave young man, again impeccably dressed, saying the impeccably correct things about his own paintings to patrons who greeted him as they walked around, striking another exactly determined mean, Charles felt—this time between modesty and self-esteem. To please Kitty he bought a picture

for five guineas—a view of an English country house as Botticelli
might have painted it if he had painted English country houses
rather badly.

"It's really very odd, Mr. Rainier," said the young man, as Kitty
proudly stuck the red star on the corner of the canvas, "but you've
chosen the best thing I've ever done!"

"Very odd indeed," Charles answered, "because I know almost
nothing about painting."

Afterwards he took them both to dinner at Kettner's, encouraging
them in a rather vulgar way to choose all the expensive items—caviare and quail and plenty of champagne. Of course the young man
was a poseur, but halfway through the meal he became aware that
he himself was posing just as artificially as the Philistine industrialist
and champagne uncle. When Turner talked about Stourton (Kitty
had evidently taken him there) and how wonderful it was to own
such a place, Charles answered: "Oh, it's an awfully white elephant,
really. The house is uneconomical and the farms don't pay. If it were
nearer London my brother could carve it up into building plots, but
as it's only England's green and pleasant land nobody wants it and
nobody can afford it and nobody will pay a decent price for anything
that grows on it."

"But it's a privilege, all the same, to keep up these old family pos-
sessions."

"It isn't an old family possession—at least not of *our* family. My
father bought it cheap because the other family couldn't afford it."

"Well, he must have admired the place or he wouldn't have
wanted to buy it at any price."

"Oh, I don't know. He liked buying things cheap. He once bought
a shipload of diseased sharkskins because they were cheap and he
thought he could make a profit."

"And did he?"

"You bet he did."

"A businessman, then?"

"Yes—like myself. But rather more successful because he had a
better eye for a bargain and also because he lived most of his life
during a rising market."

Turner gave a somewhat puzzled sigh. "Well, well, I suppose
that's the system."

"Except in Russia," Kitty interposed. Then brightly: "Roland's
been to Russia too." She must have been remembering Wal.

With a slight awakening of interest as he also remembered Wal,

Charles said: "Oh indeed? And what made *you* go there, Mr. Turner?"

"I wanted to see what it was like."

"And what *was* it like?"

The young man smiled defensively. "I don't think I could answer that in a single sentence."

"Many people do. They say it's all marvelous or else it's all horrible."

"I didn't see all of it, Mr. Rainier, and I didn't think what I did see was either."

"So you don't believe in the coming revolution?"

"I daresay it's coming, but I don't particularly believe in it." And he added, with a gulp of champagne: "Just as you, Mr. Rainier, don't particularly believe in capitalism, though you go on trying to make it work."

"I wonder if that's true."

"The fact is, Mr. Rainier—perhaps we can both admit it after a few drinks—we neither of us believe in a damn thing."

Afterwards Charles regretted the conversation and his own pose throughout it, but he remained vaguely troubled whenever he thought of Roland Turner and Kitty; he slightly disapproved of that young man, and felt avuncular in so doing. He did not see them again that year, for they were abroad most of the time, and he himself had many other things to worry about. By April of 1929 he was so exhausted from overwork that, after settling an especially troublesome labor dispute at the Cowderton works, he went to Switzerland for a holiday, despite the fact that it was not a good time of the year—past the snow season, and before the end of the thaw. He stayed at Interlaken, in an almost empty hotel, and while he was there a letter came from Kitty, forwarded from an address in Provence through London. He wondered what she was doing in Provence until he read that she was with Roland Turner, who was engaged in painting a portrait of an Indian rajah. "He's a very fat rajah," she reported, "and he's given Roland five hundred pounds to go on with, which I expect will be all he'll get out of it, because the picture gets less and less like the rajah every sitting." Charles replied from Interlaken, expressing pleasure that her fiancé had found such profitable employment—to which he could not help adding that the fee was much higher than the Rainier firm could ever have paid for catalogue illustrations. Two days later came a wire from Avignon: COMING TO INTERLAKEN DON'T GO AWAY EXPECT ME TEN TOMORROW MORNING.

During the intervening day he wondered at the possible cause of her visit, though capricious changes of plan were really nothing to wonder at where Kitty was concerned; the theory he considered likeliest was that the portrait commission had fallen through, and that she and Roland had decided to touch him, as it were, for a Swiss holiday. (He had already discovered, from other sources, that Turner's never-failing affluence was bound up with his never-failing debts and geared by his skill and charm in cadging.) He did not mind, particularly; after all, he could always go back to London if the situation became tiresome.

It was a cold bright day when he waited on the Interlaken platform. There was still a litter of shoveled snow in the gutters and against the railings, and the train came in white-roofed from fresh falls in the Simplon-Lötschberg. She was dressed in a long mackintosh with a little fur hat, like a fez, and as she jumped from the train before it quite stopped, it was as if something in his heart jumped also before it quite stopped.

"Oh, Uncle Charles, I'm so happy—I was afraid you'd take fright and leave before I got here! It seems ages since I saw you. How *are* you?"

"I'm fine." (Breaking Miss Ponsonby's old rule.) "And it *is* ages since you saw me—nearly a year. Where's Roland?"

"Not with me. I've left him. Take me somewhere for a drink—there was no diner on the train."

In a deserted restaurant-café opposite the station she told him more about it. "I found myself getting *silly*—saying silly things to all his silly crowd—there's a regular colony of them wherever he goes. But more than that—after all, I don't mind so much saying silly things myself, but it got to the point where I didn't notice when things *they* said were silly. Softening of the brain—" she tapped her head. "I simply *had* to take it in time. And I felt sorry for the poor old rajah. He was pretty awful to look at, but at least he knew what's what with women—which is more than most of Roland's friends do."

"So I rather imagined."

"Of course *you* really fixed it—that night at Kettner's."

"*I* fixed it?"

"I could see you didn't like him."

"On the contrary, I think I began to like him then—just slightly—and for the first time. He has his wits about him."

"He'd better have—they're what he lives by. But it's no good denying it—you *don't* like him. I could feel that."

"Well, I'm not as keen on him as you are."

"*Were.*"

"Oh, is it *were?* Well, in that case there couldn't be a better reason for breaking off the engagement."

"But it never pleased you to think of me marrying him. Did it now?"

"Why should that matter to you?"

"Because it *does* matter! I can't bear to do things you don't want, except when you don't want them to my face—like forcing myself on you here, I don't mind *that—*" She suddenly lowered her head into her hands and looked up a few seconds later with eyes streaming. "Can't you see you've spoilt me for other men?"

"But, my dear—that's ridiculous!"

She went on: "I'm not asking for anything. I can go back by the next train if you'd prefer it. I'll probably marry someone eventually and be quite happy, but it'll have to be a man whom you like fairly well, and who doesn't sneer because you do an honest job of work instead of battening on rich people."

"Battening on poor people is more in my line—according to your former fiancé."

"Poor Wal—I often wonder what's happened to him—I really liked him more than Roland. . . . By the way, I saw the papers—you've been having strikes at Cowderton, haven't you? Was it very serious?"

"While it lasted. That's really why I came out here—for a rest."

"Oh God, why don't you give the whole thing up? You've got enough money, haven't you?"

"For what?"

"To live on, for the rest of your life, at about a thousand a year."

"Depends on several things—how long I live, how much a thousand a year will continue to be worth, and how long people will pay me anything at all for not working. . . . But that's not the whole point, in any case."

"You mean you *want* to stay with the firm? It's still a game, as you said in one of those letters—a game you want to win even if it isn't worth playing? Haven't you won enough? . . . Or maybe it's more than a game now—it's become the lifework?"

He smiled. "Perhaps it's somewhere between the two—more than a game, but not quite a lifework yet. You know, when I first took over the job it was with all kinds of reluctance—because I'd been more or less jockeyed into it by the family crying out to be saved. Well, that was the idea, originally—to save 'em and then be off quick, before they needed more saving. Rainier's was just something that kept the family going, and I didn't respect it enormously for that.

But then, when I began to look into things personally, I found it kept a good many other families going. Over three thousand, to be precise."

"I see. Responsibility. Uncle Atlas."

"You can laugh at me if you like, provided you believe me sincere. I'm not a sentimentalist. I don't call the firm the House of Rainier, or myself a Captain of Industry, or any of that nonsense. But there *is* a responsibility, no use denying it, in owning a three-thousand-family business. If I can contrive a little security for those people—"

"But there *isn't* any security—as you said yourself when I asked you about your thousand a year. It's an illusion put up by banks and insurance companies and lawyers and building societies and everybody who goes without what he wants today because he thinks he'll enjoy it more later on. Supposing some day we all find out there isn't any 'later on'?"

"Then, my dear, will come Wal's revolution."

"And we shall all make a grab for what we can get?"

"Provided there *is* anything to get by then. If the whole thing's an illusion, then the rewards may fade equally."

"Then you try to comfort those three thousand families by encouraging them to believe in a future that doesn't exist?"

"They don't believe in it. Every street-corner speaker warns them not to at the top of his voice. What I *do* comfort them with, since you put it that way, is enough of a regular wage to buy food and pay their rent and smoke cigarettes and go to the local cinema. That keeps them satisfied to go on waiting."

"For the big grab?"

"Or for the discovery that there isn't anything left to grab."

"Which makes you one degree more cynical than they are. They don't believe in the security they accept because they're looking to the revolution, but *you* don't believe in either the security of the present or the revolution of the future!"

"Your other ex-fiancé put it even more simply, my dear, when he said I didn't believe in a damn thing."

"Well, don't you?"

"That's what I've been asking myself very carefully and for a long time, and I still can't find an answer."

"Probably because you've been asking it *too* long and *too* carefully. The answer to that sort of question ought to *fly* out—like a child when he's asked what he wants for his birthday—he always knows instantly without having to think—either a bicycle or a toy train or something. . . . Oh, I'm quite happy again now. I don't miss Roland a bit. Just talking to you freely like this makes the difference, though you don't talk to *me* freely—there always seems a brake on—I can hardly believe you once sent me those letters."

"Curious—I don't remember much about them. If you kept any, I'd like to—"

"Oh, no, *never!* That would be a really awful thing to do! And of course I know why you were so free in *them*—because you thought I was too young to understand. I was only the vehicle—the letter box, so to speak—where you posted them to another address."

A gleam came into his eyes. "What on earth are you talking about?"

"Well, what more could I have been in those days? Letters to a schoolgirl. . . . Of course I was crazy about you—always have been ever since that time at Stourton when I came up to your room and smoked a cigarette. Remember? . . . It might be fun if you loved me now—we'd have a good deal in common. I sometimes wonder why you don't."

"In my slow and careful way I've been wondering that too—ever since you stepped off the train."

"Well, why don't you—just to be curious?"

"I haven't said I don't."

"Oh *no!*"

"Would it be so very incredible?"

"It would be *fantastic!*"

"Then it *is* fantastic."

"Darling, you don't mean—" She seized his hand across the table. "You're not saying it just to be kind?"

"I don't feel a bit kind. I feel—well, let's stick to fantastic."

"But I—I—I don't know what else to say for the moment."

"You don't have to say anything."

They sat in silence, his hand changing places over hers. A train entered the station opposite; the tick of its electric engine was like a clock measuring the seconds. Presently she said: "There's the oddest thing in my mind for us to do—if it's all real and not a dream. Let's go down the Danube in a canoe, as you always wanted."

"Yes, we'll do that. And up the Amazon too, if you like." His face was very pale. "I'll take a year off—from the firm and the City and the three thousand families and everything else. Let someone else have his turn. . . ."

*   *   *

Back at his hotel that night he could hardly believe in the changed future; it was almost as if he had been another person during the

day and was now perusing with amazement a report of what had
happened to someone else. He was not regretful—far from it—but a
little bemused at so many decisions made all at once, somewhat
startled that they must all have been his own, yet ready to accept
them with a loyalty that might well become more enthusiastic when
he had had a chance to think them over.

At breakfast he compared notes and found that her emotions had
been similar only as far as a doubt as to whether he could really have
meant what he said enough to go on meaning it; he assured her
laughingly that he had and did, and immediately happiness blazed
across the rolls and honey between them as they planned the trivial
details of the day. The future was still fantastic to talk about, even
to think about, and they agreed for the time being not to give themselves the even heavier task of explaining it to others. No one expected him in London before the end of the month (the Rainier
board meeting was on the thirtieth), and no one knew she was not
still in Provence, except Roland and his crowd, who did not count.
Jill was in the Aegean, cruising among the antiquities but taking
(one suspected) very little notice of them. He and Kitty could have
at least two weeks in Switzerland before returning to announce the
astonishing news to the family and to the world. Of course they
could send the news by letter, but somehow to pull the lever that
would release all the commotion even at a distance required a certain fortitude; they decided to enjoy those two weeks first of all.

And so began an interlude that might have been in another world,
and almost was. They stayed for the first week in Interlaken, making
it a center for mountain trips into the high Oberland. The weather
improved after the last big snowfall of the year; the sun dried the
drenched meadows, so that they were able to walk by the lakeside
to Giessbach, and up the Lauterbrunnen Valley as far as the lower
slopes of the Rothal. It was pleasant to see the industrious Swiss
polishing up their ballrooms and cocktail bars and funicular railways
in readiness for what was to come; but pleasanter still to tramp along
the cleared roadways in face of the sun and snow. During the second
week they discovered the hotel on the two-mile-high Jungfraujoch,
where there was nothing to do but talk and absorb the physical atmosphere of being above and beyond the earth. They liked it enough
to stay there till the last day before the necessary return to England.

That last day came, and with the descent to natural levels a curious
deflation of mood that was easy to interpret as sadness at leaving a
place where they had been so happy. Throughout the long rail journey through Berne and Basle to Boulogne the mood persisted—

seemed impossible to shake off, being perhaps a physical effect of the changed altitude, they both agreed. They reached London amidst driving rain and had dinner in a restaurant near Victoria Station, saying all the time and over and over again how wonderful it had been in Switzerland and how sorry they were to have returned. The Rainier board meeting was four days away, and it was understood that no announcement of future plans should be hinted at to anyone until then.

The board meeting came, and with it all the commotion. He had not guessed how considerable it would be. He had suspected that the family would not be altogether pleased, but he hadn't realized they would have so many reasons for being displeased. He soon found that they regarded his year's absence from Rainier's as a form of abdication amounting almost to desertion—in spite of the fact that they had long been jealous of what they called his "domineering" over the firm's affairs. Then also, those who had hoped their children would inherit his personal fortune strongly resented his marriage to anybody at all; he hadn't anticipated that, even remotely. And finally, all except Jill (and in one sense even including Jill) were manifestly and desperately jealous of his choice. Only Chet seemed to have any genuine tolerance of the idea—a tolerance not quite reaching the point of enthusiasm. He had so long joked about the need for Charles to "hurry up" that now Charles *was* hurrying up he could not withhold somewhat rueful good wishes.

The party at Stourton to celebrate the engagement was not a successful affair.

Then, in June, quite suddenly, Chet died after a heart attack, and plans for the marriage in July were postponed till autumn; it would have been impossible, in any event, to leave England during all the legal complications that ensued.

The marriage was finally fixed for October. Charles took Kitty to dine at Kettner's again one night in late September, and for some reason the same mood came upon them as during the journey back from Switzerland five months before. She suggested that, on his side, it was due to news in the evening paper—a big stock-market crash in New York, with inevitable repercussions in London.

He was too honest with her to accept that as a reason. "I'm not a speculator. Rainier's dropped five shillings today, I notice, but it doesn't affect me or the firm—they can go down ten times as much before it'll begin to worry me. Matter of fact, everything's been pushed too high lately, especially in America. I could make a lot of money now if I backed my opinion."

"What opinion?"

"That the fall will go much further."

"How would you make money by backing your opinion?"

"Selling short, as they call it. That means—"

"I know—I learnt all about it at Kirby when we used to gamble in Rainier shares. Remember?"

"You must have lost everything."

"Nearly everything. About thirty-two pounds all together." She laughed. "Well, why *don't* you sell short?"

"I will, if it amuses you. But I'd have no other reason."

"Yes do it—to amuse me. Please, Charles."

"Then there's two things I have to do at the office tomorrow morning." He took out his notebook and made a pretense of writing something down. "Sell short to amuse Kitty. Also get Miss Hanslett to send out the wedding invitations."

"Who's Miss Hanslett?"

"My new secretary. You saw her last time you called."

"Oh, that quiet girl?"

"I suppose she's quiet. I certainly wouldn't want her to be noisy."

"Darling, how soon can we leave—afterwards?"

"You mean for our world tour? Maybe next month. It'll be too late for the Danube, though, this year. We'd better do the Amazon first. Or the Nile."

"No, not the Nile—Jill's there."

"What's she doing?"

"Looking at the tombs, I suppose, and having a good time."

But the laugh they rallied themselves into failed to shift the mood that made him, as soon as dinner was over, confess that he felt tired and would prefer an early night in bed. He dropped her at Jill's new house in St. John's Wood, where she was living with a cook-housekeeper, and kept the taxi for his own journey to Smith Square. But his apartment seemed so inexplicably cheerless that after a drink and an attempt to feel sleepy, he called another cab and drove round the West End till he found a film that looked tolerable enough for whiling away the rest of the evening. He stayed in the cinema less than an hour, his restlessness increasing all the time, so that at last he walked out and paced up and down the thronged pavements till past midnight, longing suddenly for the sun and snow of the Jungfraujoch, yet knowing that it was only a mirage of what he would still long for if by some miracle he were to be transplanted there.

Usually when he could not sleep he was quite satisfied to stay up reading, often until dawn; but that night he felt he would be far too restless to concentrate on any book, so he bought tablets and took several on his return to Smith Square. They gave him a heavy unrefreshing sleep, from which he woke about noon to find a penciled letter from Kitty at his bedside. It had been delivered by hand early that morning, and contained, in effect, the breaking of their engagement and an announcement that she was leaving immediately to join her stepmother in Luxor.

PART THREE

The first gray smudge was peering over the hills and it seemed that we both saw it together.

"Well, we've talked all night—and for the second time. Aren't you sleepy yet?"

"No. . . . You were telling me about that letter, the one Kitty left for you. Didn't it give any reasons?"

"Plenty. But I really think we'd better go to bed if we're to be in any decent condition tomorrow. The crowd will soon be on us, worse luck."

"Then why do you have them here?"

"That's part of another story. Well, I must have a nightcap, even if it *is* morning. Have one with me?"

We went down to the library, feeling our way in the dim dawn shadows without switching on any of the house lights. Meanwhile he continued: "I'd show you that letter if I had it here, but it's locked up in my safe in the City. I admit I'm sentimental about it—a little puzzled also. It's the last word I ever had from her, except picture postcards from all kinds of places. What happened to her afterwards is what she said would happen—except that it didn't last for long. She married a man she met in Egypt—she was quite happy—and he was a man I liked when I met him, but I didn't meet him till after she was dead. He had plantations in the F.M.S. and she went out with him there and died of malaria within six months."

He bent over the decanter, his shape and movements ghostly against the gray pallor from the windows. The moon had gone down, and it was darker than at midnight.

"And then?" I said.

He handed me a drink and raised his own.

"The rest," he declaimed half-mockingly, "is a simple saga of success. I flung myself into business with renewed but disciplined abandon: I sold short and made more money out of the slump than I'd ever done out of ordinary trading; I accepted directorships in other companies and became what they call 'a figure in the City'— I even assumed the burden of two other family heritages, by taking over Stourton and by allowing myself to stand for my father's old Parliamentary seat of West Lythamshire. And a few years later, my affairs having more than survived the storms of 1931 and the doldrums of 1932, I married a lady who had become quite indispensable to me in this struggle for fresh fame and fortune—Miss Hanslett, the quiet girl. That again turned out to be an astonishing success. You never know what these quiet girls can do. From being quiet, she became one of the busiest and cleverest of London's hostesses—and the miracle is, she's *still* quiet—you'd hardly know the machine's running at all."

"So different from Miss Hobbs—but that, I suppose, is because you chose her yourself."

"Or else *she* chose *her*self. She was just a girl in the general office first of all, until one evening I was working late and she invaded my private office to ask outright if she could work for me personally. Said she knew the other girl was leaving and she was certain she'd be better than anyone else. After that I simply had to give her either the sack or the job."

"Anyhow, *you* made the right choice there."

He laughed. "Oh yes, and I soon knew it. She was everything she promised. I've nothing but praise for her. I'd never have made so much money or acquired such style in after-dinner oratory but for her. She's intensely loyal, tremendously ambitious for me, and personally charming. I love her more than most men love their wives. She's guided my career—in fact she's almost made a personally conducted tour of it. I never do anything, in politics or business, without seeking her advice. She runs Stourton and Kenmore like a pair of clocks—she doesn't care if I'm in or out to lunch or dinner, or if I go to India or South America for six months or merely to Brighton for a week end. She's everything a man like me could wish for in a wife —always provided—" He paused and took a drink, then added: "Always provided he's completely satisfied to be a man like me."

"And aren't you?"

He took my arm. "Let's save up something for another night. I'm going to bed, and after all this, I really think I shall sleep. Tell Sheldon not to wake me till the guests begin to arrive."

The guests began to arrive in groups during the following afternoon, but I did not see Rainier till tea time, when he appeared on the terrace to greet the assembly; and from then throughout the week end I had no chance to talk with him alone. Nor with Woburn either, for that young man, after initial shyness, turned into a considerable social success. Observing him from time to time I felt there was a certain scientific detachment in his obvious effort to make good at his first fashionable houseparty (he had told me it was his first, and that he had never mixed in that class of society before); it was as if he were exploring himself, discovering his own powers; experimenting with the careless flatteries, the insincere attentions that make up the small change of such occasions; finding that he could do it just as well as people born to it, perhaps even a little better after practice. He was clearly a very adaptable and cool-headed young man, and the whole party was a good deal pleasanter for his being always at hand to pass interesting conversational cues, to make up a bridge four, to play a not offensively good game of tennis, and to dance with otherwise unpartnered matrons. One could almost read in his face the question, too wondering to be smug: Is this all there is to it?

Mrs. Rainier was the perfect hostess as usual, and I should have been lost in admiration at everything she did had it not been a repetition on a larger scale of what she habitually did at Kenmore. All, in fact, was as gay and brilliant and smooth-running as usual, but something else was not *quite* as usual—and I don't know how to describe it except as a faint suspicion that the world was already swollen with destiny and that Stourton was no longer the world—a whiff of misgiving too delicate to analyze, as when, in the ballroom of an ocean liner, some change of tempo in the engines far below communicates itself to the revelers for a phantom second and then is lost behind the rhythms of the orchestra.

The simile was Rainier's as we drove back to London on Monday evening, leaving Woburn and Mrs. Rainier at Stourton. Within a few weeks the same misgiving, many times magnified, had become a headline commonplace; trenches were being dug in the London parks; the curve of the September crisis rose to its monstrous peak. Rainier lived at his Club during those fateful days and we were both kept busy at all hours transcribing reports, telephoning officials, and listening to the latest radio bulletins. Diplomatic machinery had swung into the feverish gear of guesswork and divination: Was Hitler bluffing? What sort of country was this new Germany? Would Russia support the Czechs? When would the bombers come over? Every chatterer could claim an audience; journalists back from Europe were heard more eagerly than ambassadors; the fact that all seemed to depend on the workings of one abnormal human mind gave every amateur psychologist an equal chance with politicians and crystal gazers. And behind this mystery came fear, fear of a kind that had brought earlier peoples to their knees before eclipses and comets—

fear of the unknown, based on an awareness that the known was no longer impregnable. The utter destruction of civilization, which had seemed a fantastic thing to our grandfathers, had become a commonplace of schoolboys' essays, village debating societies, and after-dinner small talk; for the first time in human history a sophisticated society faced its own extinction not theoretically in the future, but by physical death perhaps tomorrow. There was a dreadful acceptance of doom in all our eyes as we sat around, in restaurants and at conference tables and beside innumerable radios, listening and talking and drinking, the only three things to do that one could go on doing—paralyzed as we were into a belief that it was too late to act, and clinging to a last desperate hope that somehow the negation of an act might serve as well.

That negation was performed, if performed is the word; talking, listening, and drinking then merged into a sigh of exhausted relief, and only a few Cassandra voices, among whom was Rainier's, murmured that no miracle had really happened at all. But national hysteria urged that it had, and that one must not say otherwise, even if it hadn't. Anyhow, the crisis passed, the rains of autumn soaked into half-dug trenches, and as the days shortened and darkened the Kenmore lamplight glowed again in the faces of *diseuses* and diplomats—Sir Somebody This and the Maharanee of That, the successful novelist and the Wimbledon winner, delegates from somewhere-or-other to the something-or-other conference, as well as visiting Americans who thought they were experiencing a real pea-souper fog because the sun of a November midday had turned red over the roofs.

I went to a good many of those lunches, and somehow, I don't remember exactly when, it became a recognized thing that I should have a place at all of them unless my duties with Rainier called me elsewhere.

Often they did. Many days during that strange, almost somnambulist winter of 1938–1939 I sat in the Gallery of the House of Commons, listening to dull debates and hearing Big Ben chime the quarters till I saw Rainier get up and push his way through the swing doors with that casualness which is among the specialties of House procedure—a form of self-removal that implies neither rudeness nor even indifference to the speech in progress. Then he would dictate letters in a Committee Room, or order tea, or we might stroll along the usually empty Terrace, watching the last spears of sunset fade from the windows of St. Thomas's Hospital, or staring over the parapet at a train of coal barges on their way upstream. It was at such mo-

ments that I came to know him most intimately, and to feel, more
from his presence than from words, that the years he no longer talked
about were still haunting; that he was still, as two women had said,
vainly searching for something and never at rest. Yet outwardly, and
to others, there were few signs of it. Indeed, the disfavor into which
he fell as a result of his attitude towards official policy seemed to
come rather as a release than as a suppression. It was not that he
blamed the government for what had happened at Munich; such
blame, he said, when history assessed it, would doubtless be spread
over many years and many personages, of which the men of 1938
were but last in a tragic line. He did, however, blame those who
had stepped out of panic only to sink back into hypnosis. "These
are the last days," he said to me once. "We are like people in a
trance—even those of us who can see the danger ahead can do nothing to avert it—like the dream in which you drive a car towards a
precipice and your foot is over the brake but you have no physical
power to press down. We should be arming now, if we had sense,—
arming day and night and seven days of the week,—for if the Munich
pact had any value at all it was not as a promise of peace to come,
but as a last-minute chance to prepare for the final struggle. And
we are doing *nothing*—caught in the net of self-delusion and self-
congratulation. We don't realize the skill and magnitude of the conspiracy—the attempt to reverse, by lightning strokes, the whole
civilized verdict of two thousand years."

Such talk, during the winter of 1938–1939, was heresy in a country
that permitted heresy, but could not regard it as in good taste. People
began to remark, in advance of any argument about him, that they
liked Rainier—this also was a bad sign in a society where likings
are rarely expressed except by way of fair-minded prelude to disparagement. And one reflected that there had always been something
against his chances of attaining high office—something expressed by
his political enemies when they praised him as "brilliant," and by
his political friends when they doubted if he were altogether "safe."
Such doubts were now running high.

In the City, however, safety and brilliance were not held as in-
compatibles by gatherings of grateful shareholders at annual meetings in the Rainier Building. Here also it was my duty to accompany
him, handing out appropriate documents and keeping his memory
jogged against forgetfulness of such things as—"You will be glad to
know that during the past year we have opened a new factory at
West Bromwich where we are now manufacturing a model especially designed for the Colonies." He made such announcements with

a solemnity in which only I, perhaps, detected any ironic note; similarly there seemed to me a touch of disdain in his bent for handling complicated masses of figures, a touch that did not detract from the enormous confidence reposed in him by enriched but usually mystified investors. Nor was that confidence misplaced. Once I said to him: "Leaving sentiment out of it, you haven't done so badly. You saved the family inheritance, you rescued the money of hundreds of outsiders, and you kept intact the jobs of a whole army of workpeople. You did, in fact, everything you set out to do."

"There's only one thing more important," he answered, "and that is, after you've done what you set out to do, to feel that it's been worth doing."

That was the day when he took me down to the sub-basement of the Rainier Building to show me the result of certain constructional work that had been in progress there for several weeks. "I've allowed it to be supposed that these are new storage vaults," he told me, as we entered the first of a series of empty catacombs, "but actually I had another thought in mind—and one that it would be too bad to thrust on a group of happy dividend collectors. But the fact is—and entirely at my own personal expense—I've made this place bomb-proof. So you see, *something's* been worth doing." He walked me round like an estate agent. "Comfort, as well as safety,—there's an independent heating plant,—because it's no good saving people from high explosive just to have them die of influenza. And another reason—the greatest man of the twentieth century may have to be born in a place like this, so let's make it as decent as we can for him. A steel and concrete Manger—sixty feet below ground . . . that's why I've had to keep it a big secret, because you couldn't expect the investing public to swallow *that.*"

But we liked the City—"the City of Meticulous Nonsense," he called it once, after an annual meeting at which somebody had used the adjective in praise of his own attention to the firm's affairs. "*Meticulous,*" he echoed, afterwards, "really meaning *timid*—and how right that it should nowadays be used as a compliment, since so many of the most complimented people nowadays deserve it! Meticulous little people attending meticulous meetings, passing meticulous votes of thanks for meticulous behavior!"

One rainy Saturday we waited several minutes while the homeward rush-hour crowd swarmed in front of the car, taking no notice of the horn until a man, just an ordinary mackintoshed fellow with (I remembered) a piece of garden trellis under his arm, called out:

" 'Ere, give the bloke a chawnce!"—whereat the crowd, heeding just as casually as they had been heedless before, made way for us to pass. There was no resentment in their faces because we had an expensive car or because we kept them waiting a few seconds longer in the rain, no social significance in the appeal to give the bloke a chance, no indication of who the bloke was—I or Rainier or the chauffeur. The very absence of all these things was English, Rainier said—something offhand but good-humored, free but obedient, careless but never heartless.

"But tell that," he added, "to the Indians in Amritsar, to the Chinese who read the notice in a Shanghai park, 'No Dogs or Chinese Allowed,' to the tribesmen in Irak, to the peasant in County Cork, to the . . ." But then he laughed. "God, how we're hated! It isn't so much because we really deserve it. Even at the bottom of the charge sheet I could quote Santayana's remark that the world never had sweeter masters. *Sweet*—a curious adjective—and yet there *is* a sweetness in the English character, something that's almost perfect when it's just ripe—like an apple out of an English orchard. No, we're not hated altogether by logic. It's more because the world is *tired* of us—*bored* with us—sickened by a taste that to some already seems oversweet and hypocritical, to others sour and stale. I suppose the world grew tired of the Romans like that, till at last the barbarians were excused for barbarism more readily than the Caesars were forgiven for being tough. There come such moments in the lives of nations, as of persons, when they just can't do anything right, and the world turns on them with the awful ferocity of a first-night audience rejecting, not so much a play it doesn't want, as a playwright it doesn't want any more. . . . But wait till they've experienced the supplanters—if we are supplanted. A time may come when a cowed and brutalized world may look back on the period of English domination as one of the golden ages of history. . . ."

I remember that afternoon particularly because as we were waiting for the traffic lights in Whitehall we saw Nixon at the curbside vainly signaling a taxi and Rainier had the car stopped to offer him a lift. Bound for Victoria to catch a train, he chattered all the time during the short drive, finally and quite casually remarking: "Oh, you remember that fellow Ransome who took us to tea at his house in Browdley that day when his wife wasn't there?"

Rainier looked up sharply.

"Rather sad business," Nixon continued. "She'd gone out to buy a cake, as Ransome thought—must have been hurrying back, because she was carrying it as she ran into the bus . . . killed instantly . . .

poor chap was in a terrible state, so I heard. Only been married about a year."

We drove on in silence after dropping Nixon in the station yard; Rainier's face was strained, tense, as if he had suffered a personal blow. Halfway to Kenmore he tapped on the window and ordered the chauffeur to turn and drive back. "Let's hear somebody play the piano," he said. "That's the best cure for the mood I'm in."

We drove to the West End, while I searched the *Telegraph* for recital announcements. The only one I could find was of the first and only appearance in London of Casimir Navoida, who would give a mixed program of Beethoven, Chopin, Brahms, and Ravel at the Selsdon Hall. I had never heard of Navoida, and the fact that Rainier hadn't either lent no optimism to my expectations. We found a photograph on the rain-sodden posters outside the Hall—the conventionally somber, heavy-lidded profile brooding over the keys. That too was not encouraging, nor was the obviously "paper" audience of only a few score. Nor, for that matter, were the explanatory notes in the printed program—composed, Rainier grimly suggested, by some schoolgirl in a mood of bibulous *Schwärmerei*. With less distaste we read a paragraph about the performer, though even that was vague enough—merely mentioning a Continental reputation, tuition under Leschetizky (misspelt), a prix-de-somewhere, and an ancient press-agent anecdote beginning—"One morning, at the So-and-So Conservatoire . . ." Then the door at the rear of the platform opened and this fellow Navoida walked to the piano, gave a hinge-like bow to half-hearted applause, and began. He did not look much like his photograph, though a description could not have omitted the same points—the gloomy profile, wrinkled nape, and upflung hair. We listened with tolerance, soon aware that his playing was not exactly bad. When the interval came I noticed a woman in the seat beyond Rainier's fumbling for a dropped program; presently he stooped and retrieved it for her. She thanked him with a foreign accent and added: "You think he plays well?"

Rainier answered: "He might be good if he weren't out of practice."

"You are a critic?"

"Only to myself."

"You are not on one of the newspapers?"

"Oh dear, no."

She seemed both relieved and disappointed. "I thought you might be. I suppose they *are* here."

Rainier looked round and included me in the conversation by say-

ing: "Notice anybody? *I* don't. . . . I'm afraid Saturday afternoon's
a bad time in London."

Then Navoida came on again and played the Chopin group. At
the next interval she said: "You are quite right. He is out of practice.
He played cards till four this morning."

Rainier laughed. "Stupid of him, surely?"

"Oh, he doesn't care. He lost much money, also. If only people
would realize that he *can* play so much better than this—"

"Why *should* they? If he chooses to drink and gamble the night
before a concert—"

"Oh no, not *drink*. He *never* drinks."

"No?"

"But gambling is in his blood. It is in the blood of all the Navoidas.
If he travels by autobus he will bet on how many people get in at
each stop."

Rainier looked slightly interested. "How do you know all this about
him?"

She had just time to reply, as the piano began again: "I am his
wife."

I could judge that throughout the Brahms Sonata Rainier was feeling somewhat embarrassed at having discussed the pianist so frankly,
but when the next interval came she gave him no time to apologize.
"Oh, I could *kill* him for being so bad! The foolish boy. . . . Maybe
it was a mistake to come to England at all."

Rainier answered: "Oh, no need to feel that. But your husband's
concert agent ought to have chosen a better day for a first appearance. Londoners like to get away to the country at week ends."

"Even when it rains?"

"My goodness, we never bother about rain."

"*Ach,* yes, your London climate . . . when it is not rain, it is fog.
. . . I understand."

I winked at him, apropos of this foreign belief that English
weather is the worst in the world; it is not, Rainier had once said,
but the convention is useful in that it enables an Englishman to appear modest by conceding something that, whether true or false, is
of little consequence. All the time that Madame Navoida was be-
moaning London rain and fog I was glancing at her sideways and
judging her to be forty-five or so—younger, at any rate in looks, than
her husband. The light in the concert hall was not particularly kind,
and her make-up had either been put on hurriedly or else had got
blurred by raindrops; her eyes were brown and rather small, but her

forehead had a generous width that somehow compensated; it was
an interesting face.

During the Ravel I whispered this to Rainier and received his
reply: "I don't give a damn about her face. And I don't give a damn
about this Ravel either. I only know she amuses me and I'm more
cheerful than I was an hour ago. . . ."

For the next few minutes I heard the two of them in whispered
conversation; then he turned to me. "They're Hungarians, but she
lived for a long time in Singapore—hence the English. She also speaks
French and German—besides, of course, Hungarian. Writes poetry
in all four, so she'd have you believe. Also worships Romance with
a capital R. Reads Dekobra and D'Annunzio, but prefers Dekobra—
so do I, for that matter. . . . Altogether rather like a female spy in
a magazine story—every minute I expect her to say 'Hein' and produce a bundle of stolen treaties out of her corsage. And she says
such delicious things—like—'Ach, your English climate—' and that bit
about gambling being in the blood of all the Navoidas. . . . I'm trying to think of something half as good as what she'll say next—remember that game we used to play?"

That was one of the fooleries we would sometimes indulge in during our morning car journeys to the City. There was a certain newspaper shop at a street corner in Pimlico, and outside it, every Tues-
day, appeared a picture poster advertising that week's issue of a
publication called *Judy's Paper;* and this poster always showed an
evening-clothed couple in some highly dramatic situation, captioned
by such a sentence as "He refused her a ring" or "She lied to save
him." Most Tuesdays, before we reached the shop, Rainier and I
would try to invent something even triter than what we should presently discover, but we never succeeded, so hard is it for the sophisticated mind to think in the natural idiom of the ingenuous. But it
made an amusing diversion, for all that.

After further whispering he turned to me excitedly. "She's *said* it!
I *knew* she would! She's just told me that we English are so *cold!*"
At that moment Navoida finished the Ravel and Rainier was able to
answer her amidst the applause. I heard him say: "Madame, we are
not cold—it's merely that we have to be warmed up, especially on
wet Saturdays. So I beg you to make allowances for us during the
rest of your stay here."

"We are leaving tomorrow."

"So soon?"

"Casimir has a concert in Ostend on Wednesday."

"You'd better take care of him there. It's a great place for gambling."

"Oh, that will be all right. We shall go to the Casino and have champagne and Casimir will be lucky—he always is at roulette. It is cards he is no good at—especially poker." (She pronounced it "pokker.") "When I saw him playing poker with some Americans at the hotel last night, I knew he would be a bad boy today."

"I thought you said he didn't drink?"

"Only champagne. But of course it is so expensive in England. When we were in Singapore we drank nothing but Heidsieck all the time. A bottle every meal. It prevented him from being dysenteric."

"Probably it also prevented him from being Paderewski."

"You mean it is not good for him? But consider—if it pleases him, is he not entitled to it? What is the life of a concert artist nowadays? Nobody cares—there is no musical life as it used to be—in Berlin, in Leipzig, in Wien. Only in America they pay an artist well, but I do not want him to go there again."

"Why not?"

She whispered something in Rainier's ear and then added: "Of course I forgave him afterwards. He was faithful according to his fashion."

Rainier let out a shout of sheer glee. "What's that? *What?*"

She repeated the sentence. "Do you not know the poem by one of your English poets, Ernest Dowson?" And she began to recite the whole thing from beginning to end, while Casimir, in whom I was beginning to feel a deeper interest after these varied revelations, appeared on the platform to play the Chopin "Black Key Study" as an encore, muffing the final octaves and finishing on a triumphantly wrong note in the bass. "Perhaps you would now like to meet him?" she concluded.

So we trooped round to the little room at the back of the platform where a few mournfully mackintoshed women were loitering while the pianist scrawled his signature across their programs in a mood of equal mournfulness. The entrance of Madame Navoida brought a touch of life to these proceedings, and I noticed then a certain vital quality that made her still an attractive woman, despite sagging lines and the bizarre make-up. As soon as the autograph seekers left she approached Casimir as one making a stage entrance, kissed him resoundingly on both cheeks, and cried: "*Casimir, mon cher, tu étais magnifique!*" Then, for a moment, she gabbled something incomprehensible and turned to Rainier. "He speaks Hungarian best. I have to tell him he is wonderful now, but soon I shall tell him he was awful

—*atrocious!* Poor boy, he is always tired after a concert—please excuse him. He says he has a headache."

Rainier answered: "That's too bad! I was about to suggest that you both had dinner with us somewhere—that is, if you had nothing else to do."

Her face lit up. "Oh, but we should be *enchanted!* It is so kind of you. I am sure his headache will get better. But there is one thing I must tell you beforehand—he will not dress. Not even a smoking. Only for the casinos where they will not admit him otherwise—and then he curses all the time. So if you do not mind—"

"Not at all. We probably wouldn't dress ourselves, anyway."

"Then he will be delighted." She turned to her husband. "Casimir, this is—" And of course another turn. "But I do not know your name?"

I had guessed it would come to that, and I remembered that moment on Armistice Day when all Rainier's pleasure had disappeared at the enforced disclosure of his identity. I wondered if it would be different with foreigners to whom his name would almost certainly be unknown.

But he answered, with a sort of gleeful solemnity: "Lord Frederic Verisopht—and this—" with a bow to me—"is Sir Mulberry Hawk. . . ."

Having arranged to meet them at seven at Poldini's we spent the interval at Rainier's club, where his spirits soared fantastically. When I reminded him of an engagement to speak that evening at the Annual Dinner of the Gladstone Society he told me to wire them a cancellation on account of urgent political business. "That's all very well," I answered, "but then somebody will see us dining at Poldini's with a couple who look like a rather seedy croupier and a soubrette out of a prewar musical comedy."

He laughed. "Not if we do what nobody else does nowadays—engage a private room."

"And what was the idea of introducing me as Sir Somebody or other?"

"To find out whether she reads Dickens. *You* evidently don't. . . . Well, that was *partly* the reason. The other was to give her a thrill. I'm sure titles do. Poldini's will too—it's got that air of having seen better and more romantic days. I rarely go there, so the waiters don't know me, and I've never been in one of their private rooms since my uncle took me when I was twelve years old. That's a story in itself. I don't think I ever told you about him—he was a charming and very shortsighted archdeacon, and the only one out of my large collection of uncles whom I really liked. He liked me too, I think—we often used to spend a day together. One evening during the Christmas holidays, we felt hungry after a matinée of *Jack and the Beanstalk*, so as we were walking to the nearest Underground station he said, 'Let's go in here for a snack'—and it was Poldini's. I think he mistook it for some sort of cheap but respectable teashop—anyhow, we walked in, all among the pretty ladies and the young men-about-town; we were the cynosure of every eye, as novelists in those days used to write—because it wasn't at all the kind of place a Church of England dignitary would normally take his schoolboy nephew to, and my uncle, with his white hair and flashing eyes (the drops he had to put in them made them flash), must have looked rather like Hall Caine's Christian about to create a disturbance. . . . Anyhow, old Poldini,—he's dead now,—scenting something funny about us, pretended all his tables were booked and asked if we'd mind dining upstairs—so up we went, my uncle blinking his way aloft without a word of protest, and presently Poldini showed us into a cosy little room furnished in blue and gold, with a very thick carpet and a convenient chaise longue against the wall and gilt cupids swarming in a suggestive manner all over the ceiling—in fact, Poldini took charge of us completely, recommending à la carte dishes and serving them himself, and as the meal progressed my uncle grew more and more surprised and delighted—still under the impression it was an A.B.C. or some such place; and when the bill came I snatched it up and said I'd stand treat, and he said, 'My boy, that's very generous of you'—and by God, it was, for it took all the money he'd just given me as a Christmas present. But I never let him know, and to the end of his life he always used to tell people he'd never enjoyed a better meal than at that eating house off the Strand . . . *eating house*, mind you!" He took a long breath and added: "So that's where we'll dine tonight—among the ghosts of the past—a couple of milords entertaining the toast of the town—and rather battered toast, if you'll pardon two bad puns at once."

When I look back on that evening I remember chiefly, of course, the incident that crowned it; but I can see now that the entire masquerade was somehow Rainier's last and rather preposterous effort to tease a way into self-knowledge, and that the climax, though completely accidental, was yet a fitting end to the attempt. I realized also, even if never before, how near he was to some catastrophic breakdown—partly from overwork, but chiefly from the fret of things that could not be forgotten because they had never been remembered. And all that day, ever since meeting Nixon, the fret had strengthened behind an increasing randomness of acts and words.

We drove to Poldini's through the rain, and were glad to find the place reasonably unchanged—still with its private rooms upstairs, little used by a generation that no longer needs such an apparatus of seduction, and therefore slightly melancholy until gardenias and ice buckets revived a more festive spirit. Then, with some commotion, the Navoidas arrived, the pianist rather pale and glum in a long overcoat with an astrakhan collar, and Madame very florid and voluble with heavy gold bangles and ancient but good-quality furs, obviously bewitched (but by no means ill-at-ease) at the prospect of dining intimately with English nobility. We soon discovered that both of them were equally accomplished champagne bibbers, but whereas Madame grew livelier and gayer with every glass, her husband sank after the first half-dozen into a settled gloom from which he could only stir himself at intervals to murmur to the waiter a demand for "trouts"—for there had been some confusion over his order, due perhaps to the waiter's reluctance to believe that anyone in 1939 would ask for *truites bleues* in addition to Beluga caviare, steak *tartare,* and English *rosbif.* But all that too, and to Rainier's feverish delight, was in the halcyon tradition—the age of monstrous dinners and fashionable appendicitis, the one most often the result of the others.

Presently, after the popping of the fourth magnum, Madame grew sentimental and talked of her romantic adventures in all parts of the world—a recital garnished with copious quotations from the poets, of whom she knew so many in various languages that I began to think it really must be a passion with her quite as genuine as that for Heidsieck; she liked amorous poetry best, and there was something perhaps a little charming in the way she obviously did not know which was too hackneyed to quote, so that from a worn-out tag of Shakespeare she would swerve into a line from Emily Brontë or Beddoes. A few words she wrongly pronounced or did not understand; she would then ask us to correct her, quite simply and with an absence of self-consciousness that made almost piquant her theatrical gestures and overstudied rhythms. Suddenly I realized, in the mood of half-maudlin pity that comes after a few drinks yet is none the less percipient, that she was a sadly disappointed woman, getting little out of later life that she really craved, without a home, a wanderer between hotels and casinos, listening to the same old Brahms and Beethoven in half-empty concert halls, tied for the rest of her days to a flabby maestro, yet alive in her illusion that the world was still gay and chivalrous as a novelette.

After Rainier had called for more cognac he asked if she had any ideas for spending the rest of the evening, because he'd be glad to go on to a show if she fancied any particular play. She answered, with enthusiasm: "Oh yes, it is so kind of you—there is one place I have always wanted to go because I have heard so much about it —your famous old English music hall!"

Rainier said how unfortunate that was, because the famous old English music hall no longer existed; there were only assortments of vaudeville turns and dance bands.

"Then perhaps we could go to see Berty Lowe."

"Berty Lowe?"

"A man at the hotel told me this morning he was acting in London somewhere, and I should like to see him because I once knew an Englishman in Budapest who used to do imitations of him. He always said Berty Lowe was the greatest comedian of the famous old English music hall."

Rainier had asked the waiter for an evening paper and was now glancing down the list. "Yes, he used to be quite funny, but I haven't heard of him in London for years—he's a bit passé, you know . . . well, he's not at the Coliseum or the Holborn Empire . . . that rather limits the possibilities . . . wait a minute, though—'Berty Lowe in *Salute the Flag* Twice Nightly at the Banford Hippodrome'—"

She clapped her hands ecstatically. "Oh, I should love to go there!"

"But it's miles away in the suburbs—" he was beginning, but suddenly then I could see the mere caprice of the idea seize hold of him; to drive out to Banford to see Berty Lowe at the local Hippodrome was in the right key of fantasy for such an evening. He handed me the paper. "They call it a riot of rip-roaring rib-tickling—doesn't that sound awful? Wish you'd ring 'em up and book a box for four at the second house."

"*Salute the Flag*," echoed Madame, with hands clasped. "Oh, I know I am going to love it if it is about soldiers. The Englishman I knew in Budapest was a soldier. It was during the war, but he wasn't interned at first, because the Hungarians always liked the English, but when he began to send me flowers every day with little notes hidden in them—written in English, of course—the police arrested him for espionage, but when they translated the notes—oh, *mon dieu*, you should have seen their faces—and *his*—and *mine*—because, you see, he was crazily in love with me—*crazily*—not a bit like an Englishman! Oh, how I wish I had made them give me back those notes. . . . Casimir, of course, was mad with jealousy."

Casimir, no longer capable of being mad with jealousy, looked up as a dog will on hearing his name mentioned, then shook his head with a bemused belch over his unfinished *crêpes Suzettes*.

I went out to telephone.

An hour later we were sitting on four very uncomfortable cane chairs as the curtain rose on *Salute the Flag*. It had been a mistake, I could see, to have engaged a box; the orchestra seats would have been much more comfortable, and further away from certain plush hangings which, on being merely touched, shook out clouds of dubious-looking dust. I gathered from the way we were escorted to our seats, and also from the fact that the other boxes were empty, that our arrival had created a little stir; it would be odd, I thought, but perhaps not absolutely catastrophic, if some member of the audience were to recognize Rainier. However, no one did, despite the fact that some of the actors played at us outrageously—even, by the end of the show, making jokes about "the gentleman in the box who's fast asleep." It was true; Casimir was fast asleep. Madame awakened him several times, but he slumped forward again almost immediately; soon she gave it up as a bad job.

As for the play, it had been (I guessed) an originally serious melodrama on a wartime theme, dating probably from 1914 or 1915; its villains had then been Germans of impossible villainy and its heroes English soldiers of equally impossible saintliness. A quarter of a century of lucrative adaptation, however, had merged both the villainy and the saintliness into a common mood of broad comedy burlesque; such patriotic speeches as remained were spoken now only to be laughed at, while the hero's first appearance was in the always comic uniform of a scoutmaster.

But Madame was puzzled. During the intermission she said: "I cannot understand why they laugh at some of the lines. When the recruiting sergeant made that speech about the British Empire, what was funny about it?"

"It's just our English sense of humor," Rainier explained. "We think recruiting sergeants *are* funny. We think long speeches are also funny. The British Empire has its funny side too. So put them all together and you can't help making an Englishman laugh."

"But it was a *patriotic* speech!"

"Englishmen think them the funniest of all."

"But in Austria, if anyone laughed at a patriotic speech there would be a riot and the man would be arrested."

"That just proves something I have long suspected—that Austria isn't England."

"You know Austria?"

"I once spent a few days in Vienna on business."

"Ah, you should have stayed longer and gone to the Semmering and then to Pressburg down the Danube in a steamboat."

"Curious you should mention it, but that was one of my boyhood ambitions. But in a canoe, not a steamboat."

"Oh, but that would be more wonderful still! Why did you not do it?"

"Because when I first wanted to, I hadn't enough money—then later, when I had enough money, I hadn't the time . . . and today, whatever I have, there isn't any Austria."

"Ah yes, it is so sad. But let us not think about it—see, the curtain rises!"

She said that so much like a musical-comedy cue that I almost expected to see her jump down to the stage and begin a song. However, *Salute the Flag* was doubtless better entertainment. It continued to be equally hilarious during its second half, though Berty Lowe, as the heavily mustached German general, was actually less funny than some of the smaller parts; there was one especially that had the audience holding their sides—when an English subaltern entered his colonel's tent (the colonel being a German spy in disguise) to exclaim, between chattering teeth and amidst paroxysms of stammering—"The enemy advances—give the order to attack, or, by heaven, sir, I will myself!" As a rule I do not care for jokes based on any physical defect, but I must admit that this particular player brought the house down by some of the most ludicrous facial contortions I have ever seen—the whole episode being topped by the final gag of a doorknob coming off and rolling across the stage when he banged his exit.

It was difficult to keep up or down to such a level, but the play romped on with a good deal of vulgar gusto until the last scene, evidently the dramatic high-spot of the original play, when the heroine, threatened by the villain with a revolver, cried: "You cannot fire on helpless womankind!"—whereat another woman, of suggestive male appearance and elephantine proportions, invaded the stage from the wings brandishing weapons of all kinds from tomahawk to Mills bomb. Crude, undoubtedly; but the Banford audience loved it, and were still laughing throughout the perfunctory finale in which all the cast rushed on to the stage to chase off the villain and line up for a closing chorus.

As we left the theater I saw that Rainier's mood had changed. He almost bundled Madame and her husband into the car, and spoke very little during the ride back to London; she chattered to me for a while, but Rainier's moods had a queer way of enforcing their atmosphere upon others, and she also was somewhat subdued by the time we reached their hotel in Russell Square and set the two of them down on the pavement.

"Good-bye, my lord," she said to Rainier, evidently remembering her manners but not the name. But she remembered mine. "Good-bye, Sir Hawk."

Casimir nodded grumpily as she took his arm to help him up the hotel steps. The last we saw was her effort to get him through the revolving door. It should have been funny, but perhaps we had had enough laughter for one evening; it wasn't funny, therefore, it was somehow rather sad.

"Of course she's ruined him," Rainier commented, as we drove away towards Chelsea.

"What makes you think that?"

"His playing. I could tell he was good once."

"Well, he's ruined her too. She can't get much fun out of life, watching over him wherever they go. Incidentally, I think she was rather shocked by our rough island humor."

"Probably it was too unsanitary and not sexy enough for her."

"And then that fellow's stammer. I suppose on the Vienna stage you couldn't have an officer stammering—only a private."

"God, yes—that stammer . . . they kept it in—and the doorknob coming off as well. . . . But the gag at the end was new."

"Sounds as if you've seen the show before."

He was thoughtful. "Yes, I think I have."

"Not surprising. It's been played up and down everywhere for years."

"But more than that—more than *seeing* it before—I—I—" He turned to me with a curious abrupt eagerness. "Do you mind if we drive around for a while before going home?"

"Of course not. . . . But what's happened? You look—" I stopped, but he cut in sharply: "Yes, *tell* me—what's the matter with me—*how* do I look?"

I said, meeting his eyes and speaking with as little excitement as I could: "You look as you did when I first saw you staring at a mountain because you thought you recognized it—through the train windows that Armistice Day."

"*Armistice Day,*" he repeated. Then he added, quietly, almost casually: "I was in hospital . . . I mean on that first Armistice Day— the first one of all. The *real* one." He suddenly clutched my sleeve. "Yes, I remember—I was at Melbury!"

I said nothing, anxious not to break any thread of recollection he was about to unravel, and afraid of the tension in my voice were I to speak at all.

"There were so many hospitals," he went on. "I was at Sennelager first—then Hanover. Then they exchanged the shell-shock and t.b. cases through Switzerland. So back home—Birmingham for a time— then Hastings—and another place near Manchester . . . then Melbury. That was the last of them. . . . I'd like to go to Melbury."

I still couldn't answer; I was afraid of breaking some kind of spell. He seemed to read this into my silence, for he went on, in a kindly voice: "Do you mind? Or are you very tired?"

"No, I'm not tired." My voice was all right, but I was still apprehensive, and more so than ever when I realized he wanted to go to Melbury that very night, immediately. I added something about Hanson being probably tired, even if we weren't—after all he'd driven us to Banford and back, and to ask him now to make another excursion into the distant suburbs . . .

"Yes, of course—glad you thought of it." He was always considerate to servants. "We'll drop him here and send him home by taxi. Then I'll drive—or perhaps you'd better if you think I've had too much to drink." He was already reaching for the speaking tube, and had given the new instructions before I could think of anything else to say at all, much less frame an objection. Hanson pulled up at the curb, showing no more curiosity than a good servant should. But it was still pouring with rain, and he must have thought it odd to choose such a night for a pleasure drive.

Rainier moved next to me in the chauffeur's seat; as I drove off he said he hoped I knew the way.

"Through Stepney and Stratford, isn't it?"

"Don't ask me—I've never been there since—since the morning I left."

"You remember it was a *morning?*"

He turned to me excitedly. "Did I say morning? Yes, it *was* . . . and if I can only *see* the place again—"

"You won't see much tonight, I'm afraid."

"I didn't see much last time, either—it was too foggy. God—that's something else. . . . Just let me talk on anyhow. Don't feel you have to answer—I know it's hard to drive these juggernauts on a wet night —why does my wife always buy such monsters?—and we have four of them."

"Nothing to stop you buying a small car yourself if you wanted."

"But I'm not interested in buying cars."

I laughed and said: "Well, you can't have it both ways. If you're not interested in cars, you can't blame Mrs. Rainier for buying the kind she thinks is suitable for a rich man who isn't interested in cars."

"True, true. . . ." The side issue had lowered the tension.

We drove through the almost deserted City, past Aldgate and along the wide, brilliant, rococo Mile End Road. It was midnight as we crossed Bow Bridge, five minutes past as we reached the fork of the road in Stratford Broadway; I had to drive slowly because of the slippery tram rails. Once I stopped to inquire from some men drinking at a coffee stall; they waved us on into the deepening hinterland of the suburbs. The slums here lost their sinister picturesqueness, became more and more drably respectable: long vistas of lamplit roads, with here and there a block of elementary schools rising like a fortress over the roof tops, and at every shopping center the same names in a different order—Woolworth, Maypole, Sainsbury, Home and Colonial, Lyons. We passed an old-fashioned church with a new-fashioned sign outside it, proclaiming the subject of next Sunday's sermon—"Why Does God Permit War?"—and that set Rainier improvising on the kind of sermon it would be—"very cheerful and chummy, proving that God isn't such a bad sort when you get to know Him"; and then abruptly, in the tangental way so characteristic when he was inwardly excited, he talked again of his favorite uncle the archdeacon. "*He* never preached a sermon on 'Why Does God Permit War?' To begin with, I don't suppose he ever thought about it, and if he had, he'd probably have answered 'Why shouldn't He?' He took it for granted that the Deity minded His own business, and that 'God's in His Heaven' was just Browning's way of putting it. All this craze for bringing Him down to earth and appealing to Him at every turn would have struck my uncle as weak-kneed as well as in appallingly bad taste. And yet, in his way, and on the outskirts of Cheltenham, he lived an almost saintly life. He would never kill insects that strayed into the house, but would trap them in match boxes and set them free in the garden. He approved of hunting, though, and thought the smearing of a girl's face with fox blood after her first ride to hounds was a rather charming custom. All in all, I don't suppose he was any more inconsistent than the modern parson who tries to combine Saint Francis, Lenin, and Freud into one all-embracing muddle."

We drove on through Leytonstone; there the tramlines ended and we could put on a little speed. It was just after one o'clock when we reached the market square in the center of Melbury; I pulled up and looked to him for further instructions. He was peering through the window and after a moment I wound the window down on my side. The rain had increased to the dimensions of a storm, and a solitary policeman sheltering under a shop awning called out to us: "Looking for somewhere?"

Rainier turned at the sound of the stranger's voice.

"Yes, the hospital," he answered. "Where's the hospital?"

"You mean the new one or the old one, sir?"

"The old one, I think." Then in a sudden rush: "It's on a hill—has big gates and a high wall all around it."

The policeman looked puzzled. "That don't sound much like either of 'em." Then, as I was about to thank him and drive off, he came towards the car, leaned in, and said, with a glance across me to Rainier: "You wouldn't be meanin' the *asylum*, would you, sir?"

PART FOUR

He was so tired of stammering out to a succession of doctors all he knew about himself that eventually he jotted it down on a single sheet of notepaper for them to refer to at will. He had recently been transferred to Melbury from another military hospital, and the change had somewhat upset him, because it meant beginning everything all over again—contacts with new doctors, nurses, and patients, the effort to find another corner of existence where people would presently leave him alone. Besides, he didn't like the place—it was too big, too crowded, and altogether too permanent-looking. Overworked psychiatrists gave him treatments that were supposed to have done well in similar cases, but perhaps it was part of his own case that he didn't feel any similar cases existed, though he admitted there were many worse ones; he also felt that the doctors—grand fellows all of them, he had no specific complaints—aimed at raising a statistical average of success rather than his own individual cure.

That particular morning in November he began the regulation mile along the cinder paths, glad that the fog had kept most of his fellow victims indoors. Only alone did his various symptoms ever approach vanishing point, and amidst the fog this sense of aloneness was intensified so reassuringly that as he continued to walk he began to feel a curious vacuum of sensation that might almost be called contentment. Walking was part of the encouraged regimen at Melbury; extensive grounds surrounded by a fifteen-foot spiked wall permitted it while an army greatcoat kept the cold air from penetrating his thinnish hospital uniform.

Suddenly, as he neared the main entrance where the name had been painted over (though it was still readable in burnt letters on brooms and garden tools—"Property of the So-and-So County Asylum")—suddenly, as the heavily scrolled ironwork of the gates loomed through the fog, a siren screamed across the emptiness beyond—a factory siren, already familiar at certain hours, but this was not one of them, nor did the sound stay on the single level note, but began soaring up and down in wild flurries. A few seconds later another siren chimed in, and then a third; by that time he was near enough to the gates to see two uniformed porters rush hatless out of the lodge, shouting excitedly as they raced up the shrouded driveway. For the moment—and he realized it without any answering excitement—there was no one left on guard, no one to stop him as he passed through the lodge into the outer world, no one to notice him as he walked down the lane towards the town. Behind his mute acceptance of things done to him, there was a slow-burning inclination to do things for himself, an inclination fanned now into the faint beginnings of initiative; but they were only faint, he had no will for any struggle, and if anyone ran after him to say "Come back" he would go back.

Nobody ran after him. The lane turned into the main road at the tram terminus; a small crowd was already gathering there in groups, chattering, laughing, greeting each newcomer with eager questions. Nor had the sirens stopped; they were louder now, and joined by tram bells, train whistles, a strange awakening murmur out of the distance. He walked on, still downhill, edging into the roadway to avoid people, glad that the fog was thickening as he descended. Soon he was aware of some approaching vortex of commotion, of crowds ahead that might cover all the roadway and envelop him completely; he felt as well as heard them, and a nagging pinpoint of uneasiness expanded until, to relieve it even momentarily, he turned into a shop at the corner of a street.

The inside was dark, as he had hoped, revealing only vague shapes of counter, shelves, and merchandise; it seemed to be a small neglected general store, smelling of its own shabbiness. The opening door had tinkled a bell, and presently, as his eyes grew used to the dimness, he saw an old woman watching from behind the counter— thin-faced, gray-haired, rather baleful. He tried to ask for cigarettes and began to stammer. He always did when he talked to others, though he could chatter to himself without much trouble—that was one of the points he had noted for the doctors, though he suspected they didn't believe him, and of course it was something he couldn't prove. Just now, with all the extra excitement, his stammer was worse than ever—not a mere tongue-tie, but a nervous tic that convulsed his entire head and face. He stood there, trembling and straining for speech, at last managing to explode a word; the woman said nothing in answer, but after a long scrutiny began sidling away. He relaxed when she had gone, hoping she would just return with the cigarettes and not oblige him to say more, wondering if she would think it odd if he stayed to smoke one of them in the shop. Anyhow, it was good to be alone again. Then suddenly he realized he was not alone. A girl had entered, or else had been there all the time and he hadn't noticed; she too was waiting at the counter, but now she turned to him and began urgently whispering. "She's gone to fetch somebody —she knows where you're from."

He stared hard, trying to isolate her face from the surrounding shadows.

"You *are*, aren't you?"

He nodded.

"She knows you're not supposed to be out."

He nodded again.

"Not that I'd blame anybody for anything today. The war's over— you know that? Isn't it wonderful . . . ? And you certainly don't *look* as if you'd do any harm." She smiled to soften the phrase.

He shook his head and smiled back.

"Well, if you *have* given them the slip, I wouldn't stay here, old boy, that's all."

He smiled again, a little bewildered; somebody was talking to him normally, casually, yet personally too. It was a pleasant experience, he wished it could go on longer, but then he heard the old woman's footsteps returning from some inner room behind the shop; with a final smile he summoned enough energy to walk away. A few seconds later he stood on the pavement, blinking to the light, aware of the prevalent atmosphere as something pungent, an air he could not breathe, a spice too hot for his palate. Shouts were now merging into a steady sequence of cheers, and through the pale fog he saw a tram approach, clanging continuously as it discharged a load of yelling schoolchildren. He turned away from the clamor into a side street where two rows of small houses reached upwards like flying buttresses astride a hill; presently he came to a house with a dingy brass plate outside—"H. T. Sheldrake, Teacher of Music." He spoke the name, *Sheldrake*, to himself—he always tested names like this, hoping that some day one of them would fit snugly into an empty groove in his mind. No, not Sheldrake. There was the sound of a piano playing scales; he listened, calming himself somewhat, till the playing stopped and shrill voices began. That made him move on up the hill, but he felt tired after a short distance and held to a railing for support. Just then the same girl caught up with him.

"What's the matter?"

He smiled.

"I followed you. Thought you looked a bit off-color."

He shook his head valiantly, observing her now for the first time. She was dressed in a long mackintosh and a little fur hat like a fez,

under which brown straight hair framed a face of such friendly eagerness that he suddenly felt it did not matter if she saw and heard his
struggles for speech; rather that than have her think him worse than
he was. He wanted to say: You should see some of the other fellows
up there—what's wrong with me is *nothing*—just a stammer and not
being able to remember things.

While he was planning to say all this she took his arm. "Lean on
me if you like. And talk or not, whichever you want. Don't be nervous."

After that he decided to say merely that he was not really ill, but
only tired after walking further than usual; he began bracing himself to make the effort, smiling beforehand to console her for the
ordeal of watching and listening. Then a curious thing happened;
it was like taking a rush at a door to break through when all the
time the door was neither locked nor even latched. He just opened
his mouth and found that he could speak. Not perfectly, of course,
but almost as easily as if he were talking to himself. It made him
gasp with an astonishment so overwhelming that for the moment he
expected her to share it. "Did you hear *that?* I wasn't so bad *then*, was
I?"

"Of course you weren't. Didn't I tell you not to be nervous?"

"But you don't know what a job I have, as a rule."

"Oh yes I do. I heard you in the shop. But that old woman would
scare anybody. Where d'you want to go?"

"I don't know."

"Well, this street doesn't lead anywhere."

"I was just—walking."

"But weren't you trying to get away?"

"Not—not exactly. I hadn't any real plans. I just came out because
—well, because there was nobody at the gate."

"Do they look after you all right?"

"Oh yes."

"I've heard they're a bit rough with some."

"Not with me."

"All the same, you don't really *like* the place?"

"Not—not very much."

"Then you oughtn't to be in it, surely?"

"There's nowhere else, until I get all right again."

"How can you get all right again when you're not happy in a
place?"

He had often asked himself the same question, but he answered, parrying the idea: "Perhaps I wouldn't be very happy anywhere—just now."

"But the war's over—doesn't that make any difference?" She came near to abrupt tears, then dashed a hand to her eyes and began to laugh. "Silly, that's what I am—everybody's gone silly today. Seems an awful morning to end the war on, doesn't it?—I mean, you'd almost think the sun ought to shine—blue skies—like a picture. . . ." She almost cried again. "Shall we stroll down?"

She gripped his arm as they slowly descended the hill. His walk was pretty good, and he was suddenly proud of it—just the faintest shuffle, nobody would notice. When they reached the piano teacher's house he hesitated. "I'd rather not get mixed up with the crowd—if you don't mind."

"Righto—we'll keep well away." She added: "So you don't like crowds?"

"Not very much."

"Or hospitals?"

He smiled and shook his head.

"Well, that's fine. If I keep on trying I'll really get to know you."

They both laughed; then she said: "There's a place where we could get some hot coffee, if you like *that*."

The Coronation Café was a cheap little place along the Bockley Road, patronized mostly by tramway men on duty who stopped their vehicles outside and dashed in with empty jugs, leaving them to be filled in readiness for the return trip. All day long these swift visitations continued, with barely time for an exchange of words across the counter. But today, the eleventh of November, 1918, drivers and conductors chatted boisterously as if they were in no hurry at all, and passed cheery remarks to the couple who sat at the marble-topped table in the window alcove. They could see the man was a soldier by his greatcoat, and it was a good day for saying cheery things to soldiers. "Wonder 'ow long it'll take to git the rest of you boys 'ome, mate?" . . . "Maybe they'll march 'em to Berlin now and shoot the old Kaiser." . . . "Seems queer to 'ave the war end up like this—right on the dot, as you might say." . . . "Wouldn't surprise me if it's just a rumor, like them Russians comin' through." . . . "But it's all in the papers, see—it sez the Germans 'ave signed a what's-a-name—means *peace*, don't it?" All this and much else in snatches of news and comment. The proprietor always answered: "You're right there, mister"—"That's just what I always said meself," or, if the remark had been especially emphatic: "You 'it the nail straight on the 'ead that time, mister." Towards noon the fog grew very thick in-

deed and drivers reported crowds still increasing at the busy centers;
workpeople had been sent home from offices and factories, as well
as children from all the schools. Then the trams stopped running,
impeded by fog and crowds equally, and as there were no more
customers at the Coronation Café the proprietor set to work behind
his counter, polishing a large tea urn till it glowed in the gloom like
a copper sun. Presently he came over to the table. He was a little
man, pale-faced, bald, with watery eyes and a drooping mustache.

"Wouldn't you two like a bite o' somethin'?"

The girl looked to her companion, saw him frame a word and
then begin to struggle with it; she intervened quickly: "Sounds a
good idea. What have you got?"

"Eggs, that's about all. 'Ow d'yer like 'em—soft or 'ard?"

Again she looked across the table before answering. "Oh, mid-
dling'll do."

"That's the ticket. That's 'ow I like 'em meself. And two more
coffees?"

"Righto."

"Keep yer warmed-up a day like this. War's over, they say, but
anybody can die of pewmonia."

"That's a fact, so bring those coffees quick."

He went away chuckling; then the girl leaned across the table
and said: "Don't look so scared. He won't bite."

"I know. But I'm always like that with strangers—at first. And besides—I don't think I've enough money."

"Well, who cares about that? I have."

"But—"

"Now don't start being the gentleman. You were telling me about
yourself when that fellow came up. Go on with the story." He stared
at her rather blankly till she added: "Unless you'd rather not. Your
mind's on something else, I can see."

"I'd just noticed that sign outside." He pointed through the window to a board overhanging the pavement above the café doorway
—the words "Good Pull-Up for Carmen" were dimly readable
through the fog. "Carmen," he muttered. "That gives me something
—why, yes . . . Melba."

"Melba? Oh, you mean the opera?" She began to laugh. "And
Melba gives me peaches. What is this—a game?"

"Sort of. I have to keep on doing it, one of the doctors says—part
of his treatment. You see, I've lost my memory about certain things.
It's like being blind and having to feel around for shapes and sizes."

"I'm terribly sorry. I didn't realize, or I wouldn't have laughed."

"Oh, that's all right—I'd rather you laugh. I wish everybody would laugh. . . . Now what was it you were asking me before?"

"Well, I was wondering why you had to be in a hospital at all, but now of course I understand."

"Yes—till I get thoroughly better. I daresay I will—eventually."

"And then your memory'll come back?"

"That's what they think."

"But in the meantime what are you going to do?"

"Just wait around till it happens, I suppose."

"Isn't there some way of tracing any of your relatives and friends? Advertising for them, or something like that?"

"They've tried. Some people did come to see me at the hospital once, but—I wasn't their son."

"I'll bet they were disappointed. You'd make a nice son for somebody."

"Well, *I* was disappointed too. I'd like to have belonged to them —to have had a home somewhere."

He then gave her some of the facts he had written out for the doctors—that he had been blown up by a shell during 1917, and that when he recovered consciousness he was in a German hospital somewhere, unidentified and unidentifiable. Later there had been an exchange of wounded and shell-shocked prisoners through Switzerland, and by this means the problem had been passed on to the English—but with no more success. He had been a pretty bad case at first, with loss of speech and muscular co-ordination, but those things had gradually returned—perhaps the memory would follow later. Altogether he had spent over a year in various hospitals, of which he liked the one at Melbury least of all. "Mind you," he added, seizing the chance to say what he thought of saying before, "I'm miles better than some of the others. You'd think so too if you saw them."

"And that's why *you* shouldn't see them at all. Doesn't exactly help you, does it?"

"No, but I suppose all the hospitals are so crowded—there's no chance to separate us properly."

The proprietor, coming up with the coffee and eggs, saw them break off their conversation suddenly. "Gettin' a bit dark in 'ere— I'll give yer a light," he murmured, to satisfy a dawning curiosity. Standing on a bench he pulled the chain under a single incandescent burner in the middle of the ceiling; it sent a pale greenish glow over their faces. He stared at them both. "You don't look so chirpy, mite. Feelin' bad?"

"He's just tired, that's all." And then, to get the fellow out: "Bring a packet of cigarettes, will you?"

When he had gone she leaned across. "That's what you were trying to ask for in the shop, wasn't it?"

"Yes, but I didn't really need them."

"Oh, come, I know what you need more than you do yourself. Don't be scared of that little chap—he means all right."

The proprietor returned to their table with the cigarettes. "Looks to me as if 'e might 'ave the flu, miss. Lots o' flu abart 'ere. Dyin' like flies, they was, up at the 'orspital a few weeks ago."

When he had gone again she comforted: "There now, don't worry. If you don't like it here, let's eat and then we'll be off."

"It isn't that I don't like it, only—only I'd rather them not come after me, that's all."

"Why should they?"

"He mentioned the hospital. He knows I'm from there, just as you did when you first saw me. It's in my face—the way I look at people. I haven't a chance—even if I knew where to go. They come round the wards every night at six. If I get back by then there'll be no trouble."

"You really mean to go back?"

"There's nothing else to do." He smiled wanly. "You've been very kind to bring me here."

"Oh, don't talk like that."

"But you have. I'm grateful. Maybe I'll be more satisfied now, because I shall know I'm not really well enough to be on my own —*yet*."

They ate in silence for a few moments after that; then she went up to the counter and paid the bill. "One and tenpence, miss. Can't make it any more or I would. An' if I were you, I'd get your pal 'ome pretty quick. 'E don't look as if 'e ought to be aht, an' that's a fact."

A moment later the fog was curling round them in swathes, fanning the sound of cheers over distant invisible roofs. She took his arm again as they walked to the next corner, then turned through quiet residential roads away from the center of the town. But at one place jubilant householders were dancing round a bonfire, and to avoid passing through the blaze of light they made a second detour, along alleys that twisted more and more confusingly till, with a sudden rush of sound, they were back in the main street, caught in a madder, wilder throng. Already the war had been over for several hours, and the first shock of exultation was yielding to a hysteria that dis-

guised an anticlimax. The war was over . . . but now what? The
dead were still dead; no miracle of human signature could restore
limbs and sight and sanity; the grinding hardships of those four years
could not be wiped out by a headline. Emotions were numb, were
to remain half-numbed for a decade, and relief that might have eased
them could come no nearer than a fret to the nerves. A few things
were done, symbolically; men climbed street lamps to tear away the
shades that had darkened them since the first air raids in human
history; shop windows suddenly blazed out with new globes in long-
empty sockets. The traffic center at Melbury was like a hundred
others in and around London that day; the crowds, the noise, the
light, the fog. Beyond a certain limit of expression there was nothing
to say, nothing much even to do; yet the urge to say and to do was
self-torturing. So, as the day and the night wore on, throngs were
swayed by sharp caprices—hoisting shoulder-high some chance-
passing soldier on leave, smashing the windows of tradesmen
rumored to have profiteered, making a fire of hoardings that proclaimed slogans for winning the now-extinct war, booing the harassed police who tried to keep such fires in check. From cheers to
jeers, from applause to anger, were but a finger touch of difference
in the play of events on taut nerves.

Presently a girl summoning help for a soldier in hospital uniform
who had fainted provided a new thrill—compassion; within a few
seconds the crowd was entirely swept by it, pressing in on the two
donors with cries of pity, indignation, and advice to do this and that.

"Give 'im air! Keep back there! Pick 'im up and carry 'im inside—
I got some whiskey—give the poor chap a nip. . . . No, 'e shouldn't
'ave no alco'ol, not without a doctor. . . . Phone the 'orspital, they'll
send an amberlance. . . . Christ, I wouldn't let 'im go there if 'e was
my boy—they kill 'em, that's what they do up there."

Presently a few men carried the soldier from the pavement into
a grocery, whose owner nervously unbarred his front door to repeated knockings. Inside the shop the stream of advice would have
continued indefinitely, but for the girl, who kept saying she would
take him home.

"Better 'ave a doctor first, miss."

"I'll get a doctor when he's home."

"Where's 'e live?"

"Not far away."

"Wounded badly, was 'e?"

"No, he's all right—just fainted, that's all. See, he's coming round
now—if I can get him home—"

"Your 'usband, lidy?"

"That make any difference?"

"Come to think of it, I seem to 'ave seen your face before."

"Maybe you have, old boy, but that doesn't mean I'll stand any of your lip. Come on now, and give me a hand. If I could get a cab—"

"Not much chance o' that, miss, not on a night like this."

But the shopkeeper, anxious to get them all off his premises, whispered to her, while the others were still arguing the point: "I've got a van and my son'll drive you. Think your friend can walk to it?"

"Oh yes, I'm certain he can. Let's try."

It proved to be a large van, smelling of miscellaneous foods and soaps; its driver was a thin youth who easily made room for them on the front seat. After he had inched his way out of the yard he lit a cigarette and began proudly: "You ain't supposed to drive these vans till you're eighteen, but Dad don't tell nobody. Where to, miss?"

"D'you know the Owl—the other side of Bockley?"

"You bet I do. Biffer's place?"

"That's it. But stop in the lane just before you get there."

"Right you are. Won't arf be a journey though, in this fog. 'Ow's the patient?"

"Fine. You keep your eye on the road."

"That's all right. I could drive round 'ere blindfold. Aren't you on at the Empire this week?"

"If there's any show at all. They said there wouldn't be tonight."

"I saw the show in Bockley last week. Jolly good."

"Think so? I thought it was rotten. Look where you're driving."

"Sorry."

"Good of you to take us, anyhow, even if we do get killed on the way."

"Don't mention it. Be in the army meself next year."

"Not now the war's over, will you?"

"Won't they 'ave me because of that?" He looked puzzled and rather disappointed.

"Maybe they will—if you live that long."

"Pretty quick, ain't you, miss? Reminds me of that scene you 'ad in the play, when you kept tellin' orf that fat old gent with the mustaches. I could 'ave larfed."

"Why the devil didn't you then? You were supposed to."

"My dad'll stare when I tell 'im it was Paula Ridgeway. 'E didn't recognize you. Went to the show same as I did, only 'e don't see so well lately."

They drove on, slowly, gropingly, chattering meanwhile, avoid-

ing the main streets as far as possible, and especially the road junc-
tions and shopping centers where crowds were likely. Melbury and
Bockley were adjacent suburbs, completely built over in a crisscross
of residential roads that afforded an infinity of routes; but once beyond Bockley the rows of identical houses came to an end with the
abruptness of an army halted, and the wider highways narrowed and
twisted into lanes. They pulled up eventually at the side of a hedge.

"'Ere y'are, miss. The Owl's just rahnd the corner. Sure I can't
tike yer no further?"

"This'll do fine. We can walk now."

He helped them out. "Sure you know where y'are?"

"Yes—and thanks." She was fishing in her bag for a coin when he
stopped her. "No, miss—you send me a signed picture of yourself,
that's what I'd rather 'ave. . . . 'Is nibs feelin' better? That's good.
Well, it's bin a pleasure. Good luck to both of you. Good night, miss."

She waved to him and he drove off, leaving them alone.

"Where are we going?"

"Home—at least it'll do for one."

"But—I—I have to get back to the hospital!"

"We'll see about that tomorrow."

"But this place—I don't understand—"

"It's the Owl Hotel if you like the word. Call it a pub to be on the
safe side. I know the landlord."

"Will he mind?"

"The odds are he won't even know, old boy, not in the state he'll
be in tonight."

She guided him a little way along the lane, then through a side
gate into a garden where the shapes of trees loomed up at regular
intervals. "Lovely here when the summer comes—they serve teas
and there's a view."

"What name was it he called you?"

"Paula Ridgeway. It's not my real name, though. What's yours?"

"Smith—but that's not real either."

"You don't remember your real name?"

He shook his head.

"Well, Smith's good enough. Come on, Smithy."

As they found their way along a path, the silent blanket of fog
was pierced by a murmur and then by a paleness ahead, the two
presently merging into a vague impression of the Owl on this night
of November the eleventh, 1918. A two-storied, ivy-clustered, steep-
roofed building, ablaze with light from every downstairs room, and
already packed with shouting celebrants of victory; a friendly pub,

traditional without being self-consciously old-world. Established in
the forties, when neighboring Bockley was a small country town, it
had kept its character throughout an age that had seen the vast
obliterating spread of the suburbs and the advent of motor traffic;
it had kept, too, the sacred partitions between "private" and "public"
bars—divisions rooted in the mythology of London life, and still ac-
ceptable because they no longer signify any snobbish separation,
but merely an etiquette of occasion, dress, and a penny difference
in the price of a pint of beer. Even the end of a great war could
not shatter this etiquette; but with the sacred partitions still between,
the patrons of both bars found community in songs that were roared
in unison above the shouting and laughter and clatter of glasses.
They were not especially patriotic songs; most were from the music
halls of the nineties, a few were catchy hits from the recent West
End revues. But by far the most popular of all was "Knees Up, Mother
Brown," a roaring chorus that set the whole crowd stamping into the
beer-soaked sawdust.

On the threshold of the Owl, Smith felt a renewal of nervousness,
especially as the girl's entry was the signal for shouts of welcome
from within. She pushed him into a chair in an unlighted corner of the
lobby. "Stay there, Smithy—I won't be long." A group of men pressed
out of the bar towards her, dragging her back with them; he could
hear their greetings, and her own in answer. He sat there, waiting,
trying to collect his thoughts, to come to terms with the strange sequence of events that had brought him to a noisy public house in
company with a girl who was something on the stage. A few people
passed without noticing him; that was reassuring, but he suspected
it was only because they were drunk. He decided that if anyone
spoke to him he would pretend to be drunk also, and with the safe-
guarding decision once made the waiting became easier. He
watched the door into the bar, expecting her to emerge amidst a
corresponding roar of farewells, but when she did come, it was
quietly, silently, and from another direction. "I managed to get away,
old boy, and believe me it wasn't easy. Come on—let's go before they
find us."

She led him through another door close by, and up a back staircase
to the first floor, turning along a corridor flanked by many rooms;
she opened one of them and put a match to a gas jet just inside.
It showed up a square simple apartment, containing an iron bed
and heavy Victorian furniture. He stared around, then began to
protest: "But how can I stay here? I can't afford—"

"Listen, Smithy—the war stopped this morning. If that's possible, anything else ought to be. And you've got to stay somewhere." She began to laugh. "You're safe here—nobody's going to bother you. I told you I know the man who runs this place—Biffer Briggs—used to be a prize fighter, but don't let that frighten you. . . . It's cold, though—wish there was a fire."

She suddenly knelt at his feet and began to unlace his boots. Again he protested.

"Well, you *must* take your boots off—that's only civil, on a clean bed. I'll come up again soon and bring you some tea."

He took off his boots as soon as she had gone, but the effort tired him more than he could have imagined. The day's strains and stresses had utterly exhausted him, in fact; he almost wished he were back at the hospital, because that at least promised the likelihood of a known routine, whereas here, in this strange place . . . but he fell asleep amidst his uneasiness. When he woke he saw her standing in front of him, carrying a cup of tea. She placed the cup on the side table, then fixed the blankets here and there to cover him more warmly. She was about to tiptoe away when he reached out his hand in a wordless gesture of thanks.

"Awake, Smithy?"

"Have I been asleep?"

"I should think you have. Four solid hours, and this is the third cup of tea I've made for you, just in case. . . . God, I'm tired—tell you what, old boy, I've had just about enough of it downstairs."

"It's late, I suppose."

"One A.M. and they're still hard at it."

"Do you live here?"

"Not me—I just know the Biffer, that's all. I reckon *everybody's* living here tonight, though. Hope the noise won't keep you awake—it'll probably go on till morning."

"I shan't mind."

"You sleep well?"

"Sometimes."

"Lie awake thinking about things?"

"Sometimes."

"About who you are and all that?"

"Sometimes."

Her voice softened with curiosity as she looked down at him. "Drink it up, Smithy. What does it feel like—to think of the time before—before you can remember?"

"Like trying to remember before I was born."

She gave his hand an answering touch. "Well, you're born again now. So's everybody. So's the whole world. That's the way to look at it. That's why there's all this singing and shouting. That's why I'm drunk."

"Are you?"

"Well, not really with drinks, though I have had a few. It's just the thought of it all being over—I've seen so many nice boys like yourself, having a good time one week and then by the next . . . Oh well, mustn't talk about *that*—better not talk any more about anything; you're too sleepy, and so am I. How about making a bit of room?"

Without undressing, except to slip off her shoes, she lifted the blankets and lay down beside him. He felt her nearness slowly, luxuriously, a relaxation of every nerve. "Tell you what, old boy, I'm just like a mother tonight, so cuddle up close as you like and keep warm. . . . Good night, Smithy."

"Good night."

"And Paula's the name, in case you've forgotten that as well."

But he felt no need to answer, except by a deeper tranquillity he drew from her, feeling that she was offering it. The crowd were still singing "Knees Up, Mother Brown" in the bars below. It sounded new to him, both words and tune, and he wondered if it were something else he had forgotten. He did not know that no one anywhere had heard it before—that in some curious telepathic way it sprang up all over London on Armistice Night, in countless squares and streets and pubs; the living improvisation of a race to whom victory had come, not with the trumpet notes of a Siegfried, but as a common earth touch—a warm bawdy link with the mobs of the past, the other victorious Englands of Dickens, Shakespeare, Chaucer.

Presently, as he lay listening, he fell asleep in her arms.

In the morning he had a temperature of 103. He didn't know it; all he felt was a warm, almost cosy ache of all his limbs, as well as a trancelike vagueness of mind. She didn't know it either, but his flushed face and incoherent speech made her telephone for a doctor. A majority of the other occupants of the Owl on that first morning of Peace were also flushed and incoherent, though from a different cause. The Biffer himself, sprawling, disheveled, and half undressed, snored loudly on a sofa in the little room behind the private bar; Frank, the bartender, boastful of never having touched a drop, languished in sober but melancholy stupor on the bench in the public bar, watching the maids sweep sawdust and broken glasses into heaps. Other persons, including a second bartender, a waiter, and several dilatory patrons who had either declined or been unable to go home, were not only fast alseep in various rooms and corridors, but likely to remain so till many more hours were past. It had been a night in the history of the Owl, as of the world.

The only doctor who heeded the call proved, on arrival, to be extremely bad-tempered. As she met him in the lobby he took a sharp look round, eyeing distastefully the prostrate figures visible through doorways. "Daresay you know how busy I am—three Bockley doctors down with the flu—I'm trying to do the work of five men myself, so I hope you haven't brought me here for nothing. I know Briggs—known him for years—he drinks too much and I've told him he'll die of it—what more can I do? A man has a right to die as well as live the way he chooses—anyhow, a doctor can't stop him." By this time she had led him upstairs and into the bedroom. He walked across to the bed, took one look, and swung round angrily. "What's the idea? Who is he?"

"He's been a soldier. He's ill."

"But I thought it was Briggs. . . . You had no right to drag me out here—who *are* you?"

"A friend of the Biffer—like yourself."

"Well, I've no time for new cases."

"But he's *ill*. Can't you see that?"

"How much did he drink?"

"Nothing. It isn't that."

"How do you know?"

"I was with him."

"You're his wife?"

"No."

"Well, what *is* he to you? And what's he doing here? You call me away from my regular patients—you tell me it's urgent—I hurry here because Briggs is an old friend—" But by this time he had drawn back the blankets. "Why, God bless my soul, the man's in his uniform. . . ."

"I told you—he's been a soldier."

"He's still a soldier—he belongs to a hospital."

"Aren't you going to help him at all?"

"Can't interfere in a military case—all I can do is notify the authorities. What's the fellow's name? . . . Ah, here it is—"

"But he's *terribly* ill."

"He'll be sent for."

"But you can't leave him like this!"

"You don't need to instruct me in my duty."

Smith half heard all this as he lay on the bed, his mind tremulous with fever and his body drenched in perspiration; he heard the door close and then saw her face coming towards him out of a mist.

"I bungled that, Smithy. I'm afraid the old boy's gone back to tell 'em you're here."

He smiled. He didn't care. She seemed to read that in his face. She went on: "Yes, you think it doesn't matter, you'd just as soon go back—but *would* you, when you once got there? You don't really *want* to be in a hospital again. . . . Or *do* you?"

He smiled again, more faintly. He was too ill to speak.

"Well, if you die, it'll be pretty hard to explain you being here, but if you weren't going to die I wouldn't be so pleased at having let you go. So you'd just better stay here and not die, Smithy."

He kept smiling as if the whole thing increasingly amused him.

Thus it happened that when, towards twilight, the doctor revisited the Owl, striding into the lobby in an even greater hurry and temper than before, she met him there with answers rehearsed and ready.

"Well, young lady, I've made arrangements about that man. The Melbury Hospital will send an ambulance this evening."

"But he's gone!"

"*What?*"

She repeated: "He's gone."

The doctor flushed and seemed on the verge of an outburst, then suddenly began to cough. She thought he looked rather ill himself. When he could regain breath he said more quietly: "You'd better do some explaining. Where has he gone? How did he get away?"

She offered him a chair. "Maybe he wasn't so ill. Perhaps he was just drunk, as you said."

"Nonsense! He's a shell-shock case, if you know what that is—has delusions that people are against him. Men like that can be dangerous—might have a crazy fit or something." He began to cough again. "Now come on, don't waste any more of my time. Tell me where he is."

She was facing him steadily when all at once his coughing became worse; he struggled with it for a while and then gasped: "Where's Briggs? Let me talk to *him* about this."

"He's out."

"Well, I'll call again later when I've finished my round." He seemed to have a renewal of both energy and anger as he stalked out of the room, for he shouted from the doorway: "It's all a pack of lies you've been telling—I know that much!"

But he did not call back later when he had finished his round.

In fact he never did finish his round. He collapsed over the wheel of his car half an hour later, summoning just enough final strength to pull up by the roadside. It was a lonely road and they did not find him till he was dead. The flu of 1918 was like that.

Later in the evening a military ambulance drove up to the Owl and drove away again after a few minutes. The Biffer was emphatic in his assurance that there must have been some mistake—nobody on his premises was ill. But he called the driver and the two attendants into the private bar and hospitably stood them drinks.

The flu had other victims: Biffer Briggs himself, Frank the bartender, Annie the maid; they recovered. But an old man named Tom who for decades had odd-jobbed in the Owl garden died quietly, like ten millions more throughout Europe; indeed the war during all its years had not taken so many. But because the larger claims were made without horror they were surrendered without concern, and the Owl was far less perturbed when three fourths of its occupants were ill and near to death than on a night some months before when a German air raider had dropped a solitary bomb in a meadow miles away.

Meanwhile Lloyd George was organizing his khaki election; the world grew loud with promises; the ex-Kaiser was to be hanged; the losers must pay the whole cost of the war; the armies of the victors were all to come home and find work waiting for them; the new world was to be one of peace and plenty for Englishmen. Among all the promises a few things were real and immediate: a vote for the women, and gratuities to the men as they put off their uniforms—sums in cash that ranged from the field marshal's fortune to the private soldier's pittance. The morning these were announced Paula took the newspaper upstairs along with the breakfast tray, but said nothing till she was holding a thermometer to the light. "Well, Smithy, you're down to nearly normal, so I reckon I can tell you the other good news—the government owes you some money." She read him the details and added: "So stop worrying—you'll be able to pay for everything soon."

"But in the meantime?"

"*Now* what's bothering you?"

"I hate to seem inquisitive, but—I mean—you—you probably aren't so well off as—as to be able to afford—to help me—"

"Darling, I'm not well off at all, but helping you isn't bankrupting me, either. And why should you hate to seem inquisitive?"

She sat on the bed waving the thermometer happily. "I'm afraid you're too much of a gentleman, old boy. After all, you don't know *what* you are, do you? Maybe you're a lord or an earl or something. Can't you remember going to Eton? You talked a good bit lately while you were in a delirium, but it was all war stuff—not very helpful. You've been pretty bad, incidentally—know that? This morning's the first time you've dropped below a hundred." She poured out a cup of tea. "All the others caught it too—good job *I* didn't."

"You've been living here?"

"Living and lifesaving. The flu closed the theater so I'd have had nothing else to do, anyway."

"I still don't see how you can afford to help me like this."

"Darling, I'll let you into a secret—I'm not paying for your room, but if it makes you feel better, you can turn over anything you like as soon as the government gives you the money."

"That's another trouble. I can't be demobilized till I'm officially discharged from hospital."

"Well, hurry up and get better, then they'll discharge you quick enough."

"But—in the meantime—don't you see?—I can't *hide*—like this—in somebody else's house!"

"But you don't have to hide. I've talked to the Biffer about you already."

"You mean he knows I'm here—and where I come from?"

"Yes, and he doesn't mind. Doesn't give a damn, in fact. I knew I could fix it."

"But—why does he think you're doing all this for me?"

"Well, why do *you* think I am?" She laughed. "It's just a hobby of mine. Now listen to this—it's the Biffer's idea, not mine. He says for the time being—when you've got over this flu and are strong enough—why don't you do a bit in the garden same as old Tom used to? If you *like*, that is. Might be good for you to have a quiet job in the fresh air—you wouldn't have to talk to people much. And it's lovely here when the summer comes."

Something flicked against his memory. "You said that once before."

"Did I?"

"The night we came here—as we walked through the garden in the fog. You said—'It's lovely here when the summer comes.'"

"Well, it certainly is, but I don't remember saying it. And you're the one who's supposed to forget things!"

"That's why I'm always trying to remember them—things that have happened before."

The Biffer's not minding was a mild way of expressing his willingness to co-operate. He was, in truth, delighted to join in any outwitting of authority, which he visualized as the same malign power that had placed so many restrictions on his wartime management of the Owl. Jovial, obese, and somewhat thick-witted after the hundreds of collisions his skull had withstood in years gone by, he remained the product of an early education that had taught him to read printed words with difficulty and to believe them with ease; so that he did indeed believe the things he could read with least difficulty—which included the sporting pages of the daily papers, Old Moore's predictions, and "powerful articles" by the more down-writing journalists of the day. He had a few fierce hatreds (for such things as red tape, government interference, and Mrs. Grundy) and a few equally fierce affections, such as for Horatio Bottomley, "good old Teddy" (meaning the late King Edward the Seventh), and Oxford in the Boat Race. He took pride in the oft-repeated claim that "there ain't a more gentlemanly House than the Owl in all London," and that it should shelter a victim of the things he most hated added zest to a naturally generous impulse. "Pack of Burercratic busybodies," he exclaimed, during his first meeting with the victim. "Just let 'em come 'ere, that's all. I've still got strength to give 'em what I gave the Gunner!" What he had given the Gunner (at Shoreditch on May 17, 1902) was a straight left hook in the fourteenth round—this being the peak of his career, and one which, in money and fame, he had never afterwards approached. But he had bought the Owl with the money, and the fame, carefully husbanded too, had survived pretty well within a ten-mile radius of his own brass-bound beer engines.

So Smith began to work in the garden of the Owl; and in the meantime President Wilson crossed the Atlantic to be cheered as a new Messiah in the streets of London, Rome, and Paris; English, French, and American troops held the Rhine bridgeheads; the first trains crept again through the defiles of the Brenner; and in the great cities of central and eastern Europe revolution and famine stalked together.

It was the Biffer's second-favorite boast that from the garden of the Owl you could see "the Palace" on a clear day—the Alexandra Palace, that was, seven miles west across the Lea Valley; in the other direction the trees of Epping Forest made a darkly etched panorama that grew brown, and then suddenly green, as spring advanced. There was only preparatory gardening to be done until that time, but then the grass grew long in a single week and a line of daffodils flowered in every window box. Hardly anyone visited the garden during the daytime, and by evening, when a few already preferred to take their drinks out of doors, Smith was in bed and asleep, except

on Sundays, when Paula would generally pay a visit if her show
were playing in or near London.

Of course he knew she didn't come to see him only, but chiefly
the Biffer and the crowd in the bar, who all seemed to be her friends
and greeted her with vociferous cordiality; naturally she spent a good
deal of the time with them, and it wasn't easy to get away for a
solitary chat with a semi-invalid. She managed it, though, as a rule,
meeting him in the garden and walking with him along the Forest
paths as far as the big beech trees. He enjoyed such walks, because
it was dark and he still shrank from meeting people; but he also
shrank from the thought that he might be dragging her away from
much livelier company in the bar. He tried to tell her this.

"Don't you worry, Smithy. I won't let you bore me."

"But you have such a good time with the crowd."

"I know—that's because I like people. Can't help it. But don't think
so little of yourself—you're included. Gives me plenty of fun to see
you getting better like this, week by week."

"Yes, I think I *am* getting better."

"You only *think* you are?"

"I still don't like to talk to people, though." He tried to explain.
"It isn't so much fear of them as a sort of uneasiness—as if I really
oughtn't to be alive, and everybody knows it and wonders why I still
am. I know that's foolish, but it isn't enough to know—I've got to *feel*,
before I can free myself."

"You will, Smithy. You'll suddenly feel you're free as air one of
these days."

"If I do, I'll have you to thank—chiefly. You've given me so much
of your time."

"Oh God, don't start being grateful. Listen, I'll tell you something.
If you oughtn't to be here, neither should I, and I wouldn't be, but
for luck. A house I was living in was hit by a bomb—I was asleep
in one room and two people were killed in the next. I wasn't going
to tell you that—thought it might upset you to be reminded of the
war, but now maybe it'll cheer you up to think we're both like that.
They did their best to finish us off, Smithy, but we managed to trick
'em somehow or other. That's the way to feel, and it's easier now the
war's over and there's a future."

"I'd like to feel that, if I could."

"You will. You'll go on getting better, and then one night I'll see
you in the front row of the stalls, watching the show."

"Yes, I'd like to see you act."

"Oh, don't come for that reason. I don't act—I'm just a comic."

"I *will* come, when I'm better."

"That's a promise, now!"

There wasn't only the question of his reluctance to meet strangers. Any prospective employer, no matter how sympathetic, would ask for details of his history, his army discharge papers and so on, and if it came out that he'd escaped from a mental hospital, the authorities would certainly send him back there, at least for tests and observation, and if he *were* sent back, even for a short time, he felt terribly certain he would get worse again. There was nothing for it but to stay where he was and be thankful for such a sanctuary; it was really an astounding piece of good fortune ever to have found it. So he stayed, pottering about the Owl garden and gradually returning to the world of ordinary awareness. There came a day when he could open a newspaper and face whatever catastrophe the turn of a page might reveal; another day when he could pick up an exciting novel without perilously identifying himself with one or other of the characters. He was recovering.

Sometimes while he was busy in the garden the landlord, puffing and sweating in his shirtsleeves, would bring out a couple of pints of beer. He took a naïve, childlike interest in his protégé. "Easy does it, mate—don't work your head off. Seen the paper? They 'aven't 'anged the old Kaiser yet, but it looks like they'll do for this chap Landru—supposed to have murdered twenty women—what d'you think of that?"

Smith didn't have to answer much, because the Biffer was always glad to talk, especially about his favorite diversion, which was a word competition in a well-known weekly paper. He usually sent in several entries; they consisted of some supposedly apt comment on a selected phrase. The prize-winning comment generally had wit, or at least a double meaning; but the Biffer could never grasp that, and his hard-wrought efforts were invariably trite, and just as invariably failed to score. But every night in the private bar he would discuss them with his regular customers, and in the daytime he was glad enough to add the new gardener to his list of consultants. The latter, encouraged to take a rest from work and study the weekly contest, soon developed an inkling of what might stand a chance, and from time to time made suggestions that the Biffer dutifully incorporated into his own efforts. Suddenly one of them won a prize of a hundred pounds, and never since his epic fight with the Gunner had anything happened to give the Biffer a greater feeling of elation. His first response was to insist on an equal split, paid over there and then in five-pound notes, for he believed (more truly than he realized) that the gardener's emendation might have helped. But that was not all. In the Owl bar that same evening, under stress of many drinks and congratulations, he could not withhold credit as well as cash from his collaborator. "Quiet well-spoken sort of chap—stammers a bit—been shell-shocked in the war. Matter of fact, they 'ad 'im locked up in that big guv'ment hospital at Melbury till the poor chap got away. I reckon that's a fine joke on them guv'ment busybodies—a feller they make out is off 'is chump goes and thinks up something that wins a hundred quid!" And the more the Biffer contemplated this extremely ironic circumstance, the more he repeated and elaborated it over a period of several hours and before changing audiences.

A few evenings later Smith was tidying up in the greenhouse; but it was a Sunday and there had not been much to do. It was hardly time for Paula to come yet, even if she did come; he knew she was at Selchester that week—perhaps it was too far away. The uncertainty as to whether she would come or not made a curious little fret inside him; it didn't matter so much if she wasn't coming provided he hadn't looked forward to it in advance. That brought him to a realization of how much he did look forward to her visits. Of course, now that he was getting better he didn't expect to see her so much; she had been kind while he was ill, he mustn't trade on that. And another thing was curious—his memory of the night she had brought him to the Owl, every word she had said, little intimacies of physical presence, details that swung like lamps amidst the background of fever and delirium. He could hardly believe that certain things had happened at all, that she had so comforted him throughout that long night of Armistice. There had been no other nights like that, there never would be, neither in his life nor in the world's. He could not expect it; and it was natural that their relationship, begun in such a wild vacuum of despair and ecstasy, should by now have become a more normal one.

Suddenly the greenhouse door opened and she stood there in the sunlight, breathless. "Oh Smithy, you've got to go—immediately! Drop those things and don't stay here a moment longer. I'll pack your bag—I'll find where everything is—meet me in the Forest by the beech trees in half an hour! But go *now*—don't waste any time—"

"But what's the matter? What on earth's happened?"

"Two men from Melbury Hospital talking to Biffer in the bar. They've come for you."

"For *me?*" He stared at her, bewildered at first, then enraged and indignant. "They want to take me *back?* They *still* want to get me?"

She ran to him, holding him, trying to stop his cries. "Don't shout—

and don't argue—just go as I tell you!" She pulled him out of the
greenhouse and across the garden to the side gate. "Wait for me—
you know where—I shan't be long."

They met again, under the trees. He was calmer; he had waited,
smoking cigarettes and thinking things out. The day had been hot
and pockets of warm air lingered amidst the fast-cooling shades. The
Forest was very beautiful, and something in him was beginning to
respond to beauty, as to anger and indignation also. He sprang to
eagerness as he saw her approach, carrying bags and parcels. They
stood still for a moment, while she regained her breath. "It's all right
—nobody saw you—we're safe so far. The men have gone—the Biffer
got mad and said he'd give 'em what he gave the Gunner." She
laughed. "But of course that wouldn't help—they've got the law on
their side—the law and the doctors. . . . I didn't say much to Biffer.
He means well, but as soon as he's had a few drinks he tells all he
knows, which isn't much as a rule, but it's too much just now. So he'd
better not know about us till he finds out."

"Us?"

"Well, of course. We're going together, aren't we?"

"But how can—I mean—"

"Are you being the little gentleman again?"

"It's not that, but isn't it time—"

"Listen, Smithy, I'm only trying to help you—"

"I know that, but it's time I began helping myself."

"What a moment to think of it!"

"It isn't that I'm not grateful, but—"

"I know, you feel independent. Well, go on your own then, but
where will it take you? You haven't an idea. One place is as good
as another, what's wrong with Selchester then? I'm there for the week
and after I've gone you can do as you like. . . . You've got those
ten fivers in your pocket, haven't you?"

"Yes."

"Then hand over half to me."

He did so, willingly and seriously; she took them with a laugh.
"Thanks, Smithy—you'll feel better now."

They reached Selchester late at night, after a confused journey
by various trains and buses; but all the way he had been aware of
a barrier rising between them, so that at Selchester Station she summoned a cab and did not suggest that he accompany her. "You'll be
all right, Smithy—the town's full of pubs and lodgings—I reckon you'd
rather choose one yourself. I lodge with the company, of course.

Well, good night—you're safe here if you look after yourself, and you will, won't you?" She leaned up and gave him a sudden kiss—the first she had ever given him, but he knew it meant less than her hand touch the first time they had met. "Good night, old boy," she repeated.

"Good night, Paula."

When her cab turned the corner and he was left alone with the crowd of strangers in the station yard, he felt suddenly, hopelessly lost. It was a sensation of sheer panic for the moment, but he conquered it—as if he had seen a loathed insect and shudderingly ground it with his heel. He walked into a near-by hotel and engaged a cheap room under the name of Smith. They gave him a very small attic with dormer windows and a view over the railway goods yard; throughout the night he kept waking up with a start whenever express trains screamed by, but somehow he did not mind that kind of panic; it was the inner kind that paralyzed him—or rather, could not quite paralyze him any more, since he had fought it, alone and so terribly, after she had gone. How comforting, as well as fearful, that word *alone* was; he wanted aloneness, because it was the hardest training ground for the kind of strength he also wanted; and yet, once he had that strength, he knew he would not wish to be alone. And he knew, too, that his feeling for Paula was no longer an eagerness to submit, like a child; but something positive, strong enough to demand equality, if there were ever to be any further relationship between them at all. He knew there probably could not be. That warm outpouring pity had saved his life, but he could only keep his life from now on by refusing it. Lying awake that night in the Station Hotel, he made up his mind that he would not try to see her in Selchester that week; she would be busy, no doubt, with rehearsals and performances; and he, too, ought to be busy—looking for a job if the town offered any, and if not, deciding where else to go.

For five days he walked about Selchester alone. He visited the Cathedral, sat for hours in the Close under the trees, spent an afternoon in a very dull municipal museum, watched the trains in and out of the railway station, read the papers in the free library. None of these pursuits involved conversation, and—except to waitresses and the maid at the hotel—he did not utter a word for anyone to hear. Sometimes, however, during walks in the surrounding country, he talked to himself a little—not from eccentricity, but to reassure himself of the power of speech. There were a few factories also that he scouted around, wondering if he should ask for a job, but sooner or later he always found a door with a notice "No Hands Wanted." He knew that subconsciously he was glad, because he still feared the ordeal of cross-examination by strangers.

One rainy afternoon he sat in the refreshment room at the railway station, drinking a third cup of tea that he did not want and staring at an old magazine that he was not reading. Curious how one had to simulate some normal activity or purpose in life, even if one hadn't one, or especially if one had a secret one; in a town café he could not have stayed so long without attracting attention, but at the station it was merely supposed he was waiting for a train. Trains were things people waited hours for; one did not, unless one were peculiar, wait hours for a desire to clarify itself. But that was what *he* was waiting for. It was Saturday; he had been in Selchester almost a week. He had a definite desire to go to the theater and see the show, but he could not decide until he felt certain what his desire signified. If it were weakness, an urge to go back on his pledge to himself, he would not give way; he could endure plenty more of the aloneness, it would not break him. But, on the other hand, supposing it were not weakness but strength—supposing it meant that he could now walk into a theater as normally as into a library or museum, could face the crowd and the lights and the excitement without a qualm?

He had walked past the theater several times and had judged the kind of show it was from bills and photographs; nothing very uplifting, but probably good entertainment, and it would be interesting to see what she was capable of. Thus, he made his desire seem casual, normal, almost unimportant, until suddenly he decided he was strong and not weak enough to go. He got up and walked briskly to the counter to pay for the tea. "Gettin' tired of waitin'?" remarked the girl, with mild interest. "The Winton train's late today."

"Yes," he said, smiling. "I think I'll get a breath of fresh air."

He left the station and walked through the rain to the center of the city, feeling more and more confident.

It was an odd thing, this loss of memory; he could not remember personal things about himself, yet he had a background of experience that gave him a certain maturity of judgment. He had probably been to many theaters before, just as he had probably been to schools and received a decent education. There were things he knew that he could only have picked up from schoolbooks, other things that he could only have learned from some forgotten event. It was as if his memory existed, but was submerged; as if he could lower a net and drag something up, but only blindfold, haphazardly, without the power of selection. He could not stare into the past; he could only grope. But by some kind of queer compensation, his eyes for the present were preternaturally bright; like a child's eyes, naïve, ingenuous, questioning.

In such a mood he sat in the third row at the first house of the Selchester Hippodrome that night and looked upon a show called *Salute the Flag*, described on the program as "a stirring heart-gripping drama, pulsating with patriotism and lit by flashes of sparkling comedy." Actually it was a hangover from wartime, having begun in 1914 as a straight melodrama with no comedy at all, but with many rousing speeches that audiences in those days had liked to cheer. Then, as the war progressed and the popular mood changed from that of Rupert Brooke to that of Horatio Bottomley, the patriotic harangues were shortened to make room for the writing in of a comic part, which speedily became such a success that by 1918 the show had developed into a series of clowning episodes behind which the dramatic structure of what had once been a very bad play appeared only intermittently. Nobody knew the authorship of the original, or of any of the later accretions; successive actors had added a gag here and a gag there; every now and then the show became too long, and the parts left out were naturally those that elicited neither laughs nor cheers, no matter how essential they were to the original plot. But nobody minded that—least of all the audiences who paid their ninepences and shillings in the few remaining small-town English theaters that had so far escaped conversion into cinema houses. *Salute the Flag* had certainly helped to preserve the very existence of such a minority; it had also made a great deal of money for a great many people. Probably, in the aggregate, it had been more profitable than many a better-known and well-advertised West End success.

Smith found it endurable, even before the moment when Paula appeared. Her part in the play was trivial, that of an impudent girl at a hotel desk who got people's bedrooms mixed up, but in one of the other scenes she stepped out of the part for a few impersonations in front of the drop curtain; he thought them pretty good, not from any definite competence to judge, but because of the warm vitality that came over the footlights with them, her own rich personality, full of giving—even to a twice-nightly audience. Evidently the audience too were aware of this, for they cheered uproariously, despite the likelihood that few had seen the originals, which included Gerald du Maurier, Gladys Cooper, Mrs. Pat Campbell, and the ex-Kaiser. They cheered so much that she came on again to give an impression of a society woman telephoning her lover, all smiles and simperings, in the midst of grumbling at her maid, all scowls and snarls—a bit of broad unsubtle farce that demanded, however, a sure technique of changed accents and facial expressions. She did not appear again till the final scene in the last act, when the heroine, a nurse, unfolded a huge and rather dirty flag in front of her, and with the words "You kennot fahr on helpless womankind" defied the villain, who wore the uniform of a Germany army officer, until such time as the entire rest of the company rushed on to the stage to hustle him off under arrest and to bring down the curtain with the singing of a patriotic chorus.

Smith was halfway down the aisle on his way out of the theater when an usher touched him on the arm. "Excuse me, sir, one of the artists would like you to go behind, if you'd care to. She says you'd know who it was."

He hesitated a moment, then answered: "Why, of course."

"This way, sir."

He was led back towards the stage, stooping under the brass rail into the orchestra, stepping warily amidst music stands and instruments, then stooping again to descend a narrow staircase leading under the stage into an arena of ropes and canvas. The usher piloted him beyond all this into a corridor lined by doors; on one of them he tapped. "The gentleman's here, miss." A moment's pause. "I expect she's dressing, sir—you'll excuse me, I've got to get back."

Again, after the usher had left him, he felt the beginnings of panic, but it was different now—an excitement that he fought only as much as he wanted to fight it. And the door opened before he could either yield or conquer to any extent.

"Oh, Smithy—Smithy—you kept your promise!"

She dragged him into the room with both hands and closed the door. It was a shabby little dressing room, with one fierce light over a mirrored table littered with paints and cosmetics; playbills and an old calendar on the wall; clothes thrown across a chair; a mixture of smells—grease paint, burnt hair, cigarettes, cheap perfume, Lysol. She wore a dressing gown over the skimpy costume in which she was soon to appear again.

"I didn't see you till the end—glad I didn't—I'd have been so excited I'd have ruined the show."

He said, smiling: "I enjoyed it very much—especially your part."

"Oh no, Smithy, you don't have to say things like that. . . . Tell me how you are! Better, I can see—or you wouldn't be here. But what have you been doing with yourself all week?"

"Oh, just looking around. Have to find some sort of a job, you know."

"Any luck?"

"Not so far. I somehow don't feel Selchester's a very good place to try."

"We're going on to Rochby next week. More chance in a place like that, maybe."

"I daresay I'll get something somewhere."

"And you *feel* better?"

"Oh yes—fine."

The call boy shouted through the door, "Five minutes, miss."

"That means I've only got five minutes." She paused, then laughed. "I do say intelligent things, don't I?"

He laughed also. "They keep you pretty busy—two shows a night."

"Yes, but this is Saturday, thank heaven. You'd be surprised what a rest Sunday is, even if you spend most of it in trains."

"You leave in the morning?"

"Ten o'clock."

"But it isn't far."

"About three hours. We have a long wait at Bletchley. Somehow that always happens. I seem to have spent days of my life waiting at Bletchley."

"I don't think I know Bletchley."

"Well, you haven't missed much. There's nothing outside the station except a pub that never seems to be open. Oh God, what are we talking about Bletchley for? . . . I've got some money of yours, you know that? Or did you forget?"

"No, but—"

"Well, I'd better give it back since I'm off in the morning." She began to fumble in her dress. "I carry it about with me—doesn't do to leave fivers lying loose."

"Oh, but you mustn't—"

"Well, you don't think I'm going to *keep* it, do you?"

"I—I—never thought about it, but—"

"*Did* you think I was going to keep it?"

"Well—I don't know—it would have been quite fair—after all, you'd done so much—"

"Listen, you little gentleman—I kept it because I thought I'd have to help you again, and I thought you'd feel better if I was spending your own money! But now you *are* better, thank God, and you don't need my help, so here you are!" She pushed the notes into his pocket. "I've got to go on again in two minutes, so don't make me angry!

You'll need that cash if you're looking for a job. . . . What sort are
you looking for?"

"Any kind, really—"

"Outdoor or indoor?"

"I'm not particular about that, provided—well, you know some of
the difficulties—"

"You're scared they'll ask you too many questions? What you'd
really like is for someone to stop you in the street and say—'I don't
know who you are, or what you've been, and I don't care either, but
if you want a job, come with me.' Isn't that the idea?"

He laughed. "Yes, that's exactly the idea, if anyone would."

"You wouldn't mind what the job turned out to be, though?"

"I think I could do anything that I'd have even the faintest chance
of getting."

"Figures? Keeping books?"

"Oh yes."

"A bit of talk now and again—even to strangers—in that charming
way you have?"

"I wouldn't *choose* that sort of job, but of course—"

"You mean you're still bothered about meeting people?"

He hesitated. She went on: "Well, leave that out. What about a
bit of carpentry mixed up with the bookkeeping?"

"Why carpentry?"

"Why not? . . . Back at the intelligent conversation, aren't we?"
The call boy knocked again. "Well . . . I suppose it's got to be good-
bye till we meet again—unless you want to see the show through
twice—you'd be a fool if you did."

"Perhaps I could meet you somewhere afterwards?"

"We always have supper together on Saturday nights—all the company, I mean—it's a sort of regular custom, wherever we are. Of
course I could take you as my guest, but there'd be a crowd of
strangers." Abruptly her manner changed. "Smithy, would you really
come?"

"Do you *want* me to come?"

"*I* wouldn't mind a bit, it's what *you* want that matters. You're
free as air now—that's how you always hoped to be. And they can
be a rowdy gang sometimes. So please yourself, I'm not inviting you
anywhere any more . . . but if you *are* coming, say so now, then
I can tell them."

He felt suddenly bold, challenging, almost truculent. "I'll come,
and I don't care how rowdy they are."

She flashed him a smile as she slipped off the dressing gown and put final touches to her make-up. "Number 19, Enderby Road—that's near the cattle market—about eleven-thirty. You don't need to hang around here for me—just go straight to the house at the time. I'll come sharp—ahead of the others. See you then."

The rain had stopped; he took a long walk in the washed evening air, then sat on a seat in the Cathedral Close and smoked cigarettes till the chime of eleven. He could not quell his nervousness at the thought of meeting so many strange people for the sort of evening party that was a weekly custom of theirs—that in itself made him an outsider. He half wished he hadn't said he would go, and it occurred to him that of course he didn't have to—if he failed to turn up, that would be the end of it. But the reflection, though tantalizing up to a point, had the stinging afterthought that he would then not see her again.

Enderby Road was a quiet cul-de-sac of Edwardian houses, most of them let to boarders; Number 19 looked no different from the others, but had a gas lamp outside the front gate. He waited there, watching for her after the Cathedral clock chimed the half-hour; it was comforting to reflect that nobody knew him yet—he was just an anonymous man standing under a lamppost. Presently she turned the corner, her walk breaking into a scamper as she saw him. "On time, Smithy—I mean *you* are, *I'm* not. But I hurried to be ahead of the others—I didn't even stop to clean off the make-up."

She led him into the house. "Wait in the hall while I go up and finish."

He waited about ten minutes; the hall was dark and smelt of floor polish with an added flavor—which he took practically the entire time to detect—of pickled walnuts. Near him stood a bamboo hall stand overloaded with hats and coats; the staircase disappeared upwards into the gloom with thin strips of brass outlining the ascent. Voices came from a downstairs room. He wondered what he should say if anyone came out of one of the rooms and accosted him, but when the thing happened it turned out to be no problem at all; the voices stopped, a thin old man with a high domed forehead suddenly emerged through one of the doors, collided with him, murmured "Pardon," and disappeared along the passage. After a moment, he returned, collided again, murmured "Pardon" again, and re-entered the room. Then the voices were resumed.

Soon after that she came down the stairs two at a time, to whisper excitedly: "Now I'm ready."

They entered the room, in which—despite the voices—there was only one person, the thin old dome-headed man; he was sitting at the dining table with a large book open before him, propped against the cruet. The domed head rose over the book as from behind a rampart.

"Mr. Lanvin—this is Mr. Smith."

"A pleasure to meet you, my dear sir." He smiled, but did not offer to shake hands. Then he closed the book slowly, and Smith could see it was a Braille edition. Somehow that gave him peculiar confidence; Lanvin could not *see* him, could only judge him by his voice; so for the time being he had only one thing to concentrate on.

Lanvin was placing the book exactly in its place on a shelf; it was clear he knew by touch and feeling every inch of the geography of the room. "So you are to join the weekly celebration, Mr. Smith?"

"That seems to be the idea. I hope you don't mind."

"Mind? I'm a guest like yourself, though I've been one before. I warn you—they're a noisy lot—though no noisier than I used to be in my young days. If they weary you later on, come over and talk to me."

Smith said he certainly would, and Mr. Lanvin began to talk about Shakespeare. It seemed he had been reading *The Merchant of Venice,* taking the various parts in various voices. "I used to be quite a good Shylock, though I say it myself—and of course it's a fine acting part, and the trial scene has wonderful moments. But taking it all in all, you know, it's a bad play—a bad play. Why do they always choose it for school use? The pound of flesh—gruesome. The Jewish villain—disgustingly anti-Semitic. And a woman lawyer—stark feminism. . . . Oh, a bad play, my dear sir. You're not a schoolmaster, by any chance?"

"I'm afraid not."

"Because if you were, I should like to . . . but never mind that. Since my eyes compelled me to retire from the stage I've spent a great deal of my time reading, and do you know, the Braille system gives one a really new insight into literature. You see, you can't skip —you have to read every word, and that gives you time to think for yourself, to criticize, to revalue—"

Meanwhile the door had reopened and a heavily built, red-faced, pouchy-eyed man stood in the entrance, waiting till he was quite sure he had been seen before stepping further into the room. Eventually he did so, exclaiming: "Paula, my angel, so *this* is the friend you spoke of!"

She completed the introduction; the red-faced man's name was Borley. He lost no time in dominating the scene. "Fine to have you with us, old chap." And then, dropping his voice to an almost secret parenthesis and leaning over the table with the gesture of one about to unveil something: "I don't know if you've ever noticed, but the food in English boardinghouses is always in inverse proportion to the size of the cruet. The larger the cruet, that is, the worse the food. Now this is a perfectly *enormous* cruet." He gave it a highly dramatic long-range scrutiny. "You'd think it ought to light up or play music or something—it's really more like a municipal bandstand than a receptacle for Mrs. Gregory's stale condiments."

Just late enough to miss these remarks the landlady entered with a trayful of small meat pies. Smith had to be introduced to her also, and it was Mr. Borley who made haste to do this. "Mrs. Gregory, I was just remarking on the quality of your food, and I perceive from yonder succulent morsels that all I have said will soon be amply demonstrated!" Whereupon Mr. Borley delivered a portentous wink all round the room while Mrs. Gregory bounced the tray on the table without much response. She looked so completely indifferent to the bogus compliment that Mr. Borley's joke was somewhat dulled. "Glad to serve you all," she muttered. "I do my best, as the saying goes—consequently is, I keep my reg'lars."

"You not only keep us, Mrs. Gregory, but *we* keep *you*—and proud to do it!"

She shuffled out of the room, leaving Mr. Borley to proffer the dish of pies with an air of controlled distaste. "Well, the risk's yours, Smithy. Don't mind if I call you Smithy, do you? That's what *she* calls you."

Rather to his surprise, after all this, Smith found the pies excellent. He said so to Mr. Borley, adding that he was even hungry enough to have another.

"Right you are, then—and fortified by your example I'll even try one myself." Mr. Borley then began eating and hardly stopped throughout the entire rest of the evening. He added, with his mouth full: "But if you're a hungry man, God help you at Mrs. Beagle's!"

Smith did not see how the food at Mrs. Beagle's, whoever and wherever she was, could be any concern of his, but he had no time to explore the point because another member of the party had just arrived—a young man in tweeds, puffing at a pipe, almost like a magazine advertisement of either the tweeds or the pipe; he had a pink, over-handsome, rather weak face to which only premature dissipation had begun to lend some interest. Once again Mr. Borley officiated at the introduction, and while he was still performing two other persons entered, one a pale thin girl with a large nose and spotty complexion, the other an elderly silver-haired man of such

profoundly sorrowful appearance that the beholder could not keep
back a first response of sympathy. Mr. Borley had to summon all his
technical powers to hold attention against such competition, but he
did his best by shouting the further introductions.

The silver-haired man smiled and bowed, while the girl marched
on Smith, delivered a crunching handshake, strode to the window,
stared out for a moment as if deeply meditating, then swung round
with husky intensity. "Oh, Mr. Smith, hasn't it been a wonderful day?
I'm *sure* you're a rain lover like me!"

Smith felt somewhat cheered by a feeling that in this encounter
all the others were standing round to see fair play, especially when
the tweedy youth nudged him in the ribs. "Don't worry about her—
she's always like that. Why Tommy married her nobody can imagine
—not even Tommy any more . . . can you, Tommy?"

Here a sharp-nosed, jockey-sized man, with bloodshot blue eyes
and straw-colored hair came across the room to be introduced, shook
hands wordlessly and continued to do so while he glanced around
with concentrated expressionlessness. Presently, turning his eyes on
Smith, he whispered: "What made you first take an interest in slum-
ming?" He went on, before Smith could think of any reply: "We're
just a low vulgar crowd. Rogues and vagabonds, they called us in
Shakespeare's time—am I right, Lanvin? We have no homes, we live
in dingy lodginghouses in every middle-sized town in England, we
know which landlady counts the potatoes, which theater's full of
fleas, and which has a roof that leaks on the stage when it rains.
None of your high-class West End stuff for us—we lure the coppers,
the orange peel, and the monkey nuts, and we spend our one-day-
a-week holiday chewing stale sandwiches in Sunday trains."

Mrs. Gregory then came in with what was evidently the main dish
—quantities of fried fish, chip potatoes, and hot peas; meanwhile Mr.
Borley had been out and now reappeared carrying a crate of bottled
beer. The party began to find places at the table while the sorrowful-
looking man, whose name was Margesson and whom one would have
expected to speak like an archbishop, boomed across the table, quite
unsorrowfully and with the zest and accent of an auctioneer: "Ladies
and gentlemen, may I remind you that we shall soon be at the mercy
of Mrs. Beagle." Here followed a chorus of groans and catcalls. "So
I'm not going to keep you from the really serious business of the
evening, which is to eat the last decent meal we shall have for a
week. Before we begin, though, and speaking as the senior member
of this company,—bar Lanvin, who's a permanent resident,—may I
offer you a welcome, Mr. Smith, and beg you to take no further

notice of that truncated nitwit Tommy Belden, nor of that moon-faced stewpan, Richard Borley, nor of . . ." He had an insult for each of them, culminating in the arrival of a fat over-powdered woman with a large smile she bestowed upon everyone from the doorway, whereupon Margesson turned on her and exclaimed: "Now, Miss Donovan, you old bag of bones, don't stand there ogling the men—come and meet our guest, Mr. Smith, commonly called Smithy—"

And so it went on. Not till weeks later, when he had got to know them as human beings, did he realize that they had behaved with extra extravagance that evening in order to put him at his ease, and that the insults were a convention in which they took particular pride —the more horrific and ingenious, the warmer the note of friend-liness indicated. A climax came when Margesson, at the end of din-ner, rose to make an appeal on behalf of an actor whom they had formerly known and who had fallen on bad times. Margesson's speech began: "Ladies and gentlemen, if such there still are among this depraved and drink-sodden gathering—some of you, even in your cups, may remember Dickie Mason, one of the dirtiest dogs who ever trod the boards of a provincial hippodrome—"

The party lasted till after three in the morning, and was only then dissolved at the energetic request of Mrs. Gregory, who said the neighbors were being disturbed. Towards the end of it, Margesson took Smith aside and said: "Well? Can you stand us?"

Smith answered with a laugh: "I think so. I'm having quite a good time, anyhow."

"The train's at ten tomorrow morning."

"Yes, Paula told me."

"Some people sleep late, that's all."

That seemed another odd remark, but he didn't begin to grasp its significance till later on when several people shook hands or clapped him on the back with the remark: "See you tomorrow, Smithy."

Paula walked with him to the corner of the road. He said: "I'm really glad I came—they're a warmhearted lot, and it's nice of them to expect me to see them off in the morning."

"I'd better tell you what else they expect. They think you're com-ing with us—to Rochby and all the other places."

"But—"

"Now don't begin to argue. Maybe I've bungled again—you've only got to say so, and the whole idea's dropped. But there's a job for you if you want it. In fact it's just about a hundred jobs rolled into one—you'll find that out, if you take it on, and if you don't like it or something better turns up, then you're free to go like a shot."

He said quietly: "What did you tell them about me?"

"Just part of the truth. I said you'd been ill, that you were better now, that you were a friend of mine, and that you wanted a job. . . . But all that didn't get it for you—don't worry."

"What did, then?"

She laughed in his face. "I may as well go on telling the truth, even if you hate me for it. I think it was probably because they could all see you were such a gentleman."

Afterwards he realized the meaning behind the remark. The other members of the company were *not* gentlemen, nor ladies either, in the restricted sense of the word. They could act the part, successfully—even terrifically; no duke or baronet ever wore an opera cloak or swung a gold-knobbed cane with such superb nonchalance as Mr. Borley—indeed, it is extremely probable that many a duke and baronet never possessed an opera cloak, or swung a gold-knobbed cane at all. And that, of course, was the point. The gentlemen in *Salute the Flag* lived up to the ninepenny-seat idea of gentlemen; they were much realer than the real thing. So also in speech and accent nobody could approach Paula for aristocratic hauteur: when, in her impersonation of a duchess, she exclaimed to a footman, "Do my bidding, idiot!" the blue blood became almost as translucent in her veins as in those of Mr. Borley when the latter addressed the German officer—"You contemptible hound—you unmitigated cur—you spawn of a degenerate autocracy!"

In private life, so far as members of a second-rate touring company could enjoy any, they tended to keep up the manners and moods of their professional parts, combining them with a loud geniality expressed by a profusion of "old boys" and hearty backslappings; yet behind all that they well knew the difference between the real and the too real, and how the same difference was apt to be recognized by others. Hence the usefulness of Smith. He had a way with him, despite—or perhaps *because* of—his shyness, diffidence, embarrassments, hesitations. Where Mr. Borley's loud and overconfident "Trust me till the end of the week, old chap" failed to impress a country tradesman, Smith could enter a shop where he wasn't known and ask for what he wanted to be sent to his hotel without even mentioning payment. And where even Mr. Margesson could not, with all his sorrowful glances, persuade a small-town editor to print as news a column of disguised and badly composed puffery, Smith could rewrite the stuff and have the newspapers eager for it.

No doubt it was for somewhat similar reasons that Nicholas Nickleby became a success with the company of Vincent Crummles —except, of course, that Nicholas graduated as an actor. Smith did not aspire to that, but he speedily became almost everything else —advance press agent, scene painter, bookkeeper, copy writer, toucher-up of scenes that were either too long or too short or not wholly successful, general handy man, odd-jobber, negotiator, public representative, and private adviser. He was always busy, yet never hurried; always pleasant, yet never effusive; always reserved, yet never disdainful. In short, a perfect gentleman.

There certainly could not have been devised a more likely cure for all that remained of his mental and temperamental difficulties. The constant meetings with strangers, the continual handling of new problems and thinking out of extempore solutions, the traveling from one town to another, the settlement in new lodgings—all combined to break down the pathological part of his shyness; yet shyness still remained, and with it there developed an almost ascetic enjoyment of certain things—of rainy hours on railway platforms with nothing to do but watch the maneuvers of shunting in a goods yard, of reading the numbers on houses in a strange town late at night, knowing that one of them hid a passing and unimportant destiny. His work also brought him into contact with average citizens of these many provincial towns—the barber, the tobacconist, the stationmaster, the shopkeepers who were given a couple of free seats in exchange for a playbill exhibited in their windows, the parson who sometimes preached a sermon attacking the show as indecent (good publicity if you could get it), sometimes the parson who came himself with his wife and children, but most often the parson who neither attacked nor patronized, but just passed by in the street with a preoccupied air, recognizing the smartly dressed strangers as "theatricals" and therefore in some vaguely opposite but no longer warring camp. One of these clerics, with whom Smith got into conversation, commented that the Church and the theater were now potential allies, being both sufferers from the same public indifference—"Your leaky roof and my leaky roof are the price paid for the new cathedrals of Mammon." Whereupon he pointed across the street to a new cinema advertising a film which, so it turned out after further conversation, they had both of them recently enjoyed.

Smith saw a good deal of Paula during these busy days and even busier evenings, but somehow their relationship did not seem to progress to anything warmer or more intimate. Outwardly he became just as friendly with a few of the others, especially with young Ponderby, the tweedy youth, whom he grew to like. Ponderby was not much of an actor; his job depended entirely on the possession of astoundingly conventional good looks. In *Salute the Flag* all he had was a couple of lines; he rushed into the general's headquarters with the cry: "The enemy are attacking! Give the order to advance!"— whereupon the general, who was a spy in disguise, was supposed to look sinister while Ponderby backed towards the door, delivering his second line as an exit: "Or if you don't, sir, then, by heaven, I will myself!" This was designed to bring a round of applause, and by careful attention to timing and movement Ponderby usually got one. Margesson, who managed the company, was very strict about everyone getting his "round." There was a technique about such things: you stood in the doorway, hand on the doorknob, staring hard and throwing your voice up to the farthest corner of the gallery—if the "round" didn't come, or came too sluggishly, you rattled the doorknob and repeated the final line with greater emphasis.

One Saturday, in the town of Fulverton, Ponderby spent the morning drinking in an attempt to destroy the effect of too much drinking the night before; by midafternoon, when he and Smith happened to be alone together in the lodginghouse, it was clear that he could perform in the evening only with extreme hazard, if at all. He had done this sort of thing several times before, so Smith neither believed nor disbelieved a story of bad news from home; but he felt some sympathy for the youth, especially as he knew this latest offense would probably cost him his job. Ponderby knew this too, and as the hour approached for the first show he took quantities of aspirin and pick-me-ups, all of which only added to his symptoms of physical illness. By six o'clock he was begging Smith to take over his part, as the only way by which Margesson might be placated; after all, provided the show wasn't interfered with, Margesson might not care —the part was so small, and the clothes would fit too. Smith was reluctant to agree; he didn't feel he would be any good as an actor, even in the least possible part; but then Ponderby wasn't good either, so that argument didn't carry far. And it was undoubtedly true that the part, though small, was structurally important, so that a last-minute cut would be extremely awkward; and Saturday, also, was the best night for Fulverton audiences. Everything forced him to an eventual consent, subject to Margesson's approval; but he still did not like the idea.

He went to the theater earlier than usual and found Margesson in

the midst of some trouble with scene shifters; when he said that
Ponderby was ill and he himself could take his part, Margesson
merely answered in a hurry: "Had too much to drink again, I suppose. . . . All right then—mind you get your round."

He did not have any chance to tell Paula about it, but the news
that he was taking Ponderby's part caused little surprise; he was
such a handy man, and the part was only two lines—there seemed
nothing very remarkable about the arrangement.

He was a trifle nervous as he changed into the uniform of a British
second lieutenant, but not more so than he often was at times when
people would never guess it. Quite a natural nervousness too; he
knew that many actors and public speakers were always like that,
it was really abnormal not to be. Something in the look of himself in
the mirror struck a half-heard chord in his submerged memory; he
did not come on till the middle of the last act, so he had time to
smoke cigarettes and try to catch the chord again, but that was
stupid; the more he stared at himself in the mirror, the less he could
remember anything at all. Then suddenly, with a frightening stab of
panic, he asked himself what Ponderby's lines were—he had never
thought of memorizing them, because he assumed he knew them
so well; he practically knew the whole show by heart, for that matter
—they all did. But now, when he sought to speak them to himself,
what the devil were they? He tried to visualize that part of the play:
the general at his desk, twirling his mustaches and muttering *"Hein"*
under his breath—that was to show he was a spy in disguise; then
Ponderby rushing in—"The enemy are attacking! Give the order to
advance!" Now why should a second lieutenant tell a general what
to do? Never mind—that was part of the play. Anyhow, Ponderby
backed across the stage—not too quick, though—give the general
time to give some more twirls and look suspicious; then on the exit—
"Or if you don't, sir, then, by heaven, I will myself!" That was it; and
wait for the round. . . . He said it all over again to himself: "The
enemy are attacking—give the order to advance—or, if you don't, sir,
then, by heaven, I will myself!" Twenty words—the smallest part in
the show. Saying them over a third time, he heard the call boy's
"Ready, sir."

He went out into the wings, standing where he could see the
general at his desk. The general (little Tommy made up with comic
mustaches) was rifling drawers with a terrific amount of noise (exactly as a spy wouldn't do), glancing through piles of paper in search
of a stolen treaty—even if it were there, he was going through them
so fast that he couldn't possibly find it; but that again had to be done

or nobody would get the point—anything else was what Margesson called "this damsilly West End pansy-stuff where you come on the stage and light a cigarette with your back to the audience and call it acting." Smith stood there, waiting for the cue, which was the word "*Hein.*" He felt a little queer; he was going to do something he had never done before; it would be awful if he did it badly, or didn't get his round; the only comfort was that Ponderby did it pretty badly himself.

Suddenly he heard the general say "*Hein.*" It electrified him, like a word spoken inside his own head; he felt his feet as items of luggage that didn't belong to him as he marshaled them for the forward rush. His first impression was of a dazzling brilliance and of the curious fact that there was no audience at all; then, as he stared to verify this, faces swam out of the darkness towards him: row upon row, stalls, boxes, circle, balcony, all were returning his stare from tens of thousands of eyes—quizzically, he thought at first, as if they were aware that this was the supreme moment of all drama and were anxious to compare his performance with previous ones by Irving, Coquelin, and Forbes-Robertson . . . but then, with a flash of uneasiness, he saw malevolence too, as if they hated him for not being Irving, even for not being Ponderby. He knew he had to conquer this uneasiness or it would conquer him, just as he knew he had to rush up to the general's desk and say "The enemy are attacking—give the order to advance!" He saw Tommy eyeing him watchfully—that was part of the play, but Tommy's eye held an extra watchfulness, as if he were hating him too—for not being somebody else.

And then a very dreadful thing happened; he began to stammer. It was the old, the tragic stammer—the one that made his face twist and twitch as if he were in a dentist's chair; he stood there, facing the general, facing the audience, facing God, it almost seemed, and all he could do was wrestle with the words until they came, one after another, each one fighting to the last. The audience began to titter, and when he crossed the stage to struggle with the rest of the words they were already yelling with laughter. "Or if y-y-you d-d-don't, sir, then, b-b-by G-G-God, I w-w-will m-m-myself!" The laughter rose to a shriek as he still stood there, waiting, trembling, with lips curving grotesquely and hand fumbling at the door; and when he finally rattled at the knob till it broke off and rolled across the stage into the footlights, the whole house burst into hilarious shouting while the lads in the gallery stamped their feet and whistled through two fingers for over a minute.

He got his "round" all right.

He left the stage in a daze, somehow finding himself in the wings, passing faces he knew without a word, yet noting for agonized recollection later that some looked anxious, others puzzled, a few were actually convulsed with laughter. Alone at last in the dressing room he closed the door, locked it, and for several minutes fought down an ancient resurrected hell of fear, mental darkness, and humiliation. Several knocks came at the door, but he did not answer them. Later, when the wave had passed over and he knew he was not drowned but merely swimming exhausted in an angry sea, he summoned enough energy to change his clothes. By that time the play had reached the final scene in which all the company would later be on the stage—he waited for the cue, "You cannot fire on helpless womankind," followed by the cheers and rough-and-tumble of the rescue party. Backstage would be deserted now; he unlocked his way into the corridor and escaped through the stage door into an alley by the side of the fire staircase. As he turned the corner he could see a long queue already forming for the second performance, which reminded him that Ponderby's part must be played by someone else in that; Margesson would have to arrange it; anyhow, that was a trifle to worry about, a mere pinhole of trouble compared with the abyss of despair that he himself was facing.

Of course he must leave; they would not wish him to stay; he could offer no explanation, because there was none that would not repeat his humiliation a hundredfold.

Hurrying across Fulverton that night, across the brightly lit Market Street full of shoppers, through the side roads where happy people lived, it seemed to him that someone was always following, footsteps that hastened under dark trees and dodged to avoid street lamps; an illusion, perhaps, but one that stirred the nag and throb of countless remembered symptoms, till it was not so much the ignominy of what had happened that weighed him down as the awareness of how thinly the skin had grown across the scar, of how near his mind still was to the chaos from which it had barely emerged. He hurried on—eager to pack his bag and be off, away from Fulverton and the troubled self he hoped to leave by the same act of movement; for surely place and self had some deep association, so that he could not now think of Melbury without . . . and then the renascent fear in his soul took shape; they were *still* trying to get him back to Melbury —they had been trying all the time, while he, falsely confident during those few weeks of respite, had gone about with an increasing boldness until that very night of self-betrayal. And such stupid, unnecessary self-betrayal before a thousand onlookers, among whom was one, perhaps, who did not laugh, but rose from his seat and quietly left the theater, taking his stand on the pavement where he could watch every exit. . . . Suddenly Smith began to run. They should not get him—never again. He stopped abruptly in the next patch of darkness, and surely enough the footsteps that had been following at a scamper then also stopped abruptly. He ran on again, dodging traffic at a corner and almost colliding with several passers-by. It was man to man, as yet—the enemy were attacking, give the order to advance! He turned into the short cut that led directly to his lodgings—a paved passageway under a railway viaduct. Then he saw there was a rope stretched across the entrance and a man standing in front of it.

"Sorry, sir—can't get by this way tonight."

"But—I—what's the idea? Why not?"

"Can't be helped, sir—it's the law—one day a year we have to keep it closed, otherwise the railway company loses title."

"But I must go—I'm in a hurry!"

"Now come on, sir, I'm only doing my duty—don't give me no trouble—"

Suddenly he realized that there was more than one enemy; this man was another; there were thousands of them, everywhere; they probably had the district surrounded already. . . .

"Come along, sir, act peaceable—"

"*Peaceable?* Then why are you carrying that gun?"

"*Gun?* Why, you're off your chump—I've got no gun! D'you mean this pipe?"

But he wasn't taken in by that, any more than by the nonsense about the railway company and its title; he jumped the rope, hurling the fellow aside, and ran along the passageway; in a couple of minutes he had reached the lodginghouse, whereas it would have taken ten by the road.

He had hoped to have the place to himself, knowing that on Saturday nights most landladies did their week-end shopping. But he had forgotten Ponderby, who shouted a slurred greeting from the sitting room as he passed by to climb the stairs. "Hello, Smithy—get along all right? Knew you would—nothing to it—damn nice of you, though, to help me out. . . ."

He heard Ponderby staggering into the lobby and beginning to follow him upstairs, but the youth was very drunk and made long pauses at each step, continuing to shout meanwhile: "Was Margie wild? I'll bet he would have been but for you. Why don't you come

down and have a drink with me—you deserve it. . . . Friend indeed
and a friend in need—that's what you are—no, *I'm* the friend in need
and *you're* the . . . oh well, never could understand the thing properly. What're you doing up there? Not going to bed yet surely? What
time is it? Maybe *I'd* better go to bed, then they'll all know I've been
ill. . . . What's that? Can't hear what you say. . . ."

Smith repeated: "No, don't come up, I'm coming down."

"All right, Smithy—I'll go down too and get you a little drink. Must
have a little drink—you deserve it."

By this time Smith had packed; he was naturally a tidy person,
and having to do so regularly had made him expert and the job
almost automatic. As he descended the stairs he felt calmer, readier
to do battle with the forces arrayed against him; and that made
him feel a little warm towards the weak healthy boy who never did
battle at all, but just drank and debauched himself in a bored, zest-
less way. He turned into the sitting room, where Ponderby lay
sprawled again on the sofa, head buried in the cushions.

"Hello, old boy—was just mixing you a drink when this awful
headache came on again. Don't mind me—sit down and give me all
the news."

Smith did not sit down, but he took the tumbler, which was almost
half full of neat whiskey, poured most of it back into the bottle,
and sipped the remainder. He did not usually drink, but he hoped
now it might help to steady his nerves, might give him greater calmness for the journey, wherever that was to be.

"Tell me all the news, Smithy. Don't mind me—I've got an awful
head, but I'm listening."

Smith said there was no particular news to tell.

"Oh, I don't mean the theater—damn the theater—I mean *news*.
Heard the paper boy in the street an hour ago—shouting something
—went out and bought one—there it is—couldn't read it, though—my
eyes gave out on me. What's been happening in the world?"

Smith stooped to pick up the paper with momentary excitement;
was it possible that already . . . no, of course not—an hour ago was
actually before the thing happened, apart from the time it would
take to make a report and get it printed. He glanced at the headlines. "Seems those two fellows have flown across the Atlantic—Alcock and Brown."

"Flown across the Atlantic? That's a damn silly thing to do—but
I'll tell you what, it's better than being an actor. Well, drink a toast
to 'em, old boy—what d'you say their names are?"

"Alcock and Brown."

"Alcock, Brown, Smith, and Ponderby—drink to the lot of us. Sounds like a lawyer's office—that's the job I used to have—in a lawyer's office. Damn good lawyers, too—wouldn't touch anything dirty. That's why they got so they wouldn't touch me. Rude health like mine in a lawyer's office—out of place, old boy—sheer bad taste— frightens the clients. So one fine day I did a skedaddle from all that messuage. Know what a messuage is? Lawyer's word. . . ."

Smith said he must go, if Ponderby would excuse him.

"*Go?* Not yet, surely—wait till the others come—don't like to be left alone, Smithy."

"I'm sorry, but I really must go now."

Then Ponderby raised his head and stared.

"Right you are, then . . . but good God, what's the matter? Been in a fight or something?"

"I've got to go. Good night, Ponderby."

"Nighty night, Smithy. And don't think I'll ever forget what you've done."

You won't and neither will anyone else, Smith reflected, picking up his bag and hat in the lobby and walking out of the house. Nobody saw him. The night was warm and dark. He wondered why Ponderby had asked if he had been in a fight, and at the first shop window he stopped and tried to catch his reflection in the glass. He smiled—he had forgotten to comb his hair; it showed even under his hat, rumpled as if—well, yes, as if he had been in a fight. That was easy to repair, since he carried a pocket comb, and at the same time he took out his handkerchief to wipe the perspiration from his forehead. Then he did more than smile, he actually laughed, because of the color of the handkerchief afterwards. He had forgotten to clean off the make-up. All the way across Fulverton, then, he must have been looking like that—if anyone had seen him, but nobody had— until Ponderby. Oh yes, there was the man with the gun—but it had been very dark just there, under the viaduct. He wiped off the make-up and threw the handkerchief over a fence.

He knew they would go to Fulverton Station first of all, especially for the night train to London; but he was not such a fool as to do anything so obvious. There was a station about twelve miles away, on a different line—Crosby Magna it was called; if he walked throughout the night he would be near the place by dawn and could take the first train wherever it went. He did not feel particularly tired; the whiskey had fortified him, and a certain rising exultation as he left the outskirts of Fulverton kept him tramping at a steady three miles an hour. It must be just about the close of the second performance by now; they would be taking curtain calls, then chattering in the dressing rooms, looking forward to the usual Saturday supper at the lodginghouse. A decent crowd; he had been happy with them. He began to look back upon that life with a certain historic detachment; it was all over, and it would have had to be over soon, anyway, for a reason that now, for the first time, he admitted to himself. He had been growing too fond of that girl; gradually but insidiously the feeling had been growing in him, so that soon the only freedom he could have found would have been either away from her or with her altogether; it would soon have become impossible to keep on seeing her continually and meaninglessly in trains, dining rooms, theater backstages: impossible much longer to have suppressed the anxieties he had already begun to feel about all the chance contacts of their daily lives—whether she would be in or out at a certain hour, or would happen to sit next to him here or there, or who the man was who met and talked with her so long after the show. Such things had not mattered to him at first, partly because he had been so humble about himself—why should she bother about him at all, what had he to offer? She loved life, she loved people —be honest about it, she loved men. He had even, at first, experienced a sardonic pleasure in seeing her warm to the chance encounters that fill the spare moments of stage life—his look, as he said good night to her when he was going home to bed and she to a party somewhere, had often contained the message—Have a good time, you've done all you can for me, the rest I must do myself; so thank you again and good luck.

That was his message to her now, as he walked from Fulverton to Crosby Magna and heard the chime of midnight from a distant clock. But he knew that it could not have been so had he stayed with the company, so that actually his leaving was well-timed, an escape from bondage that would soon have become intolerable.

He reached Crosby Magna towards dawn—a small deserted country station on a single line. There was a time-table pasted up from which he discovered that the first train was a local to Fellingham at ten minutes past five. He had over an hour to wait, and spent it leaning against his bag on the station platform. He felt rather drowsy; it was pleasant to rest there, with the sunrise on his face. Presently he realized that a man was staring down at him.

"Waiting for the train, sir?"

"Yes."

"It's due in now. I'll get you a ticket. Where to, sir?"

"Er . . . Fellingham . . . single . . ."

He dragged himself to his feet and followed the man into the small booking hall.

"Fellingham, there you are, sir. Not traveling with the company this time?"

"*What?*"

"Couldn't help recognizing you, sir—I was at the theater in Fulverton last night. Very funny indeed you was, sir—funniest bit in the whole show. Well, here's your train, sir."

He insisted on carrying Smith's bag and choosing a compartment for him, though the train was practically empty. It was, indeed, one of those trains that seem to exist for no reason at all except to wander through the English countryside at hours when no one wants to travel, stopping here and there at places where no one could possibly have any business, especially on a Sunday morning, and all with an air of utter vagrancy, like that of cattle browsing or a woman polishing her nails—a halt here for several minutes, then an interval of movement, even a burst of speed, then a slow-down to hardly a stop at all, and so on. Fellingham was only forty-odd miles from Crosby Magna, but the journey, according to the time-table, would take over two hours. But it was pleasant enough to look out of the window on field and farmstead in the early morning, the lonely roads disappearing into a hazy distance, a stop for the guard to throw out a parcel to a man who stood by a crossing gate waiting for it, long maneuvers of shunting in and out of sidings to detach various empty wagons. No sound when the train stopped save that of the brakes creaking off the wheels and the breeze rippling the grasses in near-by fields. Whenever he put his head out of the window at a station, another head, red-haired and a boy's, was leaning out three coaches in front, and this somehow began to suggest that he and the boy were alone on the train—final survivors of something or else first pioneers of something else.

Presently the horizon began to show a long, low-lying cloud, but a few further miles revealed it as a line of hills—rather high hills, they looked, but he knew they could not be, because there were no high hills in that part of England.

Of course he would not go all the way to Fellingham; that would make the trail too easy, especially after the porter at Crosby Magna had recognized him—unfortunate, that had been. He would get out at some intermediate station and make his way elsewhere across country.

The train had stopped again by the time the hills became clear—a station called Worling. He thought this would do as well as any other, and was just about to jump down to the platform when his bag flew open, spilling some of the contents on to the compartment floor; by the time he had them repacked the train was off again. But it did not really matter; one place was as good as another.

The train cantered on, like horses now more than cattle, steadily, at a good pace, as if anxious to reach some friendly stable; the track wound more closely into the uplands and soon entered a long shallow valley under a ridge that rose rather steeply at one point into two rounded summits; you could not tell which was the higher, but neither was very high—maybe seven or eight hundred feet, with a saucer-shaped hollow between. Just under the hill the roofs of a village showed amongst the trees, but the train turned capriciously away from it, choosing to stop at a station called Rolyott that was nothing but a shed in the middle of fields. He got out there, handing his ticket to the solitary porter, who stared at it for a moment and then said something about Fellingham being three stations further on; Smith smiled and said that was all right, and as the train moved off again the redheaded boy who was always looking out of the window saw him smiling and smiled back. That made him feel suddenly cheerful. And besides, the air was warm, blended with scents of hay and flowers, and the tree-hidden village looked tempting even at the end of a long road; he set out, walking briskly. A few hundred yards from the station, withdrawn into a hedge so that no one could see it save by search or chance, a broken signpost pointed to the ground, and he had to climb through nettles to decipher its stained and weather-worn letters: "To Beachings Over, 1 Mile."

He walked on, murmuring the name to himself, as he always did with names—Beachings Over, Beachings Over; and then Beachings Over came into view—a group of gray old cottages fronting a stream over which slabs of stone made bridges. There was a square-towered church as well, a public house called for some undiscoverable reason the "Reindeer"—a ledge in the stream where the water sparkled as it curled over green reeds. And beyond the village rose the sunlit ridge—one hill now quite clearly higher than the other, but only a little higher, and between them that gentle turfy hollow.

He crossed one of the stone bridges. A man coming out of a house stared with friendly curiosity and said "Good morning." A fluff of wind blew a line of hollyhocks towards him. An old man was clipping a yew hedge along the vicarage wall. A sheep dog stirred in the shade and opened a cautious eye as he passed. He felt: This is home; if they will let me stay here, I shall be at peace. He turned off the

road by a path towards an open field that climbed steeply. Near at
hand was a cottage, with a buxom elderly woman tending the garden. "There'll be a nice view from the top this morning," she said
knowingly as he came near. "Five counties they say you can see, on
a clear day." He smiled and then she said: "Leave your bag here if
you like—it'll be quite safe."

"Good idea. . . . Thanks very much. And could I—perhaps—trouble you for a glass of water?"

"Water if you like, sir, but cider if you prefer."

"Well, yes indeed, if it's no trouble."

"No trouble at all, sir—I'll just have to go round to the stillage."

"*Stillage?*"

"That's where we keep it, sir, being that cool off the stone, you'll
be surprised."

She came back with a pint-sized mug, which he drained gratefully.

"Glad you're enjoying it, sir—it's good cider, that I do say, though
I brewed it myself."

He wondered if he should offer to pay her, but she saw his look of
hesitation and added with swift tact: "Don't you worry, sir—you're
very welcome. Maybe when you've climbed up and down again
you'll feel like some cold beef and pickles and a nice raspberry tart—
we serve meals, you know, all day on Sundays."

"You get many visitors?"

"Hardly a one, but we're ready for 'em if they come. Gentleman
once told me this was the prettiest village in all England."

"Certainly it might be. . . . Well, thank you again—perhaps I will
want that meal."

He resumed the climb, feeling glowingly free after the drink and
without his bag. The sky was dappled with clouds like sails, the smell
of earth and grass rose in a hot sweetness. He walked steadily,
stopping only to look back when a chime floated upwards from the
church tower; Beachings Over, its gardens and roofs, lay in the fold
of the valley as if planted there. He climbed on till the ridge was
close at hand, beyond the next field and the next stone wall, the
two hills curving against the sky. After a little time he reached the
saddle between, and there, hidden till the last moment, lay a pool
of blue water, blown into ripples under passing cloud shadows. It
looked so cool he took his clothes off and bathed—there in sight of all
the five counties, so it amused him to think. Then he lay in the sun
till he was dry, feeling the warmth of sun and cider soaking into

every nerve. Presently he dressed, found a shady spot under a tree, and closed his eyes.

The sun on his face woke him; it had moved round the sky but was near the horizon and no longer hot. His glance followed the curve of the hill and came to rest on the already graying pool; he was surprised to see a girl there, perched on a jutting rock and paddling her feet. He watched her for a moment, quietly fitting the picture into his mind before recognition came, and with it a curious mounting anger because he suddenly knew why it was he had grown so desperately in love with her; it was because she had made him so, because she followed him about everywhere, because, from the moment of their first meeting, she had never let him go—despite all acting and casual behavior and false appearances. And she had followed him even to Beachings Over.

Aware that he was watching her, she turned and then came towards him, high-stepping barefoot over the grass.

"Smithy—you're really awake? Why did you run off like that? Were you ill? What's been the matter? . . . The woman at the cottage said you were here—said you'd left your bag, so you'd have to come down, but I didn't want to wait, and yet I have waited—hours—while you've been asleep. . . ."

"I'm—I'm—sorry."

"For keeping me waiting? It's *my* fault—I could have wakened you any time, but you looked so tired and you hadn't shaved—I guessed you'd been out all night somewhere."

"But I'm so terribly sorry—no, not for that—for what happened before then—at the theater—"

"Oh, *that?* Darling, you shouldn't ever have taken it on, but it didn't matter—got the biggest laugh in the whole show—Margie even said he'd change the part if Ponderby could do it that way, but he was afraid he couldn't. Anyhow, he's going to keep in the bit where the doorknob comes off—that's good for a laugh any time."

"But do they think I did it *deliberately?*"

"I told them you did—I swore you fixed the whole thing with Ponderby just for a gag; Ponderby said you had too, I made him—they all thought it was marvelous, but then they think you *are* marvelous, anyhow."

"*Marvelous?*"

"Well, you know—unpredictable. One of those shy ones who suddenly blaze out and startle everybody and then go shy again. What'll you do next? Maybe fly the Atlantic like those two fellows. Maybe murder somebody or elope with a duchess. It's all part of being a gentleman. You're privileged—like the boys on Boat Race Night."

"Paula—why do you talk like that?"

"Well, it's true, isn't it?" She bent over him. "There's such an indefinable *je ne sais quoi* about you, darling."

"What did you follow me here for?"

"To bring you back, of course."

"But I'm not coming back."

"Oh, it's only Sunday evening—there's no show till six tomorrow night in Polesby—you don't have to make up your mind till tomorrow afternoon."

"I'm not coming back. I *can't* go back. Don't you realize how I felt—"

"I know—don't try to tell me—I saw you on the stage and I was the only person who knew for certain you weren't acting—because I'd seen you like that before, in the shop at Melbury. Remember?"

He said grimly: "It wouldn't be very easy to forget—any more than last night."

"Except that you're not *bound* to go on the stage, ever again, so what does it matter? Whereas at Melbury you were like that all the time—except with me."

"Yes, except with you."

"Maybe there's something about me too—so far as you're concerned."

He moved restlessly. "There was something then, but there's a barrier between us now, compared with how we were in those days."

"There's only this between us, Smithy—I remember when you needed me, and I'm sure I'm not going to hang around when you don't need me any more. But I thought you might need me today— that's why I'm here."

"*I* feel just the opposite—you were so generous when I *did* need you I've hated to feel you could still do things out of pity as you're doing now."

"That's not just the opposite—it's the same."

"It's why I've kept away from you, anyhow, because I *can* do without you, I know I can, I *must*."

"Oh God, don't boast. I can do without you too, for that matter. Let's be independent as hell. Let's each fly in different directions and wonder why for the rest of our lives." She began to pull on her stockings. "Aren't you hungry?"

"Now you mention it."

"Let's go down. The woman at the cottage said she could give us—"

He interrupted, laughing: "I know. Cold beef and pickles and raspberry tart."

"I said we'd have it."

"You're right about that."

He helped her to her feet and they stared about them for a moment. "Smithy, how *did* you manage to find such a heavenly place?"

"As so many things happen—pure chance. My bag flew open as I was going to get out of the train somewhere else. How did you find I was here?"

"Darling, it was so *easy*. I asked at Fulverton Station, and they said you hadn't been there, so of course I thought of Crosby Magna—"

"*Of course?* Why of course?"

"Well, it was pretty obvious you'd think it *wasn't* so obvious—and then the porter there remembered you, and the guard remembered you'd walked towards the village, and the woman at the cottage said you were up here staring at the five counties,—it *is* five, isn't it?—everybody remembered you, old boy. You aren't terribly good at making people forget you."

"They certainly won't forget my performance last night."

"Back again on the same old subject? I told you they all thought it was marvelous."

"Then why did they think I didn't stay for the second show?"

"I told them it was because you suddenly got scared of how Margie would take it—I said it was just like you, to put on a gag like that and then get scared about it."

"Seems to me you thought of *everything*."

They began the descent amidst the gathering twilight, striding down upon Beachings Over as from the sky. A curl of blue smoke rose from the huddle of roofs, the church bell was ringing for evening service. Something in the calm of that darkening panorama kept them silent till they were within sight of the cottage; then she said: "Oh, by the way—I told the woman you were my husband."

"Why?"

"Because she'd have thought it queer for me to be chasing up a hill after any man who wasn't."

"Is there anything *else* you've told anybody about me?"

"There isn't yet, Smithy, but there might have to be. I'm always ready."

She took his arm as he unlatched the gate that led through an avenue of hollyhocks to the cottage. It was small and four-square, with windows on either side of the front door; at one side of the porch a board announced "Good Accommodation for Cyclists." The

woman who had given him the cider led them smilingly into a room
that opened off the flagged lobby; it was evidently the parlor,
crowded with old-fashioned furniture, pictures, and photographs.
A yellow piano with a fretwork front lined with faded silk occupied
most of one wall; an oval mahogany table stood in the center. The
single window was tightly closed, yet the room smelt fresh and
pleasant. He opened the piano and struck a few of the yellow keys;
the strings twanged almost inaudibly. Inside the closed space of
the room they felt embarrassed to begin a conversation, especially
while the woman kept chattering in and out as she prepared the
table. She told them her name was Mrs. Deventer and that her husband had been a sailor, so badly injured at Jutland, poor man, it
was a mercy he died. "But there, there, that's all over now and never
no more, as the saying is. . . . You'll take some nice ripe tomatoes
with your beef, perhaps, sir? And how about a drop of something
to drink—there's my own cider, but if you'd prefer anything else
my girl can run over to the Reindeer and fetch it. . . . 'Tain't far,
you know—nothing's very far in the village—that's what I always
feel when I go into Chelt'nam—that's our nearest town, you know—
I go there oncet a year, or maybe twice—it's a wonderful place, but
my, it does so make you tired walking through all them streets—we
ain't got only the one street here, and that's plenty when you're
gettin' old. . . ."

She talked and talked, bringing in everything she could think of
till the table was crowded with tomatoes, lettuce, cheese, a huge loaf
of bread, a pot of tea in case they wanted it, and a jar of chutney,
her own special make. At length there could not possibly be anything
else to bring in, and she left them reluctantly, with a slow smile
from the doorway.

He said: "Well?"

"Well, Smithy?"

"You look thoughtful, that's all."

"Darling, I was just wondering what you had against me."

But the door opened again—Mrs. Deventer bringing in a lighted
lamp. "I thought you'd maybe want it. Longest day of the year,
round about, but it still gets dark. . . . Maybe you'll be stayin' the
night? You've missed the last train either way by now, I suppose you
know that. Of course there's rooms at the Reindeer, but mine's as
good, I always say, and cheaper too."

The yellow lamplight glowed between their faces after she had
gone.

"Possessive woman," he remarked. "*My* cider, *my* girl, *my* chutney, *my* rooms."

"Room, she *said*. Didn't you see the notice outside—'Good Accommodation for Cyclists'? But I don't suppose one has to be a cyclist."

He said, after a pause: "I don't know why you should wonder about me like that. How could I have anything against you? Except for the same reason that I couldn't."

"Too subtle, darling, unless you tell me what the reason is."

"I love you."

Her voice leapt to the reply: "Smithy, you *do*? You do *really*? I've loved you ever since I first set eyes on you—as soon as I saw you in that shop I thought—there's my man. Because I'm possessive too—*my* man, *my* chutney, *my* room—all mine." And suddenly she took his hand and leaned down with her cheek close to it. "I could have killed you, though, while you lay on top of that hill, fast asleep. *Killed* you. . . . Oh, God, I'm so happy. . . . What's the name of this place?"

"Beachings Over."

"Beachings Over. . . . I'll get *us* from *that*—forever. Remember the game you used to play with names?"

Later, in a room so consecrated to cyclism that even the pictures were of groups of pioneer freewheelers, he asked her if—when he had fully recovered—if he did fully recover, of course—and if he found a job that could support them both—if and when all those things happened—would she marry him?

She said she would, of course, but without the delay. "I think it's only two weeks they make you wait."

"But—" He seemed bewildered by her having stolen, as usual, the initiative. Then he said, slowly and with difficulty: "I'm not *right* yet. I'm not even as near to it as I thought I was. For half an hour last night I felt the return of everything bad again—black—terrifying. I'm better now, but less confident."

She said she didn't mind, she would look after him, because she had just as much confidence as ever.

"And there's another thing—"

"*Another*, Smithy?" She was trying to mock him out of his mood.

"Wouldn't they ask me a lot of questions at the registry office?"

"You mean questions about yourself that you couldn't answer?"

"Yes."

"They might ask you one question *I* never have—and that is if you've been married before."

"Of course I haven't."

"How can you be certain, old boy, with that awful memory of yours?"

He pondered to himself—yes, how *could* he be certain? He hadn't any logical answer, and yet he felt fairly certain. When people had visited him in those hospitals, relatives of missing men who hoped he might turn out to be someone belonging to them, *he* had similar hopes, but only of finding a home, parents—never a wife. Did that prove anything?

She watched the look on his face, then added with a laugh: "Don't worry—I'll take a chance on it if you will."

Eventually it was agreed that they should go to Polesby the next day, announce their plans to the company, and ask for a few weeks' holiday. She was sure Margesson would agree, if they approached him fairly and squarely; he liked both of them, and the slack season was on. They rose early and took a walk to the end of the village, discussing a future of which Beachings Over seemed already to have become a part. "Oh, Smithy, isn't it beautiful? I didn't see it like this yesterday—I was so worried about finding you—but it's just the sort of place I've always dreamed of. I know that's sentimental—but stage people are—they love the sweet little cottage idea, though most of them would be bored to death if they ever got one—mercifully they don't, as a rule—they either die in the poorhouse or save enough to buy a pub on the Brighton Road. . . ."

She chattered on, and soon it was time to walk back to the cottage for Mrs. Deventer's excellent breakfast, pay their bill, and assure her they would return soon for a longer stay. The old lady was delighted, keeping up the farewell greetings all the way down the avenue of hollyhocks to the front gate. By the time they passed the post office the morning papers were just being unloaded; Smith bought one and scanned the front page during the mile-long tramp to the railway station. Mostly about Brown and Alcock, he told her, summarizing the newly announced details of the first Atlantic flight in history. Not till they were settled in the train did she glance at the paper herself. Then, after a few moments' desultory reading, she looked up with a suddenly changed expression. "*Smithy!*"

"What's the matter?"

"I don't want it to come as a shock to you, but there's something here that looks as if—" she hesitated and then gave a short laugh— "as if they can't come up to you . . . for being crazy."

"Who can't?"

"Brown and Alcock."

"But I don't know what you mean."

"Better read this—and don't let it upset you—probably it's not anything serious."

She handed him the paper, pointing to a small paragraph on an inside page. It was headed "Assault under Viaduct—Fulverton Man Injured," and ran:—

That he was assaulted by an unknown man was the story told to the Fulverton police last night by Thomas Atwill, railway policeman, who was found unconscious under the Marshall Street viaduct at a late hour. Taken to the Cottage Hospital, Atwill stated that he had been on plain-clothes duty to prevent pedestrians from using the footpath under the viaduct, it being necessary to do this for one day each year in order to preserve the company's legal title to the right of way. Shortly after nine o'clock a man endeavored to break through the temporary barrier erected for this purpose, and when Atwill sought to remonstrate with him, he received a severe blow on the head. Describing his assailant as young, rather tall, and clean-shaven, Atwill said he was a gentleman, not a "rough." The police are investigating the unexplained disappearance of a member of a local theatrical touring company.

He put aside the paper, stared at her for a moment, then let his head fall slowly into his hands. When he looked up he was very pale. The train was stopping at Worling, where a crowd of farm workers waited on the platform. She had only time to say: "Darling, if anyone gets in, don't look like that."

Nobody got in, and his controlled features relaxed.

"Oh, Smithy . . . you don't remember?"

"I remember jumping over—it wasn't a barrier—just a rope. And if I hit the fellow, it was accidental—a push that made him fall, maybe with his head on the pavement—I didn't look back, I was running." He added, leaning forward with both hands on her knees: "I do want you to know that I'm not a homicidal maniac rushing about committing crimes and then forgetting about them. When I said that last night for half an hour I felt the return of all the bad things, I meant things in my own mind—fears that I had to fight down . . . but they were in my own mind, and I *did* fight them down, I *never* lost control. I want you to believe that—no matter who else disbelieves it."

"I believe it, Smithy. But there are—as you say—people who wouldn't."

"I know that."

"We mustn't go to Polesby."

"*I* mustn't. *You* can. You're in no danger—on your own." He cried out, with sharp bitterness: "Perhaps you'll stay clear of me after this."

Ignoring that, she said: "Probably the man isn't seriously injured if he recovered consciousness so soon—"

"You don't need to comfort me."

"But it's true—the whole thing'll blow over if he's not badly hurt— and also if we don't go to Polesby. London's a better idea. If we change at Saxham we can get a London train from there. We'll find somewhere to stay—where no one will know who we are. London's the best place for that. We both have enough money to last for a time."

"But what about you—your job? They'll expect you at Polesby tonight. They'll know we're together."

"They'd be fools not to know that, anyway. I swore I'd never come back unless I brought you with me. . . . Darling, don't look so anxious. *I* believe you. This is just bad luck—it somehow doesn't count. . . ." She took his troubled head in her arms and rocked it gently against her. "I can't help laughing, though, at one thing." She picked up the paper and reread, crooningly, as to a child: "'Atwill said he was a gentleman, not a rough.' That's you all over, Smithy— I always said so."

They left the train at Saxham, but had just missed the best London train of the day; four hours to wait for the next. The interval was pleasantly spent in strolling about the ancient town. The second London train came in late, and they were told to change again at Santley Junction—"but it all helps," she said, "if anyone were trying to follow us." They reached Santley towards dusk and had to cross a platform crowded with waiting passengers. When the next train came in, also late, it was already so full that only tussling and scrimmaging could make further room; but eventually this was accomplished and they found themselves in a compartment occupied by an uncountable number of shouting children, all in nominal charge of an elderly, shabby, but bright-eyed clergyman who gestured apologies for his own inability to subdue the din. "It's been their great day," he explained, forcing a way for the newcomers. Then he helped them, quite unnecessarily, to put up their bags and parcels on the rack, adding with a smile: "Not hostile—only heedless." As soon as the train restarted the children shouted with renewed abandon, leaning out of the windows, jumping on the seats, breaking into song choruses that were taken up by other children in adjacent compartments until the whole train, nearing London, became one long pandemonium streaking through suburb after suburb, over bridges across blazing highways, through smoke-filled tunnels, past rows of back gardens from which shirt-sleeved householders watering their flowers looked up to wave good-humoredly, alongside commons where lovers did not stir as the sudden crescendo engulfed them. At short range, however, it was harder to ignore, a sheer wall of sound behind which three adults, lips to ear and then ear to lips, could only contrive an intermittent mouthing of words.

"It's their annual outing," said the parson, still feeling some need to apologize. "We aim at discipline but—" He gave a little wrinkled smile.

Smith nodded, and Paula, from the other side, whispered loudly in his ear: "If this bothers you, let's get out at the next station and find another compartment."

"No, no, it's all right."

And later, from the parson: "I hope you don't find their high spirits too exhausting."

"*They* don't, evidently," she answered.

"I know—amazing, isn't it? Don't believe I ever shouted like that when I was a boy. *Terrific!*"

"Good thing you keep a sense of humor about it."

"Oh yes. I don't mind the row so much, but I'm scared when they lean out like that—I've warned them over and over again but I can't make them listen."

Smith suddenly intervened: "Do you think *I* could? Perhaps coming from someone else—a stranger? . . . Now boys, supposing you stand away from those windows!"

The different voice, pitched over the wall of sound, somehow reached its goal; the swarming clusters turned, sharply disconcerted, nonplused, ready for rebellion but sensing control; then the different voice continued, releasing them a little: "That's right, sit down— plenty of room for all of us. What about another song?"

From further along the train came the chorus of "Keep the Home Fires Burning"; they joined in it, one by one, a gradual deafening surrender, while the stations flashed by more frequently and the suburbs merged into the slums. She whispered in his ear exultantly: "Smithy, how marvelous! And to think I was afraid they were bothering you!"

The parson was also pleased. "I really am extremely obliged to you, sir."

"Not at all."

"*Astonishing!*"

"Just as much to me, I assure you. I didn't know I could deal with 'em."

"You must have a knack. . . . I haven't any—with children. You're going to London?"

"Yes."

"In a great hurry when you arrive?"

"Not particularly."

"I wonder whether you could spare, then—say five minutes? I always have trouble with them at railway stations, and the Mission's only across the street. If you would . . ."

"Certainly—if I can. The magic may not work the second time."

"Let's have faith that it will."

At the terminus it was as if the whole train burst open, a human explosion on to the platform, yells and bangings of doors while the parson watched Smith bring gradual order out of the chaos. Then began the slow marshaling of two hundred youngsters into line, their realization that a new personality was in command, and their acceptance of the inevitable—truculent at first, then indifferent, finally quite cheerful. But the operation took considerably more than five minutes; it was over a quarter of an hour before the children had all been escorted through the busy station precincts to a side street whence they could be safely dismissed to their homes.

The parson stood beaming on the pavement. "I really cannot express my gratitude. I hope you haven't been too much delayed."

"Oh no."

"You mean you had no plans for—the evening?"

"Well—er—nothing special."

"Then I wonder—if you *really* have nothing else to do—it would give me great pleasure if you'd both dine with me—"

It was Paula who answered, in the instant way in which she decided everything: "Why, yes, we'd be glad."

The parson wrinkled another smile and began fumbling his way through a passage running by the side of the Mission building into an unkempt garden; beyond it stood a large ugly soot-black three-story house. He unlocked the front door, admitting them into a lofty hallway totally unfurnished down to the bare boards of the floor. "I don't think names are at all important," he said, ushering them further into a room, "but mine is Blampied."

"Smith," said Paula.

He offered them chairs, following their glances round the room with a perverse pride. "Isn't this a terrible house? It was built in 1846, when parsons were supposed to live in style. Twenty rooms— I only use five. Kitchen, bathroom, bedroom, this, and my house-keeper's. This is the best. We live in squalor punctuated by small simple meals of excellent quality—onion soup tonight, if you happen to like it."

Meanwhile an elderly gaunt-faced woman was preparing the table, showing neither surprise nor any other emotion at the presence of guests, and needing no instructions from the parson. Presently the three were sitting down before big bowls of the soup; there was nothing else but cheese, he warned them, but they could have more soup if they wanted. It was so good that they did, and asked for it with enthusiasm. Meanwhile the parson chattered on, a cordial, increasingly inquisitive host.

"You two people have much further to go?"

Smith said: "No, not very far."

"You live here in London?"

"Er . . . yes."

"Don't let me keep you, but don't go till you want to."

She said: "Oh, there's plenty of time." It was as if she were reluctant to leave.

"Yes, the buses and trams run late. I expect you can get to your home that way."

"I—I think so."

"You only *think* so?"

"Matter of fact, we haven't got a home—yet. We've got to look for one."

Smith flashed her a warning glance, but she went on: "I don't suppose it'll be very hard."

The parson's curiosity seemed to become less rather than more as he responded: "If it's the slightest help to you, please stay here for the night. My housekeeper can find you bedding, and there are fifteen rooms to choose from."

"That's awfully kind of you, but—"

"Just as you please, of course. Only I thought your husband looked tired."

"He's not my husband—yet."

The parson smiled. "To be sure . . . but after all—fifteen rooms? Enough—one would think."

Then suddenly she said: "Maybe, as you've got a sense of humor,

you can help us. . . . We want to get married, but it has to be quiet
—we don't want anyone to know—"

"Runaway?"

"Yes, that's it . . . maybe you know of a registry office somewhere
near?"

"There's an office nearly across the street, but for sheer quietness,
why don't you allow me to marry you in my own church? Hardly
anyone ever comes to any of the services—it would be the most un-
noticed marriage I could possibly imagine. . . ."

So they were married at St. Clement's, Vale Street, London, N.W.,
and as they left the church after the ceremony newsboys were racing
down the street offering extra editions—"Peace Treaty Signed at
Versailles." It was June 28, 1919. The bridegroom bought one of the
papers on his way with his bride to their home further along Vale
Street—a tall Victorian house that possessed the initial advantage of
being owned by a deaf old woman who lived in the basement and
offered the higher floors for rent. She had agreed to let them have
two big furnished rooms, plus bath and kitchenette, for a pound a
week; there was also an oblong walled garden they could share with
other tenants, but of course they never did. After several weeks of
living in the house they still hadn't said more than "Good morning"
and "Good evening" to the people who occupied the floors above
and below; and an especially odd thing was that the man who
lived above was a policeman.

But they were happy. It was strange, in a way; they had hardly
any money and so far no jobs, and they were half scared of every
knock on the door, because a daily visit to the newsroom of the free
library revealed that the police were still probing what had already
attained some small renown as "the Fulverton case." The victim was
said to be "still improving," but that began to seem almost ominous,
since anything short of recovery showed how seriously he had been
hurt; and one morning there was an even worse sound in the news
item: "Hospital authorities at Fulverton report no change in the
condition of Thomas Atwill, who is still suffering from head injuries
as a result of an assault by an unknown man under a railway viaduct
three weeks ago."

The unknown man felt sincere remorse over the fate of the innocent Atwill, but even that could not dim the joys of a partnership
that was half fun, half fear, so that every falling asleep was like an
unspoken prayer for safety and every waking up a miracle of sur-
vival. Sometimes they would hear the policeman clumping down

the stairs and back again in his heavy boots, and she would run to
the window to look out and come back saying—"It's all right, Smithy
—it's there—go to sleep." That was a joke between them, because
they had once agreed that nothing in the world could be more reassuring than a London policeman, half-dressed, going downstairs
at midnight to put out an empty milk bottle on a front doorstep—a
symbol that no harm would come, that God was somewhere over the
policeman's roof and theirs.

They felt their chief danger might come from a chance recognition
in the streets, and for this reason they avoided the better-known
parts of London where country visitors might be expected to sight-
see; they also kept indoors most of the day, discovering almost with
surprise how quickly the time passed and how little the restrictions
bothered them, provided they were together. They would do most
of their shopping late at night, economy combining then with prudence, for just before closing time in those unfashionable districts
the butcher and green-grocer and fishmonger would sell off cheap
what was left of their day's supplies. While she was bargaining
Smith would often stop to listen to some street-corner orator ha-
ranguing the multitude—the multitude consisting, as a rule, of a few
apathetic onlookers, workingmen with one hand round the bowl of
a pipe and the other in a trouser pocket. "The typical English attitude," Blampied commented afterwards, "good-humored, tolerant,
vaguely skeptical—skeptical just as much of the truth as of lies. What
a lot it will take to move men like that, but when they *do* move—*if*
they ever move—what a cataclysm!"

They were beginning to feel a friendly intimacy with the parson,
all the friendlier because his attitude was such a quaint mixture of
particular inquisitiveness and general incuriosity. He could put the
most intimate questions—once he asked: "Are you and your wife so
united that you could use the same toothbrush?" Yet he never mentioned or fished for information about Smith's background or parentage, until one day, when they were having dinner with him as they
had come to do rather often, he suddenly asked: "What shall I say
if somebody traces you here and questions me about you?"

They stared at him with such disconcerted blankness that he
added: "Didn't you say it was a runaway marriage?"

They knew him so well by then that they did not particularly
mind having betrayed themselves by the startled stare; and the fact
that his later remark gave them an easy cue for evasion tempted
them all the more to tell him nothing but the truth. Paula looked
across the table to Smith, caught and exchanged a glance, then began:

"Yes, it was certainly runaway, but probably not the kind you're imagining. We aren't likely to be troubled by objecting parents. Mine are both dead, and his are . . ." She looked again at Smith.

Blampied nodded, as if satisfied, but Smith addressed him with a smile: "There wouldn't be much point in deceiving you, would there?"

"Depends what you want me to do. If you want me to lie about you to others, at least you must tell me the truth about yourself."

"That sounds a rather unusual standpoint—for a clergyman."

"Perhaps I'm a rather unusual clergyman."

"Well, here's an unusual story."

"Good . . . go ahead."

Smith then spoke briefly of his war injury and resultant lack of memory. He called it a *lack* now, not *loss*—"because I don't *feel* any loss. It doesn't really bother me any more—there are days and nights when I never even think about it . . . but there it is, all the same. Perhaps I ought to have told you when you married us."

"Why?"

"Well, signing my name in the register. Smith may not be the true one."

The parson, sitting at the head of the table, half rose and extended his arms over their shoulders. "But it was *you* I married," he said, "not your names."

"So it doesn't matter?"

"Not a bit. And it's perfectly legal and binding. Is that all you have on your conscience?"

"Not quite all." Encouraged by a further look from Paula, Smith went on to relate the incongruous mishap to Thomas Atwill under the railway viaduct. Blampied listened with increasing interest; once or twice his face twisted into a smile; they were so accustomed to his taking the oddest possible view of things that it did not surprise, although it considerably relieved them when at the end of the re-cital he began to laugh. "It's the idea of a *railway company* having a right of way that tickles me! Know anything about rights of way?"

This seemed a side issue, but most of Blampied's conversations avoided anything in the direct line of argument. Smith said no, not very much.

"They're trying to close them all over England. You must come with me sometime on one of my crusades. I make a nuisance of my-self on village greens every now and again—just by way of a holiday from London. I inform the villagers of their ancient heritage—the commons and the pastures and the paths across the fields that the landlords have stolen and will go on stealing, whenever they get the chance. A clerical predecessor of mine, John Ball by name, made a similar nuisance of himself six hundred years ago or thereabouts—but I think he must have been much more of an oratorical spellbinder." He added, coming back to the point, "So *that's* why you two children are in hiding? You're afraid that if anything should happen to Thomas Atwill—"

"Oh, he'll get better all right," Paula intervened hastily, "but even when he does it could be troublesome if we were traced because —because—" She looked across the table, adding: "We've told you so much we may as well finish—don't you think so, Smithy?"

Smith said: "I mentioned that the war injury affected my memory. It also—at one time—had other effects. They sent me to Melbury— the big hospital for shell-shock cases. I was on their dangerous list."

"You mean liable to die?"

"Well no—liable to live—but dangerously."

Again Blampied laughed. "I see. I really begin to see."

They both joined him in laughing, glad to ease their embarrassment by so doing. Then the parson came behind Smith, putting his arm affectionately round the young man's shoulders. "You needn't worry. The reputation of crank and misfit gives me a certain freedom of reply. If, for instance, I'm asked if I know anyone named Smith, and I say I never heard the name before, it'll merely give rise to an extra legend. . . ."

The more they came to know Blampied the more they realized his remarkableness and the less they felt they completely understood him. At their first meeting in the train he had seemed just the timid, unworldly parson of fiction, almost of caricature, bearing his cross in the form of Mission boys he could not control and summer outings he must have loathed. Later he showed himself more perplexingly as a mixture of ascetic and gourmet—only onion soup for dinner, but how good it had to be. Later still, when he described "crusades" that had sometimes led to rough-and-tumble fights on village greens and once at least to his own imprisonment, he almost became the conventionally unconventional "fighting parson." And beyond that, but by no means finally, there was the visionary, the mystic. It was not easy to analyze or estimate the sum total, and many persons with whom he came into contact had long since given up the task as either hopeless or unprofitable. But one could not meet and talk to him for ten minutes, in any one of his moods, without an impression of stature—mental, moral, psychic, or perhaps

some blending of all three. And he had also (as Smith found out
when he came to work for him) an astoundingly various collection
of intimate friends.

Most of these friends lived abroad, so that occasions for personal
meetings were rare; but he corresponded, regularly and volumi-
nously, and it was this task that had lately made him aware of failing
eyesight, and so of the need for someone to help him with it. Smith
gladly volunteered, and it became a habit that two or three mornings
a week Blampied would dictate slowly while the other took down in
a longhand that soon developed into a private shorthand, marked
by curious abbreviations and a general meaninglessness to the outsider. Afterwards, at his leisure, Smith would rewrite or type the
letters in full. They went to most of the corners of the world—a hotel-
keeper in Yokohama, a university professor in Idaho, a train con-
ductor on the Orient Express, an Austrian soldier lying wounded in
a hospital in Salzburg, an editor in Liverpool, a rubber planter in
Johore, a woman head of an advertising agency in Brisbane . . .
these were a few out of the twenty-odd. All, it appeared, were people whom Blampied had met at one time or another. "I used to
travel a good deal, before the war put an end to it, and now, I fear,
I have neither the zest nor the money to resume. But for a few shillings' worth of stamps each week, I can almost achieve the same object. . . . This morning, for instance, I shall write to M'sieur Gaston
Auriac, Rue Henri Quatre, Antananarivo, Madagascar. We met only
once—on a steamer between Capetown and Durban, but we talked
for long enough to make the discovery of each other. Maybe you
were surprised when I asked you whether you and Paula could use
the same toothbrush? You see I have never married, so I don't know
whether physical oneness goes as far as that—but I do know that in
the realm of mental and spiritual things there can be a similar oneness—the knowledge that yours and mine are no longer yours and
mine, but *ours* for every possible use. And this awareness, once acknowledged by both parties, lasts forever. Gaston and I may disa-
gree about this and that, but because our thought processes are in
the same world, there's a sense in which we can use each other's
minds. We're both impervious to sentimentality and mob optimism, and both of us also, if I may so express it, are accustomed to
think proudly. . . . We found that out during our three-hour talk
seven years ago, and though we have never met since, we both know
that it must still be true, despite all the changes that have taken
place in the world about us. . . . Just now, we're in the midst of
an argument as to the right way to treat Germany now the war's

over. Gaston thinks the Allied armies should have pushed on to Berlin, even at the cost of an extra year of fighting, and then have broken Germany into fragments, acting with ruthless severity on the lines of *delenda est Carthago*. . . . I, on the other hand, would have offered terms of simply astounding generosity—lifting the blockade the day after the Armistice, forbearing to ask for meaningless and uncollectable reparations, and inviting all the defeated countries into an immediate conference on equal terms to discuss the disarmament and rehabilitation of Europe. As you can imagine, we're enjoying as violent a discussion as the somewhat intermittent mails to Madagascar will permit. But the point is: both of us are still thinking proudly. Gaston is no frenzied sadist wishing to destroy for the sake of destroying; I am no milk-and-water humanitarian yearning over a defeated enemy merely because he is defeated and has been an enemy. Both of us have the same aim in view—the cure of the thousand-year-old European disease; both methods have succeeded at various times throughout history—his, I admit, more often than mine. Either might succeed today. But what will *not* succeed, and what we both know will not succeed, is the unhappy mean between the two—the halfway compromise between sentiment and vengeance— the policy of *safe* men playing for *safety*." He added, smiling: "So you see, Mr. Smith, why it did not shock me the other day to hear that you had been classed at one time as a dangerous man. All my friends are dangerous men."

Smith came to enjoy the work of transcribing these letters, and sometimes also he helped with Church and Mission activities, especially those for which Blampied had little ability, such as children's organizations. He found that his experience on the train had been no fluke, but the result of an apparently inborn aptitude for handling youngsters. Even the most stubborn, and from the worst slum homes, responded to his instinctive offering of ease and discipline; in fact it was the most stubborn who liked him and whom he liked the most. He began holding classes in the Mission building, classes that did not invade the religious field (which he did not feel either the inclination or the authority to enter), but touched it variously and from neglected angles—classes on civics, on local history, on London and English traditions. He was so happy over all this that it came to him with a sense of retrospective discovery that he must *like* children— not sentimentally, but with a simple, almost casual affection. "You'd have made a good schoolmaster," Blampied once said, and then, when Smith replied he wasn't sure he'd care to spend all his time with children, the other added: "Exactly. Good schoolmasters don't. Anyhow, you can help to make up for the fact that I'm a bad parson."

"Do you really think you are?"

"Oh yes. Ask anybody round here. People don't take to me. I haven't an ounce of crowd magnetism. And then I'm lazy. Only physically, I think, but then that's the only kind of laziness most people recognize."

"I think you're old enough, if you don't mind my saying so, to be forgiven a certain amount of physical laziness."

"Yes, but I'm not lazy in the forgivable ways. If I went to Lord's to watch the cricket they'd think I was a sweet old clergyman who deserved his afternoon off, but as I'm only lazy enough sometimes to go without a shave—"

Smith laughed, knowing what he meant, for while it could not be said that the parson neglected his professional duties, it was certainly true that he made no effort to make himself either a worldly success or a beloved failure—the two classifications that claim a roughly equal number of adherents among the clergy. Nor, despite the fact that he inclined to High Church fashions, did he join the fanatical brotherhood of those who systematically disobey their bishops; his own disobediences were personal, casual, almost careless—wherefore his bishop disliked him all the more. So did various influential parishioners to whom he refused to toady; while the poor, to whom he also refused to toady, rewarded him with a vast but genial indifference. A few devoted lay workers ran the adjacent Mission, but they were not devoted to *him,* and when they pushed on him such tasks as the supervision of the annual outing it was with the knowledge and hope that he would have a bad time. Nor did they care for his church services, which they thought cold and formal; they realized, correctly, that he was not the kind of cleric to "drag the people in," and from time to time they plotted, more or less openly, to have him supplanted by some energetic slum parson who would unite both Church and Mission into a single buzzing hive. But it is by no means easy to dislodge a parson of the Church of England, and Blampied had suffered no more than a gradual reduction of dues and stipend during his twelve years of office.

He was, in fact, though he hardly realized it because his wants were so few, very close to the poverty line. He wore the shabbiest clothes; he lived on the simplest and cheapest of foods, though always well-cooked; he paid cash to tradespeople, but owed large sums to local authorities for taxes and bills of various kinds. About a month after his first meeting with Smith, his housekeeper fell suddenly ill and died within a few days; he was a good deal upset by that, but admitted that it had saved him from having to get rid of her, since he could no longer afford the few weekly shillings for her part-time services. It was then he suggested to Smith and Paula that they should move into the house and live rent-free in return for similar help; they were glad to consent, since their own money was rapidly dwindling.

Out of the unused fifteen they chose two large attic rooms with a view over roof tops northward as far as Hampstead and Highgate, and it was fun to begin buying the bare necessities of furniture and utensils, searching the Caledonian Market for broken-down chairs that could be repaired and reupholstered, discarded shop fittings usable as bookshelves, an old school desk that showed mahogany under its coating of ink and dirt. Gradually the rooms became a home, and the entirely vacant floor beneath encouraged a kinship with roofs and sky rather than with the walls and pavements of the streets.

Towards the end of September Blampied received a quarterly payment which he chose to devote to a crusading holiday rather than to paying arrears of his borough council rates; having invited Smith and Paula to join the expedition, he took them for a week into rural Oxfordshire "making trouble wherever we go," as the parson put it, though that was an exaggeration. The question of country footpaths was, he admitted, his King Charles's Head—every man, he added, should have some small matter to which he attaches undue importance, always provided that he realizes the undueness. Realizing it all the time, Blampied would puzzle over ancient maps in bar parlors, inquiring from villagers whether it was still possible to take the diagonal way across the fields from Planter's End to Marsh Hollow, and generally receiving the answer that no one ever did—it was much quicker to go round by the road, and so on. "I reckon you could if you tried, mister, but you'd 'ave a rare time gettin' through them nettles." A few more pints of beer would perhaps elicit the information that "I remember when I was a kid I used to go to school that way, but 'twouldn't be no help now, not with the new school where it is." Yet those, as the parson emphasized, drinking his beer as copiously as the rest, were the paths their forefathers had trod, the secret short cuts across hill and valley, the ways by which the local man could escape or intercept while the armed stranger tramped along the highroads. All of which failed to carry much weight with the Oxfordshire men of 1919, many of whom, as armed strangers, had tramped the highroads of other countries. They obviously regarded the parson as an oddity, but being country people they knew that men, like trees and unlike suburban houses, were never exactly the same, and this idea of unsameness as the pattern of life meant that (as Blampied put it) they didn't think there was anything *very* odd in anyone being a *little* odd.

Several times the parson spoke on village greens to small, curious, unenthusiastic audiences, most of whom melted away when he suggested that there and then they should march over the ancient ground, breaking down any barriers that might have been erected during the past century or so; but in one village there was a more active response, due to the fact that the closing of a certain path had been recent and resented. It was then that Blampied showed a certain childlike pugnacity; he clearly derived enormous enjoyment from leading a crowd of perhaps fifty persons, many of them youngsters out for a lark, through Hilltop Farm and up Long Meadow to the gap in the hedge that was now laced with fresh barbed wire. Smith found he could best be useful in preventing the children from destroying crops or tearing their clothes; he thought the whole expedition a trifle silly but pleasingly novel. Actually this particular onslaught had quite an exciting finish; the owner of the property, a certain General Sir Richard Hawkesley Wych-Furlough, suddenly appeared on the scene, backed by a menacing array of servants and gamekeepers. Everything pointed to a battle, but all that finally developed was a long and wordy argument between the General and the parson, culminating in retirement by both sides and a final shout from the General: "What the hell's it got to do with *you*, anyway? You don't live here!"

"And that," as Blampied said afterwards, "from a man who used to be Governor of so many islands he could only visit a few of them once a year—so that any islander might have met his administrative decisions with the same retort—'What's it got to do with *you?* You don't live here!'"

The notion continued to please him as he added: "I was a missionary on one of those islands—till I quarreled with the bosses. I always quarrel with bosses. . . ."

Gradually Smith and Paula began to piece together Blampied's history. Born of a wealthy family whom he had long ago given up no less emphatically than they had him, he had originally entered the Church as a respectable and sanctioned form of eccentricity for younger sons. Later, even more eccentrically and with a good deal more sincerity, he had served as a missionary in the South Seas until his employers discovered him to be not only heretical, but a bad compiler of reports. After that he had come home to edit a religious magazine, resigning only when plunging circulation led to its bankruptcy. For a time after that he had dabbled in politics, joining the early Fabians, with whom he never quarreled at all, but from whom he became estranged by a widening gulf of mutual exasperation. "The truth is, Smith," he confessed, "I never could get along with all the Risers-to-Second-That and the On-a-Point-of-Orderers. If I were God, I'd say—Let there be Light. But as I'm not God, I'd rather spend my time plotting for Him in the dark than in holding committee meetings in a man-made blaze of publicity!"

He formed the habit of talking with the two of them for an hour or so most evenings, especially as summer lagged behind and coal began to burn in a million London grates. To roof dwellers it was a rather dirty but strangely comforting transition—the touch of smoke-laden fog drifting up from the river, the smell of smoldering heaps in parks and gardens, the chill that seemed the perfect answer to a fire, as the fire was to the chill. For London, Blampied claimed, was of all cities in the world the most autumnal—its mellow brickwork harmonizing with fallen leaves and October sunsets, just as the etched grays of November composed themselves with the light and shade of Portland stone. There was a charm, a deathless charm, about a city whose inhabitants went about muttering, "The nights are drawing in," as if it were a spell to invoke the vast, sprawling creature-comfort of winter. Indeed no phrase, he once said, better expressed the feeling of curtained enclosure, of almost stupefying cosiness, that blankets London throughout the dark months—a sort of spiritual central heating, warm and sometimes weepy, but not depressing—a Dickensian, never a Proustian fog.

Those were the happy days when Smith began to write. As most real writers do, he wrote because he had something to say, not because of any specific ambition to be a writer. He turned out countless articles and sketches that gave him pleasure only because they contained a germ of what was in his mind; but he was never fully satisfied with them himself and consequently never more than slightly disappointed when editors promptly returned them. He did not grasp that, because he was a person of no importance, nobody wanted to read his opinions at all. Presently, by sheer accident, he wrote something that fitted a formula; it was promptly accepted and —even more important for him at the time—paid for.

After he had worked all morning he would often set out in the afternoon with Paula on a planless excursion decided by some chance-met bus; or sometimes they would tramp haphazardly first to the left, then to the right, mile after mile, searching for books or furniture in old, gas-lit shops, and returning late at night through the narrow defiles of the City. They liked the City, the city with a capital C, and especially at dusk, when all the teashops filled with men, a curious democracy within a plutocracy—silk-hatted stock-brokers buying twopenny cups while at the same table two-pounds-a-week clerks drank similar cups and talked of wireless or motor bicycles or their suburban back gardens. And afterwards, as Paula took his arm on the pavement outside, they would be caught in the human current sweeping along Old Broad Street in a single east-ward stream, then crossing Liverpool Street like a flood tide into the vast station delta. He loved to see those people, so purposeful and yet so gentle, so free and yet so disciplined, hurrying towards the little moving boxes that would carry them home to secret suburbs—secret because they were so unknown to one another, so that a bus shuttling all day between Putney and Homerton gave one a mystical curiosity about all the people in Homerton who had never seen Put-ney, and all the people in Putney for whom Homerton was as strange as—perhaps stranger than—Paris or New York. There was something fantastic, too, in that morning and evening migration, huger in man miles than any movement of the hordes of Tamerlane, something that might well be incomprehensible to the urban masses of the fu-ture, schooled to garden cities and decentralization. But there could never be such romance as in the pull of steam through the Bishops-gate tunnels, or faces that stared in friendly indifference as trains raced parallel out of Waterloo.

He wrote of such things, and he wrote as he saw—a little naïvely, as if things had never been seen before—like the line drawings of a child, with something of the same piercing simplicity. It probably helped him, as Blampied said, to have forgotten so much about him-self, because into that absence came an awareness far beyond the personal reach—the idea of the past as something to be apprehended in vision rather than explored in memory. He wrote, too, of the countryside as he had seen it: of the men in the pubs with their red faces shy over mugs of beer—old couples outside their cottages on summer evenings, silent and close, yet in that silence and close-ness telling all there is in the world—a peddler unlatching a gate with slow steps towards a lonely house—farm workers at midday, asleep under trees—a little road over the hill, curving here and there for no reason at all . . . scene after scene, as a child turns pages in a loved picture book, yet behind the apocalyptic wonderment of it all there was something to which talks with Blampied had added shape and

quality—the vision of a new England rooted far back in the old, drawing its strength from a thousand years instead of its weaknesses from
a hundred.

"Follow that vision," Blampied once said. "Follow it wherever it
leads. Think it out. Write it down. I'd say *preach* it if the word
hadn't been debased by so many of my own profession."

"I couldn't preach, anyhow. No more public appearances for me
after the last one."

"But preaching doesn't need a pulpit. All it needs is what you
have—a faith."

"Is yours the same faith?"

"You have your vision of England, I have mine of the world—but
your England will fit into my world." He added, after a pause: "Does
that sound arrogant? Maybe. We mustn't be afraid of a secret arro-
gance. After all, we are spies of God, mapping out territory lost to
the enemy when faith was lost." His eyes twinkled as he touched his
collar. "It isn't *this,* you know, that makes me say so. Religion's only
one of the things that can die without faith. Take another, for the
sake of something you may feel I'm more impartial about—take the
League of Nations. It's sickening now of that deadliest of modern
diseases—popular approval without private faith; it will die because
it demanded a crusade and we gave it a press campaign, because
it's worth our passion and we deluge it with votes of confidence and
acts of indifference. It might have sprung alive out of the soul of a
saint; it could only be stillborn out of a clause in a treaty. It should
have been preached until we were all aflame with it; instead of
which it's been flattered and fawned upon till most of us are already
bored with it. Sometimes I've even thought we should have given it
ritual—a gesture to be made whenever the name's mentioned, like
the sign of the Cross for the faithful, or—for the faithless—blowing
out the match after the second man's cigarette." As if reminded
by that he pulled out his pipe and began to fill it as he continued:
"This is a good moment to say how much I hope you'll stay with me
here—both of you. That is, if you're happy."

"We're very happy. But I have to think of how to make a living."

"Life's more important than a living. So many people who make a
living are making death, not life. Don't ever join them. They're the
gravediggers of our civilization—the safe men, the compromisers, the
money-makers, the muddlers-through. Politics is full of them, so is
business, so is the Church. They're popular, successful—some of them
work hard, others are slack, but all of them can tell a good story.
Never were such charming gravediggers in the world's history—and

part of their charm is that they don't know what they are, just as they don't know what *we* are, either. They set us down as cranks, oddities, social outsiders, harmless cranks who can't be lured by riches or placated by compliments. But a time may come when we, the dangerous men, shall either be killed or made kings—because a time may also come when it won't be enough to love England as a tired businessman loves a nap after lunch. We may be called upon to love her as the Irish love Ireland—darkly, bitterly, and with a hatred for some who have loved her less and themselves more."

After another of their talks he told Smith of a friend of his in Liverpool, editor of a provincial paper with a small but influential circulation. Apparently Blampied, unknown to Smith, had sent some of his literary work for this man to see; and now had come a request to see not only more of the work, but the writer of it. "So I hope you'll pay him a visit, because whatever project he has in mind, or even if he hasn't one at all, I know you'll like him personally."

"Another dangerous man?" Smith queried.

Blampied nodded with an answering smile.

Smith was eager to go as soon as possible; after further communication an appointment was made for just after Christmas. Paula and he spent the intervening week in a glow of anticipation, culminating in a Christmas dinner in their own attic room, with Blampied as a guest. They decorated the place like children and found him like a third child in his own enjoyment of the meal and the occasion. Later in the evening he gave them, to their complete astonishment, an almost professional display of conjuring tricks; after which Paula offered some of her stage impersonations, including one of a very prim Victorian wife trying to convey to her equally prim Victorian husband the fact that she rather thought she was going to have a child. Towards midnight, when Blampied had drunk a last toast with them and gone down to his rooms below, they sat on the hearth-rug in the firelight happily reviewing the events of the evening, and presently Smith remarked that her impersonation of the Victorian wife was new to him—he didn't remember her ever doing it on the stage, but he thought it would have gone very well if she had.

"But it wasn't written then," she answered. "I write all my own sketches—I always did—and I wrote this one last night when you were downstairs talking to Blampied. I suppose it was on my mind—the subject, I mean—because I'm in the same position, except that I'm not going to be prim about it."

He took her into his arms quietly, sexlessly, as they sat before the fire. Those were the happy hours.

The next day, as if their happiness were not enough, Blampied brought them news of another kind. It was now many weeks since they had last seen any mention of the Fulverton case, and though they felt easier about it they still opened newspapers with a qualm. But that morning Blampied had been searching old papers for something he wished to trace and by sheer accident had come across something else. "It seems that your Thomas Atwill left hospital more than a month ago, and though of course that doesn't mean the case is closed, I daresay the news will be a load off your mind."

It so definitely was that the idea occurred to them to celebrate by doing things they had been nervous of for so long—a regular evening out. They asked Blampied to join them, but he excused himself on the score of work; before they left the house, however, he shook hands with Smith and wished him a pleasant trip, for it had been arranged that he should leave that night for Liverpool. Even though it would only be for a few days, the impending separation added spice to the evening. They went first to the Holborn Empire to see Little Tich, then for supper to an Italian restaurant in Soho. When they emerged, still with a couple of hours until train time, he saw a hansom cab swinging along Coventry Street, temptingly out of place on a cold December night, but for that very reason he waved to it, telling the man to take them anywhere, just for the ride. Under the windy sky the blaze of Christmas still sparkled in the shops as they drove away, jingling north and west along Regent Street, through Hanover Square and past Selfridge's to Baker Street, with ghosts of Londoners stepping out of their tall houses ("And if I mistake not, my dear Watson, here is our client just arriving"), bidding them Godspeed into the future; and because they both had faith in that future they were drenched in a sort of wild ecstasy, and had the cabby drive them round and round Regent's Park while they talked and laughed and whistled to the parrots every time they passed the Zoo.

Those were the happy moments.

Later, on the platform at Euston, walking up and down beside the train, she said she wished she were going with him, though she knew they couldn't afford it, the little money he was beginning to make by writing wasn't nearly enough for such unnecessary jaunts. "I know that, darling, but I still wish I were going with you, and if you were just to say the word, like the crazy man you are, I'd rush to the booking office and buy a ticket—which would be stupid, I don't really mean it—Smithy, I'm only joking, of course. But I'm part of you—I'll only be half alive while you're away—we belong to the same world, as Blampied says about his friends—"

"I know that too. There's something *right* about us—about our being together here. And Blampied wants us to stay."

"I'd like to stay too. I love that old ugly house."

"So do I. And d'you know, I don't *want* to remember anything now—anything I've ever forgotten. It would be so—so unimportant. My life began with you, and my future goes on with you—there's nothing else, Paula."

"Oh, what a lovely thing to tell me! And by the way, *he* said he hoped you wouldn't remember."

"Blampied?"

"Yes. He's devoted to you."

"I should be proud to think so, because I'm equally devoted to him." He kissed her laughingly. "Must we spend these last few seconds talking of someone else?"

"But he isn't altogether someone else. He's part of us—part of our happiness—don't you feel that?"

"Darling, I do—and I also love you!"

"I love you too. *Always.*"

"The whistle's going—I'd better get inside. Good-bye, Paula."

"Good-bye, old boy."

"That's the first time you've said 'old boy' for weeks!"

"I know, I'm dropping it. Now I'm not a touring-company actress I don't have to talk like one. I can impersonate anybody, you know —even the wife of a writer on a secret errand to an editor in Liverpool. . . ." The train began to move. "Oh, *darling*—come back soon!"

"I will! Good-bye!"

He reached Liverpool in the early morning. It was raining, and in hurrying across a slippery street he stumbled and fell.

PART FIVE

Rainier began to tell me most of this during the drive back from Melbury that night; a few minor details, obtained afterwards from other sources, I have since fitted in. We drove to his Club, because Mrs. Rainier was at Stourton; after perfunctory greetings to a few members in the lobby he ordered drinks to be sent up to the suite he usually lived in when Kenmore was not in use.

He had talked rapidly during the car journey, but now, in quieter surroundings, he seemed to accept more calmly the fact that there was much to tell that he could at last quite easily recall. Once, when I thought he was growing tired and might remember more if he rested for a while, he brushed the suggestion aside. "You see I want to tell you all I can in case I ever forget it again, and if I do, you must remind me—you *must*—understand?" I promised, and he continued: "Not that I think I shall—it's too clear in my mind ever to be lost again. I could find Blampied's old house in Vale Street now if I tried—Number 73, I think it was—or maybe 75—that much I *have* forgotten, but I suppose I can't expect memory to come back without the normal wear-and-tear of years. Or can I? Has it been in a sort of cold storage, with every detail kept fresh?"

We laughed, glad of an excuse to do so, and I said it raised an interesting point which I wasn't expert enough to decide. He then resumed: "Because I actually *feel* as if it all happened only the other day, instead of twenty years ago. That house of Blampied's, for instance—it had four dreadful bay windows, one on each side of the front door and two others immediately above in the room that wasn't occupied—the attics hadn't got any bay windows. There was a pretty grim sort of basement, too, where the housekeeper lived—she didn't have to, she chose it because she was crazy enough to like it. She was a queer woman altogether—God knows where Blampied picked her up or how long she'd been with him, but he cried when she died, and looked after her cat—which was also a queer animal, an enormous tabby—spent most of its life sleeping, probably because of its weight—it had won a prize as the biggest cat north of the Thames." He added, smiling: "I daresay you think I'm inventing this—that there aren't prizes for big cats. But some newspaper ran a competition as a stunt—two first prizes, for North and South London— and Blampied's housekeeper's cat won one of them."

No, I thought—you're not inventing; you're just enjoying yourself rather indiscriminately, as a child frolics in the sand when he first reaches the seashore; I could see how, in the first flush of recollection, the mere placement of the past, the assembling of details one after the other, was giving him an intense pleasure, and one by no means discountenanced by his use of words like "grim" and "dreadful."

He went on like that for some time, going back over his story, picking out details here and there for random intricate examination; and carefully avoiding the issue that was foremost in my thoughts. Then, once again, I saw that we had talked till dawn and well past it, for there was already a pale edge to the window. I switched off his bedroom light and pulled the curtains; far below us the early morning trams were curving along the Embankment. We watched the scene for a moment; then he touched my arm affectionately. "Time for an adjournment, I think. I know what's in your mind, it's in mine, too, but it's too big to grasp—I'm collecting the small things first. You've been good to listen to me. What have we on Monday?"

My thoughts were so far away I could not give an immediate answer, though of course I knew. He laughed at my hesitation, saying he hoped I should not lose my memory just because he had regained his. By then I had remembered and could tell him: "Anglo-American Cement—ten-thirty at the Cannon Street Hotel." To which he replied, almost gayly: "The perfect closure to all our conversation. . . ."

"Don't you want me for anything tomorrow?"

"No, I'll sleep most of the day . . . at least I hope so. . . . Good night."

If this is a difficult story to tell, it may be pleaded in partial defense that the human mind is a difficult territory to explore, and that the world it inhabits does not always fit snugly into any other world. I must admit that I found the fitting a hard one as, some thirty-six hours later, I watched the sunlight stream through stained-glass windows to dazzle the faces of Anglo-American Cement shareholders. From the report afterwards sent out with the dividend I find out that Rainier spoke as follows:—

"You will be glad to know that our sales have continued to increase throughout the year, after a somewhat slow beginning, and that prospects of continued improvement are encouraging. The government's national defense preparations during the September crisis of last year led to additional consumption of cement throughout the country, and this, at prices we were able to obtain, resulted in generally satisfactory business. During the year we opened a new plant at Nottingham which we expect to enhance production very considerably during the coming year. Your directors are constantly watchful for any opportunities of further economies, either by technical developments or by the absorption of competing companies, and with these aims in view, it is proposed, in addition to the usual dividend of 10 per cent, to issue new shares at forty-two shillings and sixpence in the proportion of one to five held by existing shareholders." (Loud applause.)

We had had no chance for private conversation on our way to the meeting, for the secretary of the company had driven with us; and afterwards there was a directors' hotel lunch that did not disperse until almost three o'clock. As I went to retrieve our hats at the cloak room I overheard comments on how Rainier had been in grand form, looking so much better; wonderful year it had been; wonderful the way he'd pulled the Anglo-American out of its earlier doldrums—remember when the shares were down to five bob?—nice packet anyone could have made who'd helped himself in those days —well, maybe Rainier did, why not?—after all, he'd had faith in himself, faith in the business, faith in the country—that's what was wanted, pity more people didn't have it.

Later, as we were driving away, I repeated the compliments to Rainier, thinking they might please him. He shook his head somberly. "Don't call it faith. I haven't had *faith* in anything for years. That artist fellow, Kitty's young man, told me that when he was drunk— and he was right. Faith is something deeper, more passionate, less derisive, more tranquil than anything I've ever felt in board rooms and offices—that's why peace won't come to me now. . . . God, I'm tired."

"Why don't you go home and rest?"

He stared at me ironically. "So simple, isn't it? Just go home and rest. Like a child. . . . Or like an old man. The trouble is, I'm neither. Or else both." He suddenly patted my arm. "Sorry—don't take any notice of my bad temper."

"I don't think you're bad-tempered."

"By the way," he said smiling, "I've just thought of something— it's a queer coincidence, don't you think?—two of my best friends I first met quite accidentally on trains . . . Blampied and your-self. . . ."

"I'm pleased you should class me with him."

"Why not? He talked to me—you listen to me—even when I want to talk all night. That's another thing I ought to apologize for—"

"Not at all—in fact if it helps you now to go on talking—to continue the recollections—"

"I don't think I've much more to say, unless there's anything you'd particularly like to know?"

There were many things I wanted to know, but for the present I felt I could only mention one of them. "Those articles you wrote, some of which were published—"

"Yes?"

"What papers did they appear in?"

"The *Northern Evening Post* took two or three—the worst. The others—don't know what happened to them. Maybe they fell in the gutter when the car hit me."

"You were carrying them—*then?*"

"Yes, I was on my way to see the editor."

"A pity you hadn't taken copies."

"It was before the days I bothered about carbon paper. You see, I never behaved like a full-dress author. I used Blampied's type-writer because he had one, but I didn't card-index anything or call the room where I worked a study or self-consciously burn any mid-night oil. Matter of fact, I was in bed by ten on most nights, and I wrote if and when I felt like it. I never thought of the word 'inspiration' as having anything to do with me—it was a continual vision of life that mattered more than words in print, but if I did get into print I had more ambition to be alive for half a day in a local paper than to be embalmed forever between covers on a li-brary shelf."

"All the same, though, those articles might have been collected in book form."

"Blampied thought of that, and Paula and I once made a choice of what we thought were the best—but I wasn't very keen on the idea, and it certainly wasn't likely any publisher would have been either. I remember it chiefly because the evening we were choosing them Blampied came in and found us huddled together on the floor with the typed pages surrounding us. He asked, 'What are you two planning—the book or your future?'—and Paula laughed and an-swered 'Both.'"

We had entered Palace Yard, passing the saluting policeman and

a swarm of newsboys carrying posters about Hitler. As we left the
car a few seconds later Rainier added: "It's odd to reflect, isn't it,
that at that very moment a few hundred miles away a man whom
we had never heard of was also planning a book—and our future."

We crossed the pavement and entered the Gothic doorway; the
House, as always, seemed restful, almost soporific, on a summer afternoon.

"And you've never written anything like those articles since?" I
queried, after a pause.

"I've been too busy, Sir Hawk, as the lady called you, and possibly
also my prose style isn't what it used to be. I did write one book,
though—or perhaps Sherlock would have called it a monograph—the
title was *Constructive Monetary Policy and an International Cartel*
—I hope you've never heard of it."

I said I had not only heard of it but read it.

"Then I hope you didn't buy it when it first came out, because
I came across it the other day on a barrow in the Farringdon Road,
marked 'Choice' and going for fourpence."

I smiled, recognizing the familiar self-ridicule by which he worked
himself out of his moods. We walked on through cool corridors to
the Terrace and found a table. As nearly always, a breeze blew over
the parapet, bringing tangs of the sea and of wharves, a London
mixture that added the right flavor to tea and buttered toast and
the special edition of the *Evening Standard*. More bother about
Danzig; Hitler had made another speech. Some Members came
along, stopped at our table to exchange a few words of greeting; one
of them, seeing the headlines, exclaimed: "Why don't they let him
have it, then maybe we'll all get some peace?"—but another retorted
indignantly: "My dear fellow, we *can't* let him have any more, that's
just the point, we've *got* to make a stand—eh, Rainier?" Rainier said:
"We've got to have peace and we've got to make a stand—that's exactly the policy of the government." They passed on, uncertain
whether he had been serious or cynical (and that uncertainty, now
I come to think of it, was part of the reason why he hadn't climbed
the higher rungs of the Parliamentary ladder).

He looked so suddenly exhausted after they had gone that I asked
if he had been able to sleep at all during the previous day and night.

"Not much. A few hours yesterday morning after you left. The
rest of the day I devoted to an investigation."

"Oh?"

"I went to Vale Street to look for Blampied's old house. It's disappeared—been pulled down to make room for one of those huge

municipal housing schemes. All that part of London seems to be changed—and it's certainly no loss, except in memories. I couldn't even find anybody who *remembered* Blampied."

"That's not very surprising."

"Why not?" He stared at me sharply, then added: "D'you mean you don't believe he ever existed?"

"Oh, he existed all right. But he died such a long time ago."

"When?"

"In 1920."

"Good God! Within a year—of—of my—leaving—like that."

"Not only within a year. Within a month. *January* 1920."

"How do you know all this?"

"I also spent part of yesterday investigating. I searched the obituaries in newspaper files and found this." I handed him a sheet of paper on which I had copied out the following from the *Daily Gazette* of January 17, 1920:—

> We regret to announce the death at the age of seventy-four of the Reverend John Sylvester Blampied, for many years Rector of St. Clement's Church, Vale Street, North London. Pneumonia following a chill ended a career that had often attracted public attention—particularly in connection with the preservation of ancient footpaths, a cause of which Mr. Blampied had been a valiant if sometimes tempestuous champion. His death took place in Liverpool, and funeral services will be held at St. Clement's on Friday.

Rainier stared at the paragraph long enough to read it several times, then handed it back. His face was very pale. "*Liverpool?* What was he doing there?"

"It doesn't say."

"I—I think I can guess. He'd gone to look for me."

"We don't *know* that."

"But isn't it probable?"

"It's—it's possible. But you couldn't help it. You couldn't help finding out who you were."

"I can't help comparing what I found with what I lost!"

"You didn't lose permanently. You've got it all back now."

"But too late." He waved his arm with sudden comprehensive emphasis. "*Isn't* it too late? I'm down to ask a question in the House shortly, but not *that* question, yet it's the only one worth asking or answering . . . isn't *everything* too late? I should have stayed in that London attic. There were things to do in those days if one had vision to do them, but now there's neither time nor vision, but only this whiff of putrefying too-lateness. It was almost too late even then, except that by a sort of miracle there came a gap in long-gathering clouds—an incredibly last chance—a golden shaft along which England might have climbed back to glory."

"Less lyrically, you mean you'd like to set the clock back?"

"Yes, set it back, and set it right, and then wind it up, because it's been running down ever since Englishmen were more interested in the price of things on the market than what they could grow in their own gardens."

"I see. A back-to-the-land movement?"

"Back anywhere away from the unrealness of counting able-bodied men as a national burden just because they're listed as unemployed, and figures in bank ledgers as assets just because they're supposed to represent riches. Back anywhere from the mood in which poor men beg me for jobs in Rainier factories and rich men for tips about Rainier shares."

"All the same, though—and you've often said it yourself—the Rainier firm gives steady employment to thousands—"

"I know, I know. But I know too that the way that made Rainier's rich was the opposite of the way to make England strong."

"Yet if war comes, won't the riches of Rainier have been of some benefit? After all, the new steelworks you were able to build two years ago, and the mass-production motor plant—"

"True—and what a desolate irony! But only *half* true, because strength is only half in tanks and steel. The other half is faith, wisdom—"

A House servant approached and said something in his ear; he answered, consulting his watch: "Oh, yes. I'll come at once." Then he added to me: "It's time for that question."

We left the table and walked through the Smoke Room to the Lobby; then we separated, he to enter the Chamber, I to watch and listen from the Strangers' Gallery.

Again, as earlier at the Cement meeting, I was in no mood for correct secretarial concentration; from where I sat the main thing that impressed me was his strained pallor on rising to speak; in the green-yellow glow that came on as dusk fell his face took on a curious transparency, as if some secret hidden self were flooding outwards and upwards. But that, I knew, was a mere trick of artificial light; the House of Commons illumination flatters in such a way, often gilding with spirituality a scene which is not, in itself, very remarkable—a few Members going through the formality which

would later entitle them to boast of having "raised the matter on
the House," than which, except for writing letters to the *Times*,
fortunate generations of Englishmen were never called upon to do
more. That afternoon the benches were thinly populated, nothing
important was expected, and I find from newspaper reports that the
following took place:—

Mr. Charles Rainier (Conservative: West Lythamshire)
asked whether a consignment of trade catalogues dispatched by
a business firm in his constituency had been confiscated by the
port authorities at Balos Blanca, and whether this was not contrary to Section 19 of the recent Trade Convention signed at
Amazillo.

The Right Honourable Sir George Smith-Jordan (Conservative: Houghley), replying for the Government, said he had been
informed by His Majesty's Consul at Balos Blanca that the reported confiscation had been only partial and temporary, affecting a certain section of the catalogues about which there
appeared to have been some linguistic misunderstanding, and
that the greater part of the consignment had since been delivered to the addressees. As to whether the action of the port
authorities had or had not been an infringement of any clause
of the Amazillo Trade Convention, he was not in a position to
say until further information had been received.

Mr. Jack Wells (Labour: Mawlington) asked whether, having
regard to the general unsatisfactoriness of the incident, His Majesty's Government would consider the omission of Balos Blanca
from the scheduled list of ports of call during the proposed
Good-Will Tour of the British Trade Delegation in 1940.

The Right Honourable Sir George Smith-Jordan: No, sir.

Immediately after that, Rainier picked up his papers and walked
out, leaving the Mother of Parliaments to struggle along with barely
more than a quorum till after the dinner hour. Meanwhile I left the
Gallery, in which a small crowd of provincial and foreign visitors
had been defiantly concealing their disappointments at the proceedings below, and met him in the Lobby; he was gossiping with strangers, but behind the façade of casualness I saw how haggard he
looked, his face restlessly twitching in and out of smiles. Seeing me
approach he made a sign for me to wait while he detached himself
from the crowd—they were constituents, he explained later, and
constituents had to be humored, especially when one's majority had
been only twelve last time. "They're so proud because they heard

me ask about that catalogue business—they have a touching belief
that a question in Parliament pulls invisible wires, sets invisible forces
in motion, works invisible miracles all over the world."

Passing through the Smoke Room again on the way to the Terrace
we saw the name "McAlister" on the notice board that announced
current speakers; Rainier smiled and said that was fine—McAlister
always gave one a chance to stroll for half an hour with the certainty
of not missing anything. "By the way, I'm dining at the Historians'
Club, so I don't think I'll need you for the rest of the evening."

"Are you down to speak?"

"I'm not on the program, but I daresay I'll be asked."

"You don't have to go if you'd rather not. I can make up some
excuse."

"What's the idea—encouraging me to shirk?"

"I thought—perhaps—you might be feeling rather exhausted."

"Not a bit of it *now*. I'm game for more than a speech at a Club
dinner. You'd be surprised if you knew what's in my mind."

We stepped into the cool evening air and began walking towards
Westminster Bridge. He had given me a cue to say what I had been
planning most of the day.

"My advice would be to put the whole thing *out* of your mind
now that it's happened at last, and there isn't a gap any longer. You
ought to be satisfied."

"*Satisfied?*" He swung round on me. "When you say that I wonder
if—if you quite realize—what it all amounts to."

"Oh yes, I do. It means that so far as there was ever anything
abnormal in your life, you're now completely cured."

We came near the Bridge, a blaze of illumination from lines of
trams, and in that light I saw such anguish in his eyes that I could
only repeat, with an emphasis that somehow drained away as the
words were spoken: "Utterly and completely cured."

"You don't *really* think that's all it amounts to? You must know
there's only one thing that matters—only one thing left for me to do."

"And that is?"

"I must find her."

So there it was squarely before us, the issue that had of course
been in my mind, that I had done a pathetic best to make him shirk
by conscientiously shirking it myself. We walked a little way in silence.

"After all these years," I said at length, "it doesn't seem very
likely."

"I must try."

"It was up to her, surely, to look for you—yet apparently she never did."

"Maybe. Maybe not. I don't care. And besides—there's my son. She was going to have a child."

"But even a return of memory can't prove it was a boy."

He smiled. "No, but I hope so. I've always wanted a boy. He'd be eighteen now. I must find him . . . both of them."

"And if by chance—not that I think there *is* much chance—but just for the sake of argument—if you *should* happen to succeed, what then?"

He answered with a certain impregnable simplicity: "Then I should be happy again."

"Possibly, but apart from your own personal happiness . . . Look here, why not think it over—not now—but later—calmly—when you're alone?"

"I'm calm now, and it doesn't particularly help me to be alone when I think. I was thinking it over very clearly all the time I was asking that question in the House."

"Yes, I could see you were—but that doesn't meet my point, which is that you haven't—you can't have—reckoned with all the complications—"

"*Complications?* You'll be telling me next I ought to consult old Truslove!"

"Actually I wasn't thinking of legal complications at all, though they doubtless exist. It's other kinds you'd find most disagreeable—newspaper publicity, gossip and scandal that wouldn't do you any good politically."

"I think I've had enough good done to me politically."

"And then of course there's your wife. Whatever your private feelings are, and of course it's none of my business, you ought at least to consider *her* position."

"Anything I ought to do now is nothing compared with what I ought to have done before."

"But that's in the past—*irrevocable.*"

"No, not if she and I can find each other again."

"It seems to me we're talking about different persons."

"Oh, I see."

We walked on for another spell of silence. Then I said: "But you don't even know that the . . . the other woman's *alive?*"

He was silent for a while. "*Do* you?" I pressed.

"No, that's true." Then suddenly: "But if she is, and I can find her, then nothing on earth will stop me—neither publicity, nor poli-

tics, nor . . ." He turned to me abruptly. "I don't want to be dramatic. Let's leave that to the journalists who'll have the job of making
a nine days' wonder of it."

"Maybe they won't. Maybe they'll have more important news, the
way events are going."

As we turned into the Smoke Room the board showed that
McAlister was still speaking. A group of Members at one of the tables
greeted Rainier chaffingly and asked him to join them; as if relieved
to be rid of the argument he gave me a nod of friendly farewell and
sat down with them, completely master of himself so far as voice
and manner were concerned. But I heard one of them say, just as
I was entering the corridor: "You look pretty washed-out, Rainier—
what's the matter? Hitler getting on your nerves?"

I went back to my rooms in Bedford Square and spent the evening
with the latest editions of the papers. But I could not keep my mind
on the fast-developing European crisis; my thoughts were full of
Rainier and his story; I mused upon his whole life as I now knew
it: childhood at Stourton, with the despotic father and adored
mother; schooldays; then the war, the hospitals, the brief unmem-
oried idyl; then the return to the routine struggle that had brought
him wealth, power, and a measure of fame. I could not but feel his
personal drama near to me as I turned on the radio for the larger
drama of our times, for that too had reached a moment of desperate
retrospect.

About midnight I strolled into Tottenham Court Road and
watched the crowd pouring out of theaters and restaurants; when
I returned there was a letter pushed under the door. It was from
Rainier, enclosing another letter. He wrote:—

> I said I would let you see that last note Kitty wrote me; here
> it is, and whatever it means to you, to me, rereading it just now,
> it meant as much more as you can possibly imagine. Yrs. C. R.

The letter from Kitty, dated September 30, 1929, was as follows:—

MY DEAR CHARLES,

I'm writing this in a hurry, but after thinking things out as
slowly and carefully as even you could—in fact I've been gathering together many thoughts I began to have the moment we
left the Jungfraujoch last April, in the train and on the boat,
and then again off and on ever since, and especially in the restaurant tonight—Dearest, it wasn't the weather or the altitude
or the stock market—it was our own hearts sinking a little, and

I'm going to face that frankly, because I doubt if you ever would or could. I can't marry you, Charles dear—that's what it amounts to. We've had marvelous times, we'd still go on having them, we have so much in common, the same way of seeing things, the same kind of craziness (though you keep yours in check more than I do)—you could make me perfectly happy if only I were selfish enough not to care or stupid enough not to notice that at some point in the final argument you waver and turn away. So here's my decision—No, darling, while it's still not quite too late; and here are my plans—I'm leaving London immediately, I'll have gone before you read this—I shall probably join Jill (wherever she is, Luxor, I think)—not tragically, but in a mood to see what fun I can find—and I usually can. I'm sending this by special messenger because I want it to reach you before you go to the office, so that you won't send out those invitations and then have to cancel them—as for selling short to amuse me, it wouldn't amuse me, I'm afraid, but if you think it would amuse you, why don't you do it? Dear Charles, I want you to be happy, to be amused, to do things because you desire them, not because you're urged or tempted; I wish we could be and do all we talked of on the mountain, but the fact is, I'm not the one for you, though God knows the mistake was excusable for both of us, because I'm *nearly* the one—I claim that much and it's something to go on being proud of. But "nearly" isn't enough for a lifetime—it would be too hard to strain after the hidden difference. And there's something else that may sound utterly absurd, but let me say it—sometimes, especially when we've been closest, I've had a curious feeling that *I remind you of someone else*—someone you may have met or may yet meet—because with that strange memory of yours, the tenses get mixed up—or don't they? But Charles, because I *am* so nearly the one, and because I love you more than anyone I shall ever marry, will you forgive me for this upset and stay friends?—K.

I went to his City office the following morning and waited till after ten o'clock (he usually arrived at nine); then I rang up his Club and was told he had left very early, giving no forwarding address. It was a day of such important engagements that I went over to the Club immediately, hoping to find out more than they would tell me over the telephone.

The porter, who knew me, said he had left about six, by car.

"Hanson was with him then?"

"No, sir, he drove alone. It wasn't his usual car—quite a small one, a brown two-seater."

"But he hasn't got a two-seater."

"Well, he went away in one—that's all I can tell you, sir. I think it was an Austin, but I'm not sure."

"And he left no message for me?"

"No, sir—no message for anybody, except that he'd be away till he got back. That was his phrase. He seemed in a very cheerful mood. I thought maybe he had some good news, but it don't look like it from today's papers."

"Well, I expect I'll hear from him—it's all right."

I went away as if I thought it really was, because I was anxious not to start gossip at the Club. Then I went back to the City office and pretended the mystery was cleared up—he'd had to go away for a few days on an important political errand; I telephoned to cancel all his appointments for the day, giving the same story, except that to those in the political world I made out it was a business errand. There were certain advantages in belonging to two worlds. I wondered if I should hear from him, by either wire or telephone as the day proceeded, but no message came, and in the late afternoon I drove to Stourton. There were several cars outside the main entrance, but none was a brown two-seater; I hadn't really expected it. Woburn met me on the threshold. "What are *you* doing here?" he greeted me, as if he owned the place.

"What are you doing here, for that matter? Still on the catalogue?"

"No, I've finished that and several more since. I'm just a guest."

"Well, that's very nice."

"There's going to be a big party this week end."

There was, and that was what I had come about. "Where's Mrs. Rainier?"

"On the terrace—dispensing cocktails and small talk with her usual glassy proficiency. Just a local crowd—they'll go soon."

"Let's join them."

I realized then, as soon as I saw her in the distance, how keenly my sympathies had been enlisted for a woman whose glassiest proficiency could hardly help her much in the situation that was now so rapidly developing. As we shook hands she seemed to me rather like a pathetic tightrope walker doing her tricks in confident unawareness that the rope was about to be cut.

The crowd were mostly neighbors whom I had met before, but there was one fresh face—Sir William Somebody, whom I knew to be a retired diplomat who lived on his pension in a farmhouse rented from the Rainiers. Mrs. Rainier introduced me with the remark that perhaps, having just driven from London, I could give him the latest news. "Sir William thinks the situation's far worse than people realize."

I passed on what news there was; then a girl called Cynthia exclaimed: "We mustn't miss the wireless bulletin. Hasn't he been making another speech today?" (It had come to the point where an unrelated "he" could only refer to Hitler.)

"Just words, nothing but words," someone else muttered.

"Better than actions, anyhow."

Mrs. Rainier intervened lazily: "Oh, I'm not so sure of that as I used to be. I mean, when you're waiting for something to happen, and rather dreading it . . ." She went on: "Have you ever been going somewhere with a crowd and you're certain it's the wrong road and you tell them, but they won't listen, so you just have to plod along in what you know is the wrong direction till somebody more important gets the same idea?"

"A parable, darling. Please interpret."

She seemed embarrassed by being the focus of attention—which was unusual of her. "No, thanks, Cynthia. That's been enough words from *me*." She laughed and came round with the cocktail shaker, refilling the glasses, including her own.

Sir William resumed: "Well, if he *does* march into Poland, we shall fight." Then suddenly he pointed to the great avenue of elms for which Stourton was famous. "Look at those trees—planted two centuries ago, deliberately, by someone who thought of a time when someone else would see them like this. Who could do such a thing today?" Nobody informed him, and after a pause to deposit an olive stone in an ashtray he went on: "The most we do is to bury things under foundation stones so that future civilizations can dig into our ruins and wonder."

We all laughed, because after a few drinks what can one do but laugh; then in ones and twos the party dispersed and drove away in its cars. I went to the library and turned on the radio for the news bulletin; Hitler's speech had been just another threat to march. Somehow one didn't believe he would; there had been crises before, ending up in a deal; so that one had the half-cynical suspicion that both sides were secretly arranging another deal and that the wordy warfare was just shadowboxing, face saving, anything but a prelude to the guns. While I was listening Sheldon entered to announce that dinner would be almost immediately, and that Mrs. Rainier had said "not dress."

"Good—since I haven't brought anything."

"I think Mrs. Rainier anticipated that."

"Very thoughtful of her."

"You left Mr. Rainier in the City?"

"Er . . . yes."

"Then you'll be going back in the morning?"

"I expect so."

He nodded and went to the door, then turned and asked: "What's going to happen, do you think?"

"Can't tell yet, but it looks pretty serious."

He said, still standing in the doorway: "I mean what's going to happen to Mr. Rainier?"

He went on, facing my stare: "You said he's in the City."

"I didn't say that. I said I left him there."

"Don't you know where he is now?"

"No."

"Isn't that rather peculiar?"

"Many things are peculiar, Sheldon."

"Are you worried about him? . . . You must excuse me, I have a special reason for asking."

"I'm sure you have. It might even be the same reason I have for not answering."

He came back into the room. "Mr. Harrison . . . has he gone away to look for somebody?"

"I really don't think I can discuss—" Then something in his glance made me add: "But supposing he had—then what?"

He smiled his slow slanting smile. "Then you don't need to worry."

"I didn't say I was worrying at all. But why don't I need to?"

"Because he won't succeed in finding the person he's looking for."

"How do you know?"

"Because he never has succeeded."

He left me then, and a few minutes later the dinner gong sounded. When I joined Mrs. Rainier in the dining room, with Sheldon standing at the sideboard, I had a feeling they had been exchanging glances if not words about me, but I could not say much during dinner, on account of Woburn's presence. As if by tacit agreement we left him most of the talking, which he kept up very agreeably throughout the meal—he was really a very adaptable young man, you would have thought him born and bred at Stourton, except that most of those who had been were so much less smoothly articulate.

I was wondering how I could shake him off afterwards, but Mrs. Rainier did it for me, saying outright that she expected I had some business to talk over, so if Woburn would excuse us . . .

"Do you mind if we have a fire?" she asked, as soon as we were alone in the dining room. I helped her to remove the heavy screen, saying something about the night being cold for the eve of September.

"It isn't that," she answered, kneeling on the hearthrug. "But it makes a more cheerful background when so many uncheerful things are happening."

Looking at her then, I realized for the first time how much more she was than merely vivacious and attractive; her face had a beauty that poured into it from within—a secret, serene radiance. She went on, stooping to the fire: "You've saved me the trouble of calling at the office tomorrow—I wanted to ask about something."

"Good job you didn't, because I'm not sure Mr. Rainier will be there."

"Oh? He's gone away somewhere?"

"Yes." I remembered him saying she was never surprised at any of his movements. "And as I don't know when exactly he'll be coming back, I was wondering about the week-end plans."

"The political situation's so serious I doubt if we'd have had the party anyway. Yes, let's cancel it."

"That's what I was going to suggest."

"Nice of you, but why didn't you telephone?" She added hastily: "Not that I'm not pleased to see you—I always am—but it gave you the journey."

"Oh, I didn't mind. I'm equally pleased to see *you*."

She laughed. "Now we've had the exchange of compliments—"

She didn't know what else to say, I could see that; and after a pause I resumed: "What was it you wanted to ask about if you had called at the office?"

"Oh yes, maybe you can tell me just as well. Why did you and Charles drive out to Melbury the other night?"

The sheer unexpectedness of the question nonplused me for a moment. In the meantime she went on: "And don't blame Hanson— he wasn't to know he'd overheard such a tremendous secret!" She was laughing.

"Oh, not—er—exactly a secret."

"Well, a mystery."

I said to gain time: "And you were going to pay a special visit just to ask that?"

"Yes, indeed—I've been terribly curious ever since I heard about it."

"Then it's my turn to say why didn't you telephone?"

"Perhaps because I wanted to see your faces when I asked you—it's so much harder to hide something that way!" She laughed again. "Won't you let me in on the puzzle? Melbury's such an odd place for anyone to make a trip to."

It suddenly occurred to me that she had to know, and now was the chance to tell her. I said: "Mr. Rainier was once in a hospital at Melbury."

In the blaze of fresh firelight I could see the laughter drain away from her face and a sudden pallor enter it; but in another second she was smiling again.

"Well, it seems a queer reason for driving somewhere in pouring rain in the middle of the night. For that matter Charles was at other hospitals too—he was pretty badly hurt in the war, you know. It even affected his memory for a time. I never knew quite how much you had gathered about all that—" She was striving to seem very casual.

"Just the main facts, that's all."

"He told you them himself?"

"Yes."

The smile remained as if fixed to her face. "Oh, I'm so glad, because it shows how close you must have been to him as a friend. He doesn't often talk about it to anybody. And to me he *never* talks about it."

"Never?"

"No, never. Isn't that strange? But then he's so little with me—and mostly we have business or politics to talk about. Our marriage is a very happy one, but it's never been—well, *close* is perhaps the word. We've never even had a close quarrel."

"But you love him?"

"Well, what do you think? I adore him—most women do. Haven't you noticed that? All his life he could always have had any pretty woman he wanted."

"So it isn't surprising that he *got* the pretty woman he wanted."

"More compliments? . . . Oh, but you should have seen the girl he was engaged to when I first became his secretary. I *was* his secretary—you knew that too, I suppose? She was much prettier than me, *and* younger. Kitty, her name was. She married somebody else and died—I can't think why—I mean why she married somebody else, not why she died—she died of malaria—I suppose there's no reason at all for that, except mosquitoes. I think they'd have been very happy—she and Charles, I mean, not the mosquitoes—but she'd have tried to make him give up the business. I know that, because she told me."

I could catch a note of hysteria subdued behind her forced face-tiousness; I said, as calmly as I could: "You knew her well, then?"

"Only by talking to her while she used to wait in the office for Charles."

"Tell me—if it isn't impertinent to ask—were you also in love with him then?"

She laughed. "Of course. Right from the first moment I set eyes on him. . . . But that didn't make me jealous of Kitty—only a bit envious, perhaps. I wonder how it would have worked out—Charles without all the business and politics. Of course he found out later I was the one to help him in that, and so I have—I've done my best to give him everything he wants—success—his ambitions . . . and yet sometimes lately I've thought . . . well, like my parable."

"Parable?"

"Cynthia called it that during cocktails, don't you remember? About going somewhere with someone and having doubts about it being the right road, but there's nothing you can do but plod along until the other person begins to doubt. And then, of course, if you admit that you had doubts all the time, as likely as not he turns on you and says—Well, why didn't you warn me?"

"Well, why didn't you?"

"Because he wouldn't have taken any notice if I had. In fact he might not even have married me—and I *wanted* him to marry me. After Kitty died he threw himself into business more than ever—which gave me my chance—oh, I admit I was quite designing about it. So was he. He found how good I was—what a valuable merger it would be. He was always clever about mergers. . . ."

"Did that entirely satisfy you?"

"No, but I thought it might lead to something that would—to the *real* closeness. But it's hard to get close when so many things are in the way. . . . May I have a light?" She was reaching for a cigarette on the side table and I could see that her hand was trembling. She added, as I held the match: "Do you want a drink in exchange?"

"I think I'd rather wait till later."

"Later? Well, how long do you expect to sit up and talk parables?"

I said then: "Mrs. Rainier, I think I'd better tell you more about the visit to Melbury."

"Oh yes, the mystery—do *please* tell me everything! What did you find there?"

She was smiling as I began to tell her, and the smile grew faint
as I proceeded, then appeared again in time for the end. I told her
all that was important for her to know—the fact of his earlier marriage, his life during those brief months immediately afterwards, and
how that life had come to an abrupt finish. I did not try to make it
easier for her by a gingerly approach to the problem, or by mini-
mizing its complexities. And I told her how he had reacted to the
recent return of memory—his first excitement, then his calmer
determination and bitter regret for the years between. Finally I told
her that though it seemed to me highly unlikely that after two decades he would succeed in tracing someone who hadn't apparently
succeeded in the much easier task of tracing him during the same
interval, and though the gap of years gave legal as well as every
other kind of sanction to what had happened since, she must be
prepared for the faint possibility; and that if it happened the publicity would be neither pleasant for her nor helpful to his position.

"He must know that too."

"Yes, but in his present mood he doesn't care."

"Oh, *he doesn't care?*" She said that so softly, so gently, still smiling. I tried to think of something to express the wave of sympathy
that overcame me; in the end I could only give her my silence.
Presently she touched my hand and said: "Thank you for telling me
all this."

"I must say you take it very well."

"Did you expect me to make a scene?"

"No, but . . . when I try to imagine your feelings . . ."

"I don't feel anything yet, at least not much, but I keep on thinking of what you said—that *he doesn't care!*"

"I know it's terrible but—"

"Oh, no, it's *wonderful!* He'd throw over everything—his future—
his ambitions—*everything*—if he could find her!"

"In his present mood he thinks so."

"Don't keep saying 'in his present mood.' Maybe his present mood
is himself, and all the other moods were false. . . . How do we
know?"

"There's one thing we do know—that people are remembered as
they were last seen—and twenty years is a long time."

She turned to me with brightly shining eyes.

"How sad that is, and how true."

"And from your point of view—how fortunate."

"Oh no, no—I wish she were still as he remembers her. I wish
there *were* such a miracle. If all of us could go back twenty years

—how different the world would be! I want him to be happy, I always have. . . . Now will you have your drink?"

"If you will too."

She went over to the table and mixed them; I could see she was glad of something to do. Stooping over the glasses she continued: "I suppose he told you a great deal more than you've told me?"

"Only details."

"Ah, but the details—those are what I want to hear. Did he remember things very clearly?"

"Yes."

"Places and people?"

"Yes."

"Tell me some of them."

I hesitated, again catching the note of hysteria in her voice; she added: "It doesn't hurt me—as much as you think. Tell me some of them. . . . You say he met her first at Melbury?"

"Yes—on that first Armistice Day."

"And they were married in London?"

"Yes."

"Where did he propose to her? Did he tell you that?"

"A village in the country somewhere—I think it was called Beachings Over."

"Beachings Over . . . an odd name."

"England is full of them."

"I know—like Nether Wallop and Shallow Bowells. . . ." She turned round with my drink. "And war coming to them all again. Do you think there's still a chance of avoiding it?"

"There's always a chance of postponing it."

"No—we've had enough of that."

"I think so too."

"But we're not ready yet, are we?"

"We're terribly unready. We missed our way years ago and found a wide, comfortable road, fine for sleepwalkers, but it had the major drawback of wandering just anywhere, at random."

"Charles always thought that, but as a rich man it wasn't easy for him to say so. Being rich tied his hands and stopped his mouth and took up his time—so that the wasted years wasted him too. . . ."

"I think he's begun to realize that."

"Yes, he's sure of something at last. . . . Another drink?"

"No, thanks."

A long pause. "There's nothing we can do about it now, is there?"

"Are you talking about—er—the country—or—er—"

"Both, in a way."

"I think one can make up for lost time, but one can't salvage it. That's why *his* quest is so hopeless."

Her voice softened. "So you think that's where he's gone—to look for her?"

"It's possible. . . . But to look for her as she *was,* and that's impossible."

The hysteria touched her voice again. "Tell me another detail— no matter how small or trivial—please tell me—"

"I think you're needlessly upsetting yourself."

"No, it isn't upsetting—it's—it's almost helping me in a way—tell me something—"

"I'd rather not, and besides, it's hard to think—"

"Oh, but you said he talked all night and you've only talked for an hour so far. There must be hundreds of things—names of places or incidents that happened here or there—or how she looked. . . ."

"Well . . . let me see . . ."

"How *did* she look? Did he remember her well?"

"He seemed to, though he never described her exactly—but he did say—I believe he said when they first met she was wearing a little fur hat like a fez. . . . Or no, I may have mixed things up—that was Kitty when she stepped out of the train at Interlaken."

"Interlaken?"

"They had a holiday there—he and Kitty."

"I know. And *she* was wearing a little fur hat like a fez? Or the other one? Or both, maybe—but wouldn't that be rather improbable?"

"Yes, of course. I'm sorry—it was like me to choose a detail I'd get confused over."

She put her hand in mine. "It doesn't matter. You've been very kind. I wish I'd known you better—and earlier. Thank you again."

"You understand that I'm anxious to help *both* of you?"

"Yes, I understand. But I don't know how you can."

"Anyhow, there's a sort of chilly comfort in thinking how unimportant all one's personal affairs are these days."

She got up and began walking to the door. "Yes, but when that sort of comfort has chilled one quite thoroughly, the warmth comes— the feeling that nothing matters *except* personal feelings . . . the what-if-the-world-should-end-tonight mood."

We shook hands at the doorway, and there she added, smiling: "Perhaps our world *is* ending tonight. . . ."

*   *   *

I stayed in the drawing room a little while after she had gone; then I thought it would be only civil to find Woburn. He was in the library, listening to the radio. "Still nothing definite. You know, if there's a war, I want to get in the Air Force." We had another drink and talked for about an hour before going upstairs.

I had asked Sheldon to call me at seven; he did so, bringing in a cup of tea. "I thought you'd wish to know the news—it just came over the wireless." Then he told me.

I got up hurriedly. It was a perfect late-summer morning, cool and fresh, with a haze of mist over the hills. Woburn had brought a small radio into the breakfast room; we hardly exchanged a greeting, but sat in front of the instrument, listening as the first reports came through. Presently Mrs. Rainier entered, stood in the doorway to hear a few sentences, then joined us with the same kind of whispered perfunctory good morning. The bulletin ended with a promise of more news soon, then merged into music.

That was how we had breakfast on that first morning of the second war—to the beat of a dance band and with the sunlight streaming through the windows of Stourton.

After breakfast we heard the news repeated, and found the strain almost intolerable. We strayed about the gardens, the three of us, then came back to the radio again; this time there were a few extra items, reports of half the world's grim awakening.

The newspapers came, but they were already old—printed hours before.

I telephoned the City office, and had to wait twenty minutes before the line was clear.

Then Woburn, after wandering restlessly in and out of rooms, said he would take a long walk. I think he would have liked either Mrs. Rainier or myself or both of us to suggest accompanying him, but we stayed each other with a glance. "He's a nice boy," she said, when he had gone.

"Yes, very."

"Does Charles like him?"

"Yes, I think so."

"I always hoped he would. I feel we've almost adopted him, in one sense."

"I sometimes think he feels that too."

"I'd like him to feel that . . . I once had a child, a boy, but he died. . . ."

"I never knew that."

"Charles would have made a good father, don't you think?"

"Yes . . . he must have been terribly disappointed."

"What will Woburn do now?"

"He said he'd join the Air Force."

She moved restlessly to the radio, where the music had suddenly stopped. Another news item: the Germans had crossed the Polish frontiers at many places; the war machine was already clanking into gear.

"I can't stand this—I half wish now we'd gone with him for the walk. Don't leave me alone here—you don't have to return to the City, do you?"

"No, not yet, anyhow. I just rang up the office. They haven't had any news or message."

"Oh . . . let's go somewhere then. I'll drive you. There's nothing else to do—we'll go mad if we sit over the radio all day."

We took her car, which was an open sports Bentley, and set out. The Stourton parkland had never looked more wonderful; it was as if it had the mood to spread its beauty as a last temptation to remain at peace, or, failing that, as a last spendthrift offering to a thankless world. We passed quickly, then threaded the winding gravel roads over the estate to an exit I had not known of before—it opened on to the road to Faringdon. Through the still misty morning we raced westward and northward; but at Lechlade the sun was bright and the clock showed ten minutes past ten. A few miles beyond Burford the country rolled into uplands, and presently we left the main road altogether, slowing for tree-hidden corners and streams that crossed the lanes in wide sandy shallows, till at last in the distance we saw a rim of green against the blue.

"Perhaps it will be a simpler England after the war," was one of the things she said.

"You're already thinking of *after* the war?"

"Of course. The *next* Armistice Day, whenever it comes."

"It'll be a different England, that's very certain. Not so rich, and not so snobbish—but maybe we can do without some of the riches and all the snobbery."

She nodded: "Maybe we can do without Stourton—and Bentleys."

"And two-for-one bonus issues."

"And guinea biographies like the one somebody once wrote about Charles's father."

"And parties for His Excellency to meet the winners of the Ladies' Doubles."

She laughed. "And champagne when you've already had enough champagne."

"How *can* we be so absurd—on a day like this?"

"Maybe it isn't so absurd."

"Where are you taking me?"

"Oh, just somewhere in England, as the war bulletins may say one of these days."

We drove on, mile after mile, till at a turn of the road the hills ahead of us sharpened into a ridge and at the same turn also there was a signpost which made me cry out, with a sudden catch of breath: "Did you see *that?*"

"I know. I wanted to come here."

"But—you shouldn't—it's only torturing yourself—"

"No, no. I promise I won't be upset—see, I'm quite calm."

"But all this probing of the past—"

"That's where the future will take us, maybe—back to the past. A simpler England. Old England."

And then we came upon the gray cottages fronting the stream, the square-towered church, the ledge in the stream where the water sparkled. We parked our car by the church and walked along the street. A postman late on his morning rounds stared with friendly curiosity at us and the car, then said "Good morning." A fluff of wind blew tall hollyhocks toward us. Somebody was clipping a hedge; an old dog loitered into a fresh patch of shade. Little things—but I shall remember them long after much else has been forgotten.

There seemed no special significance anywhere, no sign that a war had begun.

But as we neared the post office I caught sight of something that to me was most significant of all—a small brown two-seater car. I walked over to it; a man saw me examining the license. "If you're looking for the tall gentleman," he came over to say, "I think he took a walk up the hill."

I turned to Mrs. Rainier. "*Charles?*" was all she whispered.

"Might be. It meets the Club porter's description and it was hired from a London firm."

We turned off the main road by a path crossing an open field towards the hill; as we were climbing the chime of three quarters came up to us, blown faint by the breeze. The slope was too steep for much talk, but when we came within a few yards of the ridge she halted to gain breath, gazing down over the village.

"Looks as if it has never changed."

"I don't suppose it has, much, in a thousand years."

"That makes twenty seem only yesterday."

"If we meet him, what are you going to say?"

"I don't know. I can't know—before I see him."

"He'll wonder why on earth we've come *here*, of all places."

"Then we'll ask him why on earth *he's* here. Perhaps we'll both have to pretend we came to look at the five counties."

She resumed the climb, and in another moment we could see that the summit dipped again to a further summit, perhaps higher, and that in the hollow between lay a little pond. There was a man lying beside it with arms outstretched, as if he had flung himself there after the climb. He did not move as we approached, but presently we saw smoke curling from a cigarette between his fingers.

"He's not asleep," I said. "He's just resting."

I saw her eyes and the way her lips trembled; something suddenly occurred to me. "By the way, how did you know there were *five* counties?"

But she didn't answer; already she was rushing down the slope. He saw her in time to rise to his feet; she stopped then, several yards away, and for a few seconds both were staring at each other, hard and still and silent. Then he whispered something I couldn't hear; but I knew in a flash that the gap was closed, that the random years were at an end, that the past and the future would join. She knew this too, for she ran into his arms calling out: "Oh, Smithy—Smithy—it may not be too late!"